THE
PROTECTOR'S
RING

A Jonah Blackstone Novel by

JOHN DARR
BOOK ONE

I would like to dedicate this first novel of the series to my best friend Andre for his creative mind and impetus, my brother Donald for his help in world building, and all my friends who gave needed encouragement along the way.

– John Darr

THE PROTECTOR'S RING

CHAPTER ONE
THE FALLEN

How long have we been enemies, Isaiah?

Isaiah Blackstone didn't bother to answer the question that had been projected into his mind. He brandished his gleaming Reaper blades—fifteen-inch, doubled-edged weapons made of single pieces of unearthly silver metal. His wife, Janice, stood beside him, her own blades held ready.

They stood in a wide, underground tunnel. The walls, floor, and ceiling were covered in onyx slabs, long since sullied by two millennia of dust and dirt. The normally close air and dank smell was exacerbated by the number of extra bodies currently occupying the space.

At least ten attackers blocked their way. All were dressed in grey pants and matching tunics with bone-white skull symbols on the left side of their chests. Each carried a curved, jet-black scythe with a handgrip. Their eyes were a solid, milky white that was the sign they were possessed by Wraiths.

Isaiah shouted and waded into their midst, blocking the swipes of their scythes with his blades. He ducked low and brought one of his blades into the underside of an attacker's chin. His long leather Reaper coat whipped around, taking hits on the enchanted fabric as he sliced. The eyes flared as the Wraith and its mortal host died. He stabbed another in the heart, used his augmented strength to kick a third guy into his fellow henchmen while cutting a fourth man across the chest.

Janice fought at his side like a beautiful Nubian princess. Always an agile woman, she'd incorporated acrobatic techniques into her fighting forms. She somersaulted, wrapping her legs around the neck of one attacker while skewering another with a blade. She twisted her body, whirling the trapped attacker into two more.

Isaiah charged straight ahead, cutting down the last two men before reaching an ancient wooden door. The writing etched into the surface was in the Kikongo tongue, one of the languages of the surrounding countryside of central Congo. The inscription translated into *conversations with the gods.*

On the other side was a hidden underground amphitheater, used by the ancestors to receive enlightenment from the Afterworld. Isaiah and his allies had thought the location a fitting safe haven to train the first Protector in over two thousand years. But it had been compromised.

"You can't save him. Give up." Deyanira's voice penetrated his concentration again.

Isaiah shook his head, trying to ignore her. She was using an arcane enchantment to communicate directly into his mind. It was a holdover from their time together as part of the Kin: the Grim Reaper's personal guard. They had been friends, of a sort, reaping souls from worthless mortal bodies. But Isaiah didn't see mortals that way anymore.

After all, he had fallen, giving up his station as a Reaper and marrying a mortal.

Reaching deep inside his soul, Isaiah shouted, "Sakoto!" The *Yoruba* wind evocation stirred the air around him. Within seconds, a torrent of air raced through the outer doors and into the antechamber. The wind slammed into the wooden door, flung it open, and banged it against the inside wall. The sound rolled across the amphitheater.

Isaiah's breath caught. A large magical shield surrounded the entire stage area. Inside, the current Protector huddled inside his own protective bubble while no less than twenty of the grey-robed attackers surrounded him.

They slashed and sliced with their jet-black scythes but so far, they couldn't touch him. When the boy turned in Isaiah's direction, his eyes wide with terror, Isaiah silently urged him to remember the training and listen to the ring. It could do so much more, if the legends were true.

Deyanira stood to the side in her flowing red Reaper's robes. She conjured a hex and sent it at Isaiah before ducking inside the protection of her barrier.

Kulinda, he thought, evoking the blocking spell with the Swahili word. His Reaper blades glowed brighter in the darkened space. The Angel script covering every square inch of the weapons flared as he brought them down in a crossing pattern to block Deyanira's attack.

Unlike most Reapers, members of the KIN despised their former lives. As such, they hated frail mortals and even reveled in the more hideous ways humans found to kill each other. Isaiah experienced a bit of shame from his time in the Kin. He'd been full of pain and sadness over his own first Death. Taking advantage of his pain, the Grim Reaper had twisted his mind and recruited him.

But I finally saw the truth to the Grim Reaper's plan. I rebelled. "Maybe you should fall, like I did, Deyanira. Become a Fallen Reaper. Step into the light."

Isaiah expected her to laugh, but her tone was sad when she spoke directly to him. "You forget. I was a powerful sorceress in my first life. I have no light to embrace."

"Then start a new course."

"You've grown so sentimental since you've left the Kin. I would never become a mortal again."

The restorative effects of crossing through a portal had reduced Deyanira's ritualistic scars to faint lines on her pale face. A full head of red hair that spilled down to her shoulders helped her look mortal despite her claims, and that hypocrisy galled Isaiah.

"You cross over into the mortal world more than any other Reaper. I wonder what that says about you?"

He wanted to goad her, but again, she came across as sad. "I miss our arguments, Isaiah."

"I don't."

Deyanira broke the mutual gaze to focus on the struggle inside the shield. "We all have our parts to play."

Isaiah mounted the stage, keeping his blades ready in case Deyanira attacked again. He moved back and forth along the outside of the barrier, unable to help.

The young man had lost his own protective bubble and had started to phase around, moving from one location to another in a blink of an eye. It was unfortunate, Isaiah mused. The boy had never known about the supernatural world or the After Life and didn't fully understand how to listen to the ring. Isaiah groaned, wondering how much could have changed if someone with training had activated the ring.

That was the catch: only certain mortals could access the power of a Protector's Ring. This young man had been one of them, maybe the last. Now it was all lost because of a traitor in their midst.

The would-be protector continued to phase around, but he couldn't avoid the attackers. There were too many, swarming around him like killer bees. Each time he appeared, he received a cut. Blood sprayed across the floor creating a macabre design.

Finally he dropped to his knees, unable to phase anymore. The attackers charged in cutting and opening new wounds. One held a scythe aloft and brought it down, intending to slice him open from left shoulder to right hip.

The boy's bloodied hand trembled as he held the ring close to his mouth and spoke to it. As the scythe bit into his body, he screamed out in agony. At the same time, the ring flared, engulfing him and the closest executioners in a brilliant light.

Isaiah blinked in horrid surprise. He snapped into motion and rolled off the lip of the stage. He pulled Janice with him against the stage's side. They huddled there, Janice curling herself into a ball so his larger body could cover her. Isaiah made sure to pull his long coat over them both.

The storm of power erupted overhead. The sound of stone hitting stone, and occasionally his back, was deafening. When the roaring decreased and the pressure relented, Isaiah peeked from under his coat. Half the amphitheater seats had been blasted to ruins by the release of power.

He lifted his coat away, gaping at the smoking spots where the blood had been baked on it. Except for a few rips, it was whole. He stood, slipped on the coat, and offered his wife a supporting hand. "You alright?"

"Yes." Janice stood.

He leapt up to the stage.

When Janice followed, her jaw dropped. "Oh my God."

It was like a bomb had gone off, Isaiah thought.

As the dust settled, a green bubble became visible on the far side of the ruined stage. Deyanira crouched there, the release of power having stripped away her human guise. Her face was more skeletal, her head bald except for a single red ponytail in the back. Most striking was the fully visible scars on her face.

Isaiah strode to the center of the stage and found the ring, gleaming and undamaged on the scorched floor. He crouched and scooped up the source of devastation.

"Give that to me, Isaiah." Deyanira had lowered her shield and stood facing him. Her frayed and smudged red robe swished as she gestured to the ring.

Isaiah rose to his feet. "I don't think so."

Deyanira's brilliant green eyes bore into his as she raised her right hand. Instead of casting a spell, she opened a vortex.

Isaiah didn't wait to see if more of her henchmen would swarm through. He reached back, and Janice clamped her hand in his. He nudged himself and phased from the amphitheater. He used his power to enter the aether, the stuff of the supernatural realm. It allowed him to bridge the gap between his starting point and destination in seconds.

The mortal world snapped into existence around them as they reappeared seven thousand miles away in a secluded courtyard. The closely packed brick surface, surrounding shrubbery, and the Lacebark pine at the center of the space reassured Isaiah. This was the sanctuary of Isaiah and Janice Blackstone.

He paused to take a deep breath of Georgia air. The sound of chirping birds and gently rustling branches was at odds with the death they'd just witnessed. But Isaiah had another reason for taking his time. He needed to let the dizziness pass. As a Fallen Reaper, phasing was second nature to him. But the distance, after expending energy fighting and carrying someone with him, took its toll.

Janice pressed a piece of hard candy into his mouth. The sweetness gave him an instant surge of energy. "Thanks."

A tall young man had been sitting on a nearby bench. He shot to his feet and hurried over, his own undamaged long coat swaying.

Isaiah nodded to him. "We're fine, Marcus."

Marcus halted, searching their bruises and raising an eyebrow at the sight of Isaiah's smoking long coat. "What about the Protector and the ring?"

"He's dead and I have the ring." Isaiah released his wife's hand and strode a few feet away, holding the ring in his right palm.

Marcus stirred behind him. "We have to let the Alliance Council know."

"There're traitors in the Alliance. That's how they found the boy."

"But--"

Janice placed a hand on Marcus's shoulder. "He's right."

"Then what are you two planning?"

Isaiah turned. "I'm resigning from the Council."

"You can't..." Marcus sputtered.

"Yes, I can, and I want you to take my place." Isaiah held up a hand to stop Marcus from arguing. "A Council member can step down and name his replacement." Isaiah removed a golden shield from an inside pocket of his coat and held it out to Marcus. The shield's face featured three interlocking circles with outstretched wings above the center one. It was the same symbol branded into the left breast of both of their long coats. When Marcus hesitated, Isaiah skewered his fellow Fallen Reaper with his most severe glare.

Marcus's shoulders slumped a bit and he placed his slender hand on top of the shield.

Isaiah nodded. "Do you pledge to honor the Alliance and what it stands for, abiding by its edicts and rules?"

Marcus gulped. "I so pledge." Curving lines appeared on their forearms, hands, and the shield. The lines flared for a second before fading away. Marcus sucked in a deep breath, took the shield from Isaiah, and turned it over in his trembling hands. "What are you going to do?"

"The Grim Reaper wants the ring, and Deyanira will tell him I have it. So we're going to lead them on a goose chase."

Marcus slipped the shield in an inner pocket while giving Isaiah a hard look. "For how long?"

"Long enough."

Marcus furrowed his brow, making his lean brown face more hawkish in appearance. He pointed at the ring. "What about that?"

Janice slipped the ring out of her husband's hand and held it up. "We'll hide it."

Marcus shook his head. "I need to come with you--"

"You have a new job," Isaiah cut him off. "There has to be three Fallen Reapers on the Council to balance out the Mages and Mortals. You know that." He waited for Marcus to nod. Isaiah softened his tone. "And you're Jonah's godfather. You'll have to step into that role soon."

"What does that mean?"

"I'm sorry." Isaiah patted Marcus on the shoulders. "It's better if you don't know where we hide the ring." He looked away. "I have enough blood on my hands."

"None of this was your fault," Marcus said.

Isaiah didn't respond. Instead, he watched his troubled protégé come to terms with the situation. As a lawyer, Marcus had always been cool and calculating. It's why Isaiah wanted the young man to take his place on the Council. *And our son's godfather.*

When Marcus met his gaze, Isaiah sensed the final acceptance and understanding radiating from him. All Fallen Reapers could sense the emotions from others, except those trained to shield their feelings. Marcus didn't use one of those techniques, Isaiah noted, a clear sign of how close they'd grown.

Heaviness weighed on Isaiah as he stood beside Janice, and he used her nearness to draw strength. A chasm yawned before them, but they couldn't falter. He clenched his jaw, biting back the frustration. His voice grew tight as he said, "Tell the Alliance Council the ring was lost." He met Marcus's intense gaze. "Go."

A brief flash of uncertainty crossed Marcus's face. He swallowed and finally shut down his raging emotions. Squaring his shoulders, he gave Isaiah a respectful nod and phased away.

As soon as he was gone, Janice wrapped her arms around Isaiah's waist, resting her head against his chest. "We won't have a lot of time."

"I know." Isaiah wrapped his arms around her. "Maybe six months."

Janice sucked in a breath and frowned. "What about Jonah? Shouldn't we explain everything now?"

"If we do that, the others will focus on our son before he's ready." Isaiah tightened his embrace. "We can't do that." Janice nodded, rubbing her cheek against his chest. Isaiah shook her. "Are you sure about this plan to hide the ring?"

She tilted her head up to look into his deep brown eyes. He always loved the way her lighter brown eyes sparkled.

He saw the certainty in them and knew it was a result of her gift to intuit things.

"Yes, it'll work," she said. "It's the last place anyone from our world would look for the ring."

CHAPTER TWO

A BOY NAMED JONAH

Jonah Blackstone stood at a shuttle stop, gazing intently through the glass cover of a Washington Post newspaper stand. He resembled any other twelve-year-old kid with his sagging blue jeans, loose t-shirt, colored sneakers and a ball cap on his short Afro. But unlike the other kids, off enjoying the start of summer vacation, Jonah carried his book bag with him.

He had paused in front of the newspaper stand, not knowing why the headline grabbed his attention. *Death Takes a Holiday?* Maybe it was the word *death* itself. Or maybe the cartoonish drawing of the Grim Reaper, complete with skull face and scythe, drew his attention. Perhaps it was the simple fact that he had an intense interest in the subject, ever since his best friend Oliver had died the year before.

Jonah had been able to sense something awful would happen, and he had seen a strange person wearing all black and hovering around his friend. When Jonah had tried to warn Oliver about the stranger, he discovered that no one else could see the man.

He leaned closer to read as he swallowed past the lump in his throat. That's why the article drew his attention. It represented a chance of finding an answer to why he could sense Death. According to the article, no person within a two-hundred-mile radius of Washington DC had died over the past two weeks. Victims of serious accidents, the kind that normally caused instant death, were hanging on. Terminally ill patients fought back from the brink of death. The phenomenon had everyone puzzled and a little scared.

Jonah's reaction had been his normal reaction to anything that puzzled him: he headed to a library. Even though he lived in Fairfax County, Virginia, he often came to the Arlington Central library because the manager knew his mom and treated him like a guest. He figured an Internet search would be enough to look up any previous occurrences of Death Holidays.

The research had provided immediate results. Jonah's excitement grew as he found articles about another such event. Tomorrow would mark thirteen years, to the day. Goosebumps rose along Jonah's arms: tomorrow was his thirteenth birthday. That meant the last time this happened was the day he was born. It had to be a coincidence, Jonah thought.

The wind gusted around the shuttle stop, snapping Jonah out of the troubling thought. He hitched the book bag on his shoulder as he waited. Another streak of silent lightning flashed overhead, and passing adults muttered to themselves.

A cold front appeared out of nowhere, taking a few hours to make the late June temperatures plummet twenty to thirty degrees. Bulging gray clouds blotted out the sun and the strange lightning flashed all day long, but no rain fell. The overall effect was oppressive, Jonah thought.

Something strange was happening, and he could sense the crackle of tension in the air.

As Jonah gazed at the overcast sky, he hoped the strange weather wouldn't prevent his mom and dad from flying home. He missed his parents and hadn't seen them in over two weeks. They had promised to be home in time for his birthday, and he wanted to spend it with them.

He reached inside his jeans pocket, wrapping his fingers around his cell phone. Should he play his mom's message again? It felt like he'd done it a thousand times already, all the while wishing his dad had spoken in the message. Jonah longed to hear his dad's deep voice telling him that everything would be fine. The phone was out and in his hand when he experienced an annoying hitch in his stomach.

The sensation was not unfamiliar. It had been happening all this week, and each time his stomach hitched, he saw a person in black. They came in all races and nationalities. And the one thing they had in common, besides an intense fascination with him, was their unnatural stillness.

Jonah searched the people walking around him and saw a thin white man who stood on the other side of the busy Arlington Boulevard. Like the others Jonah had seen, he wore a black long coat, black pants, and black boots. Why did these people watch him? The wind kicked up a notch again and neither the man's long brown hair nor his coat stirred.

A group of office workers approached and walked right through the man as if he wasn't really there. Jonah blinked in surprise. That couldn't be right, he told himself, suddenly filled with the urge to talk with the man. He stepped off the sidewalk without thinking and a horn blared and brakes squealed.

The shuttle bus screeched to a stop just short of Jonah, and the driver started making angry gestures. Looking across the street, Jonah ignored the shuttle driver. However, the stranger was gone. That was the other thing about these people. They seemed to vanish in the blink of an eye.

The shuttle driver resorted to honking his horn as he motioned Jonah to get on or move out of the way. Jonah sighed, hitched up his book bag, and hurried around to mount the steps.

He worked his way to the very back of the shuttle to hide. His face warmed as every pair of eyes seemed to watch him. Jonah hated being the center of attention, and this was his worst nightmare. *Why do these things always happen to me?*

Even though it was rush hour and the shuttle was packed, he found an empty seat next to an elderly black woman. Being extra careful not to bump her, Jonah dropped into the seat and slipped the book bag on the floor between his feet. As he did so, the strange guy outside popped into his mind and he gazed past the woman and out the window.

His eyes hadn't played tricks on him. Those people walked through that man like he wasn't really there. Maybe there was something in the articles about strange people appearing around town. Jonah unzipped his book bag, intending to pull out the articles, but his new video game console tumbled out. He managed to catch it before it hit the ground and he placed the device on his lap. When he reached inside the book bag again, the elderly woman stirred and pointed a boney brown finger.

"That looks like an expensive little gizmo." She spoke with a squeaky little voice that fit her tiny body.

Jonah turned the small game console over in his hands. "It's a birthday gift from my aunt and uncle."

"Oh. Happy Birthday."

She offered to shake his hand. As soon as Jonah touched her, the woman's little body tensed and her free hand clutched the tiny ankh necklace she wore.

"Are you okay?"

"Yes." She took a deep breath, and offered him a weak smile. "How old are you, young man?"

"I'll be thirteen tomorrow."

"I bet you have a big party planned."

"No, not really. It'll just be my mom and dad."

"What about your relatives?"

"They live in Georgia."

"No friends?"

Jonah shook his head no. The woman studied him for a moment, then glanced down at the book bag. "Summer school?"

"I'm doing research at the library."

"Bookworm, eh?" She laughed. "My second husband was a bookworm. He kept books everywhere. It drove me absolutely crazy."

Jonah wondered what she would say about his parents' study. Bookshelves covered an entire wall, stuffed with volumes from all around the world. His parents were archeologists, and the room was a bookworm's heaven.

The woman leaned closer, and the scent of some flowery perfume tickled Jonah's nose. "I never went in for big parties, myself. Better to keep it small, I say. More cake for you."

She gave Jonah a wink and went back to staring out the window while fingering her necklace.

Jonah thought about her comments as he slid the video game console inside the book bag. He hesitated before taking out the articles; the conversation also reminded him of the day he had discovered the name of his ability. That had also been the day his best friend Oliver had died.

Jonah was understandably upset with Oliver's death, so his parents had sent him to bed early that evening. Unable to rest, he had snuck out of his bedroom and crouched at the top of the stairs. His parents were in their study with the doors closed. Jonah's heart pounded in his chest as he descended the stairs, tiptoed to the closed study doors, and peeked through the crack.

He couldn't see his dad, but he heard the desk chair creak as his dad spoke. "I talked with Marcus and the others. They agreed with me. Jonah has Death Sense."

"Are they sure?" His mom moved into view. "He hasn't shown any other signs."

"You heard Jonah. He accurately sensed the danger around Oliver. I just wonder if our son is telling us everything."

"I'd be shocked if he wasn't. He is more your son in that respect."

There was a slight amusement above the clear worry in his mom's voice. His father let out a low grunt. Both his parents remained silent for a moment. Jonah had started to move when his mom spoke again.

"Maybe we should tell Jonah everything now." His mom twisted her hands together. His dad stepped into view and took her hands in his.

"No, Janice. He'll be thirteen in a year. We follow the plan."

Jonah's mom began to cry, and his dad hugged her. Sensing they would remain that way for some time, Jonah stepped back from the door and crept upstairs to bed.

His parents' conversation filled him with fear. *Death Sense?* He had never heard of the term. However, he already had experienced it twice in his life. The first time had happened when his second-grade teacher died. The second time occurred earlier that day, when Oliver died.

The sensation started with a buzzing in his head and a slight headache. This was followed by a whisper of a person's name and, when Jonah thought about the person in danger, his headache would spike.

Cold chills and vomiting followed as the headache built into a severe migraine at the moment the person died. It was the only time Jonah would ever get sick, which made it all the more unusual.

From that night on, his parents never mentioned Death Sense, and Jonah was afraid to let them know he had listened to their conversation. So he turned to the books in the library, trying to find anything he could about his ability. Jonah decided that it only happened when someone close to him, or who he liked, was in danger. It was the reason he decided not to make any new friends.

Jonah glanced out the shuttle window again as he rubbed his forehead. He'd been trying to deny that his head buzzed today. That frightened him because the only people close to him were his neighbors the Garretts and, of course, his parents.

CHAPTER THREE
THE SEER

The evening commuters jostled each other as they rushed to catch metro trains. Jonah bumped along in the midst of the crowd until he heard someone call out his name.

"Jonah."

He stopped and spun around, causing several people to give him irritated looks as they hurried by. The voice sounded so near that Jonah wondered if someone had actually whispered in his ear. The initial rush of people thinned out, and he saw her. The little woman from the shuttle waited on the sidewalk, halfway between the shuttle stop and the gate. She beckoned to him.

As Jonah approached, he wondered if he had left something on the shuttle.

"Excuse me," he said when he reached her. "Did you call my name?"

She nodded. "I didn't want to say anything on that crowded shuttle."

"Okay…"

"When I touched your hand, I understood about you. It must be hard to be different."

"I don't know what you're talking about. I have to get home."

Jonah backed toward the gate, but the woman grabbed his forearm. "I know you can sense Death."

Jonah pulled his arm out of her grip. "You're crazy."

"Crazy? Hah! I know about the other thing you can do. You are special."

"I'm not special. I'm just a kid."

"You want to believe that, but you were never just a kid. Deep down, you understand, yet you try to hide from it."

Jonah couldn't deny her words. In fact, he had thought the same thing about himself earlier.

"Who are you?"

"I'm a Seer. You were meant to take that seat next to me today."

"That just happened."

"Child, nothing happens by accident." The Seer motioned toward the sky with a gnarled hand. "Look about you, young man. It is no coincidence that Death is behaving strangely and you turn thirteen tomorrow." She pointed at Jonah's eyes. "You see them, don't you?"

"What do you know about those people?" Jonah sucked in a breath, catching the woman's larger meaning. "What does the weather have to do with me?"

The Seer didn't answer. Instead, she held out a knobby hand. Jonah shrank away from it.

"Take my hand, Jonah Blackstone."

"How do you know my name?"

The woman shook her boney hand. "Take it."

"Why?"

"I can only see by touching."

Jonah hesitated as two competing desires warred inside him. He desperately wanted to know about the people in black and the strange weather. However, this Seer could sense all those things about him just by shaking his hand. For the first time in Jonah's life, he was afraid of receiving information. This woman could destroy his hope of being a normal kid. No, Jonah decided. He didn't want to touch her again.

Perhaps the Seer read the decision on his face because she grabbed his hand with a surprisingly strong grip. Then she added her other hand to keep him from pulling free. Jonah's Death Sense began to buzz in his head as the woman closed her eyes. Her body jerked and stiffened. The ankh necklace begin to glow. When she opened her eyes, they were milky white.

Jonah struggled in the woman's firm grip. She opened her mouth and spoke in a deeper voice.

"Yes. You are different."

Her voice seemed to wrap itself around him, chilling him to the bone and freezing him in place. Jonah was frightened, yet there was something compelling about her, something that drew on his very soul.

"Yessss," she hissed. "You will become more powerful than anyone ever imagined. You are going to change things."

The woman let out a strangled moan as Jonah's Death Sense flared, causing him to wince. A shudder went through the Seer's little body and her head flopped forward. Jonah staggered as she sagged into his arms.

"Whoa!" He gently shook her.

"Hey!" The station manager called out, stepping from his kiosk. "Is she alright?"

Before Jonah could answer, the Seer stirred and lifted her head.

Her eyes were their normal deep brown color again. And she blinked several times as if trying to focus on him.

"I'm just a little tired."

"I have some water inside." The station manager paused by the gate, watching the woman with a skeptical look.

"I'm fine." She patted Jonah on the arm. "My grandson here is helping me."

"Let me know." The manager went back to his kiosk.

The Seer turned on Jonah with an awed expression. "Don't you realize how important you are?"

"You said I will change things." The Seer nodded. "Tell me. What will I change?"

"You'll change everything, young man." Her expression shifted into a deep frown. "Trust your feelings about your parents."

"What about my parents?" Jonah asked, struggling to keep up with all the cryptic comments.

"I saw you in pain and great loss."

"No."

"Your pain will end, and things will get better. You will be happy again and among family." She patted his hand. "I'm sorry."

Jonah pulled his hand free and backed away from the Seer. When she reached out, he turned and ran through the gate to the station, trying to escape the finality in the woman's voice.

"Remember, it will get better!" she called out.

Jonah tried to block out her voice as he boarded an orange-line train. He found an empty seat and collapsed into it as fear rippled through his body. Curling up against the side of the car, Jonah pressed his head to the cool window. It took him several minutes to calm his heart and for the fear to recede.

When he reached his stop, Jonah exited the station and unlocked his bike in a sort of daze. The lightning flashed continually overhead as he rode down the sidewalk along Saintsbury drive. He didn't notice it. Instead, he filled his mind with comforting thoughts of his parents being home and waiting for him. Maybe they wanted to surprise him?

Despite grasping at happy thoughts, Jonah had to battle his own growing fear, and the frequent gusts of strong wind, as he turned onto his street. When his house came into view, Jonah's spirits drooped. The house was dark and his parents' car wasn't in the driveway.

The old woman's voice came back to him, mixing with the irritating buzzing in his head. He wouldn't accept it. She had to be wrong. His feelings were wrong. Jonah tried to push the troubling thoughts out of his head as he rode to the Garretts' house.

A bright yellow balloon narrowly missed Jonah's head as he entered the Garretts' kitchen. Little Tim, the Garretts' youngest son, let out an unrestrained laugh. A *Happy Birthday* banner hung above the entrance into the dining room and a large birthday cake was on the kitchen table.

"Ah," Mr. Garrett said. "There's the birthday boy."

Little Tim stifled his laugh, walked over to Jonah, and shook his hand. "Happy Birthday, Jonah."

"Thanks, Tim."

Mr. Garrett laughed at his son as he pulled the loosened tie from around his beefy neck. He hadn't changed out of his work clothes: a dress shirt, tie, and slacks.

"We know your birthday's tomorrow, but since you'll celebrate with your parents…"

"We decided to have a birthday dinner for you tonight," Mrs. Garrett finished, coming in from the dining room. Kim, the second youngest, followed her mom. Mrs. Garrett crossed over to Jonah and picked a stray leaf off his shirt.

"I hope you're in the mood for pizza."

"That sounds cool." Jonah slipped off his book bag and Little Tim grabbed it.

"I can take that to your room."

"You don't have to do that."

Little Tim ignored Jonah's protest, hefted the book bag, and staggered out of the kitchen. Jonah wouldn't be surprised if the curious little kid riffled through the bag. Little Tim found everything about Jonah interesting.

He stuffed his hands in his pockets, unsure of what to do with himself. He was grateful to the Garretts for letting him stay over, but he wanted to sleep in his own bed tonight instead of a daybed in the guest room again.

He knew his mom would disapprove of his negative attitude. He was about to offer to help with the balloons when Kim pointed a little finger at him.

"Mom, he's gonna see it before we're ready."

"No, he won't, Kim." Mrs. Garrett took plates from the cabinet and handed them to her daughter.

Kim balanced the plates and paused long enough to warn Jonah, "No peeking."

Mrs. Garrett nudged her daughter toward the dining room before saying to him, "Why don't you go watch the game with Tyrone?"

Jonah's shoulders slumped. He considered going to the guest room and hiding out until dinner, but Little Tim came back to help his father with the balloons. Jonah knew he'd look stupid going back there after having the boy carry his book bag. So he nodded to Mrs. Garrett and shuffled off to the den.

Tyrone Garrett lounged on the couch with the TV remote in his hands. He was a thick boy, beefy like his dad. When Jonah entered the room, Tyrone gave him a slight nod with his rounded chin before focusing on the game again. Jonah crossed to one of the armchairs and sat down.

Stocky Mr. Garrett had played college football for Howard University. Tyrone played football in Middle School. Both were avid sports fans, but Jonah just wasn't into sports like that. Neither were his parents. He'd take a good adventure book over a game any day. He suspected that was one reason Tyrone didn't want to hang out with him.

Kim let out a squeal of laughter from the dining room. Little Tim answered with a shout, and both their parents told them to calm down. Jonah slumped in the chair, rubbing his forehead. He could never get used to all the activity of the Garretts' house. Even when younger, he had been a quiet kid. And being the only child of researchers made for a quiet house. His Death Sense throbbed painfully at the thought of his parents, and Jonah tried to ignore it.

The doorbell rang several minutes later, and Mr. Garrett's heavy footfalls vibrated up into Jonah's chair as the man hurried down the hallway to the front door. The noise of wind and rattling branches rolled into the house when he answered. The delivery boy looked put out and grumbled as he handed over two large pizzas.

Mr. Garrett paid the boy, then had to use his shoulder to close the door against the howling wind.

Mrs. Garrett took the pizzas from him. "I hope you gave him an extra tip."

"I did. It's getting worse out there."

Jonah didn't say anything as he followed Tyrone and his parents into the dining room. As everyone gathered around the table, Jonah had his first opportunity to witness the birthday decorations. He was stunned. In addition to the *Happy Birthday* banner over the entrance to the dining room, balloons were tied to the backs of the chairs. Multicolored napkins were placed next to each plate. The birthday cake took up the middle of the table.

Jonah thought the decorations a little young for him, but he kept that to himself.

Mrs. Garrett sat a pizza box on either side of the cake and opened them. The aroma of pepperoni and grilled chicken wafted over the table. Any other day, Jonah would have been the first to dive in. Tonight, he didn't think he'd make it through one piece.

"The birthday boy has the honor of taking the first slice."

Jonah smiled, trying to hide the grimace on his face. He chose a piece of chicken pizza, sat down, and watched the Garretts as he took his first, small bite. Thinking about the Garretts, picturing them individually in his mind, didn't affect the buzzing in his head. They weren't in danger.

A knot formed in his stomach as dread and sadness welled up inside him. He glanced out the dining room's bay window, watching the trees whip back and forth and hoping the feeling would pass. When he turned back to the half-eaten pizza on his plate, he saw Mrs. Garrett watching him. She gave him a thin smile before hurrying out of the room and returning a moment later with the birthday presents.

Kim and Little Tim were particularly excited. "Open ours first! Open ours first!" Kim bounced up and down in her chair while Little Tim tried to keep calm.

Jonah started to open the wrapping paper when Kim reached over and ripped it. "You're supposed to do it like that, silly."

Jonah smiled and pulled off the last of the paper. Inside, he found a set of bookmarks with images of famous African-Americans and with colorful tassels. Jonah suspected the gift was Little Tim's idea.

"We thought you could use these, at the library," Tim explained.

"Thanks." Jonah put the bookmarks aside and looked up to see Tyrone holding a thin, square present.

"Happy Birthday."

Jonah took the present and opened it. Inside was a music CD.

"You don't have that one, do you?"

Jonah turned the CD over in his hands. It was the soundtrack of the latest action movie. "No, I don't." He would never have expected Tyrone to do something like this. "Thanks a lot."

The last gift was from Mr. and Mrs. Garrett. Their package was larger than the rest, and it was heavy. Jonah started to open the paper, paused, and held the package out to Timothy and Kim. "You want to open it?"

The siblings launched themselves on the wrapping and tore it off in seconds. The Garretts had bought Jonah a dark brown attaché case with gold fasteners.

"Wow. Thanks."

Opening the gifts took Jonah's mind off the dread for a time, but the cold sweats started, and he worried the Garretts would notice. When his stomach grew queasy, he put on a brave face. However, the sight of pizza threatened to make him heave.

"Can I be excused?"

Mr. and Mrs. Garrett traded glances and Jonah thought they would say no.

"It's my stomach," Jonah added.

"I can get you something." Mrs. Garrett began to raise from her chair. "Maybe some mint tea?"

Jonah stood. "I just want to go to my room." He saw the mixture of looks on everyone's faces, but he had to get away.

When the Garretts gave him silent nods, Jonah gathered up the smaller gifts and slipped them in the attaché case.

"Thanks for the presents," he said and ran off to the guest room.

Jonah didn't bother to turn on the lights. He dropped the case by the closet and lay on the daybed, watching the continual lightning flashes outside the window. He couldn't hold off any longer and allowed himself to think about his mom and dad. The pain hit him so hard that he cried out before he could stop himself. His body began to twitch and spasm at odd intervals.

Not my mom and dad. Not them! In desperation, Jonah grabbed his iPod. Maybe the music would help to drown out thoughts of his parents so he could rest.

It almost worked. Several times, he started to drowse, but an unguarded thought about his parents would enter his mind and the pain from the Death Sense would jolt him awake. Finally, fatigue won out and he descended into a troubled sleep.

CHAPTER FOUR
HIDDEN CHAMBER

Jonah dreamt that he stood outside on a round brick-and-concrete platform. Crickets chirped loudly, somewhere in the middle of the night. The tree branches rustled from an errant, hot summer breeze. The only illumination came from a full moon, which gave everything a haunted look.

About a hundred feet away, stood an old, abandoned brick building. Jonah thought the building was familiar, but he couldn't remember from where. As he puzzled over that, he sensed a change in the air pressure a second before his mom and dad appeared between him and the building.

Even in a dream, Jonah imagined that any other kid would have been surprised to see people appearing, but he wasn't. He'd seen his father do the *special thing* before.

He'd seen his father do it one night when someone threw a brick in the dining room window. His mom had grabbed him and dove to the floor. Jonah looked up in time to see his dad's body ripple, disappear, and then reappear right next to them.

Jonah could never forget because he'd done the *special thing* himself. It happened at the end of the school year, when bullies chased him into the boy's bathroom. When the bullies burst through the door, they knocked Jonah backward. Instead of hitting the cold bathroom floor, Jonah felt a rippling along his body and a second later, he found himself lying in the dirt on the elementary school's ball field.

He kept that and other experiences to himself over the last six months, feeling his parents were too busy with the move to their current house, as well as constantly coming and going on secret trips. Because of the constant travel, Jonah had spent more time as a guest at the Garretts' over the last month than he had at home. He was overwhelmed with the realization that maybe he should have at least told his parents about the people in black clothes. Shame and a little anger hit him.

Jonah called to his parents. "Mom. Dad."

His parents continued to look around without giving any indication that they heard him. Why couldn't his parents hear him? This was his dream. As he wondered about that, he began to notice other things.

His mom and dad, who normally dressed alike in jeans, hiking boots, and plain brown shirts when working, had on different clothes tonight. His dad wore a long black leather coat with a high collar that didn't hide his broad, muscular shoulders. Jonah had never seen the coat before nor the black military-styled boots, black jeans, and shirt his mother wore.

As he stepped off the platform and moved closer, Jonah became aware that his parents were also dirty and sweaty as if they'd been running. Maybe they'd been fighting, he thought. There was a patch of dirt in his dad's hair and smudges on his black coat. And his mom's naturally frizzy curls stuck out at odd angles and she had a rip on her right pant leg.

They finished searching the area and turned to face the building. Jonah followed their gaze. Now that he was closer, he could read the words carved into the crumbling stone facade: Free Public Library.

"Are you ready, Janice?" Jonah's dad took out a cylinder. With a flick of his hand, the cylinder gave off a metallic swishing sound and transformed into a bright silver blade. His dad muttered and the blade shone with a pale yellow light.

His mom nodded and made a quick movement with her right hand. Jonah heard the same metallic swishing sound and a second later, she held a long silver blade. Hers shone with a pale white light. Jonah stared at the weapons in amazement.

The blades were doubled-edged and made of single pieces of metal with strange symbols covering every surface. His mom twirled her blade once, bringing it to rest in a reverse grip. She looked like a true fighter, Jonah thought, as she mounted the front steps with his dad.

They reached the entrance, pushed open the old library doors, and disappeared into the darkness. Jonah rushed up the chipped and broken stone steps. When he reached the door, he skidded to a halt because his parents stood just inside.

"Mom? Dad? Can't you hear me?" Jonah raised his hands and waved to them, but his parents didn't notice. They moved off into the darkened space.

Jonah didn't like this dream. When he swatted at the doorframe in frustration, his hand went straight through. He reached out for the doorframe again, taking his time. Jonah thought he could feel something as the hand went through the wood. He was like a ghost. Is that why his parents couldn't see or hear him?

Jonah's heart began to race, and it was all he could do to keep from screaming until he reminded himself it was just a dream. He wasn't dead. He wasn't a ghost. While he was distracted with the doorframe, his parents had crossed the library lobby.

The old counters and railings were still in place, but the rest of the floor was empty. Jonah hurried around—and even through—one of the railings, to catch up to his parents. His dad stopped in a side hallway to jiggle a doorknob. When it didn't open, he stepped back and, raising a large boot, slammed it into the wood beneath the handle. The wood cracked and splintered as the door banged open.

Jonah couldn't understand this dream. It was like being inside a 3D environment instead of a real dream. All he could do was watch and follow as his parents entered the stairwell. They descended two flights of stairs and came out in a pitch black hallway.

His dad waved his bright blade around in graceful movements, sending rats scurrying in all directions. A blank section of mildewed wall stood before Jonah's parents. His dad moved the blade back and forth, mere inches above the surface, then ran his large hand over a particular spot.

Jonah's dad pulled a round object—a compass, Jonah noted—out of his shirt and, holding it against the wall, waited. Nothing happened for several minutes until a low rumble filled the hallway. The vibration rippled up through the floor and shook his parents, but Jonah didn't feel anything. The wall rippled like water and an opening appeared. Jonah's jaw dropped as the darkened hole expanded, sounding like brick sliding across brick. The opening stabilized into a perfect circle. His dad calmly held the blade inside the hole.

"You first?" His mom nodded toward the opening.

"Of course." His dad stepped through and paused just inside to reach back and grip his mom's hand. The dim light from the blades dropped below floor level as they descended out of view.

Jonah crossed to the opening, took a deep breath, and descended the long staircase behind his parents. He had gone down about half a dozen steps when he heard the sound of sliding bricks behind him. His parents continued on while Jonah froze, listening. The opening in the wall had closed.

He paused, wondering how they would get out. Maybe his dad could use the compass again, from this side. Yeah, Jonah thought as his nervousness eased. His dad would be able to get out. That made sense. Buoyed with that conclusion, he continued down the extremely narrow passage. It was longer than he expected, and a dim glow grew brighter until he reached the bottom.

His parents stood before two high metal doors. There was a gold symbol spanning both, three inter-locking circles with a pair of wings spread out above. At the heart of the center circle was a round hole. His dad placed his compass in the depression. It rotated ninety degrees, followed by a loud click, like a bolt being released. When his dad removed the compass, the massive doors opened on their own with a heavy, creaking sound. Lights flared on inside the room.

Jonah hurried forward to follow his parents, and his jaw dropped. The chamber was huge, with a surprisingly high ceiling. Bookshelves lined three entire walls and extended up, at least two floors. Every shelf and cubbyhole was packed solid with ancient-looking volumes. Most were vertical on the shelves, but here and there, some were laid sideways. Even the spaces between the tops of the books and shelf above were crammed with more books and rolled parchments. It was a hidden library below the old library.

"Whoa!" Jonah let out an amazed breath as he stumbled further into the chamber.

Even though everything looked ancient, modern electric lights were mounted along the entire lip that separated the walls from the domed ceiling. The illumination reflected off the smooth stone, creating a subdued yet even lighting throughout the space. Jonah thought it was like many of the libraries he had visited.

While he stared at the treasure trove of books, his parents' attention was on a large, circular ring that was positioned against the fourth wall. Jonah moved closer to give himself a better view. It was made of stone with symbols, like the ones on his parents' blades, carved into the surface.

"Why is a portal in this chamber?" His mom brushed her fingers along the ring.

"They used it to cross over." His dad pressed a large hand against the surface. "I can sense it."

"You mean her?"

Jonah's dad nodded as he rotated on the spot, scanning every inch of the chamber.

"We should leave here now," his mom insisted.

"In a minute." His dad raised his rich, baritone voice so that it echoed through the space. "Elder, show yourself. We need your help!" He waited a moment, then called out again, "Elder. We need you."

"I don't think he's coming, Isaiah."

"You're right. I had to try." He took her hand. "Let's go."

They had turned for the opening to the stairway when the sound of running footsteps grew louder ahead of two men, who came into the chamber. They were dressed in grey tunics and pants with bone-white skulls on the left side of their chests. Each carried a curved, jet black scythe with a hand grip. Their eyes were solid, milky white. As soon as Jonah saw that, his Death Sense spiked. What was it about these white-eyed people that bothered him? Were they Seers, like the old woman from the bus?

A taller, third person in a billowing red robe stepped through the opening behind them. The robe had smudges on it, and the hood was drawn forward. The three newcomers quickly fanned out, blocking the exit.

Jonah's mom made a quick motion with her left hand, causing the cylinder in that hand to transform into a second gleaming blade.

His dad pointed to the bandit in the smudged red robes. "What's the matter, Deyanira? You're looking a bit ragged. I suspect you'll have to cross back very soon."

"Give me the Protector's Ring, Isaiah, and I'll let you live." Deyanira's cold voice cut the air like a knife. Jonah marveled that his dad didn't flinch.

"Your master wants me dead."

"Perhaps. Give it to me and I can let you go." His dad began to shake his head and Deyanira snapped, "Think of your family."

"I am." Jonah's parents gave each other's hand a quick squeeze. His dad stood tall, puffing out his chest and brandishing his own blades. "You can't have the ring."

Deyanira threw back the hood and Jonah sucked in a startled breath. Scars covered her face and a single red ponytail hung off the back of her otherwise bald head. She glared at his dad.

"So be it."

The woman waved her arms in a smooth motion and conjured a greenish ball of flame. It floated in midair until Deyanira brought her hands together and shouted, "*Washa!*" The fireball shot forward.

Jonah's dad waved his blades and shouted, "*Sakoto!*" A sudden gust of wind rushed forward, snuffing out the ball of fire. His dad dropped into a fighting stance.

"Shall we finish what we started?"

Jonah heard the distinctive metallic sound as Deyanira drew out her own blades. The smooth motion made it appear as if the blades were already activated beneath her robes.

Deyanira pointed a blade at Jonah's mom. "You two take care of the woman. Leave him to me."

Panic gripped Jonah as Deyanira's henchmen closed the distance between themselves and his mom. Both men sliced the air with the scythes in practiced movements. The sound of the weapons, like an eerie whine, set Jonah's nerves on end.

However, his mom wasn't bothered by the sound, and she didn't wait for them to strike. She moved like a ninja with her blades as she rushed the nearest fighter. He swung his scythe, and she easily blocked the move. Sparks flew when the weapons connected. The fighter whirled and sliced at his mom again, but she ducked under his arm, cutting him across the leg. He leapt backward, favoring the injury.

She sprang forward, swinging at him with her right blade. He blocked that with his scythe, then was forced to use his hand to knock Janice's left blade aside. He succeeded in doing that twice more before grabbing her left wrist and using his body to push her away. Jonah's mom spun with the motion, came under the scythe, and scored a deep cut across his chest. The bandit spasmed, dropping his scythe to the ground. His milky-white eyes turned normal as he fell to the floor beside his discarded weapon.

A flash of light caught Jonah's attention. His dad and Deyanira whirled, slashed, and countered each other's blows. Their movements were interspersed with blurred attacks and strange pauses. Deyanira lunged, and Jonah's dad knocked her blades aside to land a kick to her midsection. She stumbled back, then turned the fall into a backward flip and came down on her feet.

Meanwhile, the remaining fighter rushed Jonah's mom, swinging his scythe. She managed to leap back as the weapon caught her shirt and sliced it open. The fighter brought the scythe up and down in an overhead swipe.

"Mom!" Jonah shouted.

His mom crossed her blades and caught the scythe, but the force of the blow drove her to her knees. When the attacker shoved her backward, his mom rolled with the motion, pulling the guy forward. Planting a foot on his gut, she heaved, flipping him over her head. The man landed on his back and tried to roll to his feet. Jonah's mom got to her feet first and kicked him between the shoulder blades. She followed that with a swipe across his back, and he slumped to the floor.

Green light flared as Deyanira weaved her arms, conjuring another fireball. "*Washa!*"

"*Sakoto!*" Jonah's dad shouted in response.

This time, the gust of wind stopped the fireball in midair. As his dad continued to mutter and weave his blades, the fireball turned back. It struck Deyanira, whose robe burst into green flames that she snuffed out a moment later. She spun on the spot to face the portal, a sneer twisting her face.

Five widely spaced symbols on the portal already glowed a rich yellow color. When the sixth symbol lit up, a rip formed in the portal's center. It expanded into a circular opening that grew until it reached the inner edges. Jonah shivered as a wave of cold air rolled over him. Several red-robed people stood on the other side. The portal was a doorway.

A cold, inhuman laugh filled the chamber. Jonah's dad raised his blades, staring through the opening. Deyanira flinched and dropped into a crouch. Light flared on the other side of the device from a source Jonah couldn't see and then, a huge, brilliant, red fireball roared through and into the chamber.

His dad shouted, "Get down!"

The fireball sailed over his parents' heads and hit the far wall. Books, wood, and stone exploded in all directions. The ground shook as a wave of heat and dust rolled over Jonah. He feared the entire chamber might collapse. Nightmarish red flames began to burn the precious books and the old wooden shelves. Black smoke coiled along the high ceiling like an angry living creature, causing the chamber to fill with choking fumes and intense heat. In the middle of it all, Jonah's parents huddled together.

"Dad!"

His dad turned, peering through the smoke. His eyes widened in shock. "Jonah?" His mom looked around, apparently unable to see him, but Jonah's dad looked directly at him. He took a step forward. "Jonah! How?" His dad paused, lifted his mom to her feet, and pointed through the smoke.

Her blades slipped free of her grasp and clattered on the ground as she raised both hands to her mouth. "Jonah!" She darted forward, but his dad was faster, slipping an arm around her waist and pulling her back. She struggled in his grip, slapping at his arms and glaring up at him, but he held firm. After struggling for a moment more, she finally relaxed and leaned her head against his chest.

"Mom? Dad?"

His parents faced him, both oddly composed despite the nightmarish heat and destruction around them.

"We're sorry, Jonah," his mom said.

"Just remember," his dad added. "We did everything to protect you."

"We love you, sweetheart," his mom shouted.

Alarm rolled through Jonah and he started for them, but at that moment, another huge fireball roared through the opened portal, adding to the hellish red glare from the roaring flames.

Jonah's Death Sense hurt more than ever, forcing him to his hands and knees, and he threw up. His dad faced the oncoming fireball, weaving his hands in a complex motion and shouting, "*Sakoto!*"

Jonah reached out for his parents, but everything began to waver. The sounds warped as he felt himself being pulled away. The scene grew smaller as if he were sucked through a dark, scary tunnel until nothing but darkness remained.

CHAPTER FIVE
BEARER OF BAD NEWS

"No!" Jonah shouted, in his own bed again. He squeezed his eyes shut and tried to return to the dream.

"Jonah, wake up!" He opened his eyes to find Mrs. Garrett leaning over him in her nightgown. "You were shouting in your sleep."

"I have to go back!"

"Honey, you're in the bed. You haven't been anywhere."

"You don't understand." He struggled to sit up and realized his bedsheets were twisted around his body. He'd also thrown up on himself, and the soiled pajama top clung to his sweaty skin. Jonah trembled all over; the lingering smell of burning books irritated his nose.

"Jonah, what's wrong?"

"It's my parents."

Mrs. Garrett couldn't hide the look of fear that crossed her face. "I'm sure they're all right. They'll be here tomorrow." She helped Jonah untangle himself from the messy sheets and pointed to the pajama top. "Take that off."

"But something happened to them!" His words were muffled as he pulled the offending garment top over his head.

Mrs. Garrett frowned as she gathered up the bed sheet with his smelly pajama top and hurried from the room with the balled-up mess.

Jonah slumped back on his damp pillow and glanced around the darkened room. Despite what she said, he could tell Mrs. Garrett believed him. That meant she knew something about his Death Sense. He wondered why his parents would tell her before they'd even talk to him about it. He started to tremble all over again.

Not my parents, please!

The certainty about his parents threatened to overwhelm Jonah as he lay there. Mrs. Garrett returned several minutes later with a cup of warm mint tea and a clean set of sheets and pillow case. Jonah hastily wiped the tears from his eyes as she gave him the cup.

"This should help you sleep." She motioned him to stand, unfolded the sheets, and quickly remade the bed.

Jonah lifted the cup with a shaking hand, drank some tea, and frowned. His mom had fixed mint tea for him whenever he had a bad dream. Mrs. Garrett's had a strange aftertaste. Jonah tried to concentrate on that as he got back in bed, but his mind refused to work and his eyes closed. Immediately, flashes of images from the dream sprang into his head. He forced his eyes open and was surprised to see Mrs. Garrett standing in the doorway. Wasn't she just beside the bed?

"Try to get some sleep, Jonah." She closed the door.

Alone again, he rolled over and glanced at the clock on the bedside table. It read two in the morning. He had officially turned thirteen years old. Jonah curled up under the covers and tried to keep his eyes open. He didn't want to go to sleep.

He struggled to focus on the strange dream. He'd had them before, but never anything this detailed. That chamber, the sounds and smells, were so real. And his father truly looked shocked that he was there. How could that happen in a dream? And why couldn't he control anything?

With a start, Jonah realized that thinking of his parents didn't cause pain. The buzz and headache were gone. He wanted to believe that his parents weren't in danger anymore and they would be all right. As he tried to hold on to that comforting thought, his eyes overcame his resistance to keep them open, and sleep overwhelmed him.

A cry rang out, startling Jonah out of his sleep. He sat up in bed and blinked at the muted sunlight coming through the window. He listened as someone, probably Mr. Garrett, raised his voice for a second. Then the cry subsided into the low tones of a conversation.

Jonah peeked at his clock, groaned, and rolled over when he heard another muffled voice—a male voice. He sat up in bed again. That second voice sounded familiar. *Dad?* He hopped out of bed and pulled on a shirt as he left the guest room.

The hushed conversation increased in volume as Jonah neared the Garretts' den. When he reached the doorway, all conversation halted. His spirits fell because he didn't see his father. Instead, a tall black man dressed in a long, dark leather coat stood next to Mr. Garrett. The coat was just like the one his dad wore in the dream, Jonah thought. And he recognized the man, especially the large brown eyes that never seemed to blink as they watched him.

He offered Jonah a slender right hand with a bright silver ring on it.

"Good morning, Jonah. My name is Marcus."

"I know you." Jonah shook his hand. "You work with my dad. Have you seen him?"

Marcus's eyes widened and he shook his head no.

"Jonah." Mr. Garrett gripped Jonah by the shoulders. "We need to talk to you." He ushered Jonah into the den and sat him in a chair. Then he began to pace back and forth, looking solemn.

The man's sad face frightened Jonah. "What's wrong? Is it my parents?"

The question forced Mr. Garrett to stop. "Jonah this is difficult--"

"They're dead, aren't they?" Every detail of the dream came flooding back into Jonah's mind. His breath caught as the pain hit him.

"We're sorry." Mr. Garrett knelt in front of him. "There's been a terrible accident and your parents—well, your parents were killed."

Hearing the actual words stunned Jonah even though his mind already knew the truth. His body began to tremble, and he hugged himself. Mr. Garrett patted his shoulder.

That didn't help. Images from the dream flashed through his mind, and he closed his eyes, trying to block them out.

His mind wouldn't cooperate as it replayed the entire fight. *Fight!* He didn't see an accident in the dream. He opened his eyes, staring up into Marcus's face and ignoring Mr. Garrett.

"My parents weren't attacked?"

"Can I talk to Jonah alone?" Marcus also ignored Mr. Garrett as he focused intently on the boy.

Mr. Garrett hesitated, not leaving Jonah's side as he faced Marcus. Jonah could sense the tension between the two men. Perhaps Marcus felt it, too, because he finally shifted his large eyes to Mr. Garrett.

"I'm responsible for Jonah."

"That's funny," Mr. Garrett snorted. "I never saw you around when Jonah had to stay with my family."

Marcus squared his shoulders, and his eyes seemed to bore into Mr. Garrett. Although Marcus wasn't much taller than Mr. Garrett, something about the stare clearly intimidated Jonah's neighbor.

Mr. Garrett broke eye contact first and glanced toward the kitchen. Jonah heard a sniffle and realized that Mrs. Garrett must have been crying in the other room all this time.

"I'll be in the kitchen if you need me." He gave Jonah's shoulder a reassuring squeeze before leaving the den. Marcus moved a chair to face Jonah and sat down.

"Why do you ask if your parents were attacked?" Marcus stared at Jonah in his unblinking way. When Jonah didn't answer, he continued, "I worked with your father. And I don't know if your parents ever told you, but I'm your godfather. You can trust me."

Could he trust Marcus? His parents had talked with the man about his Death Sense, but the dreams were different, and he had never mentioned them to his mom and dad. He had to say something because Marcus watched him, waiting for an answer. "My parents worked in dangerous places sometimes."

Marcus scrutinized him for a several moments, and Jonah wondered if the man could sense his thoughts.

I don't care, he thought. *I don't care if you believe me. I don't care if you believe me!*

Marcus frowned and broke eye contact. After several quiet moments in which Jonah heard the Garretts' low tones from the kitchen, Marcus finally spoke. "Jonah I know you have a lot--"

"Can I be excused?"

Marcus narrowed his eyes. Jonah wondered if he'd gone too far, but again, he didn't care. He just wanted to be alone. Marcus closed his mouth and nodded.

Jonah ran out of the den and came face to face with Tyrone, Kim, and Little Tim sitting on the stairs. Everyone froze, looking at each other. Little Tim started to say something when his big brother clamped a hand over his mouth.

The movement shook Jonah out of his paralysis. He bolted past them and down the hallway to the guest room. One thought pushed all others out of his mind as he closed the door on the world outside. *My parents are dead!*

By mid-morning, Jonah had fled to his parents' home and the solitude of his own bedroom. He lay on his high, full-sized bed and stared up at his jet fighter mobile revolving lazily overhead. He tried to remember putting it together, but images of the terrible dream kept intruding, forcing all other thoughts away.

He sat up and looked around his room. Maybe a book would help. He jumped off the bed and scanned the books on his bookshelf, but nothing interested him. He crossed to the old wooden desk that had once belonged to his dad. A thick piece of glass covered the top. Postcards, tickets, and other collectibles from all around the world were arrayed underneath: every place his parents had ever traveled.

His eyes widened when he saw the postcard with the vintage image of a library on it, the same library from his dream. He lifted the glass, dumping his pencils and notebooks on the floor, and pulled the card out. How could he forget? Not all the postcards were from overseas. Some were from places in the US.

Jonah sat down in his reading chair and stared at the card. It was small, only three and a half by five inches. His mom had told him that the library was the first one built for blacks in that South Carolina county. As soon as he thought about the chamber, the entire dream returned. Jonah allowed it to play out in his head, remembering as many details as possible. He would never forget the milky-white eyes of the attackers. The old woman's eyes had become colorless. Were they connected, he wondered. And what about the woman called Deyanira, the portal, and the strange green and red fire? And who had laughed in such an evil way from inside the portal?

Jonah held the postcard limply in his hand. Why did his parents give him the library postcard, yet never tell him about the strange chamber beneath it? What did their last words mean? How did they protect him by dying? He sucked in a breath and held back the tears. He considered tearing up the card, but quickly rejected that idea. This is where they died, and they had given the card to him for a reason.

It was something from them, a part of them. And, Jonah realized, sitting forward in the chair, he had a whole house of things that belonged to his parents, including a library. He leapt to his feet and stuffed the postcard in a back pocket as he left his bedroom.

Jonah bounded down the stairs and stopped at the threshold to his parents' study. When he took a single step into the room, he paused again as a strange, sad sensation overcame him. A slight pressure touched Jonah's ears, like going up in a plane. Marcus spoke from behind him.

"Jonah?"

He whirled around. Marcus stood beneath the archway between the kitchen and den, watching him. Jonah's eyebrows drew together in confusion.

"Where did you come from?"

"I came in through the back door."

Jonah sensed that wasn't true. He couldn't explain how; he just knew it. Besides, he hadn't heard the back door open or close. Marcus, as tall as anyone Jonah had ever met, looked over Jonah's head and into the study.

"Why were you standing in the doorway?"

Jonah stuffed his hands in his pockets and wouldn't meet Marcus's stare. "My parents never let me in there while they were away."

"You think of going into the study as being disobedient." Marcus gestured around him. "All of this is yours now. Your parents left it all to you."

Jonah bit down on his lip and turned to gaze into the study.

"I'll leave you alone." Marcus nodded and walked to the front door.

Jonah thought his godfather made a show of opening the door and leaving. He hurried over and peeked through the door's little glass window. He didn't see Marcus outside, nor a car. It was as if the man had vanished. The idea didn't bother Jonah. His dad could do it, and Marcus worked with his dad. So why couldn't he do it too, Jonah decided as he backed away from the front door.

He didn't hesitate this time as he entered the study. His eyes were drawn to the large bay window on the right. It faced out on the front yard, and today, bright sunlight streamed through the patterned shears. The little shapes cast weak shadows across his mom's desk and the front of the glass display case behind it. Both were opposite the door and closer to the window. To the left of the doorway, bookshelves covered the entire wall and were stuffed with books and journals from all over the world. His dad's desk was right in front of the huge bookcase.

Jonah crossed to the desk and pulled out the old leather desk chair. It creaked as he sat down, placing his hands flat on the desktop. After a moment, he reached over and picked up his dad's favorite paperweight, turning it over in his hands. It was heavy, even though it was a copy of an actual medallion. Every detail was faithfully reproduced, including a large crack on the side.

Next to it was his dad's gold magnifier, or eye loupe—the same kind jewelers used. As Jonah lifted it to his eye, he heard someone enter the house and move around in the kitchen. At first, he thought Marcus had returned, but when the back door closed a few minutes later, he set the magnifier down and went out to investigate.

Two thick turkey sandwiches, an apple, and a bottle of juice were on the kitchen counter. Mrs. Garrett had come over, and he'd been wrong to avoid her. She had been his mom's best friend. He promised himself to thank her and apologize when he went back to their house.

The sunlight outside had dimmed to a pale golden hue by the time Jonah left his house. Hoping to sneak into the guest room without being seen, Jonah decided to use the Garretts' front door. That plan backfired because Tyrone, Kim, and Little Tim sat at the bottom of the staircase. Tyrone quickly motioned for Jonah to be silent. An unusually quiet Little Tim and Kim sat on the stairs behind their big brother. For a second, Jonah imagined that they had sat in the same spot all day. Then he realized how dumb that sounded. Still, Tyrone's actions confused him until he heard Mr. Garrett's voice carrying from the kitchen.

"I don't think it's healthy for Jonah to be by himself."

"He's always been a quiet boy." Mrs. Garrett sniffled.

"That's my point. I don't want to speak ill of the dead, and I know Janice was your friend, but his parents should have done better. "

Jonah bristled when he heard that, but Tyrone held a finger up as Mrs. Garrett responded.

"They did fine, and Marcus is responsible for Jonah now."

"Well, I'm not too sure about Marcus, either. You've seen the way he looks at us. There's something off about that man. I can't put my finger on it."

"Jonah will be okay. He has relatives, you know."

"Thank God for that. I just hope they're good, down-to-earth people."

Mrs. Garret sniffled again before saying, "Despite what you think, those were Jonah's parents, and he loved them. So you be careful what you say around him."

"Alright. I will."

CHAPTER SIX
THE PLAN

Jonah hid in the guest room, ignoring the Garretts' attempts to get him to come out and eat dinner. When the third knock came, Jonah considered running back to parents' house until he heard a different voice.

"Jonah?" Marcus called out.

Jonah hopped off the daybed and threw the door open. "Why are you here?"

"I came for dinner. Everyone's waiting for you." Marcus held out a hand. "Let's go."

Jonah didn't think he had a choice, so he shuffled down the hall to the dining room. Marcus wasn't kidding. The Garretts waited, watching as he came in. Shame warmed Jonah's face when Mrs. Garrett gave him a sad smile.

"Thanks for the sandwiches, Mrs. Garrett," Jonah said, "and for letting me stay here."

"You're welcome." Her smile grew warmer, Jonah thought, and that made him feel worse.

He lowered his gaze. "I'm sorry I didn't come out."

"That's okay. We know you wanted some time to yourself." Mrs. Garrett glanced at her husband.

Mr. Garrett clapped his beefy hands together. "Well, let's eat." He gestured at the two empty chairs on Jonah's side of the table. Kim, Tim, and Tyrone were bunched up on the other side.

Jonah relaxed as dinner started and the adults talked among themselves. He was shocked to discover that Marcus wasn't just his godfather; the man would also function as the executor of his parents' estate.

He caught Jonah's stare. "I went by your home today to assess everything and make arrangements."

Once again, Jonah could sense that Marcus didn't tell the whole truth. He wondered if the man had gone through his parents' study after he had left. *It's mine now*, Jonah reminded himself again. He'd have to get used to that. Even so, he realized that, in his mind, all those things would always belong to his mom and dad.

After dessert, Tyrone took his brother and sister into the den to play video games. Mrs. Garrett, who had gone off to the kitchen, returned with coffee and motioned to Jonah.

"Why don't you go and join the others?"

Marcus gave him a slight nod, so Jonah rose and followed the others into the den. He didn't join in playing the videos, but sat to the side and watched. Soon he grew bored with that and decided to head back to his room. That's when he caught a part of the conversation the adults were having in the dining room.

"I think Jonah should see a grief therapist or counselor," Mr. Garrett commented. "I have a friend who specializes in that."

"I don't disagree with providing Jonah help," Marcus responded. "I only ask that you let me find a professional from our company. We have counselors on staff."

"What difference does it make?"

"Dear," Mrs. Garrett chimed in. "Let Marcus handle it."

Jonah's anger got the better of him and he whirled around—and bumped into Tyrone.

The larger boy stepped back. "You want to play me in a video game?"

"No."

Tyrone glanced at the dining room doorway. "Don't pay them no mind."

Jonah pushed past the boy, hurried to the front door, and stepped out into the hot evening. He had no clue where he was going until he stood at the bottom of the porch steps. Should he walk off around the neighborhood? Maybe he should go to the park and sit on the swings to think. Why bother? Whatever the adults decided, he knew his opinion wouldn't matter.

He walked to the driveway and leaned against the back of Mr. Garrett's sedan. Jonah stuffed his hands in his pockets and shuddered with pure frustration and loss. He wanted his parents back. He wanted life back to how it used to be. He wanted to be home, with his mom and dad talking in the next room, their voices reassuring and safe. A tear rolled down his cheek. He reached up to wipe it away just as the front door opened.

Jonah expected Mrs. Garrett to come out, but instead, Marcus walked to the driveway and stopped facing out toward the neighborhood. Jonah wondered if the man even noticed him. The sun had already set and he leaned in the shadows. As Marcus lingered, Jonah's frustration returned.

"I'm a freak," he said softly.

When Marcus slowly turned, Jonah knew the man had sensed him all along.

"You're not a freak, Jonah." Marcus stepped closer. "You a teen boy, like any other in the neighborhood."

Half-lie, Jonah told himself. "Then why are you afraid?" Marcus raised an eyebrow. "I know you're afraid of what I could tell a doctor."

"And what exactly could you say to a therapist?"

"You know. I'm different. My dad was different. I have Death Sense. I heard my mom and dad talking about it. He told you."

Marcus subjected Jonah to one of his unblinking stares for a full minute before he spoke. "What do you think a therapist would say about that?"

Jonah looked away. "They would think I'm crazy." As Jonah said it, he knew that he could never tell a therapist any of those things. That made him feel even more alone. "I can't say anything, so send me to a doctor." More tears ran down his cheeks.

"Jonah, you've suffered through a horrible loss." Jonah shook his head, but Marcus went on, "I would never send you to a regular therapist because you would need the freedom to talk about everything that's happened. And you'd need someone who would understand. I wasn't lying to Mr. Garrett. Our company has professionals. You could be totally honest with them."

"So, are you gonna do it?"

"Do you want to talk to someone?"

"I don't know." Jonah swiped at his face, smearing the wetness across it. He was glad it was dark so Marcus couldn't really see that he'd been crying.

"We'll wait to see how you do, okay?"

Jonah nodded, even though he still had the sense that Marcus didn't want him to talk to anyone, not even someone from his company. It was all too much for him to figure out, so he kept quiet as Marcus checked his watch.

"I have to go. There's a million things to arrange."

When Marcus gestured to the house, Jonah's anger flared again.

"I don't want to play video games."

Marcus raised an eyebrow. "I wasn't going to suggest that you do that."

"Oh. Sorry."

"I was going to suggest that you go inside and get some rest."

Jonah pushed off from the car and started for the porch. Marcus subjected him to one of his stares before he turned and strode down the driveway. As soon as the man had turned away, Jonah paused to glance at his godfather. That's when he noticed the black sedan parked along the street.

"You have a car?" Jonah called out.

Marcus stopped at the end of the driveway. Even in the dimness, Jonah could see the smile on the man's face. "I assure you, Jonah, I travel like everyone else." Marcus lingered for a moment, then said, "Most of the time."

When Jonah awoke the next morning, the conversation with Marcus was still on his mind. He didn't want to think about wills, estates, or any of those things, so he avoided Marcus for as long as possible.

To occupy his time during the day, Jonah began to methodically go through his parents' books. *They're my books now*, Jonah had to remind himself. He stayed there all day long, only pausing when Mrs. Garrett brought him lunch. He ate dinner with the Garretts that evening and even played video games this time. Marcus never showed up, although Jonah couldn't be sure if his godfather waited until evening to go through his house again. Jonah was sure that Marcus was searching for something.

Despite his misgivings, he continued his self-imposed exile for a third day, searching through his parents' library. He had pulled books, gone through them, and even taken notes for almost two hours when came upon an old grey hardcover book.

The faded gold letters on the side read *A Manual of History*. Jonah pulled it off the shelf and carefully removed a brittle rubber band that had been wrapped around it. The inside front cover contained an imprint of the seal from the Public Library of the District of Columbia.

Jonah's finger brushed a piece of folded notebook paper stuck inside. He turned to the marked page and his eyes were drawn to an underlined sentence halfway down the page:

The Protectors possessed powerful rings which enabled them to carry out their duties.

Jonah unfolded the piece of paper. Two words were jotted down in his dad's slanted handwriting: *Protector's Ring.* Below that was the letter *H* with a question mark. Jonah wracked his brain trying to think of anyone his parents knew with a name starting with the letter *H.*

A light knock came from the study door, and Little Tim peeked into the room.

"Wow, nice library." Little Tim saw the books on the desk in front of Jonah. "Were you studying?"

"I'm researching." Jonah closed the history book and laid it on the desk, watching the younger boy enter the room.

"What are you researching?"

"I'm looking for stories about people with strange powers."

"Can I help?"

"Maybe later."

"Oh, okay." Little Tim's eyes widened and he scooped up the magnifier, lifting it to an eye to look through. "Wow, this is cool."

Jonah quickly took the magnifier from the boy and sat it back on the desk. He considered taking it, the medallion paperweight, and a couple of other things and packing them now. He paused because he still thought of them his dad's things. They belonged here, on his desk.

Little Tim crossed to the glass display case behind the other desk and pressed his hands and nose against it, gazing at all the objects inside. The boy's breath quickly fogged the glass, causing Jonah to stir.

"Tim, does your mom know you're here?"

Little Tim turned around with a guilty look on his face. "Yes."

"She does?"

"My mom told me to come over."

"Why?"

"That tall guy wants to talk to you."

"Why didn't you tell me that?"

Little Tim shrugged. Jonah was sure the boy had begged his mom to come over so he could look around the house. He knew Jonah's parents were archeologists and thought that was really cool.

When Jonah considered it, he guessed his parents did have cool jobs. He ached with the pain of the loss, and his eyes teared up. Jonah leaned down, pretending to look in his book bag so he could wipe his eyes.

"Jonah?"

Little Tim stood beside the desk, staring at him.

"What?"

"Can I come back and see the library again?"

Jonah blinked and glanced around. "I guess so." He carefully placed the old rubber band around the grey book, slipped it in his book bag, and leaned the bag against his father's desk. A bit of fear gnawed at him, and he wondered why Marcus wanted to see him.

Jonah paused in the entrance to the den with his hands stuffed in his pockets. Mr. and Mrs. Garrett sat on the small couch while Marcus sat across from them in one of two armchairs. Mr. Garrett waved Jonah inside.

"Come on in and have a seat."

Jonah watched Marcus as he crossed to the remaining armchair. The lawyer gazed at the Garrett family photos on the fireplace mantel. As Jonah sat down, the man's large, unblinking eyes focused on him. After a moment, Marcus shifted his attention to a briefcase sitting on the coffee table and lifted a single page. Jonah noticed that he didn't disturb the other pages arrayed on the briefcase.

"Jonah." Marcus paused until Jonah focused on him. "You remember your aunt and uncle in Georgia?"

"Yeah, but I haven't seen them in a long time." Jonah glanced at the Garretts, both of whom looked a bit worried. "Why?"

"Your parents made arrangements. In the event of their deaths, and if you were still a minor, your aunt and uncle would become your legal guardians." Marcus paused. "You understand?"

"I have to go and live with my aunt and uncle in Georgia?"

Marcus nodded, watching him. What did Marcus expect him to say or do? He didn't have a choice. Then a thought occurred to him.

"What about our house? What about all my stuff and my parents' stuff?"

"Don't worry about those things. You won't move to Georgia until late July, giving you plenty of time to pack. By the way, school starts up the second week of August, so that should give you time to settle in."

"August? I'll lose a whole month from summer vacation."

Jonah was struck by Marcus's smile in response. It seemed genuine.

"I'm sorry about that. You should start thinking about everything you want to take. The company will ship and store the rest of your parents' things in Georgia so you and your relatives can go through them at your leisure."

"Does that include the library?"

"Yes. We will pack and ship your parents' entire library."

"And," Mrs. Garrett spoke up. "You should try packing a little at a time. That way, you won't let the move date sneak up on you."

Marcus nodded in agreement as he leaned forward to read the next page sitting on his briefcase.

Jonah focused on the coming move and his relatives. He didn't hate them. In fact, he barely knew his aunt and uncle or heard from them except when they sent a gift. He remembered twin cousins, a boy and girl about two years older.

What bothered Jonah was a vague feeling that something strange had happened the last time he visited, seven years ago. Even though he couldn't remember the details, the thought of going back made him nervous.

"Now," Marcus paused and exchanged a quick glance with the Garretts before he continued, "your parents' memorial service is scheduled for tomorrow."

"What memorial service?"

"We would have told you sooner, but we didn't want to interrupt your solitude."

Mrs. Garrett reached over to touch Jonah's arm. "Are you okay with that, dear?"

"No." Jonah said it before he could stop himself. A memorial service would force him to think about his parents and the fact that they were gone.

"It was wrong of us not to tell you sooner." Mrs. Garrett shot an angry glance at Marcus and her husband. "We know this can be a little overwhelming--"

Jonah pulled his arm away from Mrs. Garrett's hand and stood up. Marcus watched him for a moment and then set his papers on the briefcase. "We can talk about the rest later."

Jonah nodded, but his heart raced and his hands were balled into fists. The Garretts looked miserable and avoided his direct gaze. Marcus remained calm and stroked his clean-shaven chin while subjecting Jonah to his strange stare.

After a few more awkward moments of silence, Jonah stalked out of the den and down the hall to the guest room.

The conversation in the den flared up as soon as Jonah closed the door, so he blocked it out.

CHAPTER SEVEN
MEMORIAL SERVICE

Jonah's eyes snapped open. Something had awakened him: a loud bird call just outside his window. Jonah pulled back his curtain to find a large crow sitting in the rhododendron bush outside. The bird caught the movement of the curtain and tilted its head to watch Jonah. It let out another caw and took flight. Jonah closed the curtain and sat back in bed, rubbing the drowsiness out of his eyes. That's when he noticed the black suit hanging on the door handle.

Did I put that there? No, I didn't. Mrs. Garrett must have done that last night, after I went to bed.

Jonah slumped as the suit reminded him that today was the memorial service. He still believed that a service would make everything so final, but he also wanted to honor his parents. His mom had bought the suit for him at the start of the summer even though Jonah never wore it.

Now he would wear it for his parents' own funeral, Jonah thought as he dragged himself out of bed. He showered and dressed on autopilot before going downstairs.

As he expected, everyone wore solemn expressions when he entered the kitchen. Mrs. Garrett offered to make breakfast, but Jonah shook his head. He wasn't hungry. At ten-thirty, Mr. Garrett took Kim and Timothy to a friend's house. When he returned, Mrs. Garrett, Tyrone, and Jonah were ready to climb into the family car and head to the cemetery.

Jonah wondered if the memorial service would take place inside a chapel or at the graveside. He knew from Mrs. Garrett's conversation that his parents had chosen a historic black cemetery in Washington, DC. As Mr. Garrett steered between the large wrought-iron gates, Jonah gazed out at the headstones. Some were small and normal. Others were large and elaborate. He saw several with headstones capped with obelisks several feet high.

Jonah's Death Sense gave an unexpected twinge, and he scanned the few people scattered among the headstone. *There!* A woman in black stood absolutely still, looking down at a granite headstone that was smaller than all the rest. If not for her presence, he would never have seen the grave. A light breeze blew through the graveyard, and as he expected, the woman's black dress didn't move an inch. As Jonah concentrated on that, the woman raised her head to look directly into his eyes. In the space of an eye blink, she vanished.

Jonah sat back in the seat, thinking. His Sense wasn't as severe and intense when he saw these strange people. It was more like a warning or an alert. He nursed that thought until Mr. Garrett pulled the car to a stop.

His guess about a chapel or graveside service proved wrong. They had parked in front of a mausoleum. Rows of exterior burial crypts lined the visible side of the building.

He followed the Garretts to the front doors, where an elderly black man in a dark suit and white gloves waited. He nodded to everyone without speaking, then turned and led them through the dim interior to a bare, metal elevator. It creaked loudly as everyone stepped inside. This surprised Jonah, who had expected something fancier.

The elevator descended three floors, banged to a stop, and opened. The subdued lighting heightened the eerie feel of the place. Several people stood near an exposed niche about halfway down the wide central corridor. Four rows of folding chairs faced a simple podium and a cloth-covered table.

Mr. Garrett paused to look around. "The cemetery didn't provide enough chairs."

"Marcus told me that we'd be able to sit up front with Jonah." Mrs. Garrett started for the front row.

As they moved closer, Jonah's attention was drawn to a couple of ornate urns resting on a temporary shelf below an opened niche. They were shaped like books with widened bottoms. The urns would be placed side by side in the Blackstone niche, like books on a shelf. Tears stung Jonah's eyes and he fought to keep the pain of his loss under control. He wouldn't cry in front of everyone.

Marcus stood among a group of people Jonah didn't recognize. They were all dressed more or less alike, with the same button on their dark suit coats, so Jonah suspected that they all worked for the company. Although he was curious about the buttons, he was too far away to see their details. It took him a moment to notice a boy wearing shades standing among the group. Jonah thought he must be at least eighteen. After all, he also wore the same button.

Beside himself and Tyrone, the boy was the only other young person here. He glanced in Jonah's direction, then quickly looked away. That's when Jonah noticed the bald man with deep, dark skin.

Omar?

Jonah had met Omar three years earlier, on the same day he'd met Marcus. Omar placed a hand on Marcus's shoulder, whispering in his ear while nodding toward Jonah. Everyone in the group turned to watch as Marcus excused himself and strode over to Jonah and the Garretts.

"Thank you for coming and bringing Jonah." Marcus gestured toward the reserved seats in the front row.

Before Jonah could sit down, Marcus placed a hand on his shoulder.

"I need a word with you." Jonah thought Marcus would take him to meet his group. Instead, he walked along the front row of seats and down the main corridor. He turned to watch the small crowd as he waited for Jonah. "How are you doing this morning?"

Jonah shrugged. Mr. Garrett watched them with a curious glance, and Jonah recalled the man's comments about his godfather. He glanced up and caught Marcus giving him that unblinking stare.

"Is that all you wanted to ask me?"

Marcus finally blinked and shook his head. "I wanted to let you know this memorial will be a little different."

"What do you mean *different*?"

"Everyone will be invited to say a word or two about your parents. You'll be the last one to go."

"I don't want to say anything!" Jonah's voice carried, and people turned in his direction. He lowered his voice. "Can't you do all the talking?"

"Jonah, you're expected to say something about your parents."

"But--"

"You'll know what to say when the time comes." Marcus guided him back to his seat, gave Jonah a final nod, and walked off to greet other people.

"Are you all right, Jonah?" Mrs. Garret patted his forearm.

"Yes, ma'am," Jonah lied.

The panic rose up inside him. This—being the center of attention—is what he hated. He began to shake, and he turned in his seat to hide the reaction. As he looked around the crowd, he fought to hold back the nervousness.

The central library manager, a Jamaican man with long salt-and-pepper dreads, stood in the back with two other people from the library. The man gave Jonah a friendly nod. Jonah considered waving back, then thought better of it because his hands shook.

As he battled with the nervousness, he sensed the change in the crowd before he heard Marcus clear his throat. He faced forward. Marcus stood behind the podium, waiting. Once silence settled over the gathering, he folded his hands together on top of the podium.

"We came here today to honor the lives and memories of two dear colleagues and friends: Isaiah and Janice Blackstone. They were brave, fearless, and tirelessly worked for the benefit of all human beings." Marcus paused, reached over to the table, and pulled off the covering cloth. Jonah stared wide-eyed at the table.

A collection of buttons, pins, framed pictures, ribbons, a couple of statuettes, books, and papers covered the table. Jonah suspected that all these things belonged to his parents. Marcus selected a small medal and held it up for all to see.

"Isaiah Blackstone taught me that true compassion transcends all boundaries, circumstances, and expectations. It's a lesson that I'm still learning. I will always remember Isaiah." Marcus lowered the medal and clutched it in his hand as he stepped to the side.

For several tense moments, no one moved until the library manager walked to the front and took a small manual from the table. He turned to the crowd and held the manual high.

"Janice Blackstone taught me that real knowledge begins with knowing yourself. Only then can you truly understand others." He looked briefly at Jonah. "I'll always remember your mother." He walked back to his seat holding the manual tightly against his chest.

And so it went. One person after another gave their remembrance until finally Mr. and Mrs. Garrett went up together. Once they finished, Marcus turned to Jonah and nodded.

Jonah rose shakily to his feet and went to the table. At first, he didn't know which item to take. Then he saw his dad's golden magnifier and he picked it up without thinking. Suddenly, an idea came to him. Everyone had chosen to honor either his mom or dad. Shouldn't he honor both of them?

Jonah glimpsed something feathery. He moved aside a postcard to reveal a large feather from an actual black eagle. It belonged to his mom, and he gently lifted it in his hand. And last, he selected a framed photo of his mom and dad taken while they were on one of their archeological trips.

Jonah stepped away from the table and turned to face the crowd. His mind went blank.

What could he say about his parents that others hadn't said?

He glanced down at the feather, aware of the quiet expectation of the crowd. As the silence stretched, he heard his mom's favorite saying float through his mind, and he knew what to do.

He held up the eagle feather in his trembling hand.

"My mom--" His voice cracked with nervousness.

He heard Mrs. Garrett say, "Give him strength," in a low voice.

Jonah began again. "My mom. She tried to teach me that being alone isn't living. She showed this by the way she lived her life and by the different people she knew." He found the library manager in the crowd and nodded to him. "I'll always remember my mom."

Jonah held up the magnifier. "My dad told me to never be afraid of the new and unknown. He said that if I learned new things, I would grow into what I should become." Jonah's voice grew stronger. "I'll always remember my dad."

Next, he held up the framed photo. "What happened to my parents taught me that no one knows what will happen tomorrow. I think that we should appreciate what we have today. I will always remember my parents."

When Marcus stepped toward the podium, Jonah held up all three items. The movement surprised Marcus, who stopped.

"I remember my mom," Jonah intoned.

A couple of people from the company said loudly, "We remember your mother."

"I remember my dad," he continued.

"We remember your father." More people joined that time.

"I remember my parents."

The entire crowd responded with, "We remember your parents."

Jonah paused as the last words echoed down the corridor. Then he lowered his arms and bowed his head. Marcus stepped behind him, placing a hand on each of his shoulders.

"Well done, Jonah." Marcus gently guided him toward his seat. Jonah started to sit down, but he stopped because at that exact moment, his stomach fluttered and his Death Sense buzzed.

He quickly scanned the crowd and sucked in a quiet breath. A mysterious short man, dressed in dark clothes that made his pale skin stick out, stood back from the gathering. The man also scanned the crowd, and when his gaze came to Jonah, he blinked in surprise.

Marcus finished his closing comments and the memorial guests rose to their feet, blocking Jonah's view of the man. He dodged to the side to see around the clump of people, but the mysterious man had disappeared.

Wait, Jonah wanted to shout to the man, but his Death Sense still buzzed. The man was nearby. Jonah's excitement grew. Maybe this time, he could talk to one of these strange people.

Luckily, the Garretts engaged Marcus in conversation. Omar and the older boy stood nearby. No one paid any attention to Jonah. He made his decision and slipped away into the bowels of the crypt.

CHAPTER EIGHT
STRANGE VISITOR

The dimly lit crypt proved far larger than Jonah had anticipated. From what he could see, the crypt contained a main corridor with an arched ceiling. Then there were the four parallel side corridors and oddly spaced connecting side passages, creating a huge, underground grid.

Just when Jonah feared he would never find the mysterious man, his Death Sense gave him a jolt. He stopped and peered down one of the larger side corridors. The lights began to flicker and two bulbs went out, leaving half the hallway in shadows. *This blows*, Jonah thought as he took a step toward the darkness.

"What are you?" The voice came from the end of the hallway.

Jonah's knees shook with fear, yet something about the man drew him. He squinted into the shadows and could just make out the man's outline.

"I'm a boy."

"I can see that. The question is: how can you see us?"

"Why wouldn't I be able to see you?"

"Mortals can't see us."

Jonah shuddered, his quaking voice betraying his growing nervousness. "Why can't mortals see you?"

The man didn't respond, and Jonah began to think that maybe following him had been a bad idea.

"Who are you?" The man's voice wasn't menacing. He sounded curious.

"I'm Jonah. Jonah Blackstone."

He heard the rustle of cloth, and the mysterious man stepped under a flickering light. He had a short scar along his pale right cheek, and his stark white hair stood out in the light. The man didn't come any closer. He simply narrowed his hazel eyes.

"You're Isaiah Blackstone's natural son?"

"Y-yes."

"But that's impossible. Your father…" The man stopped, cocking his head to the side as if listening to something.

"What about my father?" Jonah moved closer, then sucked in a breath because he also heard something. It sounded like a distant call, a siren. As he tried to get a better fix on it, an image exploded in his head, causing him to grunt in pain.

He saw a young guy squirming on the ground, clutching his midsection and moaning in pain. He lay in the middle of a side street in some city, Jonah didn't know where. Another young guy knelt over him, trying, without success, to get his friend to stand. He would die soon. Jonah knew that. Despite the blood covering his shirt and ground and the ragged breaths, Jonah sensed it. Death.

Just as suddenly as the vision came, it vanished. Jonah groaned again and stumbled backward. The mysterious man darted forward, grabbing Jonah's arm and keeping him standing.

"How could you see that?"

Jonah twisted out of the man's grip. "What about my father?"

The man stared at him for another moment, then stepped back into the shadows and vanished.

"Jonah!" Marcus strode around the corner a second later, Omar and the strange boy trailing behind. "What are you doing here?"

"A man stood right over there." Jonah pointed at the patch of shadows. "He just disappeared."

Marcus turned quickly to Omar and gestured toward the spot.

Omar closed his eyes and raised a hand, palm up and fingers spread as if pushing against something. A moment later, he opened his eyes and looked at Marcus.

Realization washed over Jonah. "You can sense him."

Omar offered Jonah a little smile.

Jonah turned to Marcus. "Who are these people I keep seeing?"

"You've seen others?" Marcus traded a startled glance with Omar.

Jonah nodded, hoping that Marcus would finally tell him something. However, his godfather shook his head.

"We need to get you back. The Garretts are worried about you."

"No. Tell me what's going on."

"Jonah…" Marcus reached for his arm. Jonah stumbled back and would have fallen if the boy hadn't grabbed him with a surprisingly strong grip.

Jonah glanced up into the boy's shaded eyes.

"Jonah, this is Kevin," Omar said, inclining his bald head toward the silent boy. "Kevin, this is Jonah."

Kevin raised his chin but didn't speak. Jonah wondered if the boy was angry because he had stepped on his feet.

"Jonah," Marcus began, running his large hand over his face and down to the back of his neck. "This is not how your parents would want you to act."

"You talk about honoring my parents. They never treated me like a kid!"

"Your parents didn't tell you everything."

"So there is something going on."

Kevin snorted.

Omar chuckled and said in his deep, African-accented voice, "He's definitely his father's son, Marcus."

Marcus glared at Omar, who simply crossed his muscular arms and returned the glare. Marcus let out an exasperated breath, turned, and strode off. As he reached the corner, he shouted over his shoulder, "Bring him along!"

Omar shook his bald head as he patted Jonah on the shoulder. "It's good to see you again. You've grown over the last three years." Omar held out an arm. "After you, Mr. Blackstone."

"Can't you tell me anything?"

Omar paused, as if he might reveal something. Even Kevin turned his head to watch. Finally, Omar sighed. "I'm sorry. That's up to Marcus."

"Oh." Jonah hung his head and started back. At least Omar answered him, unlike Marcus. He didn't know if he angered his godfather and frankly didn't care. Whenever an adult treated him like a kid, his attitude jumped over rational and landed squarely on defiant and rebellious. That's how his dad described it whenever they butted heads. Depending on the degree of Jonah's stubbornness, Jonah's dad would get just as irritated as Marcus appeared to be. However, his parents took care to treat him like he had a brain.

Jonah's irritation with Marcus rose again. He saw the look Marcus and Omar had traded when he mentioned the others. Why did they try to hide it?

I'm glad I talked to one of these people.

That thought also produced more questions for Jonah. Why did the visitor say that mortals couldn't see him? He sounded as if he wasn't mortal. If he wasn't a mortal, did that mean he was immortal?

Jonah wondered how he could see immortals. He held up his hands, stared at them, and thought to himself, *I'm a person. I'm mortal. And I can see them.* As Jonah lowered his hands, the reality sunk in. He had just pissed off the one person who could possibly answer those questions.

Way to go, Jonah.

His parents' memorial service had been enough of an event. Jonah wasn't ready for the gathering at the Garretts' house. After more than one person told him how brave he had sounded, Jonah had to get away. This time, he decided to be a bit more clever because Mrs. Garrett and Marcus were keeping an eye on him.

He excused himself to use the hallway bathroom. When he came out, he paused to pretend to check his tie. Mrs. Garrett was in the kitchen unwrapping another gift of food. That left Marcus as the one to avoid.

Waiting for the right moment, Jonah was rewarded when a husband and wife came through the front door. He made a show of shaking their hands. As soon as the new arrivals moved off, he took a deep breath and slipped outside.

He set off down the street at a brisk walk, expecting someone to shout for him. He didn't breathe easier until he turned the corner and walked out of sight of the Garretts' home. Feeling safer, he slowed his pace and loosened his tie. Although he feared Marcus or Mrs. Garrett would come after him sooner or later, he didn't care as long as he had some time alone.

When Jonah reached the little neighborhood park, he crossed over to a wooden bench and sat down. Slipping in his iPod's ear buds, he lay back on the bench, and listened to the entire soundtrack Tyrone had given him for his birthday. He wanted the music to take him away, since he literally couldn't get away like he wished he could. That didn't mean he wanted to go to Georgia. He wanted another life of adventures like the ones he imagined his parents must have experienced.

The cold reality settled in and Jonah squeezed his eyes tight in an effort to prevent tears from rolling down his cheek. His parents' lives were far more dangerous than they had ever let on. And now they were gone. Could that be the reason Marcus wanted to keep him in the dark? Jonah shook his head, not wanting to let go of his anger toward his godfather. He didn't want to understand the man's point of view. He grunted in frustration as he stood.

Listening to music wasn't working, but he wavered, trying to decide where to go next. He didn't want to return to the reception, yet he didn't have a choice. However, going back didn't mean he couldn't take his time. He exited the park on the opposite side and proceeded to make a big loop through the neighborhood before reaching Sayre Road.

He'd make another right at the end of the street onto Saintsbury and head back to the Garretts'. Jonah managed to add at least ten more minutes of welcomed solitude to his walk. When he finally started up Saintsbury and his own house came into view, he slowed his pace. The urge to run inside and hide out in his room rolled over him. No, he had to tell himself. *That's the first place they'd look for me.*

He continued on, each step increasing the dread at being the center of attention. As he reached the Garretts', he didn't expect to find Tyrone standing alone at the top of their driveway, shooting baskets. The boy's tie had been loosened and his shirtsleeves rolled up to the elbow. Tyrone paused, waiting for Jonah to reach the top of the driveway before tossing him the basketball.

"Mom told me to go find you, but I figured you wanted to be alone."

"Thanks," Jonah said, feeling a brief flash of gratitude toward the otherwise standoffish boy. He took a shot at the hoop mounted to the side of the house.

Tyrone grabbed the ball. "So, you leave for Georgia?"

"Yeah."

"That bites! I hear they still fly the rebel flag down there." Tyrone did a layup, then tossed the ball to Jonah. "Why can't you stay with us? My parents can adopt you."

Jonah shook his head and did a layup. "I have to live with my aunt and uncle."

"Sorry, man."

"Yeah. Hey, maybe you could come down and visit someday?"

"By then you'll have a Southern accent and all!" Tyrone's laughter was brief. "Oh boy." He motioned to the kitchen window where Mrs. Garrett looked out. "I guess we should get back inside before my mom freaks out."

Jonah glanced at the street and debated disappearing into the safety of the neighborhood again. Making his choice, he nodded and followed Tyrone around to the front porch. As they reached the top step, the porch light began to flicker. At the same time, Jonah's stomach gave a twinge and his Death Sense buzzed.

"What's wrong with this light?" Tyrone, at least three inches taller than Jonah, easily reached up and tapped it with a finger.

Jonah turned toward the yard and almost yelled. Three people stood in the middle of the Garretts' manicured lawn, watching him. He tapped Tyrone on the arm. "Do you see those people?"

"See who?" Tyrone looked over Jonah's shoulder and shrugged.

The front door banged open and Marcus stepped onto the porch, his eyes fixed on the three strangers.

"Jonah. I think you and Tyrone should get inside."

Marcus gently nudged Tyrone and Jonah toward the front door as he stepped past them to face the strangers. Jonah reversed course and positioned himself behind Marcus, peeking around the tall man's arm. Two of the strangers, a man and a woman, stood together while the third, a tall man in a grey robe, stood off on his own.

The man and woman bowed to Marcus, then the man spoke in a somber tone. "Please give our condolences to the boy."

They waited for Marcus to return the bow. Once the ritual was complete, the pair pivoted on the spot and vanished.

Marcus turned to the grey-robed stranger. "Your job is finished. File the information in your archives and tell your master it is over."

The man continued to stare at Jonah, which drew Marcus's attention. "I told you to go inside."

Jonah wanted to tell Marcus he wasn't his dad, but at that moment, Kevin came outside. The boy reached inside his suit jacket as he descended the steps. The stranger's eyes widened and a second later, he vanished. Kevin stood on the very spot the man had occupied, scanning the area as if he expected someone else to appear.

"Who were they?" Jonah tugged on Marcus's sleeve when the man didn't immediately answer.

"Not now, Jonah."

"But I could feel them, just like all the others. And you and Kevin can see them."

"Keep it down." Marcus glanced inside the house. "We'll talk later."

Jonah told himself that he'd get answers when most of the people had cleared out. He watched Marcus talk in urgent tones to the other people from the company; the strangers seemed to have lit a fuse under them all. Jonah tried to stay close to Marcus, just in case the man let a clue slip. Mrs. Garrett intervened, though, and pulled him in to the kitchen to thank the library people. By the time Jonah got away and came back into the den, Marcus and everyone from the company were gone.

CHAPTER NINE
BLACK DOGS

Jonah wondered what would happen if he refused to pack or get ready for the move to Georgia? He had a right to be mad. Those strange people who showed up in the Garretts' yard wanted to see him. He deserved to know what was going on.

Jonah grabbed his pillow and hurled it across the guest room. He thought of all kinds of choice words to call Marcus in his mind but soon grew bored with that, so he got up, showered, and grabbed his book bag.

As soon as he stepped outside the Garretts' house and felt the sun on his face, Jonah's irritation got the better of him. He circled around the house to the backyard and got on his bike instead. Packing could wait until later, he thought, and he rode off. He didn't know where he'd go, so he cruised through the neighborhood. The park was full of kids today, but he didn't feel like being around a lot of people.

He continued to ride around his quiet neighborhood, not really thinking about anything. Eventually, he caught the metro into Arlington and the mall where he played videos games until he made his way to the Central library.

After accepting condolences from a worker who knew him, Jonah sat down in his favorite study room. But he couldn't bring himself to study anything. His mind wouldn't focus, so he sat there, letting thoughts and memories slip in and out of his head. Nearly two hours later, Jonah's resolve to oppose the adults in his life gave out, and he headed back home.

When he entered his own bedroom, he stopped. Refusing to pack would not have worked because two bulging suitcases lay on his bed. He opened them up and stared in amazement. Mrs. Garrett had neatly stuffed them with all of his school and winter clothes. He imagined she did it while he was hiding out, and that meant she had stayed home from work. Guilt nibbled at his insides as he zipped the cases closed and slumped down into his reading chair.

What would my parents tell me to do?

His father would gently squeeze his shoulder and tell him to keep going. That was his dad. Never give up. His mom would point out the positive. *At least you don't have to pack your winter clothes. And remember to thank Mrs. Garrett.*

He looked around his room. Maybe Mrs. Garrett was right and he could do a little now to avoid the rush when the time came to leave. Deciding to start with the desk, he propped up the piece of glass and scooped all the postcards and tickets into a side pocket of his book bag. His father's magnifier, the black eagle feather, and photo of his parents were already inside, remnants of the memorial service. Jonah left the two suitcases on the bed and slipped the book bag's strap over a shoulder.

Downstairs, he paused in the archway to the kitchen, staring at a legal box on the counter. A large yellow sticky was affixed to the lid with a message on it.

Jonah, I thought you would like to go through these things and decide which ones you wanted to keep. Take your time. - Marcus

He slipped off his book bag, placed it against the archway wall, and peeked in the box. It was full of his parents' things that had been at the memorial service, things no one had chosen to use in their memorials. Jonah didn't need to go through the box; he planned to keep everything. He replaced the lid and rested his hands on it as he looked around the house.

They had moved here over a year ago, just after his best friend had died. The past year had been quiet for Jonah. His parents even seemed happier. Then the full implications of the move to Georgia hit him. This place was home. And just like his mom and dad, he would never see it again.

Jonah's contemplative mood persisted for the remainder of the day and into that evening as he sat down to dinner with the Garretts. Everyone seemed in good spirits, and Jonah admitted he began to enjoy himself. His bouts of sadness about the coming move lifted. Everything went well until Mr. Garrett wrinkled up his nose during dessert.

"Do you smell that?"

"Must be a neighbor burning leaves." Mrs. Garrett sniffed the air and nodded. Now that the conversation around the table had stopped, Jonah heard faint shouts coming from outside.

"What is going on?" Mr. Garrett rose from his chair and thundered down the hallway to the front door. When he opened it, a wall of sound rolled into the house. "Oh my God!" He rushed outside, and everyone else followed.

Many of the neighbors ran or pointed down the street. Jonah looked in the same direction and froze. His house was engulfed in flames.

"No!" Jonah started toward the house, but Mr. Garrett grabbed him.

"Stay here, Jonah. It's too dangerous for you to go near it."

"I'll call the fire department," Mrs. Garrett shouted. She led Timothy and Kim back inside the house.

"Let me go." Jonah continued to struggle in Mr. Garrett's grip. "All my things are in there!"

I have to get there! The thought rolled over and over in his mind like a drumbeat. Mr. Garrett released him and spread his arms out, clearly prepared to grab Jonah if he tried to run for the burning house. Tyrone came up behind his father and also readied himself.

"My things are in there," Jonah shouted, the anger and determination surging through him. "I have to get inside!"

Mr. Garrett shook his head. "I can't let you do that."

Jonah let out a frustrated yell and darted for his house. As Mr. Garrett and Tyrone moved to tackle him, something strange happened. A rippling sensation raced over Jonah's entire body. Jonah braced himself for an impact that didn't come. He stumbled, lost his balance, and pitched forward onto the soft ground. The smell of freshly mown grass assaulted his nose.

When he rolled over and looked back, he saw Mr. Garrett and Tyrone several yards away on their own front lawn while he sprawled in the neighbor's yard. It had happened again: he'd managed to move in a blink of an eye, yet he didn't waste time pondering it and scrambled to his feet. A wave of dizziness hit, and he leaned against a lamppost in the yard to steady himself. It took Mr. Garrett and Tyrone calling out his name to clear his mind. Feeling stronger and more determined to save what he could, Jonah raced off toward his house.

Too many spectators had assembled to watch the blaze, and Jonah feared one of them would try to stop him. In fact, a few people had already noticed him running down the sidewalk. He ducked through the gate into his backyard and up to the kitchen door. He burst into the house and immediately began to gag on the smoke. Taking a moment to gather a breath, Jonah ducked low and moved through the kitchen. When he reached the entrance into the den and found his book bag, he gasped.

The fire engulfed that entire side of the house and the whole study. There was no way he could get through to save anything. When he grabbed his book bag, his stomach seized up and his Death Sense spiked.

A fierce growl came from inside the burning study. Jonah moved through the den, peered into the flames, and his heart froze. A huge, dog-like creature moved into view. It tore through the room, ignoring the smoke and flames, which reflected off its jet-black skin.

The creature paused to sniff the air, then twisted its head around to look straight at Jonah with a pair of glowing red eyes. It let out a howl, exposing double rows of sharp teeth as it moved into the study's doorway.

Jonah stumbled back, tripped, and fell on the floor near the entrance to the kitchen. The sight of the creature drained Jonah's will to move any further. Nevertheless, he tried to yell, but instead, he sucked in smoke and started coughing. His vision blurred, and it became harder to breathe. As he sank to his knees, Jonah saw the creature tense and prepare to attack.

Suddenly, the air in front of him rippled and a tall person in a long, black coat appeared, holding two silver blades. He whirled on the spot like a dark, avenging angel, slashing at the creature, which howled and rolled back into the study. The person turned around. It was Marcus! He shouted to someone behind Jonah, "Kevin, get him out of here."

Kevin stepped into view with a pair of silver blades in his own hands. He crouched beside Jonah and paused. "Maybe I should stay…"

"Get him out of here now!"

Marcus whirled around just as another dog-like creature stepped into view.

The heat overwhelmed Jonah, and he resisted blacking out. He tightened his grip on the book bag. Marcus shouted again above the roar of the flames. Kevin snapped into motion, deactivating a blade and using that hand to grab a fistful of Jonah's shirt. A rippling sensation played along his entire body, and a moment later, he and Jonah were in the backyard.

Jonah succumbed to heavy coughs for several moments, his abdomen seizing up and cramping with the violent movement. Finally, he let out a last hoarse cough and caught his breath. From inside the house came loud crashes, howls, and the sound of scraping metal. Kevin cursed under his breath and whirled on him.

"Why did you go into the house, Jonah?"

"I needed to get my book bag. It's all I have left." His vision had cleared enough for him to glare at the boy. Jonah was about to say something when a pair of strong hands lifted him to his feet and he yelled, instead.

"Are you okay?" Omar turned Jonah around, giving him the once over.

"I'm alright."

Omar turned a worried glance on the burning house. Before Jonah could say anything, a shout came from the backyard gate.

"Jonah!" Mr. Garrett and the rest of the family rushed over. "One minute I'm about to tackle you and the next, you're in the neighbor's yard."

"It's just the excitement, honey," Mrs. Garret said. "I'm sure you're wrong."

She moved her husband aside and started brushing dirt off Jonah's clothes. However, Tyrone sputtered and pointed a shaking finger at him.

"I saw him ripple and--"

"We're just glad Jonah wasn't hurt." Mrs. Garrett gave her husband and son a worried look. Her attempts to explain things away were rudely interrupted when Marcus rippled into sight less than a foot from Tyrone. The Garretts' son yelled and tumbled back onto the ground.

Omar hurried to brush dirt and soot off Marcus's long coat. Marcus actually looked a little embarrassed at the attention as he scanned the waiting people. Even though wisps of smoke rose off his coat, he seemed unhurt. Jonah's eyes fastened on a burned spot on the coat's left breast. He corrected himself because the coat wasn't damaged from the fire. There was a symbol branded into the leather: three interlocking circles and a pair of wings spread over them. It was the same symbol on the buttons all the company people had worn at the memorial service.

He wanted to ask Marcus about it, the black dogs, and so much more, but at that moment, the loud cracking of wood drew everyone's attention. They watched as the Blackstone house crumbled in on itself. Jonah slipped around the others, lost for words as everything he and parents owned burned. All that was left was the book bag at his feet. Jonah barely noticed the hand that touched his shoulder.

"I'm sorry, Jonah." Marcus's words were soft.

Mr. Garrett was anything but soft-spoken when he bellowed, "What's going on?"

Marcus spared the man a glance before turning and speaking directly to Mrs. Garrett. "We need to move Jonah tonight."

"Okay," she answered. "I'll put some clothes together."

"Wait a minute." Mr. Garrett held up his beefy hands. "No one is going anywhere until I find out what's going on. Who are you people?"

"It's not safe for Jonah here."

That comment stirred Jonah out of his shocked contemplation of his ruined house. "Why isn't it safe for me?"

Marcus raised his own voice. "Kevin, take Jonah back to the Garretts'."

Mr. Garrett moved to block Kevin, but Omar stepped right in front of the man and crossed his muscular arms.

"Honey?" Mr. Garret gulped, glancing at his wife.

She gave her husband a worried look before turning to Marcus.

"He'll be fine," Marcus answered the unvoiced question. When Mrs. Garrett started to speak, he added, "Janice told you about us?"

She nodded. "Janice told me that you might have to..." She paused, glancing into Jonah's wide eyes. Then she squared her shoulders. "She told me you might have to take Jonah away at a moment's notice."

"Then trust her decision, as she trusted you to watch over her son."

Mr. Garrett stared between Marcus and his wife. "What's this? What do you know about these people?"

Mrs. Garrett wrung her hands as she faced Mr. Garrett. "Marcus wants to talk to you, that's all." She avoided her husband's betrayed expression as she reached for her son's arm. "Come on, Tyrone."

"But Mom!"

When he pulled away, she grabbed his ear and twisted. "Now!"

Jonah was shocked by the tactic. He'd never seen Mrs. Garrett so much as raise her voice to her kids. His own mom had never done anything like that to him, either. Tyrone cupped his injured ear as he shuffled toward home, muttering to himself. He didn't dare say anything else to his mom, who marched right behind him. Jonah, following with Kevin attached to his arm, didn't blame him. Mr. Garrett remained in the yard, watching helplessly.

Jonah wondered what Marcus and Omar would do to the man, but his real interest was in Mrs. Garrett. Did she work with Marcus? Jonah knew his mom had told her a lot, more than she told him. That raised even more questions for Jonah as he walked down the sidewalk to the Garretts' house.

CHAPTER TEN
PARTING WAYS

Questions continued to overload Jonah's mind as he waited in the Garretts' kitchen. What were those two black dogs he had seen in the house? What were they doing, tearing through the library? And Marcus and Kevin carried silver blades like his parents'. They could appear and disappear. What did that mean?

All of these questions bounced around inside Jonah's head. Every time he tried to concentrate on one question, another swirled to the surface and took its place. He tried sorting it all out until Mr. Garrett, Omar, and Marcus returned.

Mr. Garrett sounded excited as he stepped into the kitchen behind Marcus. "That's going to be a real mess in the morning." He caught sight of Jonah and gave him a strange look, as if trying to remember something.

Mrs. Garrett returned to the kitchen with Kim and Little Tim trailing behind her. She had a bulging duffel bag in her hands.

"Here you go, Jonah. I packed a few of Tyrone's old things."

Tyrone, who had a dazed look on his face and never took his eyes off Kevin's deactivated blade, sat up in his chair. When he opened his mouth, Mrs. Garrett gave him a severe frown and said, "I took the clothes you outgrew and I had already planned to give away."

Tyrone settled back in his chair and kept quiet as his mom turned to Jonah. "These should hold you over until…" Mrs. Garrett glanced at Marcus, and he nodded. "Until you get to Georgia."

"Georgia?" Jonah's mind finally clicked into motion. "I thought I didn't have to go there until next month?"

"You'll have to leave sooner than we planned." Marcus shook his head. "I wish it could be tonight, but tomorrow will have to do."

"Why? Is it because of those--"

"Jonah!" Marcus gave him a warning look.

Mr. Garrett stared between Marcus and Jonah. "Because of what?"

"Because of the fire," Marcus answered, never taking his eyes off Jonah.

"Well," Mrs. Garrett interrupted, setting the large duffel bag on the floor. "I'm sure your aunt can take care of getting you some new clothes."

She spoke as if his world hadn't been turned upside down again, Jonah thought. Everything was gone: his school clothes, coats, sneakers, even the ugly tie he and his mom bought for his dad for Father's Day.

Little Tim stepped around his mother. "You're going away?"

"Yeah."

"But what about all your stuff?"

"Tim," his mother cautioned. Jonah handled the stab of pain, even though tears threatened to follow at any moment. His sides were starting to ache with the effort to hold it in, and that made his back hurt.

Little Tim's worried expression reminded Jonah of what he had left. He unzipped his book bag and wrinkled his nose at the smell of smoke. He pushed that out of his mind and found the bookmarks Tim and Kim had given him as a birthday present.

"Don't worry, Tim. I still have these." Jonah knew his voice sounded weak. Little Tim didn't mind; he held out a hand for a shake. Kim surprised Jonah when she also insisted on a handshake.

"Jonah needs to rest," Marcus announced. His voice broke the silence that settled in the kitchen and people snapped into motion.

Mrs. Garrett nodded and motioned Jonah out of the chair. Tyrone stood but hung back as his parents said their goodbyes.

"Take care." Mr. Garrett shook Jonah's hand.

"I wish you could stay here," Mrs. Garrett whispered as she gave him a hug. "But your parents made other arrangements." Marcus cleared his throat and Mrs. Garrett hurried on. "Make sure you write and let us know how things are going."

"I will. Thanks." A tear ran down Jonah's cheek despite his attempts to hold it back. He turned and let Kevin escort him down the hallway and out of the house.

A tall woman with extremely short blonde hair stood next to a large black car parked in the driveway. She was dressed in the same clothes as the others: all black. And she wore the long coat complete with the symbol burned into the left chest. When she nodded to Jonah, several earrings in her left ear tinkled.

Jonah stopped suddenly, causing Kevin to bump into him. His curiosity with the symbol overrode his other feelings. He pointed. "What does that mean?"

The woman gave him a tolerant smile but refused to answer. Kevin reached around Jonah, opened the back door, and tossed the duffel bag on the backseat. Then he waited for Jonah to climb in before he followed.

The sudden silence of the car, once Kevin closed the door, shocked Jonah. Raised voices, and blaring emergency radios from the fire trucks felt distant and unreal to him. He watched the flashing lights through the shaded window until a dark shadow blocked the view and a tap came on the glass. Kevin rolled it down and Marcus leaned in.

"I know you have a lot of questions, Jonah. We'll talk tomorrow. Right now, I need to stay here and sort out things." Marcus shifted his gaze to Kevin. "Take care of him."

Kevin nodded.

Jonah didn't dare say anything because he knew he couldn't hold out much longer. For some reason, he didn't want to cry in front of Marcus. Fortunately, Kevin rolled up the window. A moment later, the car backed out of the driveway and pulled away. Jonah turned in his seat, watching the smoldering ruins of his house out the rear window.

His home was gone. His things were gone. His parents were gone. The enormity of the loss finally hit him. Jonah sank back into his seat, buried his head in his hands, and cried. He took great, heavy sobs and barely noticed Kevin patting him lightly on the back. When his body began to shake, Kevin pulled him close and wrapped a protective arm around his shoulders. The boy didn't say anything nor seemed to mind that the tears were wetting his black t-shirt.

Jonah lost track of time. Except for the quiet hum of the car's engine, his sniffles were the only other sound. When he grew quiet, the blonde woman spoke.

"You ready?"

Jonah thought the woman spoke to him until Kevin stirred and answered.

"Why do I have to babysit, Emily?"

"Because Marcus told you to take care of him." Emily had a no-nonsense voice. Yet when she spoke again, her tone had softened. "You're doing okay with him."

"He reminds me of my little brother." Kevin shook Jonah's shoulder. "Hold on to your book bag."

Jonah suspected what would happen next when Kevin reached over and grabbed the duffel bag with his free hand.

"We're ready."

Emily swerved the car off the highway and onto the shoulder of the road. As soon as it stopped, the strange ripple sensation spread across Jonah's body. Kevin shifted beside him and a moment later, the scene around them changed.

A thickly wooded area appeared around Jonah and Kevin a split second later. With the car, and Emily, gone, Jonah realized he sat in midair, and he yelled out.

He didn't fall on the ground because Kevin held him up. The older boy hissed in Jonah's ear, "Put your feet on the ground." Kevin waited until Jonah followed his order, then shook his head. "You don't know how to change your body position when you phase?"

"No."

Kevin stared at him like he had just said he couldn't tie his shoes. Jonah's face grew hot with embarrassment.

"I didn't even know it was called phasing."

"Well, changing your body position is hard to learn."

"You mean--"

"Quiet." Kevin held up a hand.

Jonah bristled. He closed his eyes and let it pass as he thought about learning to shift as he moved. His dad must have been able to do it, and Marcus as well as Omar. Then he realized he never actually saw Omar phase. He was already in the backyard when Kevin phased them outside his burning house.

"Omar can't do it, can he?"

"No, he can't. Marcus has to give him a ride, like I did for you."

"I can do it myself."

"You didn't know where to go. Now, shut up."

"Don't tell me to shut up."

Kevin turned his back on Jonah as he scanned the surrounding woods. Jonah didn't like how the boy bossed him around, like he was a kid. He wondered if Kevin could see anything with those stupid shades on.

Kevin stirred and pointed at the book bag, which Jonah had dropped when they first appeared in the woods.

"Pick up your bag."

"No."

"Stop acting like a kid, Jonah."

When Jonah crossed his arms in defiance, Kevin's body blurred into motion, snatched up the book bag, and shoved it into Jonah's chest. The impact knocked him back. In a flash, Kevin stood over him.

"Sorry. I didn't mean to do that." He reached down and offered a hand. Jonah wanted to tell him to get lost, but he accepted Kevin's help. The older boy pulled him to his feet like he weighed nothing.

Jonah backed away from him. Kevin might look like any other urban kid, wearing a printed black t-shirt and colored sneakers. And the jeans hung just right, exposing the required amount of underwear. However, Kevin was more than he appeared to be. He was clearly strong and super fast, Jonah thought. When he picked up the book bag in his free hand, Jonah noticed the muscles in Kevin's arms, like he worked out.

Kevin turned his side to Jonah and said, "Grab one of my belt loops."

Jonah didn't know why his heart skipped a beat when Kevin said that. He moved closer, hooked his middle finger through one of the loops, and was surprised by the heat coming off the boy's body.

"You're hot." He said it without thinking. Kevin searched Jonah's face for a moment. When he grinned, Jonah's own face grew hot with embarrassment for a second time.

"I didn't mean it like that."

Kevin didn't respond. He twisted his body and phased them out of the clearing.

Once they reappeared in a new location, Jonah squinted through the dimness. He could just make out lights from a building through the thick trees. But Kevin didn't move; he just scanned the surrounding forest.

Jonah grew impatient. "Why are we waiting here?"

Kevin made a dismissive sound before answering, "I needed to make sure the way is safe and we weren't followed. It's a good thing it is. Otherwise, someone may have heard you talking."

"I didn't know."

Kevin placed a hand over Jonah's mouth. When he knocked the hand away, Kevin laughed. "Let's go, little man."

Jonah glared at the older boy and waited. He expected Kevin to grab hold of him and use his ability again. Instead, Kevin set off on foot through the sparse trees, forcing Jonah to run and catch up.

CHAPTER ELEVEN

The lights that Jonah had focused on turned out to be a fifteen-story apartment complex. All the units facing them across the busy street sported gently curving balconies and windows. Judging by the cars going in and out of the parking garage, this was an upscale place.

Kevin paused, waiting for a break in the traffic, then led the way across the road. Jonah began to have misgivings about going inside such a nice place as they approached the double glass doors. He was a mess, and he noticed that Kevin had smudges on his shirt and a little dirt in his hair. The older boy didn't hesitate to enter the lobby of polished marble, smooth granite, and shiny metal surfaces. The concierge at the front desk dropped his evening newspaper and stood, giving the boys a suspicious look.

Kevin waved almost lazily at the man, saying, "Hey, Thaddeus." He continued across the lobby like he belonged in the place.

Jonah wasn't as brave and cast several nervous glances at the concierge until they reached the elevator lobby. Only when they stepped into a plush elevator and the doors closed did he relax. The elevator was done in gold and silver metal and the back wall was one large mirror. Jonah caught a glimpse of himself and averted his eyes. He looked worse than he thought.

He focused on the floor indicator and was shocked. The elevator had already shot up several floors without so much as a vibration or sound. It reached the thirteenth floor and whispered to a stop. Kevin exited onto a quiet and well-lit hallway. It took Jonah a moment to realize the door numbers had the numbers thirteen in them. He'd never seen that before.

Jonah began to wonder if anyone lived on this level, it was so quiet. Halfway down the carpeted corridor, Kevin pulled out a real key and, unlocking a door, he waved Jonah inside.

The foyer was tiled in a light-brown slate. An entry table stood to the right with a mirror situated above it. A small closet was on the left. Jonah followed Kevin as the older boy moved into the unit. To the right, off the foyer, was an open kitchen done in stainless steel, dark cabinets, and granite countertops. Next to that was a large dining area, complete with a formal table made of dark wood that could seat eight people.

The living room had a white sofa and sitting chairs arranged around a large glass coffee table. Kevin maneuvered around these to a very modern dark green and black stone fireplace situated in the middle of a wall of floor-to-ceiling blinds. When he opened the stark white blinds, the illuminated Washington Monument shone in the blackness above darkened trees.

"Wow," Jonah said, wanting to reach out and touch the view. "Is this apartment yours?"

"It's a condo." Kevin paused, and Jonah wondered if he was going to make fun of his mistake, but the other boy simply shrugged and picked up the duffel bag. "This is Marcus's place."

He carried the duffel bag to a narrow bedroom just off the living room and dropped it on a full-sized bed covered in a red-orange spread and matching pillows. A floor lamp and table were positioned beside the bed. Jonah paused in the doorway, next to a small desk and chair. His eyes were drawn to the wardrobe beyond the bed. Beautiful color nature photos adorned the front of its doors.

"This is the guest room," Kevin explained. "The bed is all right." When Jonah frowned, Kevin smirked. "I've crashed on it a few times." He held out a hand for the Jonah's book bag. "You can leave that in here."

Jonah shook his head and wrapped his arms around it. "I'll keep it with me."

"Whatever."

Kevin slipped past him and back into the living room. Jonah followed and sat his book bag on the floor next to the white sofa. Afraid to sit down because the night's events had left him filthy, he settled on stuffing his hands in his pockets and watching Kevin. He wanted to ask questions, but Kevin turned to the window, staring into the darkness outside. Jonah glanced around, struck by how neat the condo looked, almost like a picture in a magazine.

His gaze came to a small bookshelf against the wall between the kitchen and a short hallway, just past the dining area. The bookshelf was one of those modern kinds that slanted against the wall. Instead of just books, small statuettes and pictures also occupied the shelves, including a three-sided picture holder. Jonah moved around the table to get a closer look at the pictures. Omar and Marcus stood arm-in-arm on a beautiful white beach. Marcus actually smiled.

Jonah lifted the frame, turning it over. Omar and Marcus wore cold weather gear and stood in front of a snow-covered peak with skis slung over their shoulders. In the last picture, Omar stood with a group of teenagers around him. All wore the same powder blue school uniform with *Alliance Academy* on the front. The kid's dark skin shone brightly in the sunlight and their high cheekbones and deep-set eyes resembled Omar's own features. Could this be his native country, Jonah wondered. He saw lush, green trees beyond the school that sat in the background.

The stand-alone framed photo surprised Jonah the most because it wasn't a picture at all. It was a reduced Beauty Essence magazine cover featuring Omar. He wore dark jeans and a printed shirt that opened down to his navel, exposing a well-defined chest and abs.

"Whoa."

Kevin glanced over his shoulder, his eyes narrowing when he saw the holder in Jonah's hands. "Omar's a model."

Jonah rotated the holder back to the first picture of Marcus and Omar on the beach, recalling the way Omar had fussed over Marcus. "Are they dating?"

He caught Kevin giving him that unblinking look, the kind Marcus did at times. After several quiet moments, a smile tweaked the corners of Kevin's mouth. "Something like that."

Jonah opened his mouth to ask more questions, but Kevin turned back to the window. Frustration flared inside Jonah, and like a bursting dam, the events of the night flooded into his mind. He forgot about being dirty and curled up on the uncomfortable sofa, hugging himself as he tried to hold off crying.

Kevin heard him sniffle and finally turned around. "I can't tell you what's going on."

"Why not?"

"I'm Marcus's apprentice."

"So?"

"You really don't know a lot about our world, do you? An apprentice can't share anything his mentor forbids him to tell."

"Marcus told you not to say anything?"

Kevin nodded. "I'm sorry, Jonah. I think you should know."

The front door closed and Emily strode into the living room. "I left the car about thirty miles from here."

Jonah didn't understand and hopped to his feet. "Why couldn't you just phase here?" He turned to Kevin. "Why did we have to walk through the woods and across the street?"

"This condo is protected from that sort of thing."

Emily gave Kevin a sharp look, and he shrugged in response.

Realizing Kevin and Emily had let something slip, his determination to get more out of them peaked. "You mean it's protected from those black dogs? What about the Garretts? Aren't they in danger?"

Emily took off her long coat and folded it over the back of a kitchen stool. "The Garretts' house is protected. That being said, having you stay with your neighbors tonight may have created too tempting a target."

Jonah's eyes widened when he heard that. "Who's after me?"

Pressing her lips together, Emily moved into the kitchen without answering.

Jonah leaned against the breakfast counter, watching as she prepared coffee. "Are you Marcus's apprentice?"

Kevin laughed in the background and Emily stopped in mid-motion. "God, no."

"Then why can't you tell me anything?"

Emily placed the coffee pot on the machine and pressed the ON button. "It's Marcus's responsibility, Jonah. Not mine."

She refused to meet his glare. Jonah shifted and his hand brushed against her long coat, reminding him about the symbol.

"Can you tell me about that?"

Emily finally met his gaze before looking down at her coat and shaking her head. Her refusal made Jonah want to scream and he plopped down on the sofa again, knotting his hands into fists. He couldn't remember being so frustrated in his life. He wanted information; he needed it. That's how he was. His parents had always encouraged him to seek out the facts. Now they were gone and Marcus and the others didn't want to tell him anything.

The front door opened again as Marcus and Omar entered. Marcus stopped just inside the living room and scanned the glum faces in front of him.

Even though the man towered at least two feet over Jonah, he took a step back as Jonah ran up to him.

"What happened to the Garretts? Emily says I'm a target," Jonah shouted, not caring that his voice rang through the condo. "Tell me what's going on."

Marcus glared at Emily and Kevin as he spoke. "Jonah…"

"Tell me!"

Omar dropped their coats over the back of an armchair and placed his hand on Jonah's shoulders. Jonah struggled, but he couldn't shake Omar's strong grip.

"Jonah, calm down. I know you're angry. You have a right to be angry and afraid."

"I'm not afraid!" That was true. Anger burned inside him. He was angry with Kevin, the Garretts, and with Marcus for keeping information from him. And he realized he was angry with his parents for dying and leaving him alone.

Omar gently squeezed Jonah's arms. "You wanted to know about the Garretts?"

"Omar…" Marcus spoke up.

"Your way isn't working." Omar turned back to Jonah. "Well?"

In truth, Jonah wanted to get away from all of them. But his desire to understand everything happening around him won out over the impulse to run. He wiped his eyes with the back of his hand.

Omar waited until Jonah nodded, then he said in softer voice, "I'm a Memory Charmer."

Jonah blinked. "A what?"

"A Memory Charmer. I can modify a person's memory."

Marcus let out a breath and leaned against the kitchen counter.

Jonah repeated the term silently to himself as he digested Omar's revelation. He thought he understood and asked, "You can erase memories?"

"No, I can't erase memories. I can suppress them or make them less prominent, and I can only affect very recent memories. Older ones are impossible to touch without serious damage to the person."

"You blocked Mr. Garrett's memories of what happened tonight."

When Omar glanced over his shoulder at Marcus, Jonah wondered if he regretted mentioning the ability.

"Yes, I blocked his and Tyrone's memories, but I like to say I charmed the memory."

Jonah's mind kicked into gear as something else occurred to him. "What about Timothy and Kim?"

"They never saw anything."

Emily spoke softly to Marcus as she handed him a cup of coffee. "Are we considering formally recruiting the mother?"

"She's more valuable as she is, I think."

Omar gave them an impatient look, and Jonah knew Omar wanted to keep him calm. That embarrassed him.

"I'm sorry."

"Jonah, you don't owe any of us an apology."

Marcus leaned over Omar's shoulder. "I think he should get some rest."

"No," Jonah objected. "I want to know what's going on."

"I'll talk to you in the morning." Marcus motioned to Kevin. "We have important business to complete tonight."

Kevin stalked over from the window and leaned over the sofa. "Come on, Jonah." He held out a hand. "It'll be all right."

Jonah reached for his book bag when Omar gripped his shoulder, stopping him.

"Marcus, you should tell him."

"Omar…"

"He has a right to know. He's going to Georgia tomorrow. Now's the best time."

Omar and Marcus locked gazes for several moments, during which Jonah noticed that Omar wasn't bothered at all by Marcus's strange stare. After several more moments, Marcus waved his hands in surrender.

"Fine. I'll tell him, but maybe I should talk to him alone."

"I think," Omar said, "he'll feel better with another teenager present."

Until that moment, Jonah hadn't realized that he'd moved closer to Kevin. He did feel better not being the only kid in this group.

Emily clapped her hands together. "I'll make more coffee."

Marcus nodded. "Maybe you should sit down, Jonah."

Jonah did and was relieved when Kevin perched on the arm of the sofa, hovering close by. Marcus took his time setting his coffee down on the breakfast bar. Jonah suspected his godfather was trying to find the right place to start. Finally, Marcus met his gaze.

"Jonah," Marcus began, "what do you know about Reapers?"

CHAPTER TWELVE
THE HALF-REAPER

"What do I know about Reapers?" Jonah repeated to himself, rather than to the group standing around him. "I know what they do. They take people's souls in the movies and TV shows."

"That's correct as far as it goes. What else do you know?" Marcus replied. When Jonah shrugged, he continued, "There are two additional things I want you to understand about Reapers before we go any further. When certain humans die, instead of their souls going on to their final destination, they are chosen to be Reapers. No one knows how or why those humans are chosen." Marcus paused again, and this time, Jonah realized he waited for a question.

"So all Reapers were human?"

"Yes."

Again, Marcus waited, prompting Jonah to ask, "So what's the other thing I need to know about Reapers?"

"Human souls normally move on to a final destination. Reapers help them along. And even Reapers move on, eventually." Marcus took a deep breath. "But some Reapers choose to go in the opposite direction."

"You mean Hell?"

Marcus laughed. "No, I don't mean Hell. I mean they give up their station as Reapers and become human again. It's called falling and Reapers who undergo the process are called Fallen Reapers. You need to understand both of these things to appreciate what's happening to yourself."

Jonah's mind raced with the possibilities. Why did Marcus focus on Fallen Reapers? "What does that have to do with me?" Marcus held up a hand as Jonah shot to his feet. The gesture stopped Jonah, reminding him to focus on what was happening: Marcus was finally giving the information he'd been so desperate to hear. He took a deep breath and let it out as he sat down.

Marcus nodded and continued, "You can do the things you do because you are half-Reaper and half-human."

Jonah required a full minute to process Marcus's actual words. He leapt to his feet and backed away before Marcus could stop him.

How could he be a half-Reaper? That meant that his mom or dad must have been a Fallen Reaper. All the things his father had done in the dream flashed into his mind and his eyes widened as he stared at Marcus. "My-my dad was…"

"A Fallen Reaper."

"But that's… that's…"

"Impossible?" Marcus gestured to the sofa. "Jonah, please sit down."

Jonah obeyed, drawing up his knees and wrapping his arms around them. Something icy cold gripped his heart, and his stomach burned. *I'm a Reaper, a creature surrounded by Death. Is that why my best friend died? Is this why my parents died?* Jonah's breaths came faster and faster as it grew harder to breathe.

"I'm a Reaper," he said.

"Half-Reaper," Marcus corrected.

Deep down, Jonah thought that was just as bad. He squeezed his arms tightly around his legs. Slowly, the shock began to subside and he could focus on Marcus's explanation. His mind offered up a question.

"You said that when Reapers fall, they become human. Then how did my dad have powers?"

Marcus smiled at him. "You're very perceptive. Let us say that generally speaking, Reapers do become human when they fall. However, there are ways to retain or reclaim some of their former power."

"Wow." All thoughts and fears about being a half-Reaper were forgotten for the moment as the conversation switched to his parents. "Did my mom know about my dad before they met?"

"Yes. That's why your father loved your mother so much. He found someone who accepted him. They eventually got married, and they decided to have you. That caused a lot of trouble. No Fallen Reaper ever produced a child. Many thought it impossible."

Marcus started to go on, but he stopped himself. He traded a glance with Omar, who returned an encouraging nod. Marcus focused on Jonah again.

"Your father and mother hoped that you would be normal and have a normal life. When you developed the Death Sense, they were frightened. Not everyone thought you should be kept in the dark at that point, but everyone respected your parents' wishes. They wanted to protect you from your supernatural half for as long as possible. They did it out of love, Jonah, not shame. And they sacrificed themselves to protect you."

Jonah sucked in a breath. That was exactly what his parents said to him before… Jonah shut his eyes, willing that memory away. He searched for something else to focus on as he thought about everything Marcus had revealed so far.

He glanced around at the others, none of whom watched him directly. A question came to mind, something that he'd mentioned to Kevin earlier. "Fallen Reapers like my dad can phase. And half-Reapers like me can do it."

Instead of responding, Marcus strode to the window to gaze out on the darkened view. He kneaded the back of his neck. Jonah felt a pang; his father had done the same thing whenever he thought about something important.

"You and Kevin phased tonight," Jonah continued, his mind putting more pieces together. "So, are you a Fallen Reaper or half-Reaper like me?"

Marcus shook his head. "You're the only known half-Reaper."

"Then you're like my dad."

Jonah watched Marcus as he lowered his hand, squared his shoulders, and turned to face him.

"Yes, Jonah, we are like your dad. We are Fallen Reapers."

Jonah gaped at Emily, Omar, and Kevin. It was like finding out something he knew all along but didn't recall until this minute. As usual, his mind kicked into gear as more questions occurred to him. "I can't sense you like I sensed the man at the memorial service. And I never sensed my dad or Kevin."

Marcus spread his arms to include everyone in the room. "We are essentially human now."

"But you said there are ways to keep some of the power? How, if you're human?"

"Even though we fall, we're always sensitive to the power as humans." Marcus paused and took a deep breath. Omar went over and touched his shoulder.

"Maybe you should show him, Marcus." Omar's deep voice was quiet.

Kevin stirred. "I'll do it." He stood, pulling his shirt over his head in one fluid motion. Jonah gawked at the boy, caught first by the fact that Kevin was muscular. Then Jonah's eyes were drawn to the intricate design on Kevin's neck, shoulders, forearms, and chest.

Jonah stood to get a closer look. "Are those tattoos?"

"Nah. They're patterns."

"They were etched into Kevin's skin at the time he fell," Marcus added from the window.

Jonah didn't like the sound of that and looked into Kevin's face. "Didn't that hurt?"

"Heck nah." Although Kevin tried to play it off, Jonah could sense that falling must have been very painful. Kevin slowly rotated his body so that Jonah could see that the patterns continued across his upper back.

"Why do it?" Jonah couldn't imagine anyone willingly going through extreme pain.

"The patterns are part of a binding spell and allow us to draw in power," Marcus explained. "When we're fully charged, they are black. When we use power, they turn brown." Marcus indicated Kevin's patterns; they were a deep brown. "After that, they turn deep red and finally, a light red. If one of us ever totally depleted our power, the patterns would disappear, leaving faint scars on our skin."

Jonah pointed at the intricate design. "You have patterns like these?"

"Yes, I do--"

"Although," Omar interrupted, "I see you managed not to show Jonah your own."

Omar's mouth curved into a smile, but Marcus frowned at him.

"As I was about to say, Emily has them."

Emily pulled down the neck of her shirt to show him the very tip of the pattern on her collarbone.

Jonah turned to Omar. "What about you?"

"I've always been human."

Jonah considered that answer as he continued to scrutinize the elegant, thin lines of Kevin's patterns. "So, if Fallen Reapers want to use power, they have to cut themselves like this?"

"Yes." Marcus didn't elaborate as he motioned for Kevin to put on his shirt.

Jonah thought back to his father. He'd seen him shirtless when they went to the beach. His father didn't have the patterns on his body, yet his father had used power in the dream.

"Why didn't my dad have patterns?"

"Your father became human under... different circumstances."

"What circumstances?"

"That story can wait for later." Marcus came over to the sofa. "It's important that you understand what I've already told you." Marcus nodded to Kevin, who scooped up Jonah's book bag.

"Come on," he said.

Jonah stood in a tidy three-piece bathroom, staring at his shirtless reflection in the mirror. *I'm a half-Reaper.* He ran his fingers over his chest and shoulders, trying to imagine having patterns like Kevin.

A knock came on the closed bathroom door, breaking his thoughts.

"Are you all right, little man?" Kevin called through the door.

Jonah's hands dropped from his chest. He felt a little embarrassed because he'd been thinking about Kevin. "Go away."

"We don't have all night."

After a few seconds of silence, Jonah assumed Kevin had walked off. He picked at the debris still in his hair as he studied his smudged face. When he had pulled off his stained shirt earlier and sniffed it, he nearly gagged from the reek of smoke. He finished stripping and climbed into the shower.

Refreshed from a long shower, Jonah returned to the bedroom, that was directly across the hall. Kevin sat in the little chair by the desk, holding one of his deactivated blades. The strange markings on the blade's cylinder fascinated Jonah.

"Can I hold it?" He held out a hand.

Kevin shook his head, and Jonah huffed as he got in bed and pulled the covers up to his neck. He wondered if Kevin was angry because he had taken so much time in the bathroom. The older boy laid the cylinder on the desk and nudged the door partially closed with his foot. When he took off the shades and rubbed his eyes, Jonah was surprised because Kevin didn't look any older than Tyrone Garrett.

Jonah's eyes narrowed as he watched Kevin. "How old are you?"

"Fifteen."

"I thought you were like eighteen or nineteen."

Kevin gave him a tired smile. "No."

"You work with Marcus?"

"Yes, I do." Kevin folded his shades with hard movements of his hand. Jonah thought he'd snap them in two. "Marcus still treats me like a kid even though I have to deal with the same things they do."

"You don't like him."

"No, I don't. I can't wait until I'm finished with his stupid--" Kevin stopped and shook his head. "I'm stuck with him for eighteen more months. Longer if I keep screwing up like I did tonight."

"You didn't screw up tonight."

"Yeah, I did. I disobeyed an order when Marcus told me to get you out of the house. Your safety was the most important thing."

"Why? Those strange dogs weren't after me."

Kevin leaned forward in the chair and rested his elbows on his knees. "They're called Grim Hounds."

"Grim Hounds?" Jonah's eyes widened as he recalled the creature's double row of teeth. "Are they anything like Hell Hounds? I read about Hell Hounds."

"I guess you can call them that."

Jonah's eyebrows drew together. "What were they doing in our empty house?"

Kevin avoided answering as he checked his watch.

When he stood, Jonah sat up in bed. "Where are you going?"

"They need me in the meeting."

"Can't you stay a little longer? It's cool talking to someone my age."

"I'm not your age. I'm fifteen. Besides, you need to sleep." Kevin held up a closed fist. "It's been interesting meeting you, little man."

"Don't call me that."

"Sorry. It's been interesting meeting you, Jonah."

Jonah tapped Kevin's fist with his own. "I'll see you tomorrow, right?"

"You're going to Georgia in the morning. I doubt I'll see you again for a long time." Kevin hesitated before grabbing his shades and the cylinder off the desk. Jonah had hoped the older boy would forget the blade so he could inspect it, but Kevin slipped it in the pocket of his black jeans.

"Wait," Jonah called out.

"I gotta roll."

"Marcus used his blades on those Grim Hounds."

"The blades are really old and made to fight supernatural creatures." Kevin reached for the doorknob and Jonah stopped him again.

"Are you sure I won't see you tomorrow?" Jonah suspected he sounded like a little kid, but he didn't want Kevin to leave—and Kevin didn't seem too happy about attending a meeting with Marcus. Jonah was sure of that when Kevin came back and knelt down beside the bed. Jonah rolled onto his side. Kevin stared back for so long that Jonah wondered if…

"Are you trying the Marcus stare?"

"No." Kevin finally blinked. "It's called the Reaper stare, and I wasn't trying it on you. It's just that, well, you have cool eyes. Gray."

"Oh. Thanks." Jonah experienced a funny, excited sensation. What should he say now? Should he tell Kevin that his brown eyes were nice? Would he believe that? Kevin looked at his watch again and Jonah mentioned the next thing that popped into his mind. "You have a little brother?"

"Yeah."

"Do I look like him?"

"In a way, you remind me of him."

"Is he here?"

Kevin shook his head. "He lives with a family in Chicago."

Jonah propped himself up on an elbow. "You're adopted? Is Marcus your step-father?"

Kevin laughed. "No. He's more like a legal guardian. Just don't let him know I told you that." Kevin gently pushed Jonah's head back onto the pillow. "Lay down."

"Do you ever see your brother?"

"It's been a long time. Go to sleep, little man."

"Maybe you could go visit him in Chicago." Jonah started to raise his head again, but Kevin pushed it back down on the pillow. He pinched Jonah's nose and released it.

"I used to do that to my brother. The little crumb snatcher."

Kevin stared off into space for a moment. Whenever he talked, Kevin seemed like any other fifteen-year-old to Jonah. When Kevin grew quiet, Jonah could sense the difference, the strange otherness in the boy. *Was that his Reaper side?*

Jonah hesitated, then tapped Kevin's hand to get the boy's attention. "Crumb snatcher?"

"My little brother always wanted part of whatever I had."

"I don't have a brother or a sister."

"I know." Kevin smiled and started to slip on his shades. "I'll see you again sometime."

"You promise?"

Kevin paused, his shades halfway to his face, and stared at Jonah for a long moment. He smirked and raised his hand as if making a solemn oath. "I promise you, Jonah Blackstone, that I will see you again."

Jonah thought he heard a pop. Along with the strange sound came a set of goosebumps racing all along his arms and legs, like a cool wind blowing across his bare skin.

"Whoa! What happened?"

Kevin dropped his shades on the floor. His brief playful mood evaporated.

"Jonah! How old are you?"

"I turned thirteen this past week."

Kevin swore softly to himself. "Marcus never told me that." He plucked the shades off the floor and headed for the door.

"What happened?" Jonah called out. "Why's it important that I'm thirteen?"

"Bye, Jonah."

"Kevin?"

This time, Kevin didn't allow Jonah to stop him. He flicked the light off and closed the door.

Jonah lay back in the darkness and reached up to touch his nose.

"Bye," he said in a soft voice.

He wasn't angry with older boy for not explaining that weird sensation. Kevin had made a promise to him and the certainty of it pulsed inside Jonah like a warm glow.

CHAPTER THIRTEEN
STRANGER IN A STRANGE LAND

Marcus sat alone at the dinning table, the end nearest the kitchen, sipping coffee and reading the newspaper. He paused when Jonah shuffled into view.

"Good morning," Marcus smiled. "Did you sleep well?"

"Yes, sir." Jonah's eyes widened when he saw the stack of pancakes, sausages, eggs, and toast on the breakfast counter.

"Please don't call me sir. Marcus will do." Jonah nodded, and Marcus glanced at the counter behind him. "I take it you're hungry?"

"Yeah."

"Good." Marcus nodded at Jonah's bags. "Place those in the foyer."

Jonah did as he was asked, returned to the breakfast counter and grabbed a plate. "Thanks for letting me stay here."

"You don't have to thank me." Marcus glanced at the food. "Go ahead."

Jonah's mouth began to water, blanking out all other thoughts as he helped himself to a heaping breakfast.

"Did you cook all this for me?"

Marcus choked on his coffee just as Omar came around the corner from the hallway on the other side of the kitchen.

He finished buttoning a light green shirt and said, "Marcus can't boil water." He gave Jonah a pat on the shoulder as he walked into the kitchen. "I made a little of everything. We have cereal, if you'd prefer that."

"All this is cool." Jonah sat down with his plate and paused, watching Omar set a plate of food in front of Marcus. The action reminded Jonah of Kevin's comment about the men last night. "I saw your pictures on the bookshelf."

Omar gave Jonah a piercing look as he placed his own plate opposite Jonah's and sat down.

But it was Marcus who answered. "Yes, about the photos," Marcus placed his coffee cup on the saucer. "Jonah, I don't know if you realized it--"

"Oh, I know about you and Omar."

Omar seemed to relax, but he arched one of his eyebrows. "Really?"

"Yeah." Jonah swallowed. "Kevin said you're dating."

"We're partners, Jonah. And, we don't want you to feel uncomfortable…"

"I don't."

Omar smiled and hurried into the kitchen to fetch glasses out of a cabinet. Marcus continued watching Jonah, who dug into his breakfast to prove how cool he was. Of course, it also helped that he was hungry. He devoured the first plate of food and made a second. As he sat down, he paused to gaze out the window, reminded of Kevin standing at that spot the night before. The boy's comment about his eyes popped into Jonah's mind. Was that the same thing as Marcus and Omar?

"Jonah," Marcus asked. "Are you okay?"

"Leave him alone." Omar tapped Marcus on a hand as he took his seat. "I think he's daydreaming."

"But--" Marcus's eyes widened

Jonah's face grew warm. "I'm fine."

As breakfast continued, Jonah snuck glances at Omar and Marcus without being too obvious.

Omar was friendlier than Marcus, asking Jonah questions about school, the types of music he liked, and even drawing Marcus into the conversation. Jonah wondered if Omar and his mom had been friends. They were so much alike.

Marcus reminded Jonah of his dad. He bet the only people his godfather knew were the people from work. As he gazed around the condo, a new thought occurred to him.

"Did my parents ever come here?"

"Yes." Marcus set his coffee cup down, one finger tracing the rim. "They came here from time to time." He traded a glance with Omar. "Why?"

"I just wondered." *Maybe they sat at this table and talked about me.*

Jonah became so lost in his own thoughts at that point, he didn't realize he had cleaned his plate until he tapped it with his fork several times. Omar noticed.

"You want more breakfast?"

Jonah shook his head no. Omar stood, collected the empty plates, and took them to the sink. When he came back, Omar patted Marcus's shoulders. "I'll see you at the airport, Jonah."

Omar gave Marcus a hug and patted Jonah's shoulder with his big hand before leaving the condo.

Jonah leaned forward in his chair as a question exploded in his mind, one he hadn't asked Marcus yet. "My parents didn't die in an accident, did they?"

"No, they didn't." Marcus subjected Jonah to his intense stare, waiting.

"How did they die?"

"Jonah," Marcus blinked, breaking eye contact. "Your parents were real archeologists. They searched for and recovered powerful objects for our organization."

"What kinds of powerful objects?"

"Oh, all types. There were medallions, rings, pendants, talismans, among other things. All were imbued with magical or supernatural power."

"Wow."

"There are people who would use these objects to do great harm. That's why our organization takes them and keeps them safe. It's a constant race, at times a very dangerous and even fatal undertaking."

Jonah caught the reference to his parents and let out a breath, the pang of loss feeling like he'd just been sucker punched.

"So one of these bad people killed my parents?" Jonah could picture that Deyanira woman again. She'd attacked his parents; she had to be one of the bad people who'd use the artifacts for harm.

Marcus, who had hesitated before answering, nodded. "I'm afraid so."

Jonah was relieved that Marcus admitted that much without asking why he knew his parents were attacked. Again, he thought about the dream. The bad guys wanted a ring. Clearly, that was one of those artifacts. Despite the pain of loss, Jonah couldn't deny an intense curiosity about his parents' job.

He thought about all the objects they brought home and wondered if any had magical powers. Even though most of his parents' belongings were destroyed in the fire, he still had one object. He had the paperweight, a copy of a medallion. So many things about his parents began to take on new meaning. Jonah put that aside to jump to another topic.

"Kevin said I could learn to change my position when I phase." Marcus nodded, and Jonah glanced down at his hands. "Can I be a trainee, like Kevin?" As Marcus opened his mouth, Jonah rushed on. "He's fifteen and a trainee. Why can't I do it when I'm fifteen?"

"I didn't say you couldn't train."

"You mean I can?"

"Yes, Jonah." Marcus smiled. "In fact, your parents wanted you to train."

Jonah sensed the truth coming from his godfather. He'd get to train. The thought filled his mind.

Marcus cleared his throat. "I give you my word. You can start training when you turn fifteen."

Jonah's arms and legs tingled with the same odd sensation he had experienced when Kevin made him a promise the night before. It felt less strange this time and just as certain to come true.

If his godfather felt anything, he didn't show it. He didn't seem to notice anything in Jonah, either, as he cleared his throat to continue talking.

"Your parents were heroes in the true sense of the word, Jonah. They dedicated their lives to protecting the world from bad people. It can be dangerous, so don't rush it."

Jonah nodded. "Why do I have to wait? Can't I train now?"

"There are certain things you'll learn now, but more formal training won't start until later, Jonah." Marcus raised his hand to stop Jonah's next question. "Be patient. Wait until you've settled in Georgia. For now, we'll watch over you. Okay?"

Jonah didn't want to wait, but just like the promise from Kevin, he had an inner sense that Marcus would keep the promise to train him.

Marcus watched Jonah with that unblinking stare. When he seemed satisfied, he glanced at his watch. "We better get to the airport."

"Ladies and gentlemen, we will begin boarding Delta flight 403 from Reagan National to Atlanta in twenty minutes. Please have your boarding passes ready."

Jonah peeked at Marcus, curious how his godfather could remain as still as a statue. As if sensing his thoughts, Marcus stirred, glanced at his watch, and pulled a large brown envelope out of his briefcase. He tapped the edge of the envelope on the briefcase's shell as he watched the main concourse.

At last, without looking at him, Marcus handed the envelope to Jonah, who immediately opened it and shook the contents onto his lap. A small black wallet slid out along with a new cell phone, some printed sheets of paper, and a blue envelope. Jonah picked up the wallet and opened it. Inside were twenty-dollar bills and a bankcard. He counted the money: two hundred dollars in all.

"Wow."

"I assumed you'd need cash for the trip." Marcus raised an eyebrow. "Is that too much?" When Jonah smiled without answering, Marcus frowned but continued, "The bankcard accesses the account I set up for you. A small allowance will be deposited in it every two weeks."

"You're giving me an allowance?"

"Your parents are, in a way. You already know they made me the executor of their estate. I'm also responsible for the trust that has been set up for you."

"Trust? My mom and dad left me money?"

"Yes, they did."

"How much?"

"Enough. When you turn eighteen, you can decide what to do with the remaining funds." Marcus picked up the business card and handed it to him before Jonah could ask another question. "My emergency number is on the back. If you ever need me or need something from me, call."

"Okay."

"If I don't answer, leave a message, no matter the subject. It's a safe number. Understand?"

Marcus stared right into Jonah's eyes—and Jonah, understanding, stared right back. "Yes."

"The bus ticket is for the trip from Atlanta to Mount Vernon," Marcus said, tapping the blue envelope. "When you get to Atlanta's airport, just take the airport shuttle to the bus terminal. Your plane should arrive in plenty of time to make the connection."

The flight attendant raised the mic to her mouth and announced, "At this time, we will began boarding flight 403 to Atlanta. First Class passengers can come forward for boarding."

In quick order, the groups disappeared down the gangway to the plane. Finally, Jonah's group was announced. He stuffed the wallet in his back pocket and took his place in the forming line. He got a pleasant shock when he saw Omar striding down the concourse toward them. People stared at him, and one woman hurried over. Omar stopped, spoke to her, then took a pen and magazine she held out. After signing it, he smiled and hurried on.

Marcus let out a snort, causing Jonah to glance up at his godfather. He wondered if Marcus hated that Omar drew attention. Even the flight attendant, an older woman, halted before announcing the next boarding group in order to stare. Omar seemed oblivious to it as he came over to stand beside Marcus, giving Jonah a quick wave.

Jonah lowered his gaze to the envelope in his hands as he moved toward the flight attendant checking the passes. If he boarded the plane, he would leave everything he knew, and that scared him. He'd been comfortable with Omar and Marcus this morning. They knew his parents. They knew about his abilities. They could even train him.

Jonah stepped out of line and hurried back to Omar and Marcus.

"Do I have to go?" He looked up at Omar. "Why can't I stay with you and Marcus?"

"Your parents made arrangements," Omar answered. "These are your mother's people, Jonah."

"But I've only seen them once."

"You've been there more than that." Omar leaned down to stare into Jonah's eyes. "You just don't remember right now." He motioned toward the gate. When Jonah refused to move, Omar stood straight, crossed his arms, and said, "What would your father tell you if he were here?"

Jonah swallowed. "He'd tell me not to be afraid."

"Then don't be afraid."

Jonah continued to stall as the attendant made another announcement for the rest of the passengers to board.

"How about this?" Omar smiled. "See how it goes over the summer, and we'll talk about it later." Marcus stirred, but he didn't say anything. Omar gave Jonah a one-armed hug. "Now hurry before you miss the flight."

When Omar released him, Jonah hurried to the gate. He flashed his boarding pass to the checker. Glancing back, he waved to Marcus and Omar before walking down the gangway.

Jonah's plane touched down at the Hartsfield International Airport in Atlanta, Georgia an hour and a half later. He entered the main airport terminal, expecting to hear a lot of deep Southern accents in the airport. However, most of the travelers spoke in accents as varied as those in Washington.

Jonah followed the other passengers to the designated luggage carousel. As the luggage from his flight began to arrive, Jonah wondered if he could leave the duffel bag. The clothes in it weren't his in the first place. He didn't want them. And he really didn't want the reminder of what he'd left behind.

A mother and two young kids waited nearby. When their bag slid down the chute, the kids yelled and rushed forward. The mom laughed as they struggled to pull it free of the conveyor belt.

The scene reminded Jonah of Mrs. Garrett, Kim, and Little Tim. She'd packed the duffel bag for him as a way to help and he would be wrong to abandon it. After a few more minutes, it arrived. Jonah glanced at digital clock on the wall as he scooped the duffel bag off the luggage carousel. He had just enough time to find his airport shuttle to the bus station.

The Atlanta cityscape soon gave way to the surrounding suburban malls, then scattered rural developments, and finally wooded areas and pastures. As the bus rolled down the highway, Jonah thought about his parents and the burned house. Everything he knew seemed far away. *Don't be afraid of the new and unknown.*

Jonah tried to cheer himself up with his dad's favorite quote. Marcus had said his parents were heroes, and they were. They had faced the dangerous and unknown. His dad stood up to that strange woman named Deyanira. He hadn't backed down or run. Jonah released a breath and fogged up a small patch of his window. Could he do the same thing? He didn't think so. Maybe it would be different when he turned fifteen and could train like Kevin.

Soon, Jonah's own fear returned. To take his mind off of that, he lost himself in a video game until the bus stopped in a small town. A man in military fatigues grabbed a carry-on bag and walked down the aisle. Jonah pressed his nose against the window as the man exited the bus. Two young kids, a girl and boy with flaming red hair, raced into their father's outstretched arms. The man's wife gave him a hug as the man ruffled his son's curly hair with his hand.

Jonah's vision blurred and he sucked in a breath. His dad would do the same thing to him. As he watched the family walk off, his tears obscured the scene. He let them flow as he imagined the moving, blurred shapes were the taxis dropping off passengers at Dulles, the day his parents left on their final trip.

"You need to get a haircut, mister." Jonah's mom had run her fingers over his tightly curled black hair. "It's bushy."

Jonah squirmed and ducked. "Mom, don't do that. It's embarrassing." He looked around, hoping no one saw them.

"My little boy is growing. At least an inch in the last year, and you look more like your father all the time."

Jonah stuffed his hands in his pockets and watched his dad make his way through the airport crowd. With two tall parents, Jonah knew he'd eventually grow. He just hoped he turned out big like his dad and not slender like his mom.

Once his dad rejoined them at the curbside drop-off, he took out his wallet and counted out several bills. "Don't spend all of the money at once. It should last you until we get back."

"What about my birthday?" Jonah took the money and slid it in his jeans pocket.

"We'll make it." His mom placed a hand on his shoulder. "We promise, sweetheart."

His dad held up a silver house key next. "I don't want you hanging out at home the entire time."

"I won't." Jonah frowned and slipped it on his blue Lanier Middle School key chain.

His mom raised an eyebrow. "Remember, Jonah, you're staying with the Garretts."

"Do I have to stay with them? Tyrone hates me."

"Tyrone does not hate you, Jonah."

"I guess he hides from me because he likes me?"

Jonah knew he went too far when his dad gripped his shoulder.

"Have you tried talking to Tyrone?" Jonah shook his head. "You make the first move. If he doesn't respond, at least you know you tried. Don't assume someone hates you."

"Yes, sir."

Jonah looked down at his feet. His dad lifted Jonah's chin so that they looked directly into each other's eyes.

"Never be afraid to try something new. Hear me?"

Jonah nodded.

"We better get inside." His mom checked her watch before glancing at Jonah. "Will you be okay on the metro, Jonah? Maybe we should call Mrs. Garrett to get you."

"He'll be fine, Janice." Jonah's dad flashed him a smile. "Won't you, young man?"

"Yes, sir."

"We'll call you as much as we can." His mother gave him a hug.

Jonah's dad started to shake his hand, then suddenly pulled Jonah into a hug. He ruffled Jonah's bushy hair with a big hand. "Take care, son."

Jonah watched as his parents gathered their carry-on bags and disappeared into the busy airport terminal. The images blurred and shook and he raised his head, hastily wiping his eyes as the bus moved down the highway. He put the game aside and leaned his head against the window again. Soon, he'd be in Mount Vernon. The anticipation about what lay ahead began to build and intrude on his memories of his parents.

What would Mount Vernon look like? Would it be a sleepy little Southern town? How would the people treat me, a young black kid from Washington? Tyrone had joked that Georgians still flew the rebel flag. Was that true? Jonah hated that he never got a chance to do some research. He had planned to look the place up before the fire ruined everything.

Mount Vernon must be okay. My cousins live here, and my parents wouldn't send me if it weren't safe.

CHAPTER FOURTEEN
THE HIGHTOWERS

Slipping on his book bag, Jonah stepped off the Greyhound bus and into the oven of late-June Central Georgia. By the time the bus driver handed over his duffel bag, beads of sweat already trickled down the middle of his back. He squirmed in his hand-me-down clothes as he followed the other passengers into the comparative coolness of the bus terminal.

Jonah paused, realizing he wouldn't recognize his aunt and uncle if they were standing in right in front of him. That's when he noticed a short, solidly built woman near the front doors with two lanky teenagers beside her. She waved frantically at him.

"Jonah! Over here!"

Jonah grabbed the duffel bag and quickly threaded his way across the crowded area, toward his relatives. As soon as he came within reach, Jonah's aunt pulled him into a warm embrace.

"Oh, Jonah! You've grown so much! And you're the spitting image of your mother." She released him and stood back to look him up and down. "I'm so sorry about your parents. The news devastated James when he heard." Jonah needed a second to remember that she meant his uncle on his mother's side of the family.

"We're sorry we couldn't make their memorial service. And then we got the news about the fire. Everything destroyed! Oh my Lord—I couldn't believe it. How are you holding up?"

"I'm doing okay."

Aunt Imma fussed with his clothes, which embarrassed Jonah. She wore a white blouse, black pants, and comfortable-looking black shoes. Jonah remembered seeing waitresses wearing the same kind of shoes. He wondered if his aunt had taken off work to come here.

"That Marcus fellow told us your neighbor gave you these clothes," Aunt Imma continued. "It's obvious her son's bigger than you, Jonah. We'll need to get you more clothes, unless you like them baggy. That seems to be the thing nowadays." She finished pulling and tucking and then stood back, shaking her head.

"Robert and Lynn, say hello to your cousin. What's wrong with you two?" She waved the twins forward.

"Hey, little cousin." Robert spoke with a mild Southern accent as he shook Jonah's hand first.

"Hi," Lynn said. She had a high-pitched accent like her mom. Lynn stepped forward and tried to shake Jonah's hand, but Aunt Imma nudged her in the back.

"Give your cousin a hug."

Lynn obeyed with a quick hug, then stepped back and crossed her arms.

The twins were slender and taller than their mother. Like Jonah, they had vanilla-wafer complexions and medium gray eyes.

Robert wore a simple black t-shirt, cargo shorts, and black sneakers. He had angular eyebrows, and the edges of his bushy Afro were neatly trimmed.

Lynn, on the other hand, could have stepped off a basketball court with her jersey, trunks, and high-top sneakers. Her thin braids fell to her shoulders. She tossed them with a graceful flick of her head.

Aunt Imma poked Robert in the arm. "Help your cousin with his bag." Robert sighed and took the duffel bag from Jonah. She nodded and said, "Let's get you home."

Thirteen thirty-eight Morningside Drive turned out to be a tidy, one-story brick house with a two-car garage and neatly trimmed yard. It also had a matching brick mailbox with *The Hightowers* on the side.

Jonah followed his relatives to the front door, which opened with a wave of cool air. He stopped, reminded of the dream about his parents. Robert noticed his expression.

"You okay, little cousin?"

"I'm fine." Jonah blinked.

Robert continued on inside as Lynn bumped Jonah in the back with the duffel bag.

"Well, get going. You're letting out all the cool air."

Jonah stepped into the Hightowers' foyer. There was a living room on his right and a neat dining room on the left.

Robert continued down the hallway to a large, open room. The L-shaped sofa and two well-worn armchairs looked extremely comfortable. All were positioned to face a big-screen TV above a fireplace and mantel. Game consoles sat on a TV stand beside it. A breakfast bar, on the left, separated the family room from an open kitchen. A set of sliding doors led out to a patio and a fenced-in backyard.

Aunt Imma stood in the narrow hallway that ran the entire length of the family room. A bathroom was at the end of the hallway, but she pointed at a closed door to the right of it. "That's Lynn's bedroom."

She indicated the next door, also closed, with a *keep out* sign on it. "That's Robert's bedroom. And this," she motioned to the first door off the hallway, "is your room. I'm afraid it isn't too large. It used to be your uncle's office."

Jonah suspected that meant his was the smallest room. He entered and dropped his book bag on the twin-sized bed positioned beneath a window. Jonah knew with a glance that the bed wouldn't be as comfortable as his old one. He went over and peeked out the window. It faced a narrow side yard. He turned, noting that the off-white room smelled of new paint.

Aunt Imma hovered in the doorway. "I'm sorry about the fumes. We painted a few days ago. I know it's different from your old room."

"It's nice."

Lynn slipped past her mother, dropped his duffel bag on the bed, and said, "Fantastic."

Aunt Imma frowned and brushed her hand along the top of the dresser. "I've put some of Robert's old clothes in the drawers and the closet. They should fit you."

"Thanks." Jonah slid his hands in the pockets of his oversized jeans and looked around. Compared to his old room, this looked like an empty shoebox. "Really, it's okay. And I'm sorry that Uncle James lost his office."

"He's happy you're here, Jonah." Aunt Imma smiled at him and went back into the family room.

Lynn stood in the hallway, her arms crossed and foot tapping on the floor. "Mom, I have a game. Let's go."

"Okay, okay."

Lynn caught Jonah staring at her from his bedroom doorway. "Are you into sports?"

"I played sometimes with the other kids--"

"Oh Lord, not another geek!"

"Lynn! Be nice to your cousin."

Robert came to stand beside Jonah. "Just because he likes to read doesn't mean there's anything wrong with it."

"He'll fit right in with you, Sci-Fi Boy."

Aunt Imma swatted Lynn on the arm with a fistful of letters. "Lynn, be nice."

"Robert calls me *jarhead* all the time."

"Fine impression you two are giving your cousin." Aunt Imma grabbed her purse and keys. "Robert, you entertain your cousin until I get home."

"But I have something to do at the rec center."

"Then take Jonah with you. Don't leave this house without your cousin."

Robert hung his head. "Yes ma'am."

His aunt gave Jonah another hug, then left. Lynn shot her brother a quick glance before following her mom out the front door.

Jonah turned to his cousin as soon as the door closed. "You don't have to stay."

Robert couldn't hide the relief on his face. "I really need to do something."

"Then do it. I'm okay on my own."

"Don't mention this to Mom."

"I won't."

Robert crossed through the family room and went out the kitchen door. Jonah followed, pausing in the doorway to watch as his cousin rolled a bike from a large utility shed out back. After Robert waved and rode off, Jonah went back to his new bedroom. Once he finished unpacking, Jonah lay on the new bed, gazing at the ceiling. Being here in his relatives' house made all those strange things about himself seem a little less real. He liked that.

Robert came home an hour later, and Aunt Imma soon afterward. Jonah laughed and enjoyed playing his cousin in a video game so much that Aunt Imma's return caught him by surprise.

She paused on her way to the kitchen, a grocery bag in hand, and shook her head at the mayhem on the TV screen. Jonah thought she looked happy. Maybe she assumed Robert had stayed here with him all afternoon.

Aunt Imma continued on into the kitchen to put away the groceries. Jonah's concentration was shattered when he heard his uncle call from the garage doorway.

"I'm home." Uncle James came into the family room carrying a worn brown satchel. His eyebrows shot up when he saw Jonah sitting on the sofa. "Jonah?" He bounded over and gave him a vigorous handshake. "My God, you look like Janice."

Jonah thought that his uncle also looked like his mom with his thin face, pecan tan skin, and brown eyes. Actually, Jonah's uncle reminded him of a professor with his sport coat, goatee, and round eyeglasses.

"How are you doing?" Uncle James leaned back, holding Jonah at arm's length. "Did the flight go well?"

"The flight was cool." Jonah gave up the video game and let his cousin win.

"Sorry we couldn't come up to Atlanta and get you from the airport," Uncle James said. "The memorial service took place so soon, and the news about your parents' house shocked us."

"James…" Aunt Imma had leaned over the breakfast bar. Jonah saw his uncle fighting to keep himself together as he waved to her. When he turned back to Jonah, he wore a sad expression.

"It still doesn't seem real to me. I expect your mom to call and…" He took a handkerchief from the inner pocket of his sports coat, removed his glasses, and dabbed at his eyes.

Jonah understood. Sometimes, he found himself waiting for his mom or dad to call and say they were on the way home.

"We're happy to have you here." Uncle James put his glasses back on and sat his satchel beside the armchair. Then he went into the kitchen to wash his hands before pulling salad greens, tomatoes, carrots, and other items out of the refrigerator.

Before Jonah could ask to help, Robert, who had also gone into the kitchen, reached over the breakfast bar to hand him the forks, then yanked them away.

"Wash your hands and follow me." Jonah copied his uncle and rinsed his hands at the kitchen sink. He had to duck around Uncle James to follow Robert, who had pulled a stack of plates out of the cabinet, placed the silverware on top, and marched into the dining room. They began setting the table. Lynn came home a short time later and helped them finish.

As everyone gathered around the table, Uncle James went to the china cabinet and took out a plate. A folded napkin and silverware lay on top. Uncle James placed it on the table beside Jonah and noticed the confusion on his face.

"You're wondering about the extra place setting?"

Jonah nodded.

"It's a custom in my family. We do it to honor the memory of someone who has gone home, as we say." Uncle James reached over and straightened the folded napkin. "This is for your mother."

Jonah stared at the plate for a long time. He had never heard of this before. It did remind him of the remembrance ceremony for his parents. The tightness in his chest loosened a bit. Everyone stared at him, waiting for him to say something.

"How long do you …"

"Oh, we set the place for thirty days from the time of the funeral or, in your mother's case, the memorial service."

The more Jonah talked about it, the more he thought it the type of thing his mom would have done. He looked at his uncle. "Can I set it tomorrow?"

His uncle smiled. "Of course you can."

Three hours later, Jonah slipped into bed, listening to the sounds of the Hightower house. Robert moved around in the next bedroom, the low thump of music vibrating the wall. Someone watched TV in the family room, probably his uncle, Jonah thought. He wondered if he would ever get used to the newness. Jonah yawned and in no time, he descended into sleep.

Jonah dreamed that he ran along a steep dirt road on four feet. *I have paws!* Jonah realized with a start. The paws looked like something on a dog or bear. *No, I'm a Grim Hound.*

The Grim Hound's body stumbled and lost speed. The creature shook its head from side to side, and Jonah realized it heard his thoughts. He calmed himself and the creature set off again, quickly gaining speed.

Jonah had never experienced anything like this. He wasn't the Grim Hound itself. He was a passenger in the creature's body. He swore his own hands mauled the hard ground as the creature's paws kicked up dirt. His lungs burned each time the Grim Hound drew in the hot, dry air.

He concentrated on being with the Grim Hound and began to sense the creature's thoughts. As it darted around boulders and leapt over bushes, a single idea repeated itself.

Have to find it! Have to find it!

The urgency grew inside Jonah. He needed to find it. His own heart thumped with anticipation and a little fear. The creature's master would be angry if it didn't find it.

What do I have to find? Immediately, the answer came to him: The Ring.

The Grim Hound reached the top of the hill and rushed around the clearing, digging up the dirt. Something gleamed in the sunlight, catching its attention. The creature jumped and sailed several feet. Growling with eagerness, it attacked the dirt with its massive paws.

The object turned out to be the back of a plain watch. The Grim Hound let out a frustrated sound. It gripped the watch fragment in its jaws and tossed it away with a flick of its head. The Ring wasn't here.

The beast howled in irritation, and an unpleasant ringing hurt Jonah's ear as a woman's voice spoke directly in his mind.

Come to me! Now!

A ball of smoke blossomed in midair like a dirty, time-lapse flower. The Grim Hound raced forward and dived into the swirling mass. Jonah sucked in a breath as the damp wetness of the mist touched the creature's body. He was just thinking it didn't feel that bad when a moment later, darkness exploded around them. Clinging strings of vapor blurred his vision, and as they dissipated, a cul-de-sac came into view. Stars twinkled above in the velvet-black sky.

The Grim Hound padded over to a woman in a black dress. Jonah's heart beat faster as the creature looked up. The woman's pale skin glowed in the dimness. She wore square glasses and her red hair was in a tight bun.

When she peered down into the Grim Hound's eyes, the weak streetlight revealed faint lines crisscrossing her face. The creature whined as it looked away and scratched restlessly at the asphalt road beneath its paws.

The woman pointed, and Jonah heard the unspoken command. *Go!*

The Grim Hound hunched its muscles and sprang down the darkened street. Again, Jonah let the animal move in its own way. The Hound rounded a corner, leapt over a parked car, and landed with a heavy, muffled thud behind a tall bush. When it raised its head to watch a house directly across the street, Jonah's heart stopped.

That's my aunt and uncle's house!

Something tugged on Jonah and, suddenly, he wasn't part of the Grim Hound anymore. As he shrank away from the creature, the angry, red eyes seemed to watch him.

Across that very same street, in his own bed, Jonah's eyes flew open. His heart pounded furiously as he sat up and looked at his hands. They weren't large paws anymore.

I'm out of the Grim Hound's body!

Jonah whirled around in bed and looked out his window. The darkened yard outside was empty. He caught himself. Wait. *The Grim Hound watched the front of the house.*

Jonah tried to leap out of bed, but he fell to the floor with a solid bang; his blanket had wrapped around his foot. He untangled himself and rubbed his sore elbow as he walked to the door. He looked out into the silent house and waited. No one came out of their room to investigate, so he tiptoed down the hallway toward the front door.

Just as he reached out to grip the doorknob, he thought of a better idea: the dining room had a large bay window. He slipped into the room, pulled back the curtains, and pressed his face to the glass. That was a mistake because his rapid breathing quickly fogged it and obscured his view. Jonah wiped the glass, clamped his hand over his mouth and nose, and peeked through again.

He spotted the tall bush across the street and let his eyes move to the shadows. He gasped when he saw two glowing red eyes staring back at him. The Grim Hound watched the house from the exact spot as the dream! How could that be? How could he dream about the creature?

The Grim Hound leapt into motion, shocking Jonah out of his thoughts. He threw himself back from the window, cracking his head against a dining room chair. Fortunately, he still held the hand over his mouth; otherwise, someone would have heard him scream.

After seconds of pure terror, Jonah's mind registered the fact that the Grim Hound hadn't charged the house. Even though his entire body shook, Jonah stumbled back to the window and looked out. Far down the street, the creature passed below a streetlight and disappeared into the darkness.

Jonah slumped to the floor. It took a while for him to get his racing heart under control. Slowly, the shock of seeing a real Grim Hound on Morningside Drive began to fade.

How did the Grim Hound find me in Georgia?

Jonah already knew the answer. That mysterious woman in the black dress had called the beast, and she knew exactly where he lived.

CHAPTER FIFTEEN
TEEN CENTER

"Good morning, Jonah!" Aunt Imma hummed as he shuffled into the kitchen table. She paused her stirring of a skillet full of fluffy scrambled eggs and glanced over her shoulder. "I guess you're not used to the new bed."

Jonah nodded as he sat at the kitchen table. His problem wasn't with the bed. He was tired because he had tossed and turned for two hours after seeing the Grim Hound. A real Grim Hound! That thought still scared him. Of course, he couldn't tell his aunt. He couldn't tell anyone—except Marcus.

Aunt Imma set a plate stacked with buttered toast on the table. "Lynn's gone already, so it'll just be you boys this morning. I hope you like scrambled eggs."

"Uh, scrambled is fine." The smell of eggs, toast, and bacon began to push out thoughts of the Grim Hound.

Aunt Imma pointed to the refrigerator with her spatula. "Why don't you get the orange juice?"

Jonah fetched the carton of juice and sat down as his aunt placed a dish piled with eggs and bacon in front of him.

"Robert! Come and eat your breakfast!" Aunt Imma took in Jonah's baggy shirt and shook her head. "We'll get you some new clothes this afternoon, okay? I have to get to work. Robert promised to take you around this morning. You two stay out of trouble." She winked at Jonah, grabbed her bag, and headed for the garage door.

Jonah thought about waiting for his cousin, but the smell of the food made his stomach grumble, so he ate alone. He was halfway through his breakfast when Robert emerged from his room. Within minutes, the shower was running. Afterward, Robert went back to his room without pausing to say good morning.

Maybe he's trying to avoid me.

Jonah finished breakfast and started back to his room, but changed his mind. He walked up to Robert's closed door, ready to knock, and paused when he heard his cousin's voice inside. Should he knock or just leave it alone?

The door opened, and Robert, seeing Jonah, stumbled back. "Hey, little cousin. " He snapped the cell phone closed. "You weren't listening to my conversation, were you?"

"No. I wouldn't do that." He saw the smirk on Robert's face. His cousin was just kidding. "Breakfast is still on the table…" He looked over Robert's shoulder. "Wow!"

Robert stepped back, swinging his door wide. "Come on in."

Jonah entered another world, a very fantastic one.

Overlapping posters from fantasy and sci-fi movies covered every square inch of one wall. Charcoal and pen drawings of other worldly landscapes and ships hid the opposite wall.

One of Robert's drawings caught Jonah's attention, a perspective drawing of a tear-drop-shaped vehicle soaring above a flat plane. Robert had drawn a huge building in the background, its upper portion shrouded in clouds. Jonah reached out a finger, tracing the complicated lines of the ship.

Something about it pulled at him. He could almost feel himself inside the scene. "This is really good."

"Thanks." Robert looked at the floor and absently tugged at his ear. "My mom doesn't like them. That's why I keep my door closed most of the time."

Jonah turned and tripped over a long, black case. "Whoa."

"Careful." Robert scooped up the case and leaned it against the side of his dresser. "That's my trombone. I'm in the symphonic and marching bands at school. In fact, camp starts soon." Robert sat down on the bed again. "You play an instrument?"

Jonah shook his head and noticed the floor-to-ceiling shelving unit on the other side of the dresser. DVD movies filled the top shelf while hundreds of neatly displayed CDs filled the rest.

It reminded Jonah of his own lost mp3 collection. He began pulling random CDs from the wall. Robert had a wide variety of styles, including some of Jonah's favorite soundtracks. He put them back, suddenly sober. "I've never seen anyone with this many CDs," he said softly. "I have everything loaded on my iPod."

"You can borrow mine, if you want. With a really good pair of headphones, it'll sound better."

"Thanks." Jonah looked around Robert's room again, noting a one-fourth scale Predator model, still in the box. "You're really into the fantasy stuff."

"Yeah. You should meet my friend Wick. He's into magic."

"Magic?"

Robert laughed and ran his hand over his bushy hair. "My mom would have a fit if she heard some of the things Wick talks about. We're working on a supernatural computer game together. He does the heavy research. I'm the artist and programmer." His cousin nodded to the pictures. "Most of those are designs for the game."

Jonah stood back, taking in the entire wall of drawings. Robert pulled a pair of white sneakers from underneath a pile of shoes. He paused before putting them on.

"Sorry about your parents. I can't imagine what it feels like." He stared at his sneakers. "My dad took off work for three days. I've never seen him like that." Robert finished putting on his shoes and leaned back on his unmade bed. "We liked your mom. She was cool and used to tell me and Lynn about the places she went."

"I guess it was long time ago."

"A year isn't that long."

"A year?"

"Your mom visited just before school started."

Jonah rubbed his head, trying to remember his parents coming here without him. "I didn't know my parents came down to visit."

Robert sat up. "No, just your mom. We haven't seen your dad since, well you know, when you were a baby. I think there's a picture in the den with my dad, your mom, and Aunt Ruby." Robert grinned. "Your mom has Little Jonah in her arms."

Jonah nodded. He had seen the picture the day before, but he hadn't recognized the woman beside his mom. Aunt Ruby? He couldn't recall her, yet that dread he experienced when Marcus told him about Georgia returned. Jonah rubbed his head. "A lot of things have happened to me. Sometimes, it's like a bad dream."

Robert leaned forward, watching him. Images of Grim Hounds and his strange dream popped into Jonah's mind. He relived the shock and weirdness of running through the streets of Morningside Drive. Could he tell Robert about the strange people in black or the woman with the faint scars on her face? His cousin waited with an intense expression on his face.

Jonah bit down on the urge to say anything. He hoped that Robert would take the hint. After another uncomfortable minute, his cousin leaned back on his bed.

"You'll be okay, little cousin."

"Yeah." Jonah glanced at the wall of drawings and the large artist desk that sat in one corner of the room. Pens, charcoals, rulers, erasers, colored pencils, and several unfinished drawings littered its surface. A thought struck him. "Are all of you artistic?"

"No!" Robert laughed. "My dad is the editor of the local black newspaper. Lynn is into all things sports, as I'm sure you guessed. Now, my mom always has an artsy project going on." Robert snapped his fingers. "You know, she got a commission to do an art piece for the teen center."

Robert hopped to his feet and walked over to a wall-mounted shelf that contained several red wire magazine holders. Each had the word SUMMIT on the spine. Robert tipped back a holder and thumbed through the papers inside.

"Here we go." Robert slipped out a thin newsletter and gave it to Jonah. It had a small picture of a mountain at the center top and the words *The Summit* in large blue letters. The most surprising thing was Lynn's name as editor and Robert as assistant editor. Jonah's jaw dropped.

"Is this yours?"

Robert nodded. "We do it for older kids, like us. There's an article about my mom in there. She registered for one of those art classes at the community college. A bunch of the art students submitted original works for the new center and the city picked three entries, including my mom's piece. Now we can't get her to stop talking about her latest idea."

Jonah quickly scanned through the newsletter. "This is cool."

"My buddy Wick helps out sometimes. We also do an online version as a blog." Robert's stomach grumbled, cutting off his words. He patted it.

Jonah laughed. "Maybe you should eat something."

Robert grinned and said, "Yeah. Then we head to the center."

Jonah followed Robert to a large shed in the backyard. He peeked around Robert's shoulder and saw a wheelbarrow and other gardening tools inside. Then he saw two older 12-speed bikes chained to the vertical struts.

"We're riding bikes to the Recreation Center?"

"Sure. We ride most places we have to go, unless we need to go to the County mall or downtown." Robert gave Jonah a sly smile. "You do know how to ride?"

"I rode my bike to the metro all the time."

"Is that what you call the subway in Washington?"

Jonah nodded.

Robert unhooked the first bike and rolled it out to Jonah. Then he unchained the second bike.

"I wish my mom would let me drive." Robert took the chain from the strut and wrapped it around the bar on his bike. He nodded to Jonah to do the same thing. "Mom barely lets me practice even though I have my learner's permit. I already know how to drive."

Jonah remembered Robert telling his mom that yesterday. He finished hooking his chain on his bike and gave his cousin a curious look.

"How did you learn to drive?"

"Wick's big brother lets us practice in his old pickup truck." Robert gave Jonah a serious stare and closed the shed.

"I know. I won't tell your mom. Maybe you should give me a list of all the secrets I need to keep."

Robert laughed and easily straddled his bike. Jonah sized up his bike before carefully straddling it. The bike was a little larger than his old bike and Jonah had to stand on his tiptoes to keep from hurting himself.

"Is this Lynn's?"

"Lynn has her bike. Wick gave us that one for you. I guess it's a little too large."

"You think?"

Robert laughed. "Ready to go?"

Jonah nodded and they set off.

The first several blocks on the way to the teen center were relatively flat, so they rode along with no difficulty. Then Robert began to climb a series of hills. He resorted to a switchback pattern on a particularly steep hill, and Jonah followed his lead. Robert paused when they reached the top and sounded a little short of breath when he spoke. "That's the steepest hill. And that is the Cedar Hill Recreation Center."

Jonah couldn't believe his eyes. The recreation center was an old Southern mansion with a commanding view of the surrounding neighborhoods.

"The county bought and renovated the old mansion about ten years ago," Robert continued. "The east and west wings of the original house were extended about a year ago. As you can see, we have basketball courts, four tennis courts, and a swimming pool on the other side."

The boys rode up to the center and chained their bikes to the racks near the basketball courts. Jonah followed Robert up the sidewalk, pausing when he came even with the recreation center's sign. Although the sign read *Cedar*, Jonah noticed that Robert pronounced it *Ceda* with no *r*.

Jonah hurried to follow his cousin into the main atrium of the building. He stood beside Jonah and pointed out a starburst sphere made out of thin metal rods and glittering rings. It, and two other art features, was suspended from the atrium ceiling.

"My mom did that one."

"Wow. Where'd Aunt Imma find all those rings?"

"People donated them. I think there are about two hundred and fifty. It's on the plaques." Robert nodded toward three plaques attached to the far wall.

In addition to Aunt Imma's piece, there was a hanging tangle of real children's bicycles. Most of the bikes were metallic blue, green, or red. Beside that hung the third piece, a collection of old wooden tennis rackets. They were cut so that each racket actually intertwined with the others.

"They're interesting the first few times you see them," Robert whispered. "Then you get used to them."

Jonah lowered his gaze and let out a low, "Whoa!"

Directly ahead, kids sat around colorful café tables, talking or texting their friends. A few typed away on laptops. A deli counter sold sandwiches, bottled drinks, candies, and as Jonah watched, a couple of kids got fresh, hot pizzas. He drew closer and noticed the bright blue neon cursive letters above the counter. They spelled out *Cyber Café*.

Robert tugged Jonah back toward one of the arched openings off the atrium.

"This is the East wing. You have all of the recreation game rooms with pool, ping-pong, video games, and board games. On the other side is the West wing. Through there, you have study rooms, a small library, and study tables with built-in Internet access. Administrative offices and meetings rooms are upstairs. I guess you'll want to go in the library first, huh?"

It so amazed Jonah that something like this existed in Mount Vernon that he didn't even pay attention to Robert's picking at him. He didn't want to explore only the library, he wanted to explore every inch of the place.

"So, I can hang out until we leave?"

"Sure. Don't forget we're heading to the mall later."

"Okay."

"Stay out of trouble."

Jonah frowned. "I won't get in trouble."

"I'm just kidding you, little cousin." Robert laughed, but Jonah saw the strange look in his cousin's eyes before Robert headed for the main stairs.

Once again, Jonah wondered if his cousins sensed the difference in him.

CHAPTER SIXTEEN
FRIEND AND BULLY

As Jonah approached the Recreation Center library, he slowed. Three boys about his age stood at the entrance, laughing and talking. A light-complexioned boy with curly hair snatched a cell phone from a shorter, pudgy kid, held it up, and started laughing.

"For real, Drew? No one uses this old phone anymore." He threw the phone back to Drew, who fumbled and caught it.

"What do you use, Brandon?"

"Man, please." Brandon puffed out his chest. "My dad buys me the new models as soon as they come out. And I don't stand in no dang lines, either. It's shipped right to my house. Tell your old man to come off that money he makes. Right, Antwan?"

"Yeah." Antwan, the third boy, answered with a distinct African accent. He was the tallest of the three, with dark skin and a long neck.

Brandon went quiet when he saw Jonah and openly stared, sizing him up. When Brandon didn't bother to say hello or nod, Jonah decided not to bother, either. He slipped by the boys and caught a glimpse of Drew's phone. It was just like the one Marcus had given him.

As Jonah stepped into the library, all three boys laughed, causing him to wonder if they were making fun of him. Probably, he decided and turned down the first aisle of books so he wouldn't be in their line of sight.

Instead of books, Jonah faced a tall display of popular magazines. He peeked around the display, spotted a Young Adult fiction section, and headed straight for it. A few kids were around, including a boy his age who sat in one of the brightly colored chairs along the wall. The only reason Jonah noticed him was because the boy raised his book when Jonah glanced in that direction.

Jonah paused, pretending to check out the books on the shelf. The boy kept the book held high, covering his face. At least he's quiet, Jonah thought, scanning the titles on the shelves. He chose one, began reading the back cover, and almost dropped it when the boy spoke.

"There's not much of a selection." The boy stood at the end of the aisle, peering at Jonah through black-rimmed square glasses. He wore jeans and a pale blue shirt, and his hair was in a small jet-black Afro that set off his pale skin. "I'm sorry. You're new here, right? I haven't seen you before." He clutched the book to his chest as he approached. "I'm Mike."

"Hi, I'm Jonah."

Mike's eyes widened. "You're not from here."

"How did you know?"

"You sound different."

"I'm from Washington, DC."

Mike bounced on his feet with excitement. "Wow! I've always wanted to visit Washington, DC. What's it like living in the capital?"

"Well, I lived across the river in Virginia--"

"Did you ever see the President?"

"Well, the--"

"What about the Capitol building?"

"I never--"

"Or the Washington Monument!"

"Sometimes, but--"

"I bet the museums and libraries are much better than what we have here." Mike waved at the bookshelves. "Do you like to read a lot?"

Jonah blinked several times, waiting for Mike to bombard him with another question. Instead, Mike pushed up his glasses and stared back at him. Jonah opened his mouth to speak just as Brandon loomed behind Mike.

He snatched the book from the other kid's hands. "Hey nerd!"

Mike gave a little yell and stumbled back into Jonah.

Brandon glanced at the cover and made a face. "A romance novel? You wish."

"It's not a romance..."

Brandon puckered his lips and made loud kissing sounds, causing Antwan and Drew to laugh like demented henchmen.

Jonah could feel Mike shaking with fear. He stepped in front of Mike to face Brandon. "Give it back to him."

Brandon looked Jonah up and down, a sneer on his face. Jonah grew self-conscious, his eyes catching the designer logos on the other boy's clothes. Suddenly, he couldn't wait to get to the mall and buy his own things. Brandon stepped closer; he was taller than Jonah expected.

"So you're from DC?"

Jonah blinked. "Yeah. Who're you?"

"Brandon M. Warner, the third." Jonah noticed that Brandon's snide-sounding voice didn't have a heavy Southern accent. When Brandon offered to shake hands, the light reflected off a gold watch on his wrist. "My parents built this place."

"No they didn't, Brandon," Mike spoke right over Jonah's shoulder, causing him to jump. "They gave money like everyone else."

"Yeah, that's right. They gave more than anyone else, especially your folks. So be quiet, nerd." Brandon glanced over his own shoulder. "These are my friends, Drew and Antwan."

Antwan didn't even bother to nod. He stared at Jonah with his chin held high.

Drew at least waved before stuffing his hands in his pockets. All the while, he avoided looking anyone directly in the eye. Both boys wore gold watches like Brandon's. Jonah wondered if the watches were a club thing.

"So DC," Brandon continued. "What do your parents do? Are they FBI agents, or do they work on Capitol

Hill? Antwan's uncle is an ambassador. We're always in Washington visiting."

Jonah hesitated. He wasn't going to tell Brandon his parents were dead. However, Mike saved him from having to answer. "Drew! Why do you hang out with him? You're better than that."

Drew glanced up at Mike before averting his eyes.

Brandon caught the quick look between them and turned on Mike. "I told you to shut up, nerd."

Jonah had heard enough. "Give Mike his book."

"Or what?"

Jonah didn't know what he would do. He'd spoken without thinking. It seemed that Brandon didn't know what to do next, either. They stood toe-to-toe, neither one willing to throw the first punch, and neither willing to be the first to back down. Jonah thought they'd have to stand there forever until he heard Lynn's voice.

"What's going on?" Lynn stood behind Brandon and his friends, arms crossed. Mike moved out from behind Jonah.

"Brandon has my book."

"Here," Brandon said. He shoved the book into Mike's hands. "I was just playing."

Lynn tossed her long braids behind her shoulder. "I suggest you go to the East wing if you want to play." Her voice let the bully know she meant business.

Jonah was impressed by his cousin because Brandon backed away and motioned to his friends. He bumped Jonah's shoulder as he walked by. "See you later, DC."

As the three boys walked off, Brandon glanced back at Jonah and whispered to his friends. When all three laughed, Jonah had no doubt they were making fun of him this time.

Lynn waited until they were out of the library. "Robert's leaving soon. Maybe you should wait in the café so you don't miss him."

Even though she made it a suggestion, Jonah didn't think it was one. "Okay."

He waved to Mike and followed Lynn out of the library.

"Stay out of trouble this time," Lynn said, pausing by the atrium staircase.

Jonah puffed out his chest, ready to defend himself until he saw the hint of a smile tweaking the corners of Lynn's mouth before she turned and walked off.

"I should have known," Mike said from right behind Jonah. "You look like Robert."

"Yeah, they're my cousins. I'm staying with them over the summer."

"Wow." Mike glanced around the atrium. "Over here." Mike claimed an empty café table and sat down. He slipped off his glasses as he waited for Jonah to take a seat. "Thanks for standing up to that bully Brandon. He's a total jerk."

"Was he bragging about his parents?"

"Not really. His dad is a big shot doctor, and his grandfather is an important attorney in Atlanta." Mike made a sour face. "And, of course, all the girls think Brandon's light skin and soft, curly hair are so cute."

Jonah resisted the urge to smile as he wondered exactly how Mike knew Brandon's hair was soft.

Mike slammed his fist on the table top. "Did you see him back away from Lynn? I wish I were tall like Lynn. I'd kick Brandon's butt." As suddenly as it came, the fire leaked out of Mike and the boy slumped back in his chair with arms crossed. He looked miserable.

All at once, Jonah wondered if Mike thought Brandon was cute, just like all the girls did. Maybe that's why his bullying got him so angry. Jonah didn't know why he thought that. Maybe it was a slight prissiness in Mike. Or maybe it was the guilty glance that Drew gave Mike.

Mike huffed. "I get enough pranks at home from my big brother. I don't need it here."

"Why does he pick on you?"

"He thinks reading sci-fi and fantasy is… "

Jonah understood. He'd been accused of being weird because he carried those types of books. Some kids were just plain stupid, he thought.

"What about your parents?"

"My dad agrees and my mom, well…" Mike lowered his gaze but his voice grew angry. "She never sticks up for me."

Jonah couldn't imagine a more horrible position in which to be. Except to have dead parents.

"So," Mike reached across the table and poked Jonah's forearm. "Do your parents work on Capitol Hill?"

A flash of annoyance hit Jonah. Why did everyone want to know about his parents when they heard he was from DC? He wondered how many times he'd have to dodge the question.

The irritation must have shown on his face because Mike leaned back. "I'm sorry. You don't have to tell me." Mike stood.

"No, wait. I don't mind." Jonah smiled, hoping it would cover his earlier annoyance. "My parents are researchers, so they read a lot. My dad even has a library at home."

"Wow! It must be really nice to have parents like that." Mike's brow wrinkled. "Why are you here instead of Washington?"

Jonah swallowed, not wanting to lie, but he also didn't want to reveal the awful truth about his parents.

"My parents are traveling overseas, for work. They sent me to stay with my aunt and uncle over the summer. I haven't been here in years."

"It's like you're getting to know them all over again."

Jonah nodded. "Yeah, it's strange."

"Robert and Lynn are so cool, and they do a lot of stuff. You already know about the newsletter and blog? In fact, they're probably working on them right now."

It took Jonah a moment to catch up with Mike's rapid Southern delivery, wondering if he always talked fast whenever he got excited about something.

"Do my cousins have an office here?"

"It's upstairs in the attic." Mike pointed toward the stairs.

"Attic?"

"Yes. They didn't tell you?" Jonah shook his head. "Well, I bet they're under a tight deadline."

Mike went quiet and glanced down at his hands as he wrung them together. "You know, I thought about showing them something that I wrote, you know, for the blog." He glanced at Jonah, waiting for him to say something.

"That's a good idea."

Mike's hunched shoulders relaxed a bit. "Hey! Have you met their friend Wick? He does stories about strange and weird stuff." Mike lowered her voice. "I think he's a witch."

"A witch?"

"Well, he uses a different name for it, but yes. I think he's a witch."

Jonah laughed, causing Mike to cross his arms and glare back. "What's so funny?"

"Nothing." Jonah couldn't shake the sudden image of a kid dancing around a black cauldron with a pointy hat on top of his head. The words Wick the Witch bounced around his mind. Why should that be so funny, Jonah wondered. He was a half-Reaper!

Mike narrowed his eyes as he watched Jonah. "If you don't believe me, just ask him. He hangs out with your cousin Robert all the time."

"I believe you."

Jonah honestly did believe him. Grim Hounds existed, he was a half-Reaper, so why couldn't other things exist?

Robert and Jonah returned home just moments before Aunt Imma drove up to the house and honked the horn. Jonah paused on the Hightowers' front walkway, staring at the champagne-colored vehicle.

"You have a minivan?"

Robert pushed Jonah toward the sliding passenger door.

"My dad took the van in for a checkup yesterday. Mom drove his car to get you from the bus station."

"I didn't know that."

Robert closed the side door and hopped in the front. "You caused a lot of fuss, little cousin."

Aunt Imma swatted him on the arm. "Robert, that's not true."

"You picked dad up from the repair shop and took him to work almost two hours earlier than normal!"

"Your father didn't mind at all. He was able to get some extra work done." Aunt Imma backed out of the driveway and set off for the mall.

Jonah didn't know if his cousin exaggerated. Frankly, the whole situation made him uncomfortable. He didn't like his uncle giving up his office or changing his schedule.

He knew what his mom would tell him to do. He leaned forward between the front seats. "Thank you for taking me to get new clothes, Aunt Imma."

His aunt smiled back at him. "It's not a problem, Jonah. You're part of the family now."

Green Oaks Mall was located near the Mount Vernon city limits and was a small town in itself. In addition to the mall, there were numerous chain restaurants, supermarkets, and car dealerships all within easy walking distance.

Aunt Imma pulled into a multi-level parking garage and hustled Jonah into the boy's section of the nearest department store. Although she allowed Robert to help Jonah pick out his clothes, she insisted on approving all purchases. When Jonah exited the store an hour later, he had two bulging shopping bags.

"I'll put those to the van." Aunt Imma took Jonah's bags. "I have to pick up supplies for the salon."

"No problem Mom," Robert said, leaning on Jonah's shoulder. "I'll show him the mall."

"Remember you need some shoes, Jonah."

"Yes, ma'am."

Robert watched his mom head off across the pedestrian bridge to the parking garage. Then he tweaked Jonah's ear. "Yes ma'am?"

Jonah shrugged as he batted Robert's hand away. They headed straight to the food court to get lunch. Afterward, they rummaged through the discount bins in a music store, toured the new titles in the video game shop, and then stopped at a computer store so Robert could buy parts. Jonah found it cool to hang out with his cousin.

As soon as Jonah bought a pair of new sneakers, Robert headed out of the mall's ground floor entrance. Jonah followed, taking two steps for each of Robert's longer ones.

"I need to check out the art store," Robert explained. "It's a cool place and has the biggest selection of supplies in the county."

Once they reached the store, Robert held the door open for Jonah. However, Jonah's attention was drawn to a flashing sign two doors down. It read Mystic Worlds. Jonah gave his cousin a sheepish look and hurried down to peer in the store's window. The display featured books on all kinds of supernatural, spiritual, and religious topics.

"Wick told me about this store." Robert stood beside him and tapped the display window. "It opened a few days before you got here." He nudged Jonah with his arm. "You want to go in, don't you?"

"Yeah."

"I don't know." Robert gave the display a worried look.

His attitude bothered Jonah. Robert had all kinds of supernatural pictures on his wall at home and he worked on a paranormal computer game. So why did his cousin think he shouldn't go inside the store?

"It's just a book store, Robert. What's the problem?"

"Wick told me the owner is strange."

Jonah turned back to the window. "I'll be okay. You go to the art store. I can meet you back here in thirty minutes."

"Just be careful, little cousin."

CHAPTER SEVENTEEN
MYSTIC WORLDS

Jonah didn't like Mystic Worlds from the moment he stepped through the entrance. For one thing, it didn't smell like a real bookstore—not the kind with plenty of interesting old books. This store smelled new, and the burning incense couldn't quite hide it.

Maybe it was the statuettes of dragons, winged demons, goblins, reapers, bats, and other strange things that lined the shelves along the dark walls. Or maybe it was the black counter in the back of the store that set Jonah's nerves on edge.

He tried to ignore the sensation and the nagging feeling that his cousin may have been right. Jonah walked between the short bookshelves that covered most of the floor space, glancing at various titles as he went. *Understanding the Real Matrix, Behold the Horsemen of the Apocalypse, 1000 Myths about Modern Science, Beyond the Third Eye,* and *The Wiccan Way,* just to name a few. A store clerk stepped from a back room, slid around the counter, and came up to him.

"May I help you find something?" The clerk talked with a deep voice that didn't fit his very thin appearance. What drew Jonah's attention was a cross hanging from a chain around his neck. No, Jonah corrected himself. The cross had a loop at the top and a brilliant blue stone just below that. Jonah had seen this before, in one of his parents' books. It was an Egyptian Ankh, not a cross. The clerk noticed his stare and fingered the amulet.

Jonah felt a slight tremor in his Death Sense, and he thought the clerk's eyes clouded over for just a second.

"Huh… I wanted to look around." Jonah moved down an aisle on ancient religions. The clerk followed him.

"You're a little young to be interested in these books."

Jonah deliberately turned his back on the clerk, though the hairs on the back of his neck stood on end. "I'm doing research."

"Research? School's out, you know."

Jonah's irritation with the clerk peaked. Pushing aside his uneasiness, he whirled to face the man. "It's personal research. I'm looking for information on Death Sense."

Jonah smirked at the look of surprise that transformed the clerk's face. A shiver ran down his spine when he heard a cool woman's voice. "What does such a young boy know about Death Sense?"

A tall, severe-looking woman in a dark lace turtleneck and a long black chiffon skirt stood behind him. Jonah sucked in a breath. *It's her! It's the woman from my dream.*

Unlike the dream, her hair fell to her shoulders in fiery red curls. She didn't look any older than his mom, Jonah thought. And her eyes never blinked behind her black-rimmed, rectangular glasses as she continued to study him.

Her lips curled into a sneer. "Well?"

"I don't know about it. That's why I'm doing research." Jonah emphasized the last word in an obnoxious way that would have gotten him in trouble with his parents. It had the desired effect, as the woman suddenly stiffened.

"I'm not sure I like your tone."

"I don't like being treated like a kid."

"Indeed. What's your name?"

"Why?"

"Well, if I'm going to help you find what you're looking for, Mr. —"

"Hightower."

"Thank you, Mr. Hightower. It's polite to be able to refer to my customers by name, and some of us do value politeness." Jonah's face warmed at the rebuke. The sneer returned to the woman's face. "Randy, please show *Mr. Hightower* to the appropriate section. I think we have a couple of books on Death Omens."

Randy nodded and led Jonah to the other side of the store. Despite the weird vibe he got from the clerk, Jonah was relieved to move away from the strange woman. He didn't like the way she kept emphasizing his last name as if she knew it wasn't real.

He glanced over his shoulder at her, and his Death Sense gave a funny twinge. It wasn't like the time he saw that mysterious man at the memorial service or the strangers on the Garretts' front lawn. This time, the sensation was sharper.

Jonah suspected the difference had to do with the level of danger. The strangers on the Garretts' lawn meant him no harm. This woman was dangerous and could hurt him, yet she didn't want to do that at the moment. Jonah nodded. *That's it. She's curious about me.*

The clerk made an impatient sound to get Jonah's attention. He grabbed a book off the shelf without really looking. Then he stared at the clerk until the man got the message and moved away. Jonah thought about putting the book back and leaving the store. However, when he glanced at the cover, his heart jumped into his throat.

The Death Omens book featured a hooded figure in a blood-red robe. The robe's hood was drawn forward, hiding the face except for two shining points of light where the eyes would have been. Large Grim Hounds crouched on either side of the robed person. Their mouths were open, showing off double rows of razor-sharp teeth.

Without warning, memories flooded into Jonah's mind. He saw his burning house and tasted the acrid smoke again. He remembered the raw fear the first time he encountered a Grim Hound. The light from the roaring flames had reflected off the creature's double row of teeth as it snarled at him.

Jonah shook his head to dispel the awful memories. The bookstore owner watched him with a smirk on her face, and the temptation to run from the store increased, but Jonah resisted the urge. He wouldn't let the woman scare him away. He selected another book with a shaky hand and carried them to the counter.

"I'll take these."

The owner glanced at the titles of the books before refocusing her intense gaze on him. Jonah wouldn't be intimidated. If he could deal with Marcus's Reaper stare, he could certainly deal with this woman.

Jonah stood straight and glared back at her. The clerk paused ringing up the books to watch the silent battle.

Finally, the woman frowned. Instead of looking away, she leaned forward over the counter. "You don't sound like the locals. You're not from around here."

Jonah made sure to avoid her gaze as he pulled out cash and not his bank card. He didn't want the woman to see his real name. The clerk took the money and wasted time slowly counting it. When he started to count it a second time, Jonah knew he'd have to respond to the woman. "What about you?"

"Oh, I'm new in town. I'm from the Northern Virginia area. Aren't you?" Jonah couldn't shake the feeling that he'd seen her somewhere other than the Grim Hound dream. And her voice sounded familiar, too.

"Small world, isn't it?" She smirked as she watched his expression.

"I don't know what you mean. I'm from Atlanta. I'm staying for the summer."

"Really?" She moved around the counter to stand in front of him and flicked out a hand without warning. Despite his determination not to allow the woman to scare him, Jonah stumbled backward. The woman laughed with a low chuckle that sounded like someone who'd proven a point. "It's just a business card."

When she laughed again, the faint lines across her cheeks and side of her nose seemed to move strangely in the light.

The owner noticed the direction of his stare and shook the card.

"Are you afraid?"

"No."

Jonah snatched the card from her hand. She raised an eyebrow at him. "Manners, Mr. Hightower."

Jonah kept his mouth shut. Anything he said would make him sound scared. Instead, he examined the business card. A stylized image of a Grim Hound glared out at him. The name of the store was embossed in red letters across the creature's body. Below that was the store owner's name: Neera Bledsole.

Jonah stared at the name and flinched when a hand gripped his shoulder.

Robert stood behind him. "You ready to go?"

"Yeah." Jonah grabbed his bag from the clerk and followed his cousin to the front door.

Neera called after him, "Have a nice day, Mr. Hightower."

Robert turned, a confused look on his face. Jonah pushed him out the front door. "I'll explain outside."

"Are you alright?" Robert frowned as Jonah wiped his forehead.

"I'm fine."

"You look sick."

"It's the owner. She's weird." Jonah wanted to say she was evil, but he thought that sounded over the top. At least, he did until Robert answered him.

"She's probably a witch."

"A witch?"

"Yep. I shouldn't have let you go in the store all alone."

Jonah stared at the store again. Could Neera be a witch? Was that the reason he felt strange the moment he entered the store? The other times he felt that sensation was when he saw the people in black, but they had been Reapers. Neera wasn't unDead; she walked around, talked with him, even gave him her business card.

Jonah nudged Robert's arm. "Do you believe in that kind of thing? You know, witches, Reapers, supernatural stuff?"

"Yeah, I do. A little." Robert lowered his voice. "Wick's more into it than I am."

"Is he a witch?"

Robert grinned. "He calls himself a practitioner."

"What's the difference?"

"A practitioner can do small things and is sensitive to magic. A witch is very powerful and often very evil."

"Can Wick really do magic?"

Robert looked down at his feet. "I've seen him do a few things."

"Wow."

"He told me the bookstore owner gave off a magic vibe. He could sense it."

Jonah nodded. "Well, she's creepy."

Robert didn't say anything else for a while as he stared at the passing cars. Then he glanced back at the Mystic Worlds bookstore. "If Wick could feel it, then she must be into serious magic."

Jonah thought back to the encounter at the memorial service. Omar could also sense the Reaper even though the man had disappeared. Omar said he was a Memory Charmer, but Jonah wondered if he could be a practitioner. He toyed with the idea of asking Robert about Death Sense and Reapers but chickened out and showed his cousin the book and card.

"That's the best drawing I've seen of Grim Hounds." Robert whistled as he turned the book over in his hands. "They even got the double rows of teeth. She's definitely into the weird." Robert paused, his eyebrows drew together as he ran a finger over the author's name. Hackett. "It can't be…"

"What? Do you know the author?"

"No. It's nothing." Robert shook his head and began flipping through the Death Omen book, but his hands shook a bit. Jonah stuck a finger between the pages to get his cousin's attention.

"How do you know about Grim Hounds?"

"I told you." Robert snapped the book closed, almost catching Jonah's finger. "Wick and I are working on a computer game about the supernatural. It includes Grim Hounds and other creatures." He handed the book back to Jonah, who slipped it in his shopping bag.

"I know that. You called it a Grim Hound and not a Hell Hound."

"Well…" Robert held Neera's business card in his hand. He tapped it on a finger, refusing to look directly at Jonah. "Wick found a really old book, and it had that name for them. We use the book as source material for the game's mythos."

Robert's confession was interesting to Jonah. Clearly, his aunt would consider all supernatural things witchcraft. Robert didn't hold that view, not if his best friend was a practitioner of magic. Not if they were reading old books with accurate information about the supernatural world and making a game about it.

Jonah had never even considered such things until the day he heard his dad mention Death Sense. Since then, he'd seen Grim Hounds and people who could disappear. He found out his dad was a Fallen Reaper and he was half-Reaper himself. Jonah's knowledge about the world around him continued to change in strange ways. And his cousin appeared to know more about it than he let on.

Jonah took Neera's business card from Robert and slid it in his back pocket. "Can I ask you a question?"

"Not so fast, little cousin. How do you know the name for Grim Hounds?"

"My godfather told me."

"He did?"

"I guess he's into strange stuff like you and Wick."

Jonah tried to smile, and Robert crossed his arms and glared at him. "I told you the truth about how we found out. Why did your godfather tell you about Grim Hounds?"

"I asked him," Jonah paused before plunging on, "because I saw one."

Robert's jaw dropped. "You saw a real Grim Hound?"

"I saw two inside my house the night it burned to the ground. I think they caused the fire." Jonah went on before Robert could interrupt. "And that woman in the store knows I'm from Washington. She gave me that business card to see my reaction to it."

"No way," Robert said. He let out a slow breath and ruffled his Afro as he stared at Jonah. "We thought we'd find out something interesting when you came, but this-"

"We?"

"Lynn and I." Robert snapped his fingers. "That's why you bought the Death Omen book. You thought you saw…"

"You believe me, right?"

"I don't know."

"What do you mean you don't know? You're working on that computer game. You know the real name for the Grim Hounds."

"Books and games are one thing, Jonah. Seeing real Grim Hounds in real life is another." Robert looked around. "I know you've been through a lot of things…"

"I'm not crazy." Jonah began to think he'd been a fool to tell Robert about the Grim Hounds.

"I'm not saying that, little cousin. Maybe you saw a large dog or a bear."

"A bear in a burning house?"

Robert shrugged, and the corners of his mouth twitched.

"You're not going to tell Lynn or Wick, are you?" A knot formed in Jonah's stomach when Robert smiled. "Robert!"

"Okay." His cousin held up both hands. "I won't tell Lynn."

"Or Wick."

"Come on, Wick's a cool guy. He'll believe you."

"No, Robert. I'm serious."

"I won't tell Lynn or Wick. Let's get back to the Mall. My mom is probably waiting for us."

As Jonah fell into step beside Robert, his mind swirled. Grim Hounds were real. He had confronted one. Marcus had fought them. Yet Robert couldn't accept that Grim Hounds were more than fantasy creatures.

Jonah decided to never mention the dreams, transformable blades, or the fact that he was half-Reaper. He glanced back at Mystic Worlds as the heaviness weighed on him. The strangeness had followed him to Mount Vernon after all, and he would have to face it on his own.

CHAPTER EIGHTEEN
GRIM CHASE

"Eighty-two degrees." Jonah let out a sigh as he double-checked the weather report the next morning. He glanced at his book bag and decided it would be better to travel light. He set the bag down beside the bed and pulled out a small notepad and pencil. Stuffing those into the back pocket of his cargo shorts, he set out for the teen center.

No sooner had Jonah reached the teen center when his Death Sense spiked, forcing him to wince and grip his head. A second later, he heard the familiar growl. Jonah looked around and nearly fell off his bike because a Grim Hound perched like an oversized house cat on the teen center sign.

The creature's jet black body resembled a living shadow in the late morning sun. The glowing red eyes narrowed and it opened its massive mouth to reveal the double set of razor-sharp teeth. No one else paid any attention to the creature as if it wasn't there. But Jonah noticed people shifted, not walking too close. He wondered if mortals could sense the danger even though they couldn't see it.

He locked eyes with the Grim Hound as he lifted his bike, his movements slow as to avoid triggering an attack, although he knew that was impossible, given the way his head ached. Throwing caution to the wind, Jonah slung a leg over his bike and took off.

When shouts and grunts erupted behind him, Jonah glanced back. The Grim Hound had knocked a group of unsuspecting kids aside as it launched itself off the sign. Fear surged through Jonah as the creature bounded after him. His legs pumped the pedals frantically, scrambling to pick up speed. He risked another glance behind him. The Grim Hound brushed against cars and people, creating havoc.

He couldn't worry about that as he darted into an adjacent neighborhood. The Grim Hound let out a growl, sounding much closer than it had been when he'd last looked. His heart pounded with terror and he tensed his back, expecting to feel the creature's teeth bite into him.

The panic became unbearable, and Jonah suddenly veered through a front yard. The Grim Hound leapt at the same time, missed him, and slammed into a parked car. Shattered glass flew everywhere and the car's alarm blared.

Jonah sped through the home's backyard, into an adjacent yard, and out onto another street. He made turn after turn, occasionally skidding as he fled through the unknown neighborhood of two-story homes. Finally, he reached a steep hill, and the downhill descent brought him more speed.

The houses were little more than blurs on either side of him now. For one bright moment, Jonah thought he might actually get away from the Grim Hound. That hope died as he realized the street emptied at the bottom of the hill onto a busy roadway.

He couldn't stop nor safely turn without crashing. As he neared the roadway, a gap appeared in the passing cars. Jonah plunged ahead. Horns blared and tires screeched as he dodged between the cars and into an apartment complex on the other side. He heard the impact and the Grim Hound's howl of pain as the creature tumbled into a row of parked cars. Jonah paused to catch his breath and hoped the Grim Hound was dead.

He wasn't that lucky. The beast regained its feet, shook itself, and oriented on him.

By now, the commotion had caused people from the complex to gather outside. Jonah paused. If he went toward them, the Grim Hound would hurt somebody. He turned and plunged through the shrubbery bordering the complex. The bushes poked and scratched as he fought his way through and came out in a trailer park.

Each time the Grim Hound appeared behind him, Jonah would dodge around a trailer before it could pounce. That worked until he miscalculated and came around a trailer directly in front of the Grim Hound. He dodged as the beast slashed at him. Its claws ripped the back of his shirt.

Pain exploded across Jonah's upper back and he tumbled off the bike. The only thing that saved him was the fact that the Grim Hound's momentum took it clear past him. It smashed into the wooden steps of a trailer. Someone inside screamed as the impact rocked the entire trailer.

Even though his shoulder burned with pain, Jonah hopped on his bike and raced for the trailer park's exit. He managed to reach it without the Grim Hound catching him. Crossing the road right outside the park, he sped into the empty lot of an adjacent shipping building. The black surface of the lot was like a red-hot grill. Jonah's breaths started to come in gasps, and the hot air burned his nose and throat.

He didn't know how much longer he could continue. Sweat poured down his face, and the salt from it stung his eyes. His ripped shirt stuck to the drying blood on his shoulder. Whenever it pulled free, Jonah would suck in a painful breath. Stopping or turning around wasn't an option. The rain of small pebbles as the creature's huge paws ripped into the surface of the lot came from close behind.

So he raced on. And when he reached the end of the vacant building and rounded the corner, his hope faltered. A high metal fence enclosed that end of the parking lot. Cars zoomed down the busy road on the other side, and beyond that sat an abandoned gas station.

I need to get to the other side.

Jonah's fear infused the thought. For a second, he imagined heat distortions caused the ripple in front of him. Then a familiar sensation rolled along every inch of his body. With a jerk, the black parking lot disappeared, replaced by the broken concrete and gravel lot of the abandoned gas station on the other side of the busy roadway.

Jonah skidded, lost control, and went down. His bike flipped and slammed into an old gas pump. Jonah landed next to it, smacking his injured right shoulder on the pump's concrete base.

He screamed in pain and his vision blurred with tears. A wave of dizziness prompted Jonah to roll over and throw up. Once the spasms passed, he struggled to a seated position and watched in fascination as the Grim Hound pulled itself from the mangled fence. A few cars slowed and the drivers gaped as the fence buckled without an obvious reason for its collapse.

The Grim Hound shook its head, spotted Jonah, and let out a frightening bark. Even though people couldn't see it, they hugged themselves as if a chilled wind had reached them. Jonah's own body froze with fright. He forced his memory to cough up what it had learned about Grim Hounds. They could use their snarls and barks to paralyze a victim with fear. All at once, Jonah's fear lifted and he sucked in a breath.

By that time, the Grim Hound had backed away from the fence and was charging toward it. It didn't matter if the supernatural beast couldn't paralyze him with fear; Jonah didn't have the energy to move. The Grim Hound leapt the fence in a high arc, leaped over two stalled cars, and continued on toward him. Jonah's Death Sense screamed, the pain nearly causing him to faint. There was no hope of dodging this time.

As he braced himself for the Hound's attack, the air rippled and Kevin appeared between Jonah and the Grim Hound. Unfortunately, he phased with his back to the action.

"Kevin! Behind you."

The boy whirled, his blades out. The Grim Hound leapt for him, and Kevin blurred into motion as he dodged to the left. The Grim Hound landed and turned to swap a massive paw at Kevin. He phased, reappearing behind the beast. The creature sensed him, whirled around, and snapped its jaws at Kevin's head, but the boy moved almost too fast to see as he dodged the razor-sharp teeth.

He charged the creature. When it tried to claw him, Kevin cut the paw. This deadly dance continued. Each time the creature lunged, trying to grab him with massive paws so it could use its jaws, Kevin would blur into motion or phase. When he reappeared, he'd cut the Grim Hound again along its body, causing the beast to whirl or roll away.

The Grim Hound had a body like a dog and was a large as a Kodiak bear. Jonah felt the vibrations each time its paws slammed on the ground. He began to worry for Kevin, but Marcus's apprentice held his own.

The older boy crossed his arms and dodged underneath the Grim Hound's snout. When Kevin brought his arm up and out, he sliced the creature's head off its body. Dark liquid splattered his black shirt and jeans. He delivered a blurred kick to the decapitated Grim Hound, sending the headless body into the roadway.

The severed head landed a few feet from Jonah. He stood on wobbly legs and stared in shock as the remains of the Grim Hound's head began to sizzle and melt.

Kevin turned around, covered in goo. "Jonah? Are you alright?"

Before Jonah could say anything, a horrible crunching sound came from the road. It was followed by another loud bump and screeching tires. Cars rammed into the Grim Hound's body before it started to melt. The drivers exited their cars, scratching their heads.

"Oh no." Kevin's shoulders slumped as he watched the mayhem.

Any other time, Jonah might have laughed, but not today. He had never ached this bad in his life, not even when his Death Sense spiked. His shoulder was a big mass of pain, the dizziness made him light-headed, and his bike was a mess.

Jonah willed himself to walk slowly to Kevin. His energy failed him and he started to collapse. Kevin was at his side in a blur, catching him.

"Take it easy." Kevin lowered him to the ground. "You're hurt."

Jonah's rapid breathing slowed and his legs began to ache with fatigue. Kevin hovered over him with a concerned look on his face. "I need to get you somewhere so you can heal."

"How did you find me?"

"Marcus knew you were in danger."

"Then why didn't he come?"

"You were moving, so it was hard to be accurate." Kevin wouldn't meet his eyes.

"But you came to help me."

"Yeah, well, I didn't want to wait." Kevin locked eyes with Jonah before sliding one arm under his back and the other under his legs. Jonah screamed as Kevin lifted him.

"Sorry, little man," Kevin said in a soft voice.

"Don't call me that."

Kevin turned toward the rear of the station. "You're half-Reaper, so your body can heal itself. You know that right?"

"No."

"Oh. Well, you need to rest." Kevin had almost reached the cover of the ramshackle building when someone called out.

"Hey!"

Jonah grunted at the flare of pain in his shoulder caused by Kevin whirling around. A kid with short twists in his hair, a black muscle shirt, and Army fatigue pants ran over to them.

"What happened to you?" He had a slight Jamaican accent, not Southern, Jonah noted. The curious boy offered to shake hands, then thought better of it and settled on a quick wave. "I'm Wick, by the way. I'm friends with Bobby and Lynn. And you must be their little cousin from DC." Wick's eyes narrowed as he shifted his gaze to Kevin. "Who are you?"

Jonah was caught between going somewhere to heal or finally meeting Wick. He tapped Kevin's shoulder. "Put me down."

"You're bleeding, dude." Wick's eyebrows shot up as he pointed at Jonah's shoulder.

"Can you take me home?" Jonah asked.

"Maybe we should wait for someone to look at you."

"That's not a good idea," Kevin said.

"Who's he?" Wick nodded at Kevin.

"He saw me fall off my bike and came to help," Jonah offered because Kevin had opened his mouth to respond. "I need to talk to Robert and Lynn first."

Behind them, drivers shouted to the police as they pointed at ruined cars and the mangled fence. Other cops searched up and down the street. Since the Grim Hound's remains had melted, the dents in the cars presented a big mystery.

Wick turned back to Jonah, and his eyes widened. "They were right about you, huh?"

"Who?"

"Robert and Lynn. They knew things would change with you here."

Jonah wanted to ask Wick about that, but his shoulder flared with pain again. "Help me."

"Oh, yeah." Wick pointed to a small pickup at the edge of the lot. "We need to get you in the truck."

When Kevin didn't move, Jonah whispered, "You have a better idea?"

Kevin grunted and helped Jonah to the truck. An older version of Wick hopped out of the driver's side and opened the passenger door while Wick ran back to get the damaged bike.

Kevin was extremely gentle as he set Jonah inside. He could tell the boy wasn't happy about letting him go. He didn't like it either, but Wick was already curious and the last thing Jonah needed was Robert and Lynn asking even more questions.

Jonah started to lean back, but his shoulder touched the seat and the pain returned. He rested his hands on the dashboard, leaned his head against them, and closed his eyes. "Thanks."

"No problem," Wick answered.

The driver's side door opened and the truck rocked as someone got behind the wheel.

"Oh, by the way, this is my brother, Desmond," Wick said.

Desmond nodded as he started the truck. Jonah noticed that Desmond wore jeans and a t-shirt and his hair was in dreads instead of twists like his brother. He spoke with a more pronounced island accent than Wick. "Shouldn't we get him to a hospital?"

"Just take me home," Jonah said.

"You heard the man, Desmond."

"If anything happens to him, I'll swear I be mud-ridin' when this happened, man."

Jonah didn't know anything about mud riding and didn't care. He just wanted to get home. His thoughts returned to the Grim Hound and why someone would send it in the middle of the day with so many people around.

The little voice in his mind supplied the answer. *Somebody wants me dead.*

CHAPTER NINETEEN
HEALING FACTOR

"What happened to him?" Lynn rushed to help Wick place Jonah on a kitchen chair, then leaned back with a frown. "Well?"

Wick shrugged and ruffled his twists. "He claims he fell off his bike."

Lynn pushed Jonah forward in the chair. He screamed, "Hey that hurts!"

"Oh my God. You're cut." Lynn rounded on her brother. "Get the med kit. Wick, you hold up his shirt until I can get it off."

Wick hissed when he saw the injury. "Looks like you were mauled by something, dude."

Lynn nodded in agreement. "You're gonna need stitches, Jonah."

"I can't." Jonah didn't know how to explain his cuts to a doctor, nor to his aunt, who would have to take him to the hospital.

Robert returned a few minutes later with the kit. Lynn cleaned and bandaged the cuts with practiced ease. Robert handed Jonah a glass of water and a pain tablet.

Lynn crossed her arms and tossed her braids behind her back with an angry flick of her head. She waited for him to swallow the pill before asking, "Why can't you go to the hospital? What happened?"

"A Grim Hound attacked me."

"I knew you saw it!" Wick slapped his hand on the table, causing everyone to jump. "A Grim Hound, huh?"

Lynn shushed him. "Start from the beginning, Jonah."

He began with arriving at the teen center and told them everything that had happened. When he reached the part about his escape from the creature, he felt a little light-headed and realized the pain pill must have been working. Jonah claimed he managed to weave through the traffic and the creature wasn't so lucky. A shocked silence settled over the group when he finished.

Lynn, Wick, and Robert traded serious looks.

"Why are you looking at each other like that?" Jonah asked.

Wick elbowed Robert. "Show him the drawings, Bobby."

"No," Lynn interjected. She held up her hand. "We don't have time for that now. Jonah should go to the hospital. Wick, call your brother."

"Lynn, I can't," Jonah protested. "What am I supposed to say happened to me?"

"We'll think of something. I can't let you bleed to death."

Jonah shook his head, which made his shoulder ache. "Just give me some time."

"What will that do?"

The answer was on the tip of Jonah's tongue when he stopped himself. He didn't understand it all. Kevin had been sure that he could heal if he had time to rest, and Jonah wanted to trust the boy. He wanted to know if his body could heal from more than a simple cut.

"Jonah? What's going on?"

"Let me take a nap."

Lynn shook her head, causing her thin braids to flip around. She reached for Jonah's arm, but Wick stopped her.

"I think he'll be alright."

"Wick…"

"Come on, Lynn. You need time to come up with something to tell your mom and dad. Jonah's a minor, so they'll have to know."

"You two are being weird. Well, in your case, Wick, weirder than usual."

"Gee, thanks." He winked at Jonah. "If I'm wrong, you can remind me about it forever."

Lynn crossed her arms, but Jonah thought she looked less defiant. "He could be in worse shape by then."

"I doubt it. Support me, Bobby."

Robert stirred at the mention of his name and nodded. "Let him sleep, Lynn."

"You guys are crazy." She frowned for a second, then took Jonah by the arm. Jonah feared she planned to make him go to the hospital anyway. Instead, she helped him stand. "You go lay down."

Robert helped Jonah into his room and pointed at his dirt-stained clothes.

"Time to change, little cousin."

Jonah slipped off the ruined shirt and winced, but not from the pain. The shirt was the first one his aunt had picked out. How would he explain it being destroyed in just a day? He quickly handed Robert the rest of his dirty clothes and got in bed.

"Thanks, Robert." He pulled his cover up.

"No problem."

Robert closed the door and Jonah let the pain pills do their job. His shoulder throbbed and tingled a bit. When he wiggled it, real pain made him grimace. He took a deep breath and told himself to be still and rest. Just as he settled down, he felt a pressure on his ears.

"Jonah?"

Jonah sat up and yelled as much from the surprise as the pain in his shoulder. Kevin stood beside the dresser, but he blurred into motion as he caught Jonah and covered his mouth.

"Sorry. I didn't mean to scare you."

"Whm amhfn?" Jonah smacked Kevin's hand, and he pulled it away. "What are you doing here?"

"I'm making sure you're alright." Kevin smirked at him. "You're not gonna scream like a girl again, are you?"

Jonah shoved Kevin and said, "Where did you go?"

"Around. I had to keep an eye on you." Kevin glanced at the door. "Don't tell your cousins about me."

"I won't."

"Good. I'm in enough trouble. I don't need your cousins knowing all about us."

"What did you do this time?"

"I saved you, again. Marcus is pissed with me, again."

"You mean he wanted to let the Grim Hound finish me?"

"No. It's not like that." By the way Kevin studied his hands, Jonah knew the boy was holding back details. "Like I said, you kept moving…"

"That Grim Hound chased me from the teen center."

"I know. Marcus wanted you to run away from trouble and call from someplace he could phase without being seen."

"I couldn't stop and make a phone call! The Grim Hound would have killed me."

"I know."

"And you're telling me Marcus wasn't going to help?"

"I didn't say that. As soon as you stopped, I phased before Marcus could do anything."

"Thanks. I'm glad you did it."

"You don't understand." Kevin shook his head, a worried expression on his face. "It's dangerous and against the rules to phase somewhere with other people around. I didn't even have a memory charmer to deal with any witnesses. And you saw what I did with the Grim Hound's body."

"You didn't mean to cause that accident."

"Marcus won't see it that way."

Kevin looked miserable as he toyed with the edge of the top sheet. Jonah didn't know what to do. Besides, the pill was making him sleepy and he still hurt all over. Without thinking about it, Jonah touched Kevin's hand. He didn't know what the boy would do, but Kevin opened his fingers, allowing Jonah to slide his hand over the palm, and then Kevin closed his fingers.

"Little Jonah is causing all kinds of problems," he whispered.

At first, Jonah bristled at the comment, but he noticed Kevin was smiling and relaxed. It wasn't his fault. These people and creatures kept coming for him.

That reminded Jonah of Neera. "Kevin, there's a woman in town with scars-"

"We know about Neera."

"You do?" Jonah blinked in surprise. "We think she's a witch."

"She's a sorceress, or was a sorceress." Kevin shook his head. "It can get complicated."

"Why did she send a Grim Hound after me?"

"She didn't."

"What do you mean? You fought the thing."

"Marcus tracks Neera whenever she leaves Mount Vernon. She was nowhere near here when the attack happened. I think that's the reason he hesitated. He didn't want to lose Neera unless it was needed. Plus, he hoped a Memory Charmer would arrive before one of us phased, or you would at least find a more private place to call."

Jonah started to sit up despite his injured shoulder. Kevin placed a hand on his chest and held him down. "You need to get some rest."

"Kevin. She's looking for that ring, isn't she?"

"I'm not telling you any more. Marcus is right about keeping you out of this mess."

"They killed my parents because of a ring."

"That's why you need to stay out of it, Jonah."

He didn't struggle as he considered everything Kevin told him. He had Marcus on speed dial, but had he really had the chance to call? When he was in that parking lot, no one was around. Maybe he could have called then. Kevin or Marcus could have shown up before the Grim Hound reached him.

"I'm sorry I didn't call."

"Don't apologize." Kevin leaned back in surprise. "You were great. Everyone was impressed. You're not the one in trouble."

As if to underscore Kevin's statement, his cell phone beeped. He pulled it out of his pocket, glanced at the message, and stood. "I have to go. Marcus is ready to kill me now."

"Don't leave."

"Jonah, not this again."

Kevin knelt by the bed, reminding Jonah of that time at Marcus's. He noticed the embossed symbol on Kevin's black t-shirt, the same symbol on the Reaper long coats. He touched it. Kevin stared at his hand without saying anything. Then he puffed out his chest. Jonah let his hand rest against Kevin's chest, sensing the steady heartbeat beneath his touch.

"What does that symbol mean?"

"It's the group we work for."

"Monarch? Marcus works for Monarch?"

Kevin laughed, the sound vibrating Jonah's hand, still resting on his chest. "No, it's called the Alliance. It's the real company behind Monarch."

"Oh."

Kevin took Jonah's hand and intertwined their fingers. "If you're done feeling me up, get some rest, little man. It'll help your body heal itself."

Jonah gave him a lazy smirk and didn't let go of Kevin's hand as he closed his eyes. When Kevin remained still, Jonah allowed his mind to relax, and soon he was asleep.

Jonah's eye's snapped open when someone shook his good shoulder.

"Kevin?" he said, thinking that only a short time had passed. He rubbed his eyes and saw that Lynn stood beside his bed.

"Who's Kevin? Is he the boy that Wick saw holding you?"

Oh no, Jonah thought. Clearly Wick and his cousins had a talk after he fell asleep.

"He's no one."

Lynn folded her arms, staring down at him, causing Jonah's irritation to bubble up.

"What do you want, Lynn?"

"I need to change the dressing." She held up the fresh bandage. "Now, sit up."

Jonah threw off the cover and sat obediently on the side of the bed. He yawned and looked for his watch until Lynn pinched his good shoulder. "Keep still."

"How long have I been asleep?"

"Almost five hours." Lynn placed the new bandage on the bed and started to remove Jonah's old one. "So who's Kevin? Were you dreaming about him?"

"Just drop it."

Lynn gave him a sly smile. Her expression changed when she finished peeling off the old bandage. "Oh my God! The cuts have sealed themselves."

She touched Jonah's shoulder. Pain flared, but it wasn't sharp like it had been.

"There's barely a scar. Jonah, how is that possible?"

"Well, I always healed fast." He thought back to the times he had cut himself. The injuries were always gone the next morning. The first time that happened, he had shown his mom. *That's so wonderful, sweetheart. Now, let's keep the bandage on a little longer. Okay?* In the end, she always made him wear bandages for a couple days after he knew his cuts were healed.

This situation was something else. He'd never been hurt this bad, yet his body had managed to heal, just like Kevin had told him it would.

"It tingled and itched just before I fell asleep." Jonah reached over to feel the partially healed scar. "I just ignored it."

Lynn quietly prepared a new bandage. She kept her gaze focused on her hands as she worked.

Jonah tried to look her in the eyes. "Lynn?"

"Yeah." She finished and sat back.

"I've never been sick before."

Lynn finally looked directly at him. "Never?"

"Never. People always called me extra healthy. My best friend…" Jonah paused when he thought about Oliver. "My best friend used to joke and call me Superman." Jonah laughed to himself and relaxed a bit when Lynn smiled. "I guess I'm really different, huh?"

"Jonah…" Lynn stopped and looked away. "We'll see about this later." She stood and helped him up. "Dinner's ready."

Near the end of dinner, Uncle James turned on the local news. Robert, Lynn, and Jonah listened to the anchor talk about a bizarre series of property damages and accidents in the Hightowers' part of town. Police concluded that a stray animal went on a rampage. Authorities urged residents to be on the lookout for any large animals.

CHAPTER TWENTY
THE SUMMIT

"Can I see it?" Wick asked. He had arrived in time for breakfast, but his focus was entirely on Jonah as he sat down at the kitchen table.

"See what?" Jonah paused with a spoonful of cereal an inch from his mouth.

"The scar."

"He's not a sideshow freak." Lynn poked Wick in the head as she crossed by to sit at the breakfast bar.

"But I was the only one to believe him." Wick caught Jonah's look and shrugged. "I'm sorry. This is just so cool. How can you heal like that?"

"I don't know."

Wick sat back as Robert entered the kitchen with his sketchbook. He set it on the table and announced, "Wick wanted me to show you this yesterday."

Robert flipped the sketchbook open. Jonah's insides froze when he saw the first picture of a Grim Hound. He dropped his spoon in his bowl and tried to point at the picture but regretted it when his shoulder throbbed. "That's what I saw!"

Robert flipped through the rest of the pictures, then closed the sketchbook and sat down at the table. "I'm sorry, Jonah."

Lynn slipped off her stool and gave her twin brother's head a little shove. "Why are you apologizing to him?"

"Jonah told me that he saw a Grim Hound the night his parents' house burned. I didn't believe him."

Jonah thought Lynn looked uncertain as she glared at her brother.

Wick patted Jonah on his uninjured shoulder. "I would have believed you, Padawan."

Jonah smiled at him. Robert's friend seemed to be the only one excited about his healing ability and the fact that Grim Hounds were real. On the other hand, Robert and Lynn acted careful around him, like he was a time bomb.

Wick leaned forward. "So there were Grim Hounds in your parents' house?"

"Yeah."

"You know Grim Hounds hunt for things, right?"

"Marcus told me." Jonah noticed Wick's curious look and explained, "He's my godfather, and he said Grim Hounds can show up where something bad happened."

Wick rubbed his chin as he considered that. "I don't know, Jonah. From what we've read, Grim Hounds go where they are sent. My guess is they were sent to look for something in your house."

Lynn eyes narrowed as she watched Jonah. "Do you know what they were searching for?"

Jonah squirmed in his chair; Wick was correct. And the mention of his parents' house reminded him of the dream. That strange woman had obviously sent the Grim Hounds to search for a ring. Jonah had heard it in the creature's own thoughts, in a dream he didn't want to mention to his cousins. They were on the verge of freaking out already.

"My parents found a lot of objects for their company," he answered, refusing to meet any of their eyes as he spoke. "But they didn't tell me anything."

"Grim Hounds are serious." Wick tapped the sketchbook. "They must have been looking for something related to the supernatural. You never saw anything like that?"

Lynn crossed her arms, tapping her foot on the floor. Wick toyed with the pages of the sketchbook while staring Jonah, clearly expecting him to reveal some kind of deep secret. When Jonah met Robert's oddly intense gaze, images of the silver blades flashed into his mind. Memories of holding the medallion paperweight came to him next. He even recalled the strange portal from his dream about his parents.

A chill ran down his spine. His own memories were on display, like someone else was picking through them, looking for information.

"No," Jonah said. He shook his head. "I-I don't know." The slight pressure on his mind lessened and disappeared.

Robert slumped back in his chair. Lynn stalked to the kitchen window.

"Sorry." Jonah watched his cousins, sensing their disappointment. "What do you want me to say?"

"Don't worry about them," Wick answered. Lynn whirled around with her mouth open to speak, and Wick plunged ahead in a louder voice. "Somebody sent this Grim Hound straight after him. They have to be summoned and then given their mission." He turned to Jonah. "Who did you piss off?"

Robert smacked his own forehead. "It must have been that Neera woman in the bookstore. I knew I shouldn't have let you go in there."

"Although my doubting buddy didn't mention that you saw Grim Hounds," Wick spared Robert a glance, "he did tell me about Neera. She has a cool name, by the way. Did you know that in some forms, it means creator of chaos?"

Lynn nudged him in the back of his head. "Wick, stay on the subject."

"That is on subject," Wick objected. Lynn raised a fist. "Okay, sorry." He focused on Jonah. "She gave you a business card. Can I see it?"

Jonah tried to take out his wallet, but his shoulder throbbed again. Lynn had told him the cuts may have sealed themselves, but the shoulder would probably hurt for a day or two as the deep tissue healed. Jonah thought she'd been correct, as he winced once more from the unexpected pain.

"I'll get it, little cousin." Robert pulled out the wallet and passed the business card to Wick, who held the card up with a flourish. The action reminded Jonah of a magician performing a trick.

Wick closed his eyes and began to mumble under his breath. As soon as Jonah opened his mouth, Robert motioned him to keep quiet. A second later, a glowing symbol appeared on the back of the card.

"Just as I thought," Wick announced. "Neera marked the card so she could use a tracking spell on you."

Jonah's jaw dropped as Wick held the card closer, allowing him to see the symbol. Jonah was caught between awe at Wick's skill and a lack of understanding of what the boy meant. "A tracking spell?"

Wick smiled at Jonah's confused expression and explained, "Yeah, a tracking spell is like using a locator or transmitter. She planted this card on you as a locator. The tracking spell allowed her to find you whenever she wanted. That is, as long as you keep the card with you."

Wick pulled a lighter from one of his pants pockets. His unlaced black boots clacked on Aunt Imma's linoleum floor as he rose and then walked to the kitchen sink. Pausing to glance inside the sink, he set the card on fire.

"Why are you burning it?" Jonah struggled to his feet.

"It's the only way to destroy the locator."

"Otherwise," Lynn cut in, gently pushing him back down into the kitchen chair, "Neera could use it to track you down again."

Wick let the burning card drop into the sink. Once the card was reduced to ashes, he turned on the water and rinsed the sooty pile down the drain. "Then again, we could have set up a trap."

"That would be too dangerous." Lynn frowned as she watched him. "She plays seriously."

A silence fell over the group again until Robert glanced at his sister and said, "The Summit?"

"Are you sure, Robert?"

"He's seen real Grim Hounds. We can't hold out on him, not if we want information."

The twins shared a look between them that only ended when Robert turned to Wick. "What do you think?"

Wick's twists shook as he nodded. He absentmindedly opened and closed his lighter in his right hand, watching Jonah with a thoughtful expression.

Jonah shifted his gaze away and found Robert and Lynn also watching him.

"What are you three talking about? What's the Summit? Isn't that the name of the newsletter and blog you do?"

Lynn and Wick shot Robert curious looks.

"I showed him the article about Mom." He turned to Jonah. "It's more than just a newsletter and blog, Jonah. It's a place. Well, it's all three."

Jonah followed his cousins and Wick through the recreation center atrium and up the stairs to the second floor. Adults buzzed in and out of offices. Jonah thought they would go into one of those areas, but Robert paused in front of an old wooden attic door. It had *The Summit* printed in bold black letters on a piece of plain white paper.

Jonah's cousins unlocked the door, flicked a wall switch just inside, and stood back. Lynn slipped by and up a narrow staircase. Robert, waving Jonah and Wick forward, followed behind.

The Summit turned out to be a spacious attic. The exposed wood rafters were high enough for lanky Robert and Lynn to stand without bending. The dark hardwood floor creaked slightly in places, and the stairs divided the attic into two areas. The area to the right contained two computer monitors on a large fold-up table. Stray papers and computer parts littered the top of a smaller worktable situated just beyond the computers.

"We do the newsletter and blog here." Lynn gestured at the computers. "It's our own little office." She walked around the computers to lean against a grey metal desk in the back corner. The only things on it were a small lamp, an old rotary telephone, and a black nameplate with the word EDITOR in white letters. "This used to be my father's desk, from his home office. He gave it to us when we found out you were coming."

"That's our clubhouse over there," Robert said.

He pulled Jonah into the left side of the attic and to an old, slightly sunken yet comfortable-looking sofa. Two mismatched armchairs with numerous rips in the fabric faced the sofa with a battered brown steamer trunk in between. The trunk was large, with brass rivets in the corners and metal handles on the sides. Several dog-eared magazines and a few crumpled soda cans littered it.

Just beyond the sitting area was a square card table with three folding chairs positioned around it. Jonah wondered if his cousins used it to play board games or cards, but before he could ask, he noticed the wire-frame bookcase to one side of a bricked-in fireplace. He walked over and pulled a book off a shelf. The entire thing swayed.

Wick grabbed hold of the bookcase. "I'm supposed to fix that."

"And clean up, you slob." Robert picked up the soda cans and tossed them in a metal wastebasket.

Lynn spread her arms wide. "Welcome to the Summit. What do you think, Geek boy?"

"It's totally cool," Jonah gushed before pausing and frowning. "Why do you call it the Summit?"

Lynn pulled back the makeshift curtain made from a blue bed sheet and revealed a rather large, multi-paned window.

"The rec center is located at the top of one of the largest hills in Mount Vernon, and this attic is at the top of the center."

"We also have a great view," Robert added as he steered Jonah to the window. The land behind the building sloped downhill into a wooded ravine. Beyond that, Jonah could see rooftops through the trees on the other side.

"There's a creek at the bottom of the hill," Robert whispered right over Jonah's shoulder. "It's a nice getaway area."

"Yes, Robert gets a lot of use out of that place." Lynn smirked at her brother.

Wick laughed and Robert grinned as he patted Jonah on the shoulder. "I'll show you one day, little cousin."

Jonah peered over the back of a computer monitor while running a finger along the top. "Is this what you were doing the other day?"

"We were on a deadline to finish the last blog." Robert walked around into the office section and sat at one of the computers. "Lynn does most of the reporting and story gathering. I do the layouts and any artwork." Robert leaned back and pointed to the computer cases underneath the tables. "I built these computers from parts the rec center gave us. I even run our own web server and maintain the center's website."

"That's so cool."

Wick, who lounged on the sofa, his unlaced black boots hanging over the side, lifted his head into view and smiled. "I met Bobby and Lynn three years ago when they interviewed me for a Halloween piece. Lynn doubted my ability."

"I still do sometimes."

Robert glanced at his sister. "Wick's done a Halloween story ever since."

"And they use me as a source on the unexplained and weird." He winked at Jonah. "Go ahead. Ask me the million-dollar question."

Jonah knew exactly which question Wick meant. He decided to have some fun and snatched a little notepad from beside Robert's computer, being careful to use his good arm. When he crossed over to the sofa, Wick slid his black boots off the puffy armrest so Jonah could sit there.

"Sources tell us that you are a witch?" Jonah said in an exaggerated news anchor tone. "Any comments?"

"Unfortunately, people can be cruel and judgmental." Wick sat up and screwed his face into a hurt look as he gave a dramatic sigh. "I'm just a normal guy who's sensitive to magic. I don't have a cauldron or a black cat or any of that stuff."

Jonah struggled to stay in character, even though a smile threatened to break through. "What about Neera's business card?"

"I used a little spell to reveal recently performed magic." Wick shook his head and ruffled his twists as he frowned. "I'm a practitioner, and I can do things like that."

"You two stop, please," Robert groaned.

Wick sat up straight on the sofa and gave Jonah an excited look. "My big project is a working shield."

"A shield?" Jonah slipped down onto the sofa beside him.

"It's a barrier made out of magical energy."

The more Wick talked, the greater Jonah's fascination with him and the subject of magic. Until a few days ago, he wouldn't have given it much thought.

"What does a shield do?"

"A shield protects you from other magical energy and physical objects. It could also protect you from supernatural creatures if they aren't really powerful."

"Could a shield stop a Grim Hound?"

"Well, my shield couldn't stop one, but one day, I'll be able to do it."

Jonah's mind raced with the idea of having something that could protect him from a Grim Hound. He almost told Wick about the time his neighbors accused him of being a witch, but he would have to tell them about his Death Sense, and he wasn't ready for that yet. Instead, Jonah glanced over the back of the sofa at Lynn.

She balled up a piece of paper and bounced it off her brother's head. "Show him, Robert. You made the suggestion."

Robert hopped to his feet and started across the attic, then whirled around and threw the balled-up piece of paper at his sister. Lynn caught it with a quick movement of her hand and stuck out her tongue. Robert grumbled as he continued to the rusted filing cabinet on the opposite side of the fireplace.

Lynn's reflexes amazed Jonah. She had barely moved her arm as she caught the piece of paper. Jonah must have stared at her too long because she narrowed her eyes. Without warning, she threw the ball of paper at him. He didn't even have time to think about it as his right hand shot up and caught it. His shoulder throbbed because of the effort.

"Whoa, dude. You're almost faster than Lynn." Wick whooped and patted Jonah's good shoulder. He met her gaze, pleased with himself, and she finally smiled.

"There may be some hope for you, Geek Boy."

Robert cleared his throat to get their attention. He held up a thick, rectangular box, placed it on the card table, and motioned everyone over. The ornate, golden box had two locks and strange symbols covering the top and sides. When Robert touched the small knob between the locks, recesses appeared that Jonah swore hadn't been there before. The locks clicked open and folded in on themselves, setting into the recesses so that the box's surface was seamless again.

"Wow!" Jonah said.

"Cool, eh?" Robert smiled. "It scared the crap out of me the first time it happened." He touched the knob, and the locks slid out of the recesses and snapped into place with a click.

"Can I try it?"

Robert nodded.

Jonah pressed the knob, but nothing happened. He tried a few more times, but still nothing.

"Am I doing it wrong?"

"You're doing it right."

"Then why doesn't it work?"

"The box will only lock and unlock for me." Robert pressed the knob and the locks slid away. "I found that out by mistake. I didn't even know about the locks when I first got it." Instead of pressing the knob and making the locks appear again, Robert pushed it to the right this time, Jonah observed. A release clicked and the box opened.

Robert closed the lid. "That's how I used it until the day the locks appeared."

"Why did they appear?"

"Well," Robert glanced at Wick, "I cut my finger on my art knife. A drop of blood fell on the box and before I could wipe it off, the blood disappeared."

"The box absorbed it. Blood sacrifice," Wick said, his voice an exaggerated spooky whisper. "Very cool, if you ask me."

"Anyway," Lynn interrupted, "the locks appeared and snapped into place a few seconds later." Lynn smirked at her brother. "He wouldn't touch the box after that. Too scared."

"No, I wasn't. I just wanted to be careful, that's all." Robert frowned at his sister. "I tried the knob again and discovered that when I pressed button, the locks slid into the recesses."

"Robert asked me try to it next, and nothing happened." Lynn peeked over her brother's shoulder and tapped the box. "That's how we knew that only he could lock and unlock it."

Jonah examined the box, pressing his fingers against the symbols etched into the surface. "Do you know what these mean?"

Robert shook his head. "We haven't been able to figure that out yet."

"Where'd you find it?" Jonah realized that his parents would have loved to see something like this. He had continued to study the symbols, so it took him a moment before he noticed that Lynn and Robert were staring at him. "What's wrong?"

"Jonah," Robert glanced nervously at Lynn before he continued, "Your mom and dad sent the box to me as a birthday gift, two years ago."

CHAPTER TWENTY-ONE
BIRTHDAY GIFTS

Jonah's anger and shock warred with each other. His parents had given Robert a special gift on his thirteenth birthday. Yet they had refused to even discuss his abilities with him. It seemed they trusted his cousin more than they trusted their own son.

"We're sorry, Jonah," Lynn finally added. "We thought you knew about the gifts. I mean, you're thirteen now. We decided that meant something."

"Turning thirteen is often an important event when it comes to powers." Wick patted his own chest. "That's about the age I first noticed mine. And you obviously have abilities. Didn't you get something?"

"Wick!" Lynn gave him a hard look.

Jonah ignored them as he went over to his book bag, rummaged around inside, and pulled out his old cell phone. He didn't want to get rid of this one even though Marcus had given him a new one; it reminded him of his parents—and their old voice messages were on the memory card. He found the last one from his mom and played it.

Hi sweetheart. Our flight plans have changed again. I'll send you the updated times as soon as we know. But don't worry, your father and I will be home in time for your birthday. This is an important time for you and we wouldn't miss it for the world.

Oh! Your father found the perfect gift for you and we both look forward to seeing your reaction.

Take care. We love you.

By the time it finished, Lynn stared out the attic window. Robert and Wick looked totally stunned. Jonah slowly turned the phone over in his hands. "I guess they did have something special for my birthday. They just never made it back." He sat down on the edge of the sofa, feeling ashamed for doubting his parents.

"Dude. I'm sorry." Wick sat down on the steamer trunk. "I didn't know."

Jonah shook his head. He didn't want Wick or his cousins feeling sorry for him. "It's strange to discover so many things about my parents that I never knew. And now I can't ask them anything because they're gone."

"This wasn't a good idea." Lynn frowned at her brother.

"I want to know everything." Jonah jumped to his feet and leaned over the box, looking at Lynn. "Did my parents send you something?"

In answer, Robert opened the box. Lynn took out two silver palm-sized cylinders and stood away from the table with one in each hand. She activated the cylinders and, with distinctive metallic *swish* sounds, they transformed into two silver blades.

It was actually cool seeing someone transform them up close, Jonah thought. His parents had used cylinders like those in the dream. Marcus and Kevin had also used the silver blades when they rescued him.

Jonah's heartbeat sped up as he watched Lynn. She twirled and pivoted with the blades, her moves graceful and practiced. And the blades hummed as they sliced through the air. Lynn ended her demonstration with the blades crossed in front of her. In one smooth movement, she brought herself to an upright position and collapsed the blades.

Everyone clapped as Lynn took a mock bow. Then she, Robert, and Wick stared at Jonah. He knew why. He hadn't shown any obvious surprise when Lynn activated the blades.

"My mom and dad used silver blades like those. They were really good…" Talking about his parents brought back the memory of their last fight. Jonah could feel the heat of the explosions and the sounds of his parents as they fought for their lives. He slumped down on the sofa again and buried his head in his hands. Lynn sat beside him and patted his back.

"Stop trying to hide it. If this is too much for you, tell us."

"No! It's not, and I want to know." Jonah wiped at his eyes and blinked the moisture out of them. "I'm serious." He held out a hand and Lynn gave him one of the cylinders. He ran his fingers over the strange symbols, but his eye caught a thin line of topaz inlaid along one side of the handle.

He glanced at Lynn. "How did you learn to use the blades like that?"

"I've been practicing. You know, your mom and dad didn't tell us how to activate the gifts, not directly."

"What do you mean?"

"They gave us riddles to solve," Robert explained as he tapped the archive box. "But we figured out the gifts without solving the riddles."

"I nearly lost a finger when I activated one of the blades by accident." Lynn held up the other cylinder and rotated it around in her hand. "I started taking lessons. Then my mom found out about the real blades and she locked them away. She wasn't happy with your parents about that."

Jonah was careful not to activate the cylinder himself as he handed it back to Lynn. "But how did you get the blades here if your mom took them away from you?"

"I picked the lock on the storage trunk and put some practice swords in their place, just in case Mom ever checked."

"So," Robert continued, "you can see why we keep these things a secret. Our parents would never understand them." He took the cylinders from his sister and placed them in the box. "It's kind of cool your parents owned blades."

"Yeah. I just wonder why they sent a pair to you, Lynn."

"I don't know." Lynn shrugged and gave Robert a quick glance.

During their little discussion, Wick had pulled a couple of large black books from the wobbly bookshelves. "Hey, maybe that's what they planned for you, Jonah."

"Maybe. You'd think Marcus would tell me. He has a pair of blades, and he used them on the Grim Hounds."

"No way!" Wick dropped the books on the card table.

"They're meant to fight supernatural things."

Everyone went back to staring at him until Robert moved the archive box out of the way so Wick could sit the books side by side.

"What's in those?" Jonah pointed at the books, glad for a distraction.

"My brother drove me way out to an estate sale in Ellaville." Wick opened one of the books and flipped through the pages. "The old guy who sold me the books called himself a Prophet. Local folks just thought him a nut case or a Satanist." Every page in the book contained at least one picture surrounded by tiny writing. Jonah tried to read it as Wick continued, "Bobby and I have been using the books to do research for the computer game."

"Yep," Robert added. "This is where I got the idea for the drawings of Grim Hounds."

Robert pointed to a realistic drawing of the creature, complete with the double rows of teeth. Jonah stepped back from the table before he could stop himself. He could hear the angry growls of the real creature, and his heart pounded in his chest.

Lynn watched him. "That thing must have really scared you."

"Yeah, it did. You try having a Grim Hound chase you down in the street." Jonah couldn't explain to his cousins the awful dread and fear that had come over him when he had seen it.

He shifted his eyes to the writing to avoid looking at the picture. Robert tapped the page. "See? Wick was right. It says here that people thought the Grim Hound, or Hell Hound, hunted doomed individuals. In reality, the Grim Hound hunts for objects a doomed person possesses." Robert shot Jonah a worried glance. "Sorry. I didn't mean that."

Doomed. Jonah rolled that word around in his mind. Were his parents doomed? Was he also doomed? Somebody was sending creatures after him now. Once again, Jonah caught the quick glances from the others. He had told Lynn this wasn't too much for him, and he meant it.

He found where Robert had stopped reading and continued, even though his voice shook a little. "The Grim Hound is not a dog. It is a supernatural being that assumes a canine shape when summoned. Maintaining the form requires a great deal of energy. Therefore, Grim Hounds can only stay in the mortal realm for limited periods of time."

"So," Lynn leaned against the table, eyeing Jonah. "The woman in the bookstore-"

"Neera," Wick interjected.

"This Neera woman called that Grim Hound and sent it after you. She used the card to pinpoint your location. She has to be powerful."

"Maybe she's responsible for the first ones you saw, Jonah," Robert answered before Jonah could. He snapped his fingers. "You were convinced she knew you were from DC."

"Mystic Worlds opened a couple of weeks before Jonah arrived in town," Lynn said, her lips pursed as she thought about it.

"It all adds up," Robert offered.

"We can't know for sure until we do some investigating, Robert."

"But we can't go near that store again. There's no telling what she'd do the next time. Plus, Jonah looked sick after that first visit."

"Is that true?" Lynn looked at him like she just remembered his presence.

"Well, yeah. I did feel strange being around her."

"Have you ever experienced this feeling before?"

Jonah didn't want to mention his Death Sense to her. However, he realized they needed to know more than he had revealed so far. His cousins had invited him into their inner circle and trusted him with their secrets. And, of course, he hated it when someone kept information from him. How could he do the same?

He held up his hands. "I don't want you freaking out or anything."

Wick raised his own hand immediately. "I promise you, Jonah, that I won't freak out by anything you tell me."

Goosebumps rose along Jonah's arms. Wick also blinked, looked down at his arms, and said, "Whoa."

Robert stared at his friend. "Are you okay?"

"Yeah, that was just freaky. It's like…" Wick paused and stared at Jonah.

"What?" Robert pressed, watching Wick and Jonah.

"Nothing, Bobby."

"You felt that?" Jonah asked. Wick nodded. "Why does it happen to me?"

"I want to look up something first, then I'll let you know."

"But…"

"I prom-" Wick stopped himself and offered Jonah a weak smile.

Lynn cleared her throat. "Well, if you two are done being even weirder than usual, I also promise not to freak out."

"So do I," Robert added. He and Lynn sucked in breaths, staring at the goosebumps along their arms.

Jonah took a deep breath and told them all about his Death Sense and the first times he experienced it. Lynn and Robert couldn't hide their shocked reactions.

Jonah was heartened by Wick's outrage at his old neighbors. Even Lynn's nostrils flared with anger.

"There's something else I need to tell you." Jonah paused to swallow past his nervousness. "The night of the fire, I tried to run back to my house and my neighbor grabbed me. I remembered thinking I needed to get past him and suddenly, I was in the next yard."

"What do you mean?" Lynn asked. "You slipped out of his hands?"

"No. I disappeared and then reappeared in my neighbor's yard."

Lynn was too shocked to reply. Robert leaned down to look Jonah directly in the eyes. "You can teleport, little cousin?"

Jonah smiled and shook his head. "It's called phasing, Robert."

He wanted to explain more about his rescue from the house and the trip to Marcus's apartment. The problem was Kevin. Jonah had promised the boy he wouldn't mention his name. Thankfully, his cousins were more concerned with the fact he could phase rather than the details of the house.

Robert ruffled his Afro for a moment, then gave Jonah a sly look. "You can disappear from one spot and reappear in another spot?" Jonah nodded. Robert glanced around the attic. "You can look at the bay window and…"

"I would appear there."

"Show us."

Jonah looked at the ground. "I can only do it when I'm in trouble."

"What do you think, Wick?" Lynn said, shifting her gaze from Jonah to Wick. "Is it magic?"

"It's not any kind of magic I've seen or read about. I mean, some powerful mages can make a vortex." Wick pointed at Jonah. "This is something else."

Jonah stared at Wick. "What's a vortex?"

"It's like a tunnel between two locations," Wick explained. "Real Mages are supposed to be able to do it."

"Can a witch or sorceress do it?"

"Yeah, if she's powerful enough. You worried about Neera?"

"No," Jonah lied and looked away. He was still freaked out about the dreams and feeling a bit guilty about not telling everyone he was half-Reaper. "I don't understand how I can use my power without training."

"Well, your power could be tied to your emotions." Wick held up a hand to tick off his points. "You were running away from bullies that day at school, and then your house burnt down. Those events involve powerful emotions." Wick gasped, causing everyone to look at him. "That's how you got away from the Grim Hound, isn't it?"

Jonah nodded as he experienced a surge of gratitude toward Wick. The older boy had already told him far more about his powers than anyone else, except maybe Kevin. Wick and his cousins weren't freaking out as much as he feared. In fact, as they continued to talk about his abilities and who might want to hurt him, Jonah was glad he had opened up to his cousins. They, and Wick, were trying to help him.

Jonah was nervous going outside, in the open, so he stuck with Robert and Wick for the rest of the day. Just before dinner, his phone started vibrating on the bedside table. Jonah fumbled to pick it up even though he didn't recognize the ID. But when he opened the phone, he saw he had a text, from Marcus.

Sorry to contact you so late, Jonah. Things have been extremely hectic here. Kevin told me all about the Grim Hound. I'm relieved that you are okay. I wished you'd ran in the opposite direction and called me. You know that one of us can be there in seconds.

Jonah stared at the message, wondering what else had happened that kept Marcus so busy that he couldn't call. Then a second text came in.

You shouldn't have to worry about anyone else bothering you. They know we're watching. And as much as I want you to get to know your relatives and settle into your new surroundings, you need to be prepared.

Jonah's eye's widened when he read that. *Prepare? How?* The next text came in.

I've made the decision to start teaching you to use your power. I think we should start with phasing. One of us will call you later to make arrangements. - Marcus.

Jonah tossed the phone on the bedside table with a mixture of emotions. Marcus didn't answer any of his questions—like who was after him. Why did they want to hurt him? At least Marcus promised to start training him to phase. That thought filled Jonah's mind as his Aunt Imma called him out to dinner.

CHAPTER TWENTY-TWO
PHASING LESSONS

Jonah had just finished clearing the table after dinner when his phone rang. He glanced at Aunt Imma, who was preparing the leftovers for the refrigerator, then slipped outside onto the patio and answered the call.

"What's up, little man?"

"Kevin? Why are you calling?"

"You talked to Marcus. He assigned me to train you."

"For real?"

"Yeah. Will you be alone, at home around eleven on Saturday?"

"I guess so, why?"

"I'm gonna phase down. Be ready at eleven. Backyard."

"Cool." Jonah nervously swallowed and said, "Kevin?"

"Yeah?"

Jonah just wanted to talk to Kevin. Yet his nerves failed him and the words wouldn't come out. Finally he muttered, "Nothing."

"See you then, little man."

Jonah had to admit that he was excited about seeing Kevin again, but nervous about learning to phase, too. Plus, he wasn't sure what to wear to a phasing lesson. *It's not a date*, he told himself and pulled on some athletic shorts and a plain tee.

The house seemed strangely quiet as he exited his bedroom. Lynn was off helping Uncle James at the newspaper, Robert worked on the blog at the teen center, and Saturday mornings were always the busiest times for Aunt Imma at the salon. Feeling a bit restless and alone, Jonah went outside and began pacing around the patio.

A change in air pressure alerted Jonah and he glanced at his watch. Kevin appeared right on time in the backyard, near the shed. He wore an off-white, short-sleeved workout shirt, dark blue athletic shorts, and black high top sneakers. He looked ready to go running or to a workout, Jonah thought. He began to wonder exactly what learning to phase would include.

The Fallen Reaper slowly looked around the yard before focusing on Jonah. When their eyes met, Jonah's heart fluttered a little. He felt a bit light on his feet as he approached the older boy.

Kevin raised his chin in a *whatsup* greeting. "You ready to learn phasing, little man?"

"Don't call me that."

Kevin grinned and held out his arm.

Jonah locked his arm in Kevin's while glancing toward the backyard fence. The neighbors weren't out and despite standing beside the shed and under the largest tree, someone could be watching. That raised a question for Jonah. "Why did you phase to the backyard and not inside the house? No one's here."

Kevin cocked an eyebrow, watching Jonah. "Your house is protected from that kind of thing. Marcus didn't tell you?"

"No." Before Jonah could fully digest that bit of news or ask another question, the world around him shifted and disappeared as Kevin phased them.

The first thing Jonah noticed when they reappeared was that the temperature was slightly cooler and the air less humid than it had been in Mount Vernon. The sun was just as bright, though, and he heard the lapping of water. Jonah turned to find a large, glittering lake behind them.

"Wow."

He released Kevin's arm and walked closer. They stood on a deck done in light wooden tiles, arranged on the diagonal to the building behind them. That structure and the other buildings on the opposite side of the lake all had Asian-inspired roofs. Jonah experienced a moment of dislocation when he saw that. "Where are we? We didn't phase to another country, did we?"

Kevin laughed. "No, we're still in Georgia. Come on." He crossed a little white stone bridge that connected the deck to a bamboo-covered pathway. Once there, he took the left branch in the pathway that cut across a grassy field. "This place is called Camp Alliance," he continued.

Jonah's mouth hung open as he took in his surroundings. The pathway led toward four large fields, each about half the size of a football field. A sturdy looking lean-to was set at the far end of each, with waist high shrubbery separating one from the next.

"This is a camp?"

"Yep, a training camp."

Jonah scanned the area, his face a confused mask. "Where is everyone?"

"It's Saturday. They have the day off."

Kevin entered the closest field. Jonah moved to the edge to peek over the shrubs into the next field. There were rocks and other objects of all sizes piled near the front of that one. But the one he and Kevin entered was bare except for the cut grass.

The Fallen Reaper stood near the center, arms folded behind his back. "These are ranges and we use them to train new members of the Alliance."

"Really? Who?"

Kevin nodded. "Gifted mortals, like Omar and Mages."

"Mages?"

"Spell casters, people who can use magic."

Jonah's eyes widened. "My friend Wick can use magic. Could he be a Mage?"

"You mean that kid at the old gas station? Interesting."

The idea of Wick coming here to train was cool to Jonah. And what about Lynn, he wondered. She had real Reaper's blades and could use them. Shouldn't she come here and train? Jonah started to ask about that when it occurred to him that Kevin was still an apprentice. "Are you training at this camp?"

Kevin hesitated before saying, "Yeah."

"You have to teach me phasing on your day off?"

The boy shrugged. "I'm working for the Alliance already. Besides, training you is worth a lot of credits. So let's get to it." He squared his shoulders and assumed an authoritative air. "Your state of mind is extremely important when phasing."

"Okay." Jonah blinked, thrown off by the sudden shift in Kevin's tone.

"I know you've phased before," Kevin continued, "but only when you panicked. If you want to phase without being freaked out, you have to learn to clear your mind. Watch me."

Kevin closed his eyes. The air rippled around him and he phased to the other side of the range, near the lean-to. He called out to Jonah, "Think about where you want to go. See it in your mind."

On his last word, Kevin phased to the opposite end of the range. "It only takes a split second to focus." Again, he phased. Jonah sensed the change in air pressure right before Kevin appeared beside him.

"It's like riding a bike," Kevin continued as if disappearing and reappearing was the most normal thing in the world. Jonah supposed it was, for a Fallen Reaper. Even a young one.

"Picking where you want to go and phasing can happen as fast as a thought." Kevin stepped away from Jonah.

"We'll go slow today. Think about a spot in the clearing. Now, close your eyes."

Jonah closed his eyes and relaxed his body.

"Good. When you're ready, I want you to phase."

Jonah pictured a small bush beside the lean-to. He thought about it and imagined standing next to it, but nothing happened. No ripple of air or the sensation along his skin. He knew before he opened his eyes that he stood in the same exact spot.

He let out a moan. "It's not working."

Kevin crossed his arms as he watched Jonah. "You're letting the doubt get in the way, aren't you?"

"Well, I did it before. Why can't I do it now?"

"Like I said, you were in a panic, Jonah. That panic cut through the doubt, and you phased."

Jonah's frustration kicked in and he balled his hands into tight fists. "So I can't do it now?"

"It's okay for you to doubt, at first, but don't stop there." Kevin waited for him to nod and relax again. He gently tapped Jonah on the chest with his fist. "You have to believe you can do it, inside, and you'll do it." He stepped back. "Try again."

Jonah closed his eyes and willed himself to phase several more times, and each time, nothing happened. Why would he doubt his abilities? He had done it before. He believed, he knew deep inside that he could do it. He even knew how his body responded to a phase. Could that be the key, Jonah wondered?

He thought about the small tree again. This time, he imagined the sensation along his skin and slight increase of pressure on his body. Then he told himself to phase.

When he opened his eyes, the small bush was directly in front of his face.

Kevin clapped from the other side of the clearing. Jonah started to cross to him and Kevin held up a hand.

"Hold up. I want you to phase back."

Jonah closed his eyes, thought about the spot beside Kevin, and then willed himself to phase. A moment later, strong hands gripped his arms to steady him.

"I knew you could do it." Kevin patted Jonah's shoulder.

"Yeah. It's cool!" The very idea that this would be natural was exciting to Jonah. Maybe being a half-Reaper wasn't so bad after all.

Kevin made him phase two more times. After his third successful phase, Jonah paused to rub his arms. "Why does phasing make my skin feel funny?"

"You're traveling through the Afterworld when you phase. It happens so fast that you don't realize that for a split second, your body doesn't exist in the mortal side at all."

"Whoa! That's like Night Crawler. He goes through part of Hell when he teleports."

Kevin cocked an eyebrow. "You would find a geeky way to describe it. Gee whiz."

"So the funny feeling on my skin is my body disappearing? Does it break down?"

"Not exactly. Your soul travels through the Afterworld for that split second. You carry the blueprint for your body with you and it comes out on the other side."

"Wow." Jonah thought this was the coolest thing he ever heard. Then he remembered his mom and Omar, and another question occurred to him. "Why can regular people travel with us?"

"While their own souls keep their blueprint, our power allows them to travel through to the other side with us. It can only happen for a few seconds."

Jonah sucked in a breath. "Can someone like me or you cross over for longer than that?"

Kevin stared at him for several seconds, long enough for his stare to turn into one of the uncomfortable, unblinking variety. Jonah had learned, though: he calmly waited for Kevin to answer.

Now that he finally had a teacher, Jonah couldn't wait to ask everything he'd been wondering since he'd first phased, back in Virginia. His question had been sparked by the info Wick gave him on the Grim Hound. They could be summoned into the mortal realm for certain periods of time, far more than a few seconds. Why couldn't it work the other way, with Fallen Reapers?

Kevin blinked and broke the Reaper stare. "That's a deep question for a little kid."

Jonah shoved Kevin, and the boy reacted by grabbing him into a headlock.

"You can save that talk for Marcus," Kevin said, ruffling Jonah's hair. "Today, you're learning to phase on command. Got it?"

Jonah mumbled his answer, and Kevin released him. As they continued with the phasing lessons, Jonah began to see a different side of the Fallen Reaper. The older boy took his job seriously. Each time Jonah phased, Kevin wanted him to pick another spot and phase faster.

"Try four phases in a row."

Jonah succeeded in doing four, but he paused before the final phase.

Kevin shouted, "Don't hesitate between each one. Start over, at the beginning."

Jonah grumbled but eventually, he managed to do four in a row without pausing. By that time, he swayed on his feet from dizziness.

Kevin gripped his shoulder. "Careful."

"Why do I feel so dizzy?"

"Doing multiple phases takes a lot out of you. Here, try this." Kevin handed him a piece of butterscotch candy.

At the first taste of the buttery candy, a pleasant jolt of energy ran through Jonah. He glanced up at Kevin. "Does the candy work for you?"

"It makes me feel better, but I still have to recharge. I bet you just need a little down time and you're as good as new."

"Yeah, I feel better after a nap."

"Lucky you." Kevin paused as he gazed around the range. Jonah expected the Fallen Reaper to have him perform something else, but Kevin clapped his hands together once. "That's enough for today."

Jonah glanced in the boy's face, trying to judge how the session had gone. After a few moments, he gave up and simply asked, "How was I?"

"You were great."

A knot in Jonah's stomach released itself. Kevin looked sincere, and he hadn't used that stupid nickname. Jonah's excitement about having Kevin here returned now that the lesson was over. "You want to hang out? Maybe I can see the rest of the camp."

Kevin blinked in surprise and Jonah felt his own face warm. The older boy had said before that he thought Jonah was a kid. *Surely he wouldn't want to hang out with me*, Jonah decided. He'd been stupid to even ask.

Instead of making fun of him, Kevin smiled. "You have to get back before someone misses you. I have work to do."

"Oh. Same time tomorrow?"

"No. Marcus thought you should practice doing short phases on your own."

Doubt nibbled at Jonah's insides. "Can't we do both?"

"Sorry. Marcus has me working on other things." Kevin gestured around him. "And I have camp."

Jonah gaze down the line of ranges as he thought about trying to phase alone. He'd hoped Kevin would be there because he'd feel more confident.

Kevin leaned down to look him in the eyes. "The whole point of the lesson is so you can phase on your own. A little private practice won't hurt."

Jonah nodded, and Kevin continued to stare at him. "Go hang out with your friends when you get back. Have fun and clear your mind." He tapped Jonah's chest. "Your body needs to recharge anyway." He held out an arm to Jonah. "And don't look so sad. We'll meet up again."

CHAPTER TWENTY-THREE
BASEMENT AMBUSH

After the phasing lesson from Kevin—and the fact that no more raging Grim Hounds appeared—Jonah was confident enough to go out on his own. He'd decided to check out the creek side clearing behind the Teen Center. Following the well-worn path through the grass and down the hillside, Jonah reached the clearing with little problem.

Someone, probably the older kids, had moved several large rocks and a couple of moss-covered logs around the clearing. Discarded soda cans, bottles, and wrappers littered the area. At the dead center was a shallow depression with burned sticks and matches in it.

Jonah didn't try to figure that one out. All that mattered was that the stream ran clear and the place was quiet. For now, it was the perfect place to think. He breathed in deeply, listening to the gurgling creek. Branches rustled high overhead, punctuated by occasional bird calls. He let out a slow breath, enjoying the cooler air under the thick tree cover.

Of course, his mind went straight to his incident with the Grim Hound. Despite what his godfather said, Jonah wanted to know who sent that creature. He needed someone who could give him answers and he longed to talk to Kevin again. The problem was he didn't know how to contact the boy.

At least telling his cousins and Wick about himself had lifted a weight from his shoulders. He didn't have to lie anymore and could bounce ideas off them. However, they couldn't give him all the answers he needed. In fact, his cousins hoped that he would give them information.

He closed his eyes and breathed in deeply, yet again, to clear his mind. He tried to let the sounds carry him away, but someone laughed close by in the woods.

Jonah hoped whoever it was would stay away. No luck. The laugh was much closer the second time it came, followed by the sounds of shuffling feet sliding through leaves.

An older girl and boy came around a bend further up the creek and paused when they saw him. The boy waved, and Jonah noticed the tattoos covering his entire arm. "Excuse us, little dude."

Jonah frowned as he glanced back the way they had come. The river turned sharply several yards upstream and disappeared around a hill full of the moss-covered tree stumps.

Jonah originally thought the boy was thin because the oversize shirt had fooled him. The older boy had broad shoulders and biceps that bulged when he clapped his hands. Numerous tattoos covered both forearms and he had a scar on his left arm, like someone had pressed a hot iron against the skin.

The boy coughed into his fist. "Yo, are you meeting someone down here?"

"No."

"You mind if we use the spot?"

The girl watched Jonah with a curious expression. She finally jumped and said, "You're Lynn's cousin, the one from DC."

"Huh, yeah."

The boy gave Jonah an appraising stare, like knowing he was related to Lynn made a difference somehow. "Cool. Well, if you meeting your girl or something, we can go somewhere else."

Jonah stood so quickly, he actually startled the boy and girl. "I'm not meeting anyone."

With that, he ran up the hill. The girl laughed and, for a second, Jonah thought she laughed at him. He paused to look back. The boy and girl sat side by side on a boulder, their heads very close together as they talked. Jonah shook his head. He couldn't imagine ever coming down here to make out with anyone.

He entered the recreation center, intent on playing ping-pong to let off some tension. Jonah had started toward the East wing area when a girl in a staff shirt called out to him.

"Are you Jonah?"

Fear gripped him. Had he done something wrong? "Yeah, why?"

"You know Wick?"

Jonah relaxed a bit and nodded.

"Well," the girl continued. "He wanted you to meet him in the basement."

"In the basement?"

"Ah, he works here part-time in the summer, with the custodian. The office is in the basement."

"Oh, okay."

"Follow me."

She led Jonah back through the main lobby to the elevator. He couldn't imagine why Wick needed to see him. *Maybe it has to do with magic,* Jonah thought.

When the doors opened, the girl inserted a key into a lock above the button marked *basement.* She continued to worry her lower lip as the elevator descended.

"Are you okay?" Jonah asked.

"I heard there are rats in the basement."

She made a face, but when the doors opened, she didn't hesitate to lead Jonah to a storeroom.

"There you go. He's in there." She turned and hurried off.

Jonah stepped into the room, looking around. The basement storeroom only had one light working, and it flickered. Jonah was reminded of the mausoleum crypt and the memorial service for his parents. He paused just inside the door, concentrating on his Death Sense. His stomach was calm and he didn't have a headache, so none of the strange people were around. The flickering light began to bother him, and he started down the aisles of cleaning and office supplies and old books.

He peeked through the gaps in the items on the shelves, trying to spot Wick. No one seemed to be here. He returned to the front area, by the door. Maybe he should call Wick's name, he thought. Then he heard someone behind him.

"It's about time…" Jonah turned around and paused.

Mike stood panting in the doorway, his eyes wide. "Jonah! You have to get out, now. I know what they're up to."

"What…"

"It's a trap!"

Jonah's uneasy feeling morphed into a sharp prickle from his Death Sense.

"Well, well, well. It's DC." Brandon, Drew, and Antwan stepped into view. Mike bolted into the room to stand beside Jonah.

Brandon grinned at them as he entered the storeroom. "I caught you and your boyfriend in the basement." Brandon's friends laughed, but he sneered at Jonah. "You don't have your cousin to hide behind this time, DC."

"My name's Jonah." He kept cool as his mind caught up with Mike's warning. "What are you doing down here?"

Brandon's buddies stepped into the room and moved to either side of Jonah.

"So tell me, DC," Brandon continued, ignoring Jonah's question. "Is it true what I hear? You're not visiting your cousins for the summer. You're staying here for good."

Jonah's shock must have shown on his face because Brandon laughed and took a step closer.

Mike spoke in his ear. "I'm sorry, Jonah."

"I heard your parents are dead. No one wanted you, so you came here." Brandon smirked. "Poor baby. What's it like not having a momma and daddy?"

Jonah's heart hammered in his chest as he lunged at Brandon. Drew and Antwan were prepared, grabbing and pushing him back against the shelves. Without thinking, Jonah snatched a plastic bottle of cleaner off the shelf and slammed it against Antwan's head. The boy howled and leapt back.

Mike yelled, which caused Drew to hesitate. Brandon took advantage of the confusion and punched Jonah in the stomach. He collapsed to the floor, unable to catch his breath.

Mike jumped between him and Brandon. "Leave him alone."

Jonah struggled to his feet and Antwan and Drew moved in, grabbing his arms and holding him while Brandon shoved Mike out of the way. That done, Brandon punched Jonah two more times, then drew back his fist to smack Jonah in the face.

Mike launched himself at Brandon, grabbing the bully's arm and yelling, "Stop!"

Antwan shoved Jonah roughly into another row of shelves while Brandon struggled with Mike, who wouldn't let go. He managed to free his arm, then pushed him into Jonah. Both lost their balance as they toppled over with the shelves. That section crashed into the others, causing all of them to wobble. Cleaning supplies, boxes, and all kinds of debris rained down on them. Brandon and his buddies scrambled back toward the safety of the door.

Jonah looked up in time to see an entire upper section of shelving falling toward him. Mike saw it too and let out a real scream. Jonah grabbed his arm, wishing with all his might that they were anywhere except here.

In a flash, he recalled Kevin's lesson about picking a destination. The first place that came to his mind was the last place he had visited: the clearing beside the creek. He felt the ripple along his skin and in the blink of an eye, the basement room was gone.

The soft ground near the creek replaced the hard basement floor. Jonah rolled over, saw no one else around, and let out a breath. A second later, a wave of dizziness hit him, and he scrambled to the nearest rock and sat down before he collapsed.

"Oh my God! Oh my God!" Mike shouted and crossed to the rock furthest from Jonah, sat down, and watched him with wide eyes.

Jonah took a few breaths. The cooler air and sound of the water helped the light-headed feeling pass.

Mike's voice shook when he finally spoke. "Are you a witch?"

"No."

"Then how did you do it, Jonah? One minute, we're in the basement, then we're outside." Mike stood, turning around on the spot as he rubbed his arms. Jonah noticed that he took care to keep the distance between them. "My skin felt all funny and…" Mike looked down at his chest and hugged himself. "Oh my God."

Jonah understood what he meant. Phasing was like having goosebumps all over your body, all over, even the private places. It still made him feel weird.

Mike sat down and took several deep breaths. "How did you do it?"

"When I'm in trouble, I just think about being somewhere and it happens."

"But… is it magic?"

Jonah shrugged. "All I know is it's called phasing. The first time it happened, I thought I just imagined it."

Mike's eyes went wide and out of focus, as if he remembered something. Jonah knew Mike couldn't really believe what happened even though he had experienced the phase.

They sat in silence for a while, listening to the sounds of the nearby creek. When Jonah moved, Mike jumped to his feet, pointing at him.

"I know what you are!"

Jonah's insides froze. He had expected Mike to be afraid; now he was the one fearful of what Mike would say.

"What do you mean?"

"You're a Fallen Reaper, aren't you?"

Jonah's mouth hung open. He didn't know how to respond except to deny, but Mike went on first.

"I'm right!" Mike pumped his fist in the air. "My uncle has all kinds of secret books locked away. I know where he keeps the key." He settled down, looking doubtful for the first time. "I didn't know Fallen Reapers could be my age."

Jonah shook his head, trying to get his own head around the sudden change. "I'm sorry. I never meant for this to happen."

"Are you kidding," Mike breathed. "This… is… so… cool!"

Jonah blinked in surprise. "Mike, I'm not a Fallen Reaper."

"Yes you are. I know about this stuff, Jonah. You called it phasing. Fallen Reapers do that!"

"How?"

"I told you, my uncle has all kinds of books about supernatural stuff. He owns a bookstore."

"Really?" Jonah blinked in surprise again, trying to catch up to Mike's reaction. "That's awesome."

Mike subsided, looking amused. "That's the first time anyone's said that about my uncle having a bookstore." He sat on a closer rock, peering into Jonah's eyes. "You really are into books. You're a nerd like me?" He cracked a nervous smile.

"Yeah. I guess." Jonah lowered his gaze. "Okay. You're right."

"I knew it."

"Mike!"

"Sorry."

"I'm not a Fallen Reaper."

"But--"

Jonah held up a hand. "I'm half-Reaper." Mike's jaw dropped. "My dad was a Fallen Reaper."

"I never knew about half-Reapers." Mike paused. "This is so awesome."

Jonah realized that his own fear and agitation had subsided. He was comfortable talking with Mike. "You promise not to tell anyone?"

"I wouldn't do that. You stood up for me and even saved my life just now." Mike's voice shook a little. "I promise."

Jonah glanced up the hill and around the clearing. He took a deep breath and began to tell Mike everything he knew about himself.

CHAPTER TWENTY-FOUR
RESEARCH PARTNERS

Jonah rolled his bike up Morningside drive, still thinking about Mike. All he did was go to the recreation center. He never meant to use his powers. Once he did, he had assumed Mike would accuse him of being strange, weird, or even evil. That didn't happen.

He kicked a stray rock as he pushed his bike up the Hightowers' driveway and stowed it beside Lynn's in the backyard shed. When he reached the kitchen door, he paused to peek through its little window. He may have saved himself and Mike, but Jonah had scratches and a few cuts.

He didn't see Lynn in the kitchen or den, and that was good, he decided. She would blow a fuse if she saw him like this. Screwing up his nerves, Jonah entered the house.

Music blared from Lynn's room. Excellent, Jonah thought as he hurried through the kitchen and into the den. He was just a few feet from the safety of his bedroom—and a quick nap to let his body heal—when Lynn called his name.

"Jonah, why are you sneaking through the house?"

"I'm not sneaking through the house."

She carried a basket of clean laundry. When she saw his cuts, she dropped the basket on the floor. "Can't you go one day without getting into trouble?" She went for the med kit.

"It wasn't my fault. Things just keep happening to me!"

Lynn came back, grabbed him by the arm, and sat him down at the kitchen table. He winced and moved each time she tried to clean his cuts.

"Hold still and tell me what you did this time."

"Brandon and his buddies ambushed me." He recounted the entire story, being careful to leave Mike out. By the end, Lynn's nostrils flared with anger.

"I'll break his rich little neck. You could have been seriously hurt."

"I just wish I could protect myself." Jonah sat back and rubbed his side where Brandon had punched him. "It's bad enough with the supernatural stuff happening. Now, regular kids are beating me up."

She threw away the bloody swabs. "I'll take care of that arrogant punk."

"No! You can't fight for me." If Lynn got involved again, Brandon would do something even crazier to get even. He needed another idea.

Jonah decided to avoid the teen center over the next couple of days. He didn't want to see Brandon, not that he was afraid of the bully. Jonah feared that something else would happen and he'd use his power, maybe in front of more people. He hadn't lied to Lynn. He needed a way to control himself.

He talked his aunt into dropping him off at the Twiggs County library. He was impressed at his first glimpse of the modern, three-story library, and then he stepped through the center set of double glass doors and into a spacious atrium. A light, tiled marble covered the floor, creating hard echoes as people walked across it. Jonah craned his head back to see the domed ceiling of the atrium three floors above.

Ignoring the daily newspapers and Juvenile sections directly ahead through the atrium, Jonah headed for the wide staircase to the second floor. He'd looked up the library on the Internet and knew it had a large, second-floor study section. Once at the top of the stairs, he took his time walking past the periodicals and computer rooms before entering the main study section. Floor-to-ceiling wood bookcases covered every wall. Numerous large study tables filled the center of the open space. Each one contained a raised center portion with two stubby reading lamps on top and electrical outlets and data ports on each side.

Golden afternoon sunlight streamed through the massive windows, giving the adjacent reading nooks and low-slung reading chairs an inviting quality. Jonah paused to get his bearings. Not only were there nooks spaced around the outer edge of the study area, but there were also four study alcoves.

Those were his target, and Jonah hurried over to one, placing his bag on the table. This was perfect, he thought. The alcoves had three walls of floor-to-ceiling bookshelves. The fourth side was open to the study room.

Once he settled in, and he began to pull books on Reapers, Jonah's worries about Brandon, and whether or not to tell his cousins he was a half-Reaper, receded. Jonah sunk into the familiar routine of a library. Even if it was a different building, Jonah was reminded of his own lonely, yet comforting, hours in the Arlington Central Library.

He spent the rest of that afternoon pouring over information on mythology, visions, premonitions, and Reapers. Jonah found that much of his research on Reapers never touched on the things he could do. Marcus told him that the real information had been kept from mortals, and Jonah began to see the truth of that. Putting those books aside, he focused on the ring instead. He didn't know where to begin, so he delved into everything he could find. Time slipped away, turning into the early evening hours before he went home.

Jonah's cellphone rang as he stepped out of the bathroom, body damp from a morning shower. He sprinted down the hallway and into his room, glad that everyone was gone. His aunt would go crazy if she saw his wet feet on her hardwood floors. Jonah entered his room and dived across the bed to scoop up the phone from the bedside table.

"Hello?"

There was a long pause. "Hi, Jonah."

"Mike?" Jonah tossed his towel aside. "Are you okay?"

"Yeah. I've been looking for you."

"Oh, sorry."

"Can we talk?"

"Yeah." Jonah waited for him to continue, but Mike remained silent. "I thought you wanted to talk."

"I do, just not on the phone. Let's meet."

"Sure. Where?"

Mike paused again. "Are your cousins home?"

"They're gone. Why?"

"I'll come over. We can talk on your patio."

"Okay."

Jonah wasn't sure how to read Mike's tone as he dressed and headed outside to the patio. It was only after he sat down at the wooden table that he wondered how Mike knew about the patio.

The Hightowers' backyard wasn't visible from the street because of the high fence and shrubbery. Maybe he'd been over to the house before, Jonah thought just as Mike rode his bike into the backyard. Jonah relaxed a little when Mike gave him shy smile, leaning his bike against the tree.

Once Mike had plopped down into a chair on the opposite side of the table he said, "I've been thinking and I have a question." Jonah nodded. "Can Lynn and Robert do it?"

"No."

"Do they know about you?"

"Yeah." Mike went quiet. Jonah had done some thinking of his own over the past few days. Once the panic and fear of Mike revealing his secret subsided, he had begun to go over the events of that day. "Mike, how did you know about the ambush?" Jonah waited as Mike gazed out across the backyard. "Mike?"

"Drew told me."

"Why would Drew tell you anything?"

"He didn't mean to tell me. He let it slip out while we talked."

"Why were you talking to him?"

"We used to be friends--"

"He tried to hurt us. How can you take his side?"

"I'm not taking his side. I told Drew he's stupid to hang out with Brandon."

Jonah rose from his patio chair. "Is that how Brandon found out about my parents? Did you tell Drew?"

Mike pushed himself to his own feet, facing off. It was only then that Jonah realized he leaned over the patio table with his fists clenched. He took a deep breath and sat down, pressing his hands flat against the table top.

"Sorry." Jonah glanced down at his splayed hands. "I didn't mean to yell at you."

Mike's shoulders slumped a bit. "I understand, Jonah. I didn't know about your parents, so I couldn't tell Drew anything. Besides, I would never do that."

"I wonder how Drew found out?"

Mike gulped and slumped into his chair. "It was your aunt."

"My aunt wouldn't tell Drew anything about me."

"She didn't, directly."

"Then I don't understand."

"Jonah, Mount Vernon isn't a big place, and our community is even smaller. A lot of moms go to the beauty salon where your aunt works. Drew's mom goes."

Jonah stared at him. "Does your mom go?"

Mike nodded. "Yeah, but Drew told me that your aunt mentioned you at work. She talked about your parents dying and you coming to live with them. Knowing your aunt, she probably asked people to pray for you. Drew's mom heard about it."

"And she told Drew?"

"She told him to be nice to you, maybe try to be friends and make things easy on you."

Jonah snorted. "He screwed that up."

"Parents can be stupid when it comes to their kids. Did you tell your--" Mike stopped and covered his mouth. "I'm sorry."

"It's okay. I know what you mean. My aunt and uncle don't know half the things we do," Jonah admitted, thinking about all the secrets he and his cousins kept to themselves. When Mike refused to say anything, Jonah continued, "So she wanted Drew to be my friend?"

"I told you. His father's a dentist and they have as much money as Brandon's family, but they stay on this side of town. They aren't snobs like Brandon and Antwan's folks."

Jonah shook his head. He was certainly starting to understand more and more about Mount Vernon. "How did you know where to go?"

"I saw that rec center girl talking to Brandon and I ran to the library to find you."

"I went to play ping-pong."

"Oh. Well anyway, when I saw her coming off the elevator, I made her tell me what she did and take me down there."

Jonah was amazed. He never thought Mike could scare anyone. "How did you do that?"

"I told her that my big brother would beat her up if she didn't."

Jonah couldn't stop himself from laughing. "What?"

Mike bit his lip and lowered his gaze. "My brother goes to the same high school."

"Would he do that?"

"No, but she didn't know that." Mike flashed Jonah a mischievous silver grin, showing off his braces. Jonah whooped with laughter.

"That was brilliant, Mike." Jonah laughed again until a sobering thought struck him. "Do you think they saw me phase?"

Mike stuck out his lower lip as he considered it. "I don't think they saw anything. They were running toward the door when it happened."

Mike leaned forward, scanning Jonah's face, hair, hands, and arms. He held out a hand.

Jonah hesitated at first, but not because another boy wanted to see his hand. He knew Mike wanted to see the cut. He reached across the table, letting Mike grip his hand and turn it over. Mike's eyes widened when he saw the healed cuts.

"I heal fast," Jonah explained.

After a few moments in which Mike brushed his fingers across Jonah's hand, he took a deep breath and looked Jonah directly in the eyes. "Never, ever phase me again."

Jonah burst out laughing. Mike joined him after a few moments.

"Did you hear what happened to Brandon?" he said, voice full of excitement.

"No."

Mike switched to a closer chair. "Brandon, Antwan, and Drew were caught running from the storage room. The rec center demanded their parents pay for the damage. Of course, Brandon's father refused."

"What happened?"

"He and Antwan are banned from the center," Mike said, "for the rest of the summer."

"What about Drew?"

"His father agreed to pay, so Drew's okay. Can you believe it?"

Jonah enjoyed listening to Mike talk as much as he liked hearing about Brandon's troubles. When the temperatures started to rise, they went inside to play videos. Jonah enjoyed the break from his research, so when Mike suggested they head up to the teen center, Jonah was ready to return. They spent time going through the fiction section of the small library.

Around midday, Jonah had his first real chance to try out the Cyber Café. Mike chose a table in the back and Jonah ordered them burgers at the counter. Despite enjoying himself, Jonah began watching the other kids who laughed, talked, and made plans for the evening or weekend with their friends. He glanced at Mike, who had been watching a boy two tables over until he saw Jonah watching.

"We were in the same homeroom."

Jonah nodded at the explanation, even if he didn't totally believe it. He also didn't care. He liked hanging out with Mike, and he guessed they were becoming friends. So why did he feel different, like he missed something?

I'm half-Reaper.

That's it, Jonah thought. He couldn't imagine any of the other kids ever talking about Grim Hounds or Death or Reapers. How many of them lost both parents and a home? The heaviness from his first day returned and not knowing so many answers caused Jonah to slump in his chair.

Mike watched him as he slurped the last of his milkshake. "Jonah?"

"What?"

"Are you bored?"

"No."

"What's wrong? You're frowning."

"I don't know." That was true. He didn't know how to explain that he needed information. Jonah tapped the tabletop with his fingers. "I want to find out about rings."

"Rings?"

"Yeah. Ones with power."

Mike dropped the empty cup on the table, his mouth hanging open. "This has to do with your…" he glanced around, "…your power?"

"Yeah. My parents used to find powerful artifacts like rings, medallions, talismans."

"That's so cool."

Jonah met Mike's gaze. "It was dangerous." He paused at the spasm of pain from the loss. "I tried the county library, but that didn't help. The only store I know with books on things like this is Mystic Worlds, and I can't go back in there."

"Why not?"

Jonah caught himself on the verge of telling Mike about his last bookstore visit. It wasn't that he expected Mike to freak out when he mentioned the Grim Hound, but he didn't know how Mike would respond to knowing the creatures were real. Maybe he'd save that part for later.

He smiled and lowered his voice to a whisper. "We think the owner is a witch and she doesn't like me."

"Are you serious?"

Jonah nodded and Mike squared his shoulders. "Mystic Worlds isn't the only store to have those kinds of books. My uncle owns a bookstore, remember. It's called Hackett's Emporium, and I bet he has the books you need."

Jonah sat up in his own chair. "You mean I can see the secret books about supernatural stuff?"

A shadow of doubt flashed across Mike's face. "I don't know about that. I was able to see those because my uncle went out of town one time. He has a lot of regular books on the occult."

"This is about the real things, my power."

"I know, but let's see if the regular books have anything on the rings, okay?"

Jonah agreed. This was a better option than Mystic Worlds. Maybe he'd find out what he needed. That thought cheered Jonah as they headed out of the teen center.

CHAPTER TWENTY-FIVE
THE LITTLE BOOKSTORE

Hackett's Book Emporium wasn't like Mystic Worlds at all. The bookstore was located in a small, one-story house that the county had rezoned for commercial use. It was situated on a small plot of land between a hunting supply store and a propane store. A large wooden sign was nailed above the old front porch and featured the store name in painted lettering.

Mike and Jonah locked their bikes to a metal rail out front.

"My uncle can get cranky," he whispered to Jonah as they mounted the creaky steps. "And he can be strange at times. I know he doesn't like young people in the occult section, but he's my uncle and I work here part-time, so…"

"You think he'll let us see the books?"

"Yes."

"Okay." He didn't know if Mike was sure or if he was being optimistic. He decided not to press as Mike opened the old front door, causing an overhead bell to tinkle.

Jonah stopped just inside the front door to breathe in deeply. It smelled like a real bookstore, which meant it smelled like old, used books. He knew he would find slightly abused first editions of novels the mall stores would never keep in stock.

He was reminded of all the times his mom had taken him to out-of-the-way secondhand bookstores like this. He would lose himself in the mountain of books, looking for old paperback adventures and sci-fi novels. He'd always leave with a stack of them in his hands and spend the next week being transported to strange worlds.

"Mike," he breathed, "this is fantastic."

"It's larger than it looked from outside because my uncle has two trailers attached to the back of the house. The occult section is back there."

Jonah craned his neck to see the back of the store as an old man stepped out of a side aisle. He wore blue jean coveralls and a grungy, paint-splattered cap over his curly, silver-grey hair. The bushy silver-grey mustache seemed to accent the man's frown. As he approached, Jonah could understand why Mike didn't want to cross his uncle. The man never smiled as he pulled a small paintbrush from a back pocket and started chipping dried paint off the handle with a fingernail. He didn't quite have Mike's pale oatmeal complexion, but Jonah could see the resemblance as the man eyed him.

"You related to Robert Hightower?"

"Yes, sir."

"I knew it. You got those same grey eyes. Robert never mentioned a younger brother."

Jonah opened his mouth and Mike spoke over him. "Jonah's not his brother. He's a cousin."

The old man glanced briefly at his nephew, then back at Jonah. "That so?"

Jonah nodded. "You know my cousin?"

"I used to be his art teacher. I won't hold that against ya. Business is business, I say. How can I help ya?"

Mike traded a glance with Jonah, then smiled at his uncle. "We wanted to look in the Occult section."

"I've been in enough trouble with your parents, Mike. You two a little young to be involved in that kind of stuff."

Jonah wanted to sigh because Mr. Hackett sounded just like the clerk from Mystic Worlds.

Mike didn't seem put off. "We just want to look up stuff like special rings, you know…"

Mike trailed off because his uncle's hazel eyes narrowed. Most surprising to Jonah was that his Death Sense tingled. Hackett held the paint brush in a tight grip, he noticed.

Without having to think about it, he moved in front of Mike. Only after he moved did it occur to him that Mr. Hackett would never threaten his nephew. *It's me*, Jonah thought to himself.

Mike gave Jonah a curious glance but kept silent.

Hackett also noticed his move and blinked. "You said you're Robert's cousin?"

Jonah nodded, but he didn't relax, not with his Death Sense still vibrating.

"Are you a Hightower?" The man asked.

"No. My last name is Blackstone."

Hackett blinked wildly again. "Your daddy was…"

"My dad was Isaiah Blackstone."

Hackett mouthed the name *Isaiah* as he watched them for a moment longer. The man's posture relaxed, and Jonah's Death Sense quieted, but that made Jonah suspicious.

"Did you know my dad?"

"No, I never met him."

Jonah caught the way the man refused to meet his gaze and could sense that Hackett didn't tell the whole truth. Maybe Hackett never met his dad, but he had heard the name. For some unknown reason, that made the difference to this man.

Hackett nodded once, then pointed toward the front door. "Go."

"Uncle?" Mike's shocked expression matched Jonah's.

"Come back after I clear the store."

Mike glanced around at the scattered customers and nodded. He motioned Jonah to follow.

The boys hung out at the teen center until Mike's uncle called. He'd closed up a few hours earlier than normal. That made Jonah feel a bit guilty until they arrived at the bookstore and saw the *We'll Return* sign on the front door. Judging from the position of the clock hands, Mike's uncle was giving them an hour of his time. Mike gave Jonah an embarrassed shrug as he knocked on the windowpane.

As soon as they stepped through the front door of the deserted store, Hackett led them around tottering stacks of paperback books and through the narrow aisles to the very back of the store. He paused in front of a door that Jonah knew would have been a bedroom a long time ago.

Hackett moved aside and pointed them through the opening. "Go on."

Jonah stepped into the next room and gasped. The room was bulging with paintings of dragons, knights, elves, and other kinds of fantastical things, and books crowded the space just like the rest of the store. Hackett dropped his paintbrush in a jar of turpentine to soak and then motioned them to two folding chairs in front of a cluttered wooden desk. Jonah sucked in a breath because he saw a full-sized painting of the cover from the Death Omen book.

"Your uncle wrote that book?" Jonah whispered. "I bought a copy at Mystic Worlds."

Mike leaned closer and grinned. "I could have gotten it for you at half-price, and with an autograph."

Mike's uncle cleared his throat as he squeezed behind the desk, taking care not to bang his head on a large, multicolored lamp hanging overhead. Jonah thought it looked like the type of light over a pool table in a movie.

Mr. Hackett clicked on the lamp, which Jonah thought odd. Although thick dark curtains covered the room's only window, the overhead light was on as well as a couple of lamps around the room. Then Jonah noticed that the painted lacquered sides of the multicolored lamp served to focus all its light directly on the desktop, like an elaborate reading lamp.

Hackett had turned to unlock a large black safe behind his desk, and he pulled out a very old book with burnished brass clasps. He dropped it on the desk with a surprisingly heavy thud, unhooked the clasps, and began turning through the pages, which made crinkly sounds.

When Mr. Hackett found a page he looked for, he rotated the book so Jonah and Mike could see. The page contained several drawings of rings, each with different markings, but all similar.

Mr. Hackett pressed a boney finger to the illustrations and leaned over the desk to peer at them. The lamplight cast deep shadows under his eyes, making his wrinkled face even more ominous. "Only Fallen Reapers and their allies know about these things."

Jonah had expected this as soon as Hackett reacted to his real name. "You knew my dad." Jonah didn't make it a question.

Hackett nodded. "I knew about him. Fallen Reaper. I thought they couldn't have kids."

"My mom was a mortal." Jonah shrugged. "They had me."

Hackett shook his head. "Well, I'll be…" His mouth continued to move though no words came out. He cleared his throat after a moment and said, "If you want any information from me, you'll tell me how you know about the rings?"

"My godfather told me." Mr. Hackett raised an eyebrow and Jonah rushed on, "He's executor of my parents' estate."

"Estate? You mean your parents are…"

Jonah nodded.

"How long?"

"It's been a month," Jonah answered.

Hackett sat down in the squeaky desk chair and lifted the paint-splattered cap to wipe his forehead. "They didn't tell me…" Hackett shook himself and glanced at Jonah. "I'm sorry to hear that about your parents."

"Thank you." Jonah paused until Mike nudged him in the arm. "How do you know about Fallen Reapers, Mr. Hackett?"

Mr. Hackett gazed at his nephew. "I suppose you two have been talking?"

"Yes, sir. Jonah told me all about it." Mike flashed a silvery smile.

"If your momma ever finds out…" Mr. Hackett pulled out his handkerchief and wiped his forehead again. "So be it. I've seen a Fallen Reaper before, and I know all about these rings." The old man shook his head and laid his cap on the desk. He watched them for a long time. Just when Jonah decided the man was never going to answer, Mr. Hackett leaned back in his chair.

"People called me a crackpot," he shot a glance at Mike, "because I believed in a larger truth about Angels, Demons, Reapers, and other supernatural beings. I found books that talked about these powerful rings made for human beings to balance the scales between us and the supernatural." Hackett paused, his eyes slightly out of focus as if he saw the information in his head.

"The Fallen Reaper I met confirmed my research. He told me the rings existed and one of his kind could use a ring to draw in power."

Jonah's stomach bunched into a knot.

Mike looked between Jonah and Mr. Hackett. "You said the rings were meant for humans. Fallen Reapers aren't exactly human anymore, are they? Not if they still use power."

"The Fallen Reapers are human," Mr. Hackett continued. "Even more important, they existed on the supernatural plane."

Mike shook his head. "Does that make a difference?"

Mr. Hackett snorted. "It makes a heck of a difference. Once they experienced that, they're always in tune to the supernatural. That's why they can work the binding spell to draw power." Hackett paused, raising a questioning eyebrow at Jonah. "You know about the binding patterns they use?"

"Yeah. My godfather told me about that, too."

Mike gaped at his uncle and Jonah. "Really? I didn't read about that in…" His voice trailed off at the scathing look from his uncle. "Sorry."

"I see I'll need to find a better place to hide my spare key." The sour expression remained as Hackett focused on Jonah. "Anyway, a Fallen Reaper may be able to use one of them rings."

Jonah's mind replayed the conversation between his dad and Deyanira, when he had refused to give her the ring. In fact, his dad hadn't seemed to have it at all. Jonah sat up in his chair. "Have you ever seen a real ring?"

"Not in person." Hackett waved at the books. "Only the drawings."

Once again, Jonah sensed the half-truth in Hackett's comment. Finally, he got it. Hackett knew about the supernatural world, but not everything. He heard about his dad, but never met him. He could write the book on Death Omens because he knew a Fallen Reaper. But clearly, the Fallen Reaper hadn't told Hackett everything.

Jonah leaned on the desk and pointed to the ring on the page. "Do you know what the symbols say?"

Mr. Hackett shook his head. "The writing is called Angel script."

Jonah lapsed into silence as Mr. Hackett continued, "You ever heard of the Ring of Solomon? It allowed King Solomon to command and control the demons. Well, I figure it was one of these rings."

"How many rings are there?" Mike ran his finger down the page, scanning through the text.

"As far as I could tell, there were thirty-five. They were given to chosen humans so they would have the power to serve as protectors of the secret."

Jonah sat forward in his chair. "What secret?"

"Legend says that in times of great need, a group of special humans called the Children of Light would appear and balance things out. The guardians would protect and watch over them. After the Children of Light did their thing and everything is right with the world again, the Protectors would remain behind like sentinels."

Hackett paused, scratching his head. "The problem is the Protectors have been missing for nearly two thousand years—or rather, their rings have been missing."

The words *protect* and *protectors* finally connected for Jonah. His dad had underlined a passage about Protectors and rings in the little gray book.

Did my dad actually find a ring that belonged to the Protectors? Is that why my parents were killed? They died to protect me!

He couldn't hide the pain in his voice when he asked, "What happened to the Protectors?"

"They were all hunted down and killed. I'm talking about whole families and bloodlines being ruthlessly destroyed. The rings were lost."

Mike gave Jonah a worried glance before he asked, "The rings weren't destroyed?"

"Of course the rings weren't destroyed. Supernatural beings can't even touch them, let alone destroy them."

"What about the people?" Jonah cut in. He balled his hands into fists. "You're saying all the Protectors were killed?"

Mr. Hackett nodded. "There are still groups out there dedicated to finding the rings. Foolish, if you ask me. Who wants that kind of trouble?"

"What do you mean?"

"Whenever someone has claimed to have found one of the rings, they've always disappeared a short time later. You don't need a college degree to know what happened to them."

"My dad worked for one of those groups," Jonah shouted, his anger flaring. "He found a ring!"

Mr. Hackett jumped out of his chair and cracked his head on the low-hanging lamp. Mike sprang to his feet to reach up and stop its erratic swinging.

"Your father found a ring?" Hackett managed through clenched teeth, still clutching his injured head.

"Yes."

"You said your parents died?"

"Yes."

"What happened to the ring?"

Jonah shrugged. "Nobody knows."

Mr. Hackett stared at the drawing of the rings. "Your godfather is looking for the ring, isn't he?"

"Well, I guess he wants to do the same thing my parents did." The man's blatant interest in the ring rather than his dead parents began to bother Jonah. "He wants to keep it from the…"

When Jonah paused, Mr. Hackett leaned forward under the harsh lamp light. "Who's after the ring?"

Jonah glanced at Mike as he answered, "A strange woman named Deyanira."

Mr. Hackett's light face went pale and his eyes bugged out. "Deyanira!"

"Yeah." A strange thought came to Jonah, one he never considered. "I think she's a Fallen Reaper."

"Deyanira ain't no Fallen Reaper. She's a true Reaper, young man. She's a member of the KIN!" Hackett swore under his breath.

"What's the KIN?"

Hackett stared at Jonah like he didn't recognize him. Then his expression turned to one of surprise. "Your godfather never told you?" Jonah shook his head no. "Son, the KIN are a very dangerous and evil sect of Reapers. They have totally shunned the human lives they once lived and despise mortals." Mr. Hackett sighed. "You know, they're the ones who inspired the stereotypes about Reapers. And they personally serve the Grim Reaper."

"Th-there's a Grim Reaper?" Mike stammered.

"Of course, and he's the oldest of all Reapers."

"How's that?" Jonah's dread began to grow, but he had to know more.

"Your godfather should be ashamed of himself." Hackett drew in a breath. "As I hear it, most Reapers serve their term and, they, too, move on. However, long ago, an arrogant Reaper refused to follow the rules. He's remained a Reaper for over two thousand years, gaining power and knowledge about Life and Death.

"He made himself into the Grim Reaper, a deliberate evil image, meant to strike terror in the hearts of mortals. He hated his own former human life so much that he cut up his face and always hides beneath the hood of a red robe. Many of the KIN did the same thing to their faces. They ain't a pleasant bunch. And if Deyanira's involved, that means the Grim Reaper's involved."

Jonah was stunned. He had seen the cuts on Deyanira's face. Now he understood.

Hackett surprised Jonah when he slammed the books shut. "Listen to me, both of you: get out of this and stay out of it." He held up a boney hand as Mike and Jonah both opened their mouths to protest. "No, listen to me. Your parents got killed because of what they found. That's the way it's always gone down. Didn't you listen? Those rings are dangerous because they can control the very power of the universe."

Jonah slumped in his chair.

Mr. Hackett spoke in a calmer voice. "Look, son, you're the same age as my nephew?" Jonah nodded. "You're still too young to be caught up in these things. The legend of the rings is over two thousand years old. Waiting until you're older won't make any difference. Come and see me then and we'll talk."

"But--" Jonah jerked upright in his chair when Mike kicked him. "Ow!"

They glared at each other. Mr. Hackett didn't seem to notice as he stood and waved them to the doorway. "Remember what I said. Stay away from this stuff."

Mr. Hackett rushed them out of his store, locking the door behind them. Jonah glanced at the front window as he unlocked his bike. Then he rubbed his leg and glared up at Mike. "Hey! Why'd you kick me?"

"I'm sorry, Jonah. I didn't want you to argue with my uncle." Mike glanced back at the store. "Besides, my uncle says he knows a Fallen Reaper."

"Well, so do I. Actually, I know three."

"Jonah, you trust your godfather and his friends."

"And?"

"What if Fallen Reapers aren't the same? Couldn't one be a bad person? You heard what he said about the KIN."

Jonah hadn't considered that. He just assumed that all Fallen Reapers worked with Marcus and the company. In truth, he couldn't know that for sure. As always, the more information he got, the more questions he found.

"You're right," he admitted. "Do you think we should listen to your uncle?"

Mike frowned at him. "Your parents were killed because they found the ring?" Jonah nodded. "You're lucky no one came after you. I mean, if whole families were killed."

Jonah felt a stab of guilt because Mike didn't know they had tried to kill him. Wasn't that why they'd sent the Grim Hound?

"I don't have it, Mike."

"Good."

Jonah sighed and thought about it for a long moment as Mike unlocked his bike. If all the bad guys thought he knew something about the ring, they would eventually show up again. There was only one thing he could do, something he could sense inside.

"I need to find that ring."

CHAPTER TWENTY-SIX
PRACTICE CLUB

Jonah lay out on his bed, thinking about the Protector's Tale. It occupied his mind all during dinner and afterward. It was awesome, in a way, that the ring existed. And his dad had found it. His parents had died to keep it away from Deyanira. *And to protect me.* Jonah pushed that thought away. The question was, where did his parents hide the ring? He was sure they hid it; otherwise, why would someone send Grim Hounds to search their house?

Jonah had just reached for his book bag when someone knocked on his door.

"Yeah?"

Lynn opened the door and leaned against the frame. She had something blue rolled up in one hand as she folded her arms. "You're serious about wanting to learn to protect yourself?"

Jonah had to refocus his mind before he could remember their earlier conversation. "I have to do something," he answered. "If I keep phasing, someone will catch me."

"Why don't you come with me on Saturday? I have a meeting with some friends."

"What kind of meeting?"

"You'll see." Lynn stepped into the room and held the rolled-up bundle right under his nose. "Wear this on Saturday."

Jonah took it and discovered a shirt and a pair of dark blue athletic pants. He held up the shirt. It had the recreation center logo on the left chest with the words *Practice Club* underneath.

He glanced at Lynn. "What's this?"

"It's a uniform."

"What?"

"Just do it, Geek boy." Lynn paused before closing his door. "Be ready to go at noon."

Jonah stared after her, wondering what he needed to be ready to do. *Well*, he thought. *I'll find out soon enough.*

Jonah followed Lynn for several blocks as they cruised through the neighborhoods on the Hightowers' side of town. The afternoon bike ride was easy, yet Jonah fidgeted and looked around, hoping that no one noticed that he and Lynn wore the same thing. His cousin didn't seem bothered at all.

When they reached the elementary school, Lynn led the way through the playground and down a rough incline that ended at the base of a larger, tree-covered hill. A well-worn path angled up the hillside. Lynn started up, and Jonah followed. The thick bushes and shrubs made the climb rough. Lynn made it without getting off her bike. Jonah tried, but he had to hop off his bike halfway up the hill.

He expected Lynn to say something as she waited quietly for him. When Jonah reached her, she got off her own bike and started walking toward a gap in a screen of small trees. A burly Hispanic boy with spiky black hair stepped into view, blocking their path. He wore the same light blue shirt with the logo, and darker athletic shorts.

"What's up, Lynn?"

"Hey Rico."

Rico held up his hands as he came over, exposing tattoos on his arm. "Whoa, nena. Who's this?"

"This is my cousin, Jonah."

"Cousin?" Rico stroked his thin goatee as he eyed Jonah. "I don't know about this. It's gonna cost you to get him in."

"Really?" Lynn crossed her arms and let her bike lean against a hip.

Rico flashed a devilish grin. "You have to go out with me."

"What if I promise not to rub your face in the dirt if you let him in?"

Rico placed his hands over his heart. "You wound me, nena."

Jonah thought Lynn smiled as she edged by Rico and headed for the opening in the trees. Rico watched Lynn walk away with a grin on his face. "We're destined to be together, Lynn," he said. "You'll see."

"Whatever." She motioned to Jonah. "Come on."

Jonah waved and hurried to follow his cousin. Within a few steps, they entered a large circular clearing with a hard red clay surface. The trees shielded the entire area from the view of anyone passing by on the road near the school.

At least twenty teens were scattered around the clearing, talking in loose groups. All wore the same clothing. A few kids were Jonah's age, while others were clearly older than Lynn.

Jonah grew nervous because people were pausing to stare at him. He whispered to Lynn, "What is this place?"

"It's a practice club." Lynn tapped the logo on his shirt. "Everyone here takes some form of martial arts or martial weapons classes sponsored by the rec center. We come here to practice and share what we know with each other."

Lynn placed her bag on a metal wire bench and began wrapping her wrists. "One of the counselors at the rec center started the group a while back. They thought it would give us kids something creative to do during the summer.

"We even have a few former gang members here. I'll admit the practice club keeps the guys out of trouble. Plus, we compete with other practice clubs from other towns." She finished wrapping her wrists, closed her bag, and sat it beside other bags along a strip of grass.

"We do car washes and yard sales at the center to raise money for the trips. It's not a bad way to spend your time." She nodded to a muscular older teen. "I see you're not the only newbie today." Lynn waved to the older boy. "Hey Alex."

Jonah's eye's widened when he saw the skinny kid standing beside Alex. It was Mike. He stood with his head down and hands at his sides. When Mike noticed Jonah, he perked up.

"Good to see you, Lynn." Alex waved and pointed at Jonah. "Who's this?"

"My cousin Jonah. I told you about him."

"Right." Alex and two other boys wore white-collared polo shirts. Alex had his shirt neatly tucked into his dark blue athletic shorts. He stood tall and straight with an important air about himself. A silver whistle hung from a bright silver chain around his neck.

He pulled a folded sheet of paper from his pocket. "Should I add him to the official list?"

"Yeah, I guess so." Lynn pointed to a group of the youngest kids: two boys and one girl.

"You're in the beginning group, over there." She paused to tie her braids behind her head. "Remember, I didn't bring you here to learn to beat up anyone. I just think you'd feel more confident if you learned some basic moves."

When Alex blew his whistle, everyone gathered in what were clearly pre-assigned teams.

Jonah lingered, watching another group of kids take out the practice swords. He turned to join his group and walked straight into someone.

"Yo." Jonah stumbled back and looked up to see the tough looking boy he had met at the creekside behind the teen center. His dark skin appeared to shine in the sunlight. And to Jonah's surprise, he wore a white shirt, like Alex's.

The boy crossed his muscular arms and rubbed his square chin for a moment. "Lynn told me you were coming. You're Jonah, right? My name's Vincent." He didn't offer to shake hands. Instead, he glanced over Jonah's head. "You must be

Alex's little brother."

Jonah turned just as Mike came over. Vincent gave the boy the same crossed-arm scrutiny.

Mike lowered his gaze and hunched his shoulders. "My name's Mike."

Vincent's somber face broke into a smile. He motioned them toward the rest of the group as he stepped aside. "Go and introduce yourselves, and I'll be back in a sec." Vincent ran off to talk with one of the other group leaders.

As soon as Jonah and Mike joined their group, the tallest boy, with a picky brown Afro and a long thin nose, thrust out his hand.

"Hi. I'm Anthony." He pointed to a shorter, mixed boy standing next to him. "This is Rodney, but we call him Ming, because he's Asian."

Rodney screwed up his face. "I'm not Asian. I'm from Guam."

Jonah blinked at Rodney. "You're Chamorro, right?"

"How did you know?"

"My parents went to Guam on a research project."

Rodney laughed and elbowed Anthony. "I try to tell this hick about my mom's home country all the time, but he won't listen."

Anthony shrugged and began to go through warm-up exercises.

The girl stepped forward. "My name's Lorraine." After that, she whirled away and started doing her own warm-up exercises.

Anthony did a rather impressive series of hand thrusts. Jonah wondered if he showed off for his benefit. Rodney shook his head and started his own warm-up routine.

That left Jonah and Mike with no clue what to do. They exchanged glances. Just then, Alex's voice reached their group. Jonah turned and watched as Lynn and Rico sparred with each other. Lynn's blades moved almost too fast to follow with the eye. She countered every thrust and jab from Rico's practice sword.

"I could never do that," Mike observed.

"It just takes practice."

Mike didn't look sure about that. Jonah shifted his gaze to Alex, who fingered his whistle as he prowled around Lynn and Rico. "Why does your brother have a whistle?"

"He's a drum major. Band camp started last week. I think he uses it for that."

Vincent surprised both boys by clapping his hands right over their heads. "You, new guys. Eyes over here."

He waited as Rodney, Lorraine, and Anthony stood side by side at a sort of attention and bowed. Once that was done, Vincent gave them instructions. Then he focused on Jonah and Mike. He pulled Mike's hands out of his pockets.

"Hands are at your side, in a fist, like this." Vincent demonstrated. "Feet apart, even with your shoulders. This is your ready stance."

Vincent stuck his foot between Jonah's feet to knock them further apart. When Jonah started to look down,

Vincent pocked him in the forehead with two fingers and pushed his head back. "Keep your eyes focused straight ahead."

Vincent moved back to Mike and repeated the same actions, spacing his feet apart. Jonah and Mike repeated the ready stance over and over until Vincent was satisfied. Only then did he show them the basic fighting stance.

The time flew, and before Jonah knew it, his first lesson ended. He bowed to Vincent and the others and made his way over to Lynn.

"How did it go?" she asked.

"Vincent's cool." Jonah watched Lynn zip her bag closed before he asked the question that nagged him. "I saw a couple of kids with blades like yours. How can they have Reaper blades?"

Lynn smiled. "They don't. Those blades are regular ones. Like a traditional sai weapon except without the hand guards."

"You mean like Elektra uses?"

"Yes." Lynn hefted her bag, avoiding his gaze. "Come on."

Jonah followed. "You like Elektra." When Lynn blushed, he laughed. "I never thought you'd be into fantasy."

Lynn huffed. "At least she's a woman."

As they reached their bikes and got on, Jonah held back. "Wait. I wanted to ask you something. Can I learn to use the blades?"

"You came here to learn defensive moves."

"Can't I do both?"

"Maybe." Lynn paused, adjusting the straps so her bag lay snuggling against her back. "I thought you'd want to do the sword. A lot of little geeks like you want to pretend they're a Jedi or something."

Jonah didn't say anything because he had considered doing that. However, when he saw Lynn in real action, the choice became obvious. It was personal. His parents had used blades in his dream the last time he had ever seen them alive.

"I want to learn the blades," Jonah repeated.

Lynn watched him for a long time before she nodded. "Okay, but you do it my way. Understand? No complaining, and you have to keep up the lessons with Vincent."

"Deal."

Jonah's personal training with Lynn began Sunday morning when she woke him up just before dawn.

"What?" He blinked the sleep out of his eyes as she pulled his covers off.

"Up. We're going for a morning run. Well, maybe more of a walk for you."

"But…"

"You agreed no complaining." Lynn placed her hands on her hips. "We have to do this early, before church."

Jonah pulled on his socks and sneakers and stumbled out of the kitchen door behind his cousin.

She gave him the once over as she stretched outside. "You're slender, and I bet you don't have any stamina. So we're going to start with building up your endurance."

It didn't take long for him to wake up. True to her word, Lynn started with a run but alternated with walking the first day. She did the same thing on the second day.

By the third morning, Jonah waited for Lynn's knock with his shoes on. As she had done the past two days, she spent the morning building his endurance, followed by a short karate lesson in the backyard. Robert found it amusing until Lynn threatened to use him as a demonstration dummy.

Jonah understood Lynn's method. Even though he itched to try the blades, he also wouldn't give her the satisfaction of complaining. Besides, he needed a better way to deal with kids like Brandon without fear of using his abilities, and this was it. He hoped.

Normally Jonah and Lynn fought each other for the shower after their morning run. But one morning, Lynn went into the kitchen first to make a bit of breakfast. When Jonah shrugged and started for the bathroom, Lynn grabbed his shoulder.

"You've done okay over the past four days. I'm gonna start teaching you the basic blade."

Jonah let out a whoop and pumped his hand in the air. Lynn crossed her arms and waited for him to calm himself and give her a decent bow.

"That's better," she said while pulling a banana off a bundle on the counter. "I want to eat something first."

As Jonah calmed down, Lynn's comment reminded him of how much time had passed. Today was the twentieth of July. He'd been in Mount Vernon for over three weeks. So much had happened that it felt longer to him.

Lynn tapped his forehead. "What's wrong?"

"Nothing. It's just… we only have less than a month before school starts."

Lynn glanced at the kitchen calendar on the wall beside the refrigerator. "Yeah, so? If you're worried you won't have enough time to learn…"

"No. I didn't mean that." He caught the grin on her face and relaxed. "Where are you gonna teach me the blades?"

"Where do you think?" She handed Jonah a banana. "We're going to the practice field."

Robert had come out of his room when Jonah yelled. He wrinkled up his nose as he entered the kitchen and took out the cereal. "You know, we have plenty of hot water if you two want to take showers."

Robert started pouring cereal in a bowl. Lynn threw her banana peel away, then leaned on her brother's shoulder.

"Can't, dear brother. I'm teaching Jonah to use the blades today."

"Really?" Robert forgot about the cereal. "Can I come?"

Jonah opened his mouth to tell Robert he could come along.

Lynn stopped him. "I don't think Jonah needs a crowd his first time out." She grabbed her brother's hand to stop the cereal from spilling on the table. "You're making a mess." She motioned Jonah to the kitchen door. "I'll catch up with you at the Summit."

"Just make sure you take a shower," Robert said as he scooped up the extra cereal.

Lynn stuck her tongue out at her brother.

Jonah waited eagerly as Lynn pulled a pair of practice blades out of the carry case. He pointed at them. "Where's your blades?"

"I'm not letting you use the real thing. Not yet."

"Oh. Sorry."

"I guess I should start with how to handle the blades." She demonstrated, holding the blades in a reverse grip with the blades pointed back along her forearm. "Make sure you position them like this, with your arm rotated." Lynn shifted her arm so the blade faced out, along the outside of her forearm rather than turned underneath.

"The blades are primarily defensive weapons. With your arms rotated like this, the blades can block an attack. Otherwise, your enemy would be able to cut your arms. Understand?" Lynn slipped the blades down into her hands, the hilts out toward Jonah. "You try it."

The blades are heavier than I expected, Jonah thought as he lifted them.

Lynn picked up a practice baton that leaned against a tree. "Now, get into the start position."

Jonah mimicked Lynn's hold on the blades. He thought he did it right until Lynn stepped forward, swung the baton, and smacked it against his right forearm.

He cried out, dropping the blade. "Ow! Why did you do that?"

Lynn wagged a finger at him. "No complaining." She waited for Jonah to nod. "What did I tell you? Rotate the arm. Do it again."

Jonah picked up the blade and got into position again. He concentrated on his right blade and noticed too late that his left blade wasn't in proper alignment. Lynn switched her aim and landed a blow on his left forearm. He grunted, but he didn't drop the blade this time.

In quick succession Lynn went for his right arm, the left, and then the left again. *Crack, crack, crack.* Jonah dropped the blade and rubbed his forearm. Although Lynn's strikes weren't hard, his arms were beginning to ache.

After several more successful whacks on his arms, Lynn stopped and held the baton out to him. "Here. You try it on me." She took the blades and readied herself. Jonah tried one arm, then the next. Lynn blocked each strike and made sure to hold her arms in place for a brief moment before sliding them back into a perfect ready position.

"In time, it'll become second nature to you. Now, try it again."

They switched and worked for another hour.

CHAPTER TWENTY-SEVEN
THE CHALLENGE

When Jonah set out for the recreation center later that afternoon, his forearms were still sore from the blade practice. Maybe he'd take it easy and play some board games, he thought. He locked his bike in the bike rack just as his Death Sense buzzed. For one horrifying moment, Jonah thought another Grim Hound had been sent after him. Then he heard a familiar, snide voice.

"Hey, freak." Brandon strode up to him with Drew and Antwan trailing behind. "I've been looking for you."

Jonah tried to walk around the boy.

Brandon moved to block his path. "I'm talking to you." Jonah stepped right up to him, forcing the other boy to back up before he spoke again. "My parents paid for the mess in the basement."

"That's a lie. Drew's father paid for it." Jonah looked at Drew. "Mike's right. Why do you hang out with him?"

He brushed past Brandon. When the boy reached out, Jonah blocked the other's hand.

Antwan stepped in the way, and Jonah's Death Sense spiked. Brandon repositioned himself in front of Jonah again, and Drew came up behind, boxing him in.

Brandon puffed out his chest. "I don't know how you and your boyfriend got out, but you're gonna pay."

"Ooooh, I'm really scared now."

"I hear you're part of that little practice club."

"So what if I am?"

Antwan tapped Brandon on the shoulder and said, "Challenge him."

"Yeah," Brandon nodded. "I challenge you to a blade duel."

Jonah opened his mouth to accept, but paused. Lynn would be furious with him if he accepted.

Brandon laughed. "What's the matter? You scared to face me?"

Antwan and Drew snickered.

"Just like I thought, guys," Brandon sneered. "He's a chicken."

"I accept, jerk." The words were premature, but man, he wanted to wipe that sneer off Brandon's face. "Just tell me when and where."

"Meet me on Summer's End, at the practice field. Six o'clock. Be there, freak."

Jonah nodded as Brandon walked off, his mind racing. How horribly would Lynn kill him when she heard about the challenge?

"You did what?" Lynn shouted at the top of her lungs. Jonah tried to escape to his room, but she followed, knocking his door open to continue her tirade. "This is exactly what I didn't want to happen, Jonah! How could you accept a challenge from Brandon?"

"He made fun of me."

That statement got Lynn to calm down a little. "Jonah, you do realize that it isn't Brandon that you're angry about?"

"I think nearly being killed by falling junk is enough to make me angry with him."

"You're angry about all the things that happened to you." Lynn paused, took a breath, and plunged on. "You're angry about your parents and your old house and all the things you've lost. Brandon is just a convenient excuse."

"You don't know what you're talking about! You don't know what it's like to lose your parents." His anger had spilled out before he could stop it. He expected Lynn to hit him, but she watched him with a sad look on her face. It took him a second to see he'd just proven her point.

"See what I mean?" Lynn began. "Brandon is good at hitting people's buttons. He's got yours, and he knows it. Never let your enemies control you. That's the sure way to lose."

Jonah dropped onto the bed. Lynn sat next to him.

"I used to be like you, Jonah, two years ago. When Mom took the blades away from me, I got angry. I could have done something stupid. Well, I did, in a way. I broke into the locker and took the real blades. I think my mom saw the anger in me." Lynn toyed with the end of one of her braids. "Then I met Rico, Alex, and the others and I started working with them. I can hear Rico now. 'You have to stop letting people push your buttons, nena.'"

She smiled. "I listened to him, and I don't feel the anger anymore. It's what the practice club is all about. It's helped a lot of kids."

"But you wanted to break his neck the other day."

"I can lose my temper sometimes, but I wouldn't have hurt Brandon. At most, I would have had a few words with him." She nudged him. "You know that, right?"

"Yeah, I guess so."

"Anyway, I knew if Vincent and the others could change their attitudes, I could."

Jonah nodded as he stared down at his feet. "I'm sorry."

"It's okay. The next time Brandon tries to get to you, be ready for him."

"I can't back out now, can I?"

"Are you kidding? It'll be a cold day in hell before I let that snob beat up my little cousin."

"So you'll help me?"

"Yes, I'll help you." Lynn shook Jonah's head with her hand. "Geek boy."

They started the very next day. When he groaned at the increase in the training, she put her hands on her hips. "Falling down and panting for breath is a sure way to lose."

Jonah's face warmed and he conceded her point. As he started into the routine again, the desperate run from the Grim Hound popped into his mind. He'd been at the end of his endurance. If Kevin hadn't ignored Marcus and shown up, he would be dead.

Yet, if he learned to use the blades like Kevin, he wouldn't have to run. He could defend himself, no matter what his godfather said. Buoyed with that thought, Jonah didn't complain anymore.

After he and Lynn finished, Jonah lingered on the practice field, continuing to train. He was concentrating so completely that when he noticed movement near the clearing's opening, he figured Lynn had returned. Instead, Mike stood in the clearing. He laid his bike down and walked over, making sure to keep out of the way of the practice sword.

"Jonah, where have you been?"

"Busy." Jonah continued to move through the positions.

"So it's true?" Mike asked. "You're really going to duel with Brandon?"

Jonah stopped to face him. "Yes, I am."

"But Jonah, that's crazy!"

"I have to do it."

"No, you don't. Besides, will it be fair? You're--"

"I'm what?"

Mike refused to meet his gaze. "Nothing."

"If I don't stand up to Brandon, he'll keep trying to bully me."

"He's jealous of you. Beating him won't change that."

"Backing out of the duel now won't help, either. I'm in, and that's it."

Jonah started into another exercise. Mike watched him for a moment.

"Fighting's not the answer!"

"You're in the practice club."

"Yeah, to learn to protect myself. But you picked a fight with Brandon."

"So…"

"I bet Lynn wasn't happy."

Jonah paused again, his concentration gone. Mike had hit the mark.

"Brandon's a bully," Mike pressed. "When you fight, you're no better than people like him!"

"You didn't feel that way when I helped you in the library."

"You stood up to Brandon."

"I'm doing that now."

"No! You didn't fight him. You faced him. That took courage, Jonah. This is just--" Mike slapped his hands against his legs in frustration. "We should be looking for that ring, Jonah." Mike stepped closer. "Come on. Let's find that ring. I thought it was important to you."

"It is important."

"Then forget this duel. Please. You should concentrate on finding out about the ring."

"I'm not backing down." Jonah whirled away from Mike as doubt gnawed at him. "So get over it."

Mike stood on the spot for a stunned minute before he ran to his bike. He hurried out of the clearing without looking back. Jonah hated himself; Mike wasn't wrong. He had slacked off on searching for the ring. That was true. But once Brandon was no longer a threat, he'd go back to it. For now, he needed to be ready for the Summer's End Festival, which was only a week away.

CHAPTER TWENTY-EIGHT
MIDNIGHT MEETUP

Mike didn't speak to Jonah at the Saturday club practice and avoided him all the next week. That bothered Jonah, but he'd made his decision. Besides, with another week of extra training with Lynn completed, he was confident in his ability to beat Brandon. He often found himself mimicking his dad's style with the blades, when Lynn wasn't around.

All-in-all, Jonah went to bed feeling a bit better about the coming duel. He certainly didn't expect to dream of a wind-swept clearing in some far land. Just when Jonah wondered why he was there, Marcus phased into view. His godfather stood tall, waiting.

A second later, a vortex blossomed into life and Jonah gasped as Neera, the witch from the bookstore, stepped through. Her black dress looked even more ominous emerging from the swirling mass of vapor.

Marcus shouted over the howling wind, "Why do you persist? You'll never find it."

"I will have the ring, Marcus. It's only a matter of time. Perhaps the boy knows something."

"Jonah doesn't know anything."

The woman threw back her head and laughed. Then she began circling around Marcus. "The Wraiths are upset about the boy; they think he's dangerous."

"He's just a boy, that's all."

"The son of Isaiah cannot be innocent. His very existence is a threat to everything we've built."

"You won't harm Jonah as long as I live."

Neera grinned at Marcus. "Have it your way, Fallen One."

Jonah watched in horror as the woman's features morphed into something more skeletal. He yelled as horrible scars erupted across her face. Her red hair fell away, carried on the wind until little more than a ponytail remained. The black dress changed into a long, blood-red hooded robe. She produced two glowing blades out of the folds.

Deyanira and Neera were the same person. Jonah couldn't believe he'd been face to face with the woman who helped kill his parents. He recalled Kevin's comment that Marcus followed Neera. Now he understood why.

Marcus activated his blades and dropped into a fighting stance. He and Deyanira shouted to each other and lunged. Light and pain exploded in Jonah's mind as their blades met.

He woke up in his bed with his heart racing. Somewhere out there, Marcus and Deyanira continued in a fierce battle.

The image of Marcus fighting a transformed Neera continued to haunt Jonah all the next day as he spent the afternoon, after the practice club, helping Wick research an article on the supernatural. Jonah's guilt over his fight with Mike didn't help matters. It seemed his friend was right. The ring continued to be important to everyone surrounding him.

Once or twice, Jonah felt the urge to tell Wick and his cousins about the dream, and each time, he decided against the idea. However, by that evening, he couldn't hold out any longer. At least they should know the bookstore woman's true identity.

Everyone gathered at the Hightowers' to play video games. Aunt Imma was in her art room and Uncle James had carried his stack of newspapers to his bedroom to read. That left Lynn, Robert, Wick, and Jonah free to talk as they played videos. Jonah had called Mike, but his friend had been frosty on the phone and refused to stop by.

That was just as well, Jonah thought. He'd never told his cousins that Mike knew his secret, so he could talk about Deyanira without bringing up that problem. Before Jonah could think better of the idea, he blurted it out.

"Neera's not a witch. She's a true Reaper named Deyanira." Only after he said it did he realize he hadn't given them any warning.

Robert and Wick stopped playing their video game and stared at him. They didn't even notice their players being killed on the screen. Lynn, as usual, seemed a little suspicious.

Wick sat down his controller and grinned at Jonah. "So, you're a psychic now? Did that just come in a vision?"

Lynn reached over and yanked on a couple of Wick's twists. "Be serious." She stood beside the sofa, arms folded. "How do you know that, Jonah?"

"Marcus told me. I forgot to mention it."

"How can Deyanira or Neera interact with us? Robert saw her. The store clerk works with her."

Jonah shrugged, regretting mentioning that much. "I don't know. Marcus didn't explain that to me."

Lynn scowled and Jonah gave her the best innocent look he could make. "When did you talk to Marcus?" she asked.

Jonah's mind raced and he grabbed his cell phone. "I got a text." He thought the excuse sounded lame and doubted it would fly.

"That doesn't sound like the Marcus you've told us about," Lynn offered, shaking her head.

He hopped off the sofa and headed for the patio. "I have to send him another message."

Lynn watched Jonah until he closed the patio door. He didn't lie to his cousin, and he set about typing the message that proved it. He wanted to meet with Marcus.

He didn't expect his phone to buzz in response five minutes into his video game. He gave up his turn and hurried into the kitchen to read the text.

Jonah, meet me by the backyard shed at midnight. Marcus

"Do you have more information to share?" Lynn asked as soon as Jonah came back and sat on the sofa.

"Nope."

At midnight, Jonah peeked out of his bedroom. The house was quiet. He snuck through the family room to the patio door and had almost opened it before he remembered to turn off the alarm. Once it was disarmed, he slipped outside into the hot July night. He nearly jumped out of his skin when he heard the rustle of cloth in the shadows beside the shed.

Marcus stepped into the moonlight, and Jonah noticed immediately that his godfather carried himself stiffly and leaned against a tree for support. Jonah moved to help him, but Marcus held up a hand.

"I'm fine. There's no need to worry."

The sight of Marcus's injuries brought the dream rushing back into Jonah's mind, and he forgot about his initial reason for contacting the Fallen Reaper.

"Why didn't you tell me about Neera?"

"What do you mean?"

"She's a Reaper called Deyanira and she…" Jonah choked back the rest, realizing he was about to mention the dream about his parents. "I know you fought her," Jonah admitted. "That's why you're hurt."

"How do you know that?" Marcus stepped away from the tree. "Who told you that?"

"No one told me. I saw it in a dream. You and Deyanira argued about the ring, and then you fought each other."

Even in the darkness, Jonah could see Marcus's eyes widen. "I shouldn't be surprised by your abilities." He let out a breath. "How long have you been dreaming like this?"

Jonah shuffled his feet on the soft grass and refused to meet Marcus's gaze. "I've been able to do it for a couple of years. It only happens when I'm worried about something."

"You were worried about me?"

Jonah nodded. "I know Deyanira wanted the ring my dad found." He watched Marcus as closely as he could in the dark.

Marcus shook his head. "I'm not getting you involved in that. Just keep your head down."

"Keeping my head down didn't stop a Grim Hound from attacking me."

"That's why I agreed to start your training." Marcus paused as if winded. "How did it go, with Kevin?"

"It was cool. I remembered what he said and phased to get away from a bully."

Marcus pushed himself into a standing position. "Jonah. We're not training you to use your powers on everyday… teen problems."

"I had to. Me and my friend Mike would have been hurt if I didn't."

"You phased someone with you?"

"It's cool," Jonah shouted. He cringed when his voice rang out across the quiet yard and he lowered his voice. "Mike knew about Fallen Reapers. His uncle owns a bookstore and he told us about the Protector's Ring."

Marcus stood at his full height. "Obviously you've been busy." He wiped a hand over his forehead. "I'm serious, Jonah. Phasing Mike could have been disastrous. We have ways of cleaning up or hiding our true selves from others."

Jonah sucked in a breath. "Kevin mentioned Memory Charmers, like Omar. Is that what he does?"

"Sometimes, yes. You have to be careful."

"I'm know."

"Are you practicing?"

Jonah nodded. "I'm tired of only doing it when I'm scared. It's going to get me in trouble sooner or later."

Marcus paused, gazing at Jonah. "Being able to control your phasing ability was supposed to make my job easier." Marcus gave him a tired smile, then winced in obvious pain. "We can discuss these things at another date. I need time to think about your ability to eavesdrop."

"Wait. When can I have another lesson?"

"Give me the week to regain my strength. Let's say Saturday morning?"

Jonah nodded.

"Keep practicing on your own. Good night." Marcus stepped into the shadows and vanished.

CHAPTER TWENTY-NINE
DREAM WALKING

Marcus arrived at the Hightowers' home on Saturday morning. After a brief conference in the dining room with Uncle James and Aunt Imma, he led Jonah outside to the car.

When Marcus got into the driver's seat, Jonah gave in to his curiosity. "What did you tell my aunt and uncle?"

Marcus started the car and let it idle as he answered. "I told them I wanted to spend a little time with you so we could talk about how you're adjusting."

"Oh."

"In addition to that," Marcus went on, "today, I want to take you for a little drive. I deemed it appropriate to let your aunt and uncle know you were with me."

Marcus drove them north out of Mount Vernon. Thirty minutes later, he reached a wide entrance to an open pasture. He pulled to the side and motioned for Jonah to get out. They stood beside the car, looking out over the fields.

"Observe your surroundings," Marcus began, "and remember what you see. As Kevin should have mentioned in the first lesson, phasing is about clearly picturing where you want to go in your mind."

Jonah followed his godfather's instructions and noted his surroundings. There were tree-covered hills in the distance and wide pastures on either side of the highway. This was pretty easy to picture, Jonah decided.

He frowned and turned back to Marcus. "Kevin phased to me at the old gas station. How could he picture that if he'd never been there?"

Marcus gave Jonah a big smile.

"I hoped you would notice that. When a Reaper is given an assignment, a bond is created between the Reaper and the mortal. They use that bond to locate the mortal. I'm able to perform a similar action with you."

Jonah's eyes widened. "That's how you knew I was in trouble with the Grim Hound?"

Marcus nodded.

"But Kevin showed up, not you. He doesn't have a connection to me, does he?"

"No, he doesn't." Marcus took Jonah's arm in a light grip before he could ask another question. "Are you ready?"

"Yes. What are we--"

A moment later, he and Marcus stood on a tree-covered hillside overlooking a valley below.

Marcus released Jonah. "How far do you think we've come?"

"I don't know."

"Think about it."

Jonah didn't have any idea how to do that. Marcus tapped him on the forehead. "A Reaper can feel the distance."

"But I'm not a Reaper."

Marcus smiled. "Close your eyes."

"Why?"

"Close your eyes and think about it."

Jonah obeyed. He concentrated, and to his surprise, he did feel something that he couldn't translate into words. "I can't tell for sure. I'm sorry."

"That's understandable, Jonah. You'll be able to tell when you've gained more experience." Marcus gestured around them. "We're about three miles away. I know that's farther than you've ever phased. Now, all you have to do is phase back to the car. It's simple." He gave Jonah a small wave and vanished.

"Marcus!" Jonah looked around and waited for Marcus to reappear. *Maybe he's playing a trick*, Jonah thought.

As the seconds turned into minutes, Jonah realized that Marcus had abandoned him on the hillside. At that moment, panic and doubt began to fill his mind. How could Marcus do this to him?

Jonah's heart raced and his breathing quickened. "Take me back, take me back." He said it over and over until the air rippled around him and suddenly, he stood several feet away from Marcus and the car.

Jonah ran over, shouting, "Why did you leave me there? I could have been lost!"

Marcus, who had leaned against the car when Jonah first appeared, stood tall, facing the boy for several tense seconds. At last, his shoulders relaxed and he folded his arms as he leaned against the car again. "You're supposed to be learning to phase with a clear head."

"But you left me!"

"Yes. I wanted to know if you would keep a cool head and remember all that you've learned. Clearly, you panicked and then phased here."

Shame began to slowly replace Jonah's anger. He had asked Marcus to teach him how to phase, and now he acted paranoid. Jonah shook off that sad thought, not willing to let go of all his anger.

"What if I couldn't have done it?"

"I knew you could do it. You just needed a little push."

"But what if I couldn't?"

"Jonah, I wouldn't leave you out there alone." Marcus's eyes widened and he stepped forward, gripping Jonah by the shoulders. "I'm sorry. I should have known you'd be sensitive to people leaving you."

"I'm not sensitive." Jonah shrugged out of Marcus's grip and refused to meet the Fallen Reaper's gaze.

Marcus motioned for Jonah to follow. "Come here."

He walked around to the back of the car and opened the trunk. Inside was a backpack and bottled water.

"I would have phased back to you," Marcus explained. "And if I didn't have enough power to bring us both here, we could have taken a nice hike back to the car."

"But, but what if I phased short and got lost?"

"I can sense where you are, Jonah. When I agreed to your parents' request it created a special bond between you and I." Marcus looked Jonah straight in the eye. "I'm connected to you, Jonah. I'll always be able to find you."

"Always?"

"Yes. Well, at least until you're eighteen."

Jonah's eyes went out of focus as he thought about it. "Why? Is that important in the Supernatural world?"

"No. Thirteen is the age when a supernatural being gains his or her powers. I'll always be your godfather, but you'll be an adult at eighteen, and the bond ends." Marcus paused. "It was your parents' decision." He closed the trunk. "Do you believe me?" Jonah nodded. "Now, can you do it again, with a clear head?"

Jonah turned and looked around. *Why not?* With Marcus standing behind him, assuring him he'd be there, Jonah knew he could phase back to the hillside. He stepped away from Marcus and stood in a perfect ready stance.

In a Yoda-type voice, he said, "Size matters not. Distance matters not."

Marcus cocked an eyebrow, and Jonah laughed to himself. At least Wick would have appreciated it. And with that thought, he closed his eyes, took a breath, and phased.

Marcus and Jonah rode back to Mount Vernon in an uncomfortable silence. His godfather told him he did well today, but his face didn't match his words.

After several more quiet minutes, Jonah couldn't hold back. "What's bothering you?"

"Why do you think something's bothering me?"

"You have that look."

Marcus glanced at him in surprise and laughed. "Omar always says the same thing about me."

"So what's wrong?"

"Your dreams concern me, Jonah. I've been thinking about it, and I've concluded that they must be a form of phasing. You said that when you're really worried about something, you tend to have the dreams. My guess is you're sensing the person involved and phasing to their location."

"But how can it be phasing when the people never see me? It's like I'm not really there. I'm like a ghost."

Marcus flinched when Jonah said that, then quickly spoke to cover it. "I'm not saying it's exactly like phasing. I'm suggesting that it's similar. In fact, I think…"

"What?"

"I think your soul is traveling or phasing to these locations. If not for the fact that you see things as they happen, I would call them visions. It's more like an out-of-body experience."

Jonah's jaw dropped as he considered that. He'd come across out-of-body and astral projection in his research after his first dream. He glanced at his godfather. "How about dream-walking?"

Marcus nodded. "You have to understand, Jonah, you're the first half-Reaper, so anything is possible." Marcus looked at him. "If it is your soul, that takes on a different meaning because you're half-Reaper. And nobody understands what you'll become as you mature."

"That's why Deyanira wants me dead." The statement didn't scare him as much anymore.

"For what it's worth, I don't believe Deyanira wants you dead."

"Why not? She helped kill my parents." Even as Jonah said it, he knew that wasn't totally true. Deyanira had offered his dad an exchange. She wanted the ring.

"I know it sounds unbelievable, Jonah, but no one knows what would happen if you…"

"If I what? If I die?"

Marcus stared at the road ahead and didn't meet Jonah's eyes. "I didn't want to say that."

"What could happen to me if I die?"

Marcus's hands gripped the steering wheel tightly. "The decision to turn someone into a Reaper is made at the highest levels. You're only a half-Reaper, yet you have the powers of a full Reaper, and more. You could become even more powerful."

Jonah couldn't believe it. Was everyone afraid that he could become some kind of super Reaper if he died? Could he really become dangerous?

He glanced at Marcus. "Deyanira or someone else is going to come after me, aren't they?"

"Deyanira's focus for the last year has been on the object your father found."

"You mean the ring."

Marcus let out a low breath. "Yes, I mean the ring. She meant those comments she made as a taunt for me. It's what she does."

"What about the other Reapers?"

"Despite that spat of sightings around the time of your birthday, I don't think most Reapers really know about you." Marcus glanced sideways at Jonah. "You have to stop worrying about all this."

"Why?"

"It's dangerous, Jonah. Eventually, the beings you spy on may be able to sense your presence. If that happens, they could hurt you. Just promise me you'll try."

"Okay." Jonah tapped his knuckle against the window. *Keep from worrying?* He was learning to use the blades and phase. And he had the duel with Brandon in five days. Plus his best friend wouldn't talk to him which reminded Jonah he still didn't know where to find the Protector's Ring. After all of that, he would start a new school. As he saw it, he had more than enough to worry about.

CHAPTER THIRTY
REAPERS

Jonah changed into his practice clothes and rushed to the practice field after Marcus dropped him off. Anthony, Lorraine, and Rodney were stunned when he worked out with the blade group at practice. Mike, who ignored his own training to watch Jonah, received ten laps around the clearing from Vincent. When practice ended for the day, Rodney was the only one of Jonah's original group to wave goodbye. Mike slipped out of the clearing with his brother Alex without speaking.

Jonah frowned, wondering if he should have listened to Mike and backed out of the duel. Finding the ring was important and Jonah told himself he could do both, but in reality, he couldn't. He stood, gazing at the exit and not moving to put his things away when Lynn tapped his shoulder.

"What's up?"

"Huh?" Jonah focused on her. "Nothing. You didn't tell me what I did wrong?"

"That's because you're getting better."

"Really?"

"Yeah." Lynn closed up her bag. Rico and Vincent motioned to her, and she ran over to talk with them.

Jonah gathered his things, feeling happier than he had in days, despite his trouble with Mike. But he also couldn't shake the feeling that something was up with Lynn. Even on his best days, she always found something for him to improve. Mike wasn't the only one unfocused today, Jonah decided. His waning happiness shifted to confusion when Robert and Wick waltzed into the clearing.

"What are you two doing here?"

Robert stood right beside Jonah and glanced at Lynn.

"We're betting on you killing Brandon in five days." Robert lowered his voice. "Thought we'd come by and watch practice."

Wick slapped Jonah on the back, coming around to his other side. "We wanted to make sure we're not gonna lose our money, Padawan."

Jonah didn't know whether to laugh or not. "Are you guys serious?"

Robert nodded. "The odds are on the home team to beat the kid from DC. Sorry, little cousin."

"You're betting against me?"

Wick squeezed his shoulder. "Of course we aren't betting against you. We know you have powers."

"I can't use my powers."

"Well, you can't phase in front of everyone, little cousin." Robert glanced in Lynn's direction again. "When you beat Brandon, we'll make a ton of money. It should be a great Summer's End."

"Why's it called Summer's End?"

Robert traded a disbelieving look with Wick. "It marks the last week of summer vacation, so it's called…"

"…Summer's End," Wick concluded.

"Back to business, little cousin. You need to beat Brandon."

"It couldn't hurt to use a little power, either," Wick added, giving him a wink.

Jonah opened his mouth to protest and Robert held up a finger. "Not too loud."

Jonah pushed his cousin's hand aside. "How will people know who won? You're not gonna record it, are you?"

Robert smiled. "We have that handled. You just beat Brandon. You didn't look too bad out there."

"You saw the practice?"

"Yeah." Wick pointed to the treeline. "We sat out there."

Jonah laughed, but Wick and Robert's expression sobered. Jonah understood why when Lynn gripped his shoulder.

"Let's go to the Summit." Lynn pushed Jonah toward the exit.

All at once, Jonah suspected that whatever they had planned, this was the real reason Wick and Robert had come by the practice field and the reason why Lynn had seemed distracted all session. His insides begin to squirm. *At least my Death Sense isn't going off*, he thought.

Wick dropped his large black book down on the steamer trunk. Unfortunately, it sounded like a gunshot in the quiet attic clubhouse. Robert scowled at his friend.

Wick gave him a weak smile. "Sorry."

Lynn all but ordered Jonah to sit in the spongy arm chair. Now she stood over him, arms crossed. "You've been holding out on us."

"What do you mean?"

Lynn flicked her braids over a shoulder without answering. Instead, Wick cracked open the large book, opening it to a bookmarked page.

Jonah glanced at the heading at the top and his insides froze. It said *Reapers*.

Wick cleared his throat and began reading. "Reapers collect the souls of the dead and, wow, I never paid attention to this. They can't be seen by mortals." He paused, glancing at the others. Lynn gave him an impatient wave to keep reading. He leaned over the book again. "Here we go. Reapers are able to appear at the location of their next soul reap. The term for this ability varies and includes apparrating, tunneling, portaling, and phasing." Wick sighed. "I'm sorry, dude. You told us you can phase."

Lynn snapped her fingers. "What else does it say about Reapers?"

Wick hesitated before glancing down at the book again. "Let's see. Reapers are drawn to scenes of death as part of their job. They… can sense death in general."

Robert came to stand beside Wick. "Reapers have Death Sense."

"It doesn't actually say Death Sense." Jonah tried to hold down his panic, but he could see that his cousins and Wick weren't gonna accept that lame point. And having Lynn standing right over him made Jonah feel trapped.

Thankfully, Lynn sat down on the edge of the steamer trunk, facing him. "What I don't understand is how can you have Reaper powers?"

Anger built up inside Jonah and an irrational disregard for keeping his secret overcame him. "I'm a Reaper. Okay?"

Robert gripped Jonah's shoulder. "You can't be, little cousin."

"Why not?"

"Reapers are the Undead and exist on the other side."

Wick reached over and poked Jonah in the chest. "You aren't dead, let alone an undead being."

"There's a passage in the book about Fallen Ones. Are you one of those, little cousin?"

"No." Jonah slumped under the weight of the older kids' questions. "My dad was."

Wick's eyebrows shot up in excitement. Robert and Lynn carried identical, slightly out of focus gazes. Jonah wondered if they were replaying everything they remembered about his mom and dad. After several quiet, tense moments, Lynn nodded.

"This explains everything." She gazed at Jonah. "So, what are you?"

"I'm a half-Reaper. The only one, according to Marcus."

"What's Marcus? Is he…"

Jonah nodded. "He's a Fallen Reaper."

Wick let out a slow whistle as he ruffled his twists. He seemed pleased about this, but Robert looked a bit spooked, Jonah thought.

"We talked about it," Robert said. "Lynn and I agreed that you had to be something more than, you know, a normal person. I mean, you can see Grim Hounds, sense death, and even do that phase thing? No regular person can do that."

"And we can't forget the gifts your parents sent us," Lynn added. "They aren't exactly normal. We've known for a while there was something different about your family, Jonah."

Robert nodded in agreement. "Can I ask you question?"

"Robert, don't…" Lynn shook her head.

Jonah found it odd to see his cousins disagree about something secret. That made him more curious to hear Robert's question. "Yeah, I guess."

"I'm warning you." Lynn raised her fist.

Robert blinked and looked between his sister's fist and Jonah. He swallowed and hunched his shoulder as if expecting to get hit. "Can you suck out our souls?"

"Robert!" Lynn shot to her feet and punched her brother in the bicep.

"Ow!" Robert clamped his hand over the injured arm, glaring back at his sister. "You and Wick wanted to know."

Jonah's moment of curiosity over his cousins' disagreement evaporated as the anger returned. He saw the fear in Robert's eyes and the way Lynn's hand shook as she toyed with one of her braids.

"No, I can't suck out your soul. I'm only a half-Reaper."

"That's good, little cousin."

Jonah shot to his feet, facing Robert and Lynn. "My dad never did anything like that. Marcus and Kevin didn't do that. Besides, Marcus told me that Reapers help souls, not suck them out like monsters." His voice bounced off the wooden attic ceiling.

Robert held up his hands. "Alright. I was just asking."

The anger continued to build and Jonah's pulse thudded in his ear. He started to pace back and forth until Lynn reached out for him.

"Jonah, listen--"

"No." Before Jonah knew it, he ran for the attic stairs, descending them two at a time.

Robert shouted from behind, "Stop him."

Jonah leaped down the last few steps and slammed into the attic door before he could open it. He recovered and started to pull it open as Lynn reached the top of the stairs. She was fast, but Jonah's thoughts were faster. He phased before Lynn could grab him.

Jonah appeared in the clearing by the creek behind the recreation center. *Why not use my Reaper power?* However, he took a wrong step and stumbled backward over one of the flat stones. Jonah landed hard on the ground and tumbled into the shallow water.

"Dang it!" The tepid water sloshed over him, soaking his clothes. He climbed out of the creek and sat down on the nearest flat rock. He took off his wet shoes and socks and sat there, seething with anger. He wanted to be normal, but he never was, and he never would be. That Seer back in Virginia had been right about him. He could see the fear on his cousins' faces.

It wasn't fair that all these things happened to him. He never did anything to anyone. He hated being here. He hated this place. He hated everything about his life.

Jonah wanted to scream and cry at the same time. In a fit of frustration, he took his wet sneakers and flung them away. He didn't even care when he heard them splash into the creek.

Lynn stepped into view and came over to stare down at Jonah with her hands on her hips. "If you're done feeling sorry for yourself, I have a question for you, genius."

"Lynn, I don't want to hear it…"

"Shut up and listen anyway."

Jonah shot to his feet, his hands balled into fists. For a wild second, he found himself wishing for power that would let him attack. Jonah shivered at the thought. Yet the anger over the unfairness of it all thundered in his ears.

Lynn dropped into a ready stance. "Go ahead, Geek boy."

Her nickname released a dam inside of Jonah. Before he knew it, he swung at her. His anger prevented him from concentrating and remembering everything he'd learned, and Lynn blocked all his swings and kicks but resisted pressing her advantage. Jonah grew even more frustrated.

His technique suffered, causing him to overreach with a punch. Lynn easily slipped under his arm, came up behind, and pinned him in a head lock.

"Let me go!" Jonah screamed and struggled.

Lynn obliged and shoved him forward. She also hooked her foot between his feet, causing him to trip and land face-first in the muddy creek water. When he sputtered and tried to raise himself, Lynn planted a foot in the small of his back and pushed him down. He roared in frustration as he pulled his head out of the water for a second time. She caught him up in a tight hold, planting her feet to either side to keep him from flipping her over. He struggled, pushed, and screamed, and through it all, Lynn held on to him.

Jonah smacked the water over and over again with his fists, letting all the anger, frustration, and fear out. After what felt like forever, the fit subsided and he let go of the troubling impulse to lash out. He took gulping breaths as he tried to stop the tears that splashed into the water, only inches from his face. Lynn's hold on him turned into a gentle rocking motion until the sobs gave way to slow, shallow sniffles.

She never said anything. When Jonah relaxed, she changed her grip and helped him stand, wrapping her arms around his shoulders. "Are you done?"

He nodded and she helped him onto the bank and sit down on a stone. Then she knelt in front of him and peered into his eyes.

Jonah refused to look at her at first, but Lynn tapped his forehead until he met her gaze.

She spoke in a quiet voice. "Can I ask you my question now?" She waited for Jonah to nod. "Why did you run?"

"You all think I'm a freak, a monster."

"No we don't, and we never said that."

Jonah blinked at his cousin. "Then why did Robert ask if I could suck out his soul?"

"Robert's being an idiot, that's all."

"You thought the same thing."

"Well, fine. I won't lie to you." Lynn leaned back. "Everyone knows that Reapers take souls. So yeah, I wondered about that."

"See!"

"Jonah, I know you wouldn't do that, even if you could." Lynn waited, but Jonah didn't want to yell anymore. "If you had waited, Robert and I had something to tell you."

"What?"

"We aren't normal, either." Lynn swallowed and gazed off. "I have very strong intuition about things. It runs in the women on my dad's side. My Aunt Ruby has it and your mom had it, big time."

Jonah wiped his eyes, unable to believe what he was hearing. "I didn't know that."

"Obviously. Think about it, Jonah. That's why your parents knew they could send the gifts to us. Once we had them, your mom came to talk with us all the time. I bet she had the feeling that you should be here, with us."

"What about Robert?"

"Oh, he gets images in his head when he concentrates on what someone is thinking. It works best if he's drawing, and the person is really thinking about a particular thing." Lynn lowered her gaze, causing Jonah to think she was embarrassed. "We've developed a routine for getting information from people. We've gotten good stories that way."

Jonah's eyes widened. "That's… kind of cool." He sucked in a breath, remembering the times that images exploded in his head while talking to Robert. "He did it to me?"

"Yeah. We thought you knew more about where the gifts came from. Your mom promised to tell us when…" Lynn's own eyes widened and she stood.

"What?"

"I think she meant to tell us when you turned thirteen."

"Oh."

"We weren't making fun of you." She waited a minute before starting in again. "That brings me to my last point. Jonah, you're not alone. Robert, Wick, and I are part of this, so stop trying to handle it all by yourself."

Lynn's frown was a signal, Jonah knew, that she wanted to goad him into seeing the situation as she did. He didn't know what to say, so he sat there and stared into the little creek. But he thought Lynn was right.

"Why did I get so angry?"

Lynn's expression grew serious. "You still have a lot of anger inside. I thought the practice club would help."

"I'm sorry I tried to attack you."

"Don't apologize. You need to get it out, otherwise it'll eat you up inside." She leaned forward, meeting his gaze. "We don't understand everything that's happening, so don't jump to hasty conclusions. Okay?"

Jonah nodded. "I won't."

Lynn tapped Jonah on the shoulder. "Come on."

Jonah stood up, holding his wet socks in one hand. Lynn's eyes widened as they moved from the sopping socks down to Jonah's bare feet. "Where are your shoes?"

Jonah pointed at the creek, his face growing warm with embarrassment.

"Why'd you throw them in the water?"

"I didn't mean to do it."

Lynn shook her head and muttered something about geeks as Jonah sloshed into the creek to fetch his shoes.

CHAPTER THIRTY-ONE
DEYANIRA'S CHAMBER

Jonah stood in a dank, torch-lit passageway with a low ceiling. Directly ahead, at the end of the passage, was a modern-looking steel door with a blinking display set into the stone wall. *Why am I here,* Jonah wondered, trying to puzzle out the mixture of old and new in this dream-walk. Voices and footsteps sounded behind him. He turned and saw a darkened stairway made of the same rough stone as the walls.

Marcus's warning about being detected in his dream-walks popped into Jonah's head. Before he could move, the bookstore clerk descended the stairs, followed by a young man and woman. They were engaged in an argument.

The woman voice's was an angry whisper. "You were right to attack the boy with that Grim Hound. He's dangerous."

The clerk made a sharp jerk of his head. "That wasn't my decision to make. I paid for that mistake."

"If the boy finds the ring, he'll condemn us to this plane forever." The young man pounded his own chest with a clenched fist. "The promises to our kind will mean nothing!"

The clerk whirled to face the man and woman. "You repeat the Grim Reaper's fears and propaganda. Even the most powerful of our Seers don't agree with him. As long as our king trusts the counsel of the Seers instead of the empty promises of the Reapers, none of us are to harm the boy."

The argument took place less than half a dozen feet from Jonah, pressed against the wall. He thought it lucky that they argued with each other. All three acted as if he wasn't there, and he breathed easier.

The clerk stepped by Jonah, lifting a small, round object that he wore around his neck. It wasn't the Ankh amulet, which the man still wore. This object was smaller, made of a slender piece of carved wood, and with multi-colored beads attached to one end. The clerk held it high, and a distortion appeared in the air in front of him.

The strange barrier parted like curtains as the clerk stepped forward. He passed through three more similar distortions before reaching the metal door and typing a code into the wall-mounted keypad. Jonah edged forward. Just as he crossed the first distortion, it closed, touching him. Pain lanced Jonah's arm, and he gasped.

Oh no!

Jonah darted forward, racing through the rest of the openings before they snapped closed. He came to a halt, right behind the others, to catch his breath and rub his left arm, which was still a bit numb. Wick said a shield could protect against supernatural and magical things. *If I'm a ghost in this dream-walk, that includes me.*

The first distortion continued to undulate before going transparent again. That drew the clerk's attention, and he paused with his hand on the door, eyes narrowed. Jonah remained still, fearing the man would sense him.

The clerk scanned the tunnel for several tense moments before he pulled the thick metal door open and entered the chamber. When the young man and woman followed, the door began to swing shut. Jonah hurried through with less than an inch to spare before the door closed with a thud.

The interior of the chamber was circular, with high metal walls that tapered toward a much-smaller opening at the apex. Stars twinkled in the sky, visible through the grate covering the opening. Jonah glanced down and gulped. One large symbol covered the entire floor, and it looked as if someone had drawn it with blood.

The young man and woman positioned themselves to the left of the doorway, near a cot. A pair of ominous-looking black handcuffs hung on the wall above it. Jonah shivered when he saw those, and he shifted his gaze around the chamber again. Something on the far side caught his attention. He squinted into the shadows and gasped. A stone portal stood against the far side.

An image of a huge red fireball streaking out of a similar portal popped into his mind. He clenched his fists as sweat broke out on his forehead. *Could it be the same one from the dream about his parents?* He thought the symbols on its surface were the same, but he had no way to be sure.

The clerk moved, revealing a pedestal in the center of the room. It had a simple stone base that flared at the bottom and a circular flat surface on top. A pair of lights mounted high on the wall created overlapping cones of harsh light on the pedestal. The clerk ignored it as he waited, his attention on the stone portal.

Several symbols on the portal flared, casting an eerie glow. A small hole appeared at the very center and expanded out to the edges. A sudden gust of cold air washed over them as the opening reached its full size, revealing a dark, cavernous interior on the other side.

Deyanira stepped into view in her true form as a tall, red-robed, and menacing KIN member. The ritualistic slashes and cuts were clearly visible on her pale face. Pain flared in the pit of Jonah's stomach.

He shuddered as he watched the woman turn slightly to the assembled group and bow. Several more red-robed people stood behind her. Unlike Deyanira, their hoods were pulled forward over their heads. She completed her bow and walked toward the portal.

The air around the opening shimmered as Deyanira stepped through. Jonah's jaw dropped when her body rippled and transformed. The red robe became a black, thigh-length dress. Her skeletal face lost the scars and became severe and normal. Long red hair quickly grew down to her shoulders like some time-lapse movie.

By the time she stood on this side of the portal, she had transformed into the bookstore owner, all evidence of her true form hidden.

The clerk inclined his head and waited until the portal closed before he spoke. "Welcome back."

Deyanira sneered and looked over the clerk's shoulder. "What are they doing here?"

The young man stepped forward. "We're making sure things get done."

"You haven't found the ring yet." The young woman joined the young man. "Our king is concerned."

The man and woman blinked and in that instant, both sets of eyes turned milky white.

Deyanira never took her pale green eyes off the two people. "You aren't needed, Wraiths, and you certainly aren't welcomed."

"The Grim Reaper's day is coming," the young man sneered at Deyanira. "All Reapers will have to answer for the bad choices you've made."

He pushed the clerk aside and started around the pedestal. The young woman went around the opposite side.

Jonah would have been scared if two Wraiths, whatever they were, circled toward him from both sides. Deyanira's long fingers curled like talons as she tilted her head back and laughed. "Today is not that day, so either leave willingly or I'll be forced to make you leave. I'd hate to damage those poor, innocent bodies."

The young man let out a snide laugh. "You wouldn't--"

He didn't finish speaking because Deyanira blurred into motion, shoving the woman into the wall, grabbing him by the neck and slamming him against the pedestal. With her other hand, Deyanira activated one of her blades and hurled it into the young woman's shoulder, pinning her to the metal wall. The woman howled and tried to pull the weapon free. When she touched the blade, her hands began to smoke.

Meanwhile, Deyanira had raised her free hand over the young man's head. He craned his neck around in order to stare at the clerk. "Brother! Are you going to let her do this?"

The clerk shrugged, making no move to help.

Deyanira smiled. "You've forgotten yourself, spirit. Reapers command all of you."

She pressed her hand against the young man's forehead. He screamed as a translucent shape was sucked out of his body. Jonah's jaw dropped when he saw a human spirit dressed in colonial-era clothes. That was a Wraith, he thought. Deyanira released the human and gripped the Wraith around its ghostly neck before it could escape. The Wraith let out another agonized scream, flared brightly, and exploded into smoking threads.

Deyanira turned on the young woman, whose white eyes narrowed in pure hate.

"You haven't heard the last of this, Reaper." The young woman opened her mouth in a silent scream. The Wraith poured out of her, a female with curly hair, and flowed up and through the grate. The young woman's body sagged against the blade that still protruded from her shoulder.

Deyanira pulled the blade free. When the woman slumped to the floor and groaned, Deyanira motioned to the clerk. He slid a Taser out of his pocket and calmly zapped both people.

"Leave them in the woods near the crossroads," Deyanira ordered.

The clerk nodded. "You are sending a not-so-subtle message to my Wraith brethren."

"Of course."

Jonah stared at the two bodies and suddenly, he wanted out of this dream-walk. *Wake up,* Jonah told himself. Nothing happened. Maybe if he went back to the foot of the stairs, he could do it. Jonah took a step toward the door.

Deyanira tensed and looked around the room. "Who's there?"

The clerk watched her with a worried expression. "We're alone, Deyanira."

"No, we aren't." Her eyes narrowing to mere slits like a tiger that's spotted its prey, she stepped toward the door, never taking her eyes off it. "I can sense you."

Without warning, Deyanira's hand shot directly at Jonah's throat. He had discovered in practice sessions that he had excellent reflexes. They allowed him to avoid her first attempt. However, every movement on his part enabled Deyanira to sense him more.

Her head followed his progress as he scuttled around the chamber. Jonah tried to remain calm and think clearly about his bedroom. That proved difficult with Deyanira stalking him. It took all his willpower to stop himself from taking another step. Deyanira paused.

Come on. Come on. Don't panic. Think clearly.

Deyanira stepped toward him with her hand outstretched.

"Who are you?" She looked over her shoulder at the clerk. "Is it one of your brethren?"

"I can't tell while in a human host. It's a limitation of human senses."

"Then come out of him now."

The conversation terrified Jonah. If Deyanira figured it out, she would kill him for sure, no matter what Marcus said.

Stay calm and think about the bedroom. I can do this.

Deyanira lunged forward and managed to wrap her thin fingers around Jonah's neck. She let out a wicked cackle as he twisted in her grip.

"Show yourself!"

The awful truth hit Jonah. Deyanira had said it earlier: Reapers controlled spirits. She had been able the grab the Wraith before it could escape. And if he was a ghost in these dream-walks, she could also hold on to him. Total panic suffused Jonah's body and he shuddered.

Behind Deyanira, the clerk's body collapsed to the floor as the Wraith released it. Jonah watched as an ancient Egyptian warrior floated into the air. He couldn't imagine why a being so dignified would possess a lowly clerk. The Wraith stared at Jonah.

"Who is it?" Deyanira demanded as she shook Jonah. "Answer me, Wraith!"

The Wraith shifted his gaze to her, disgust and loathing twisting his face for a brief moment, and then he smoothed his ghostly expression. "I can't be sure."

Deyanira roared in anger and activated a blade with her free hand. She couldn't see as the Wraith touched the ankh amulet, the same one the clerk wore. Light shot out from it and heat flared under Deyanira's hand. She screamed and released Jonah. Immediately, he felt the welcomed pull as he was ripped away from the dream-walk.

He awoke in his own bed and sat up, rubbing his throat. His heart raced at ninety miles an hour, and he could still feel Deyanira's hard fingers around his neck. He didn't care about the things he heard or the fact that he had watched Deyanira destroy a Wraith.

I never want that to happen again.

Jonah thought of sending Marcus a text, but he didn't want to worry him and Omar. So he tossed and turned, afraid to sleep. At last, the terror of the dream-walk faded enough for his mind to form questions. Why did the Wraith lie to Deyanira or use his amulet to help him escape?

That action bothered Jonah as much as anything else. Surely Deyanira would know what happened and punish the Wraith, maybe even kill him, like she did the other one. Jonah wondered at his concern for the ghostly warrior. He rolled that and all the other questions around in his head until he descended into a dreamless sleep.

CHAPTER THIRTY-TWO
CROSSROADS

Home from church and changed out of his Sunday best, Jonah sat at the Hightowers' kitchen table as Robert sketched. At least, his cousin tried to sketch. Robert had the sketchbook in his lap, and he slapped the pencil down on it. "You have to focus, Jonah."

"I'm sorry. I'm just thinking about that Wraith." Jonah still had to get used to his cousins knowing everything about him.

Robert arched one of his sharp eyebrows. "Lynn wants the sketches of the people as soon as possible."

"Okay." Jonah concentrated and eventually described the two young people from the dream-walk. As Robert put finishing touches on the sketches, Lynn came through the kitchen door. Wick was right on her heels.

"Excellent," Lynn said as she took the pages from her brother and left the house.

Meanwhile, Wick helped himself to a soda from the refrigerator and sat down at the kitchen table. "What's up, Padawan?"

Jonah shrugged, and Robert gave his best friend a serious

look. "He had a dream-walk."

"Dream-walk?"

"Yeah. Jonah calls them dream-walks now."

Wick blinked at Jonah. "Oh, that's a cool name. It's like astral projection." Wick's eyes widened. "That means your soul is traveling around."

With that, Robert, looking a bit shocked at Wick's words, proceeded to tell his friend everything about it. Wick leaned back in the kitchen chair and plopped his black-booted feet on the table.

Robert scowled and knocked his friend's feet back onto the floor. "My mom would kill all of us if she saw you."

"Sorry." Wick took out his lighter and played with it as he leaned back in the chair again. "When you think about it, Reapers and Wraiths kind of go together."

"You mean disembodied, super-angry human spirits?" Robert asked, his eyes widening slightly. "I thought they just floated around, haunting places. I never heard of them having a king or working together."

"Me neither," Wick said, ruffling his twists, thinking.

Jonah waited for his friend to go on, but the boy looked like he was deep in thought. Jonah tapped the table to get Wick's attention. "Are they just ghosts?"

"Oh no. They're human spirits that were killed out of time or order and didn't move on for some reason. That's why they turn super-angry and tend to haunt places."

"What does *out of order* mean? Like what it says in the Bible, where everyone has a time to die?"

"Your guess is as good as mine, Jonah."

"But the people were possessed. Can Wraiths take over you?"

Wick laughed. "No. I'm guessing these people welcomed them in. It had to involve some ritual, probably a corruption of the ancient Voodoo Loa ritual. If you heard any music in the background, that would have been a clue."

Robert gave his friend a doubtful look. "You know, Lynn's right about you."

"I'm wounded, Bobby." Wick feigned being stabbed in the chest. Robert scowled, but Jonah noticed the beginnings of a smile on his face. Meanwhile, Wick turned back to Jonah. "I'm more interested in the bookstore clerk. You saw him hold something in his hand as he walked toward the security door."

Jonah nodded, happy to be on another subject.

"Did he say anything in a strange language or do anything?"

"No. I saw the air shimmer like a force field. The clerk walked through it."

Wick snapped the lighter shut. "They have wards protecting the door."

"Wards?"

"They're basically shields, except they protect a fixed location. Wards are also stronger and more intricate. I'm sure the clerk held a talisman. It allows him to walk through the wards without having to take them down."

Jonah continued to be amazed by Wick's knowledge. A thought occurred to him. "Can you make a talisman?"

Wick's jaw dropped. "Wards are way above what I can do, Jonah. Besides, the person who made the barrier is the only one who can make the one to work on it. Talismans are individual things, like the signature of the person."

"But why use wards? Do they work on regular humans?"

"Oh yeah. They protect against anything mortal. My guess is Deyanira's more worried about something supernatural getting into that chamber."

"You mean Fallen Reapers and Wraiths?" Jonah lapsed into silence as his mind picked through the information.

Wick traded a glance with Robert. "You know, Jonah, if she has wards, I'm sure she has ways to prevent phasing into that chamber. Usually, it's a symbol called a sigil."

"She does. I saw a huge one on the floor. Deyanira used a portal to get in."

Robert startled Jonah when he jumped from his chair and hurried off to his room. He returned with a different sketchbook in hand.

"The first time you mentioned portals, I wanted to show you these." Robert placed the sketchbook on the kitchen table and showed Jonah detailed, hand-drawn images of a stone portal. Robert even included the strange symbols around its surface.

Jonah's eyes widened. "I saw this."

Robert nodded. "The portals are doorways between the mortal realm and the supernatural realm."

"You mean …."

Wick nodded. "Yep. The Afterworld. The domain of the Undead."

Jonah took the sketchbook and flipped through, his mind racing. Robert had drawings of the blades, graceful looking ships, and the irregular gaseous shape like the one Jonah had seen in the Grim Hound dream.

Robert looked over Jonah's shoulder and pointed at the gaseous drawing. "That's a vortex."

"Does it connect to the Afterworld, too?"

"It only works on this side. Have you seen one of those?"

"Deyanira can make one."

Robert's eyes widened at that and he turned on Wick. "I thought only humans could make those."

"True. Witches, sorcerers, mages, and magicians can open them."

"Then how can Deyanira do it?"

Wick clicked his lighter open and closed. After a minute, he gave it one final snap and stood, excited. "In one of your dream-walks, you said Deyanira stepped through a vortex in her human appearance." Jonah nodded, caught up in Wick's growing excitement as the boy paced back and forth. "But in the latest dream-walk, when she crossed through the portal, it transformed her from Reaper into a human disguise?"

"Yeah. Why are you smiling?"

"It's obvious. When she comes through the portal, it transforms her. My guess is that it allows her to interact with humans."

Jonah finally understood the taunt his dad had hurled at Deyanira. He said she needed to cross back over. It all made sense. "You, Robert, and everyone else could see Deyanira as the store owner because the portal makes her more human."

"Well, not exactly human," Wick corrected. "I think it's more like the Grim Hounds. They have a physical form wrapped around them. Because of the power needed to do that, they can only stay for a limited time."

"That's why she crosses back to the Afterworld," Jonah concluded.

"Correct. And being in a human form also allows her to use her old abilities. She must have been a witch or sorceress in her former life."

Robert pumped the air with his fist. "That's why she can do wards!"

Wick stood up as he and Robert touched fists, smiling. Jonah shared their excitement as he recalled Kevin's comment about Deyanira. A knot grew in his stomach and he frowned.

Wick noticed. "What's troubling you, Padawan?"

"I think that we'll have to get inside that chamber."

Robert gave him a quizzical look. "Too bad we don't have a clue where she lives."

Jonah closed his eyes and thought about the chamber and then sitting here in the Hightowers' kitchen. He wished Marcus was here to help, but he gave it a try anyway. He imagined an invisible thread connecting both locations.

And it worked. "It's outside Mount Vernon. I'd say about fifteen miles."

Wick let out a low whistle. "Dude, that is so cool." He blinked and looked at Robert. "It's probably an old house or mansion. Deyanira would need somewhere private to work her stuff."

"That's a start," Robert agreed. "I can go to the Summit tomorrow and run an Internet search of the county records."

Searching the county records turned out to be boring, Jonah thought. Robert simply created an automated search routine and let the computer do all the work, accessing various databases from surrounding counties.

Jonah peeked at the screen. "Can't you just do an Internet search?"

Robert raised an eyebrow. "Where's the fun in that? Besides, I'd have to go to each County's website. That's boring and tedious, especially when I can do it with a simple algorithm."

"Okay." Jonah set Lynn's bag down and pulled out the deactivated blades. "Here. Lynn cut my practice short to go investigate something. She wanted me to bring these to you."

Robert took the blades to the filing cabinet, took out the archive box, and locked them inside. That done, he returned to the work desk, where he opened an old laptop. He paused, glancing at Jonah. "You are ready to kick Brandon's butt in two days, right?"

"Yeah, I am." Jonah picked up a connector cable and turned it over in his hands. "What is all this stuff?"

"You got me thinking yesterday when you mentioned the keypad beside that metal door. If you're serious about getting into Deyanira's chamber, then I'll need to be able to break through the door's security." He took the connector from Jonah and placed it back on the desk. "This may look old, but it has more than enough power to get in."

"You can do that?"

"Well, I won't know until I actually see it. Still, it doesn't hurt to be prepared."

"Thanks. For listening to my hunch."

Robert paused his typing and gave Jonah an embarrassed grin. "Don't sweat it, little cousin. This is nothing. You should see Wick. He's busy trying out ways to take down a ward without getting himself killed."

"For real?"

Robert grinned. "And he has working shield bracelets. Can you believe it? He showed me. They stopped everything I threw at him. Too bad you can't use one against Brandon."

Jonah stared at his cousin in amazement, unable to think of anything to say. He sat with Robert, occasionally asking him questions. Lynn came up the stairs an hour later, humming and swinging a small bag from the café downstairs. She also had a satchel slung over her left shoulder. Without a word, she pulled out a large sub sandwich and divided it into three pieces, handing one section to Jonah and another to Robert.

"I have good news." Lynn dropped her satchel on the far end of the table and continued after taking a quick bite of her piece of the sub. "The two people you saw in your dream-walk are okay. The police picked up the woman for vagrancy. She remembered being at the roadhouse restaurant, and then nothing until the police found her."

Robert paused in his work and looked at his twin. "You know the name of the place?"

Lynn nodded, pulled a bunch of flyers out of her satchel, and placed them on the table.

"She's not the only one to have memory loss," Lynn continued. "Other people have reported waking up in strange places around town. None of them remembered how they got there. The one common element is the roadhouse."

Lynn shifted the ad for the roadhouse to the top of the pile of papers. Jonah read it.

"The Crossroads?"

"Yes. Interesting name, isn't it?"

"Wait a minute." Robert turned to his desktop computer, minimized the search window, and opened up a different file. "I knew it!"

Lynn peered over her brother's shoulder. "Knew what?"

"Wick's always going on about magic power lines." Robert clicked on an icon, and a color map of Twiggs County opened. "He made this map of Mount Vernon and the surrounding county. That roadhouse is built on a Ley line." Robert tapped the computer screen. "Wow. Looks like it's near an actual crossroads." He laughed. "That makes sense."

"Why?"

"It's an old Blues tale about selling your soul to the devil at the crossroads." When Jonah gave him a blank look, Robert continued. "My dad used to listen to this old song. I should have known it would be based on something real."

"Maybe the singer knew about Wraiths," Lynn offered.

"Could be."

Jonah pointed at the thick red lines forming the crossroads. "That's cool, but what are Ley lines?"

"Wick is better at explaining these things," Robert hedged. "Ley lines are supposed to be like magic power lines."

"We forget you're not from around here." Lynn looked up from the screen as she explained, "A lot of the newer businesses were built on the site of much older places. I bet that old roadhouse used to be something related to the supernatural."

Jonah couldn't imagine why people would build on a site like that. He shook his head in confusion. "Why are they important to Wraiths?"

Lynn glanced at Robert, waiting for him to answer. He paused as if to gather his thoughts. "Wick said that it's easier for the Wraiths to cross over at those locations. They may not be in the Afterworld, but they are on the supernatural plane."

"I wondered why they've become so active." Lynn peered over her brother's shoulder again. "The number of missing people hasn't been this high since…" Lynn glanced at Jonah, then lowered her gaze back to the screen. "Well, never."

She didn't have to say it. Jonah knew what she thought because he had come to the same realization. "It's all because of me."

Lynn glanced at him. "Jonah, what did I tell you about jumping to conclusions?"

"I'm not jumping to conclusions. I know what everyone wants." Jonah looked his cousins squarely in the eyes, took a deep breath, and said, "They want the Protector's Ring."

CHAPTER THIRTY-THREE
KAYAKS AND RINGS

"The Protector's Ring?" Robert ruffled his Afro as if trying to remember. "What's that?"

Jonah experienced a surge of embarrassment. It was Mike who had urged him to look for the ring. After all, his parents were killed because they found the Protector's Ring. An evil Reaper—Deyanira—had injured Marcus in an attempt to find it. Whole families and bloodlines were destroyed because of the ring.

Lynn gave him a shrewd look. "I think the more interesting question, my dear brother, is why does Jonah think it's all about a ring?"

Robert caught on, and he, too, looked at Jonah with the same, shrewd stare.

Lynn quickly cleared a space on the work table and sat down. Robert turned all the way around in the computer chair and leaned forward. Jonah began with the information he had learned from Mr. Hackett.

Robert leapt out of his chair when Jonah mentioned his old art teacher. "Did he say anything about me?"

"No." Jonah looked away. Mr. Hackett had certainly seemed angry with Robert about something, but Jonah didn't want to get into that at the moment. He continued on, telling his cousins about Marcus's encounter with Deyanira.

"That's how you knew about the woman from the bookstore." Lynn flipped her braids behind a shoulder with an angry twist of her head. "Is there anything else?"

"I found those words written on a piece of paper in one of my dad's books. I remembered it after visiting Mr. Hackett."

Jonah grabbed his book bag off the sofa, pulled a small grey book out, and hurried back to Lynn.

She took the small volume, turning it over in her hands. "I thought your father's library burned to the ground."

"I had this book in my bag." He slipped the folded piece of paper from the book and showed it to her.

She read it out loud. "The Protector's Ring."

"My dad must have found it."

"Then why turn around and hide it?"

"Well, Mr. Hackett says it's always been too dangerous to keep a ring."

"But your dad was a researcher, Jonah. He would have known about the ring's history. He thought the risk of finding it was acceptable. I wonder why." Lynn curled a finger in one of her braids as Robert took the piece of paper from Jonah.

"What does H mean?"

"Mr. Hackett?" Jonah suggested. "He claimed he met a Fallen Reaper, but said he never met my dad. I think he lied about that."

Robert smacked his hand on his desktop. "Old Man Hackett never told me any of this while I took art lessons."

"Get over it, Robert." Lynn leaned on her brother's shoulder until he shrugged her off. Lynn ruffled his Afro as she turned to Jonah. "I don't know. Your dad only came here once."

"Really?"

"Yep, little cousin." Robert nodded. "I told you. He came with your mom right after you were born."

Jonah frowned as he considered that. If his cousins were right, either his dad never visited again, or he had phased down to see Mike's uncle without telling anyone.

Robert swiveled his chair around to his computer and started typing. "You said Hackett mentioned the Solomon Ring. I've seen something about that, something recent." He typed furiously for a few minutes before letting out a shout.

"Dr. Francis Halliwell, a renowned collector of ancient rings, risked his professional credibility after he claimed to have found a powerful yet obscure ring called King Solomon's Ring." He gave them a significant look. "Solomon's Ring supposedly endows the wearer with extraordinary powers. Dr. Halliwell disappeared from the public scene shortly after his claims were made, thus preventing authentication of his find."

Lynn nodded. "Your dad must have found out about Halliwell and tracked down his last known location."

"Look! I found a drawing of the ring." Jonah and Lynn huddled on either side of Robert.

The image on the computer screen was exactly like the one in Mr. Hackett's book. Jonah took in the details of the mysterious ring as he recalled Hackett's comments. "Mr. Hackett told me that the Solomon Ring was actually a Protector's Ring."

"So, you still think your dad meant Hackett in that note?" Lynn gave him a questioning look, and Jonah nodded.

"Why not? All he put was… wait a minute!" Jonah snatched the piece of notepaper from the desktop where Robert had dropped it, and stared at the *H*. "Halliwell was the one who had tracked down the ring. Maybe my dad meant Halliwell."

"That makes more sense than Hackett." Lynn noticed Robert's shocked expression. "What's wrong? You don't think so?"

"Lynn! We know that name from a certain sculpture made from rings."

"Halliwell's Sphere." Lynn's eyes went wide with understanding and she glanced down at the attic floor. "Does anyone think that's just a coincidence?"

Moments later, Jonah, Robert, and Lynn stood on the second floor landing, gazing at Aunt Imma's hanging art piece. The late afternoon sunlight streamed through the high skylights and glinted off hundreds of rings.

Jonah squinted at the brilliant points of lights. "You think it's one of those?"

"Your parents sent the blades and archive box to us." Robert's voice sounded awed. "It's possible they sent the ring to our mom. That means it's been right in front of us all this time."

Jonah gazed at the rings, feeling the same growing excitement as his cousin. "Too bad we can't tell from here."

"We don't have to." Robert smacked the railing with a hand. Jonah and Lynn looked at him in confusion. "Mom kept records of every ring donated. She wanted me to make a database. It's all at the house, in her art room. We can check."

Jonah shook his head. "My dad wouldn't have told her the real name of the ring."

"He didn't have to, Jonah. I took pictures of every ring submitted."

Lynn eyed her brother. "Can you access that from here?"

"I wish I could. Mom's computer isn't on the Net. She's afraid of viruses, so I planned to connect it anyway and just not tell her."

"We'll have to wait until tomorrow to check. I'm sure Mom's home by now."

"Wait." Robert smacked his forehead. "I have band practice all day. And you're working with Jonah on the duel." When Lynn threw up her arms, Robert added, "Why don't we just ask Mom?"

Aunt Imma wasn't at home when Jonah and his cousins arrived. So instead of waiting to ask her about the records, Robert changed his mind and decided to search the art room. After about fifteen minutes of frantic looking, he slammed the last drawer and leaned against his mom's desk in a huff.

"She used pre-printed submission forms. I helped her fill them out."

Lynn crossed her arms, leaning against the doorframe and smirking. "I thought you wanted to ask about them."

Robert gave her a frosty look. "They're supposed to be here." He cast a disgusted glare around his mom's art room.

Jonah sat on the sofa in the family room, listening to the argument. He had a practice stick in his hand, flipping back and forth between ready positions. Lynn wanted it to be second nature to him by the time the duel arrived.

Wick, who reclined in the armchair, watched him until Lynn stalked out of the art room and plopped down on the sofa beside him. A moment later came the sound of the garage door closing.

Aunt Imma walked into the family room and stopped. "Goodness, I didn't expect to see all of you here." Aunt Imma started for the kitchen with her grocery bag when she noticed Robert standing in the entrance to the hallway leading to the art room. "Robert, what were you doing in there?"

Everyone froze, but Robert didn't miss a beat as he came over, took the grocery bag from his mom, and carried it into the kitchen. "Mom, what happened to all the records on the Halliwell Sphere?"

"Honey, I gave the records to the county library."

"Why'd you do that?" Robert started squeezing the box of cereal he'd just taken out of the grocery bag.

Aunt Imma smacked his hand to get him to release the box. "Well, they're going to do the database and make an interactive display for it. If you had started on it when I asked, you could have finished it. Why is it so important now?"

Robert sat down at the table and looked at his mother with a blank expression. Jonah knew his cousin didn't have a response, so he jumped to his feet.

"I wanted to know if my parents sent you a ring." His words prompted Lynn to shake her head, but he sent her a silent plea. He didn't have any intention of telling his aunt everything.

He walked into the kitchen. "I don't have many things left after the fire. I thought that if they sent you a ring, it would be cool to see it."

"Your parents did send a ring. It's part of the sculpture. I can show you if you want."

Wick gave Jonah a thumbs-up gesture as Aunt Imma began putting up the groceries. She stopped suddenly.

"You know, Jonah, your parents sent two rings: a family ring and another strange ring with a lot of funny writing on it. I never saw anything like it before. Your mother told me the most interesting story about the art collector who owned it. That's where I got the name from—Halliwell's Sphere."

Robert leapt up from the table. "Mom, I thought you read about Halliwell in your art book from class."

"Oh Robert, what does it matter now?" Aunt Imma looked at her watch and started to take out pots and pans. "Your father will be home soon. Wick, you can stay for dinner if you'd like." She began cutting up vegetables and loading them into a pot. "I wasn't going to do rings. I wanted to do kayaks."

"Kayaks, Mom? Why kayaks?" Robert threw the folded grocery bags on top of a recycling stack in the corner.

Aunt Imma smiled at her son. "Exactly! No one would expect kayaks. It would have been spectacular, but Jonah's mom convinced me it may have been too large for the small space. She suggested that I do rings and even offered to donate the first ones."

Jonah couldn't believe it. Robert, Lynn, and Wick all stared at him.

"It turned out so well," Aunt Imma continued. "I meant to thank your mother personally and have her come down and see it…" His aunt's voice trailed off and she busied herself with preparing dinner.

Jonah knew he had to say something. "My mom would have liked it."

"Thank you, Jonah." Aunt Imma paused, holding a whole butternut squash in her hands. "Life is funny. No one asked about the sculpture in months and then twice in one day, people want to know all about it."

Lynn sprang off the sofa and joined them in the kitchen as Aunt Imma began cutting the squash.

"Mom, who else asked about the sculpture today?"

Jonah had a sinking feeling in his stomach as Aunt Imma paused to answer. "This odd woman came into the shop today with long red hair that felt strange to the touch. She probably uses a lot of chemicals on it."

"Mom, what did she ask?"

"She recognized my name from an article on the recreation center, and we started talking about the sculpture. She asked where I got the rings, and I told her about the donations." Aunt Imma paused and gazed at the grim looks on the faces around her. "Honestly, what's gotten into all of you? It's not a secret. It's in every article written about the center." She pointed at Robert and Lynn with the half-cut squash. "That includes your blog, if I'm not mistaken."

"Aunt Imma?" Jonah got her attention. "Did you tell the woman my parents sent rings?"

"She asked about any strange ones and I mentioned the one your mom sent. That's when she told me about her bookstore with the funny name."

Everyone spoke at the same time. "Mystic Worlds."

Aunt Imma blinked at them and nodded. "Yes, that's the name. Doesn't sound like any bookstore a good Christian would visit, does it? Anyway, she said she'd be interested in seeing a ring like that one. I told her she could see it anytime she wanted because it's still on display in the center." Aunt Imma turned her attention to the steaming pots on the stove.

Lynn motioned to the back patio. Everyone followed her outside and sat around the patio table.

Robert was the first to speak. "So what do we do?"

"We stop her, that's what we do." Jonah pounded lightly on the table with his fist. "We have to get the ring before Deyanira does."

Wick gave him a slight nod. "I agree with Jonah. We have to get it first."

"We will, but I think Deyanira will wait until Thursday." Lynn eyed Jonah. "She can't do anything while the place is set up for the Summer's End celebration."

"Oh, yeah. That's right." Robert nodded. "With the extra vendors in the parking lot, there are too many people around, even at night."

Jonah watched the others nodding, but he didn't get it. "Why wouldn't she try tomorrow night, after the celebration?"

"That's break down night, little cousin. The vendors won't clear out until late Thursday."

Wick tapped Jonah's fist with his own. "Plus the rec center goes into shut-down mode for a week. It'll be the perfect time for Deyanira to go for the ring."

Jonah looked off across the darkening backyard. He wanted to do something now, not in two days.

Lynn nudged his chair with her foot. "There's another very good reason for you to hope Deyanira waits." When Jonah didn't say anything, she continued, "Haven't you forgotten something, Jonah? The Summer's End duel is tomorrow evening."

"I know that." Jonah held up the practice stick.

Lynn nodded and leaned forward with a serious expression. "We go on Thursday night." Everyone nodded.

"We'll have to wait until late. I think midnight should be late enough."

"Lynn!" Jonah lowered his voice when everyone waved for him to keep it down. "Deyanira could be there by then."

"Think about it." Lynn gave Jonah a thump on the head. "We have to wait until my parents are asleep. Otherwise they'd notice us leaving." She continued staring at him until Wick changed the subject.

"If Deyanira is back in town, shouldn't Marcus be nearby?"

"I don't know." Jonah hadn't had time to think that far ahead yet.

"Well, I hate to say it, Jonah." Lynn gave him a thin smile. "Marcus would be a big help. You haven't heard from him?"

"No." When everyone continued to watched him, Jonah held up his hands. "I'll give him a call."

Robert glanced through the patio doors. "Dad's home."

Jonah worried so much about Deyanira getting the ring that he barely ate any dinner. The twins were just as keyed up, and none of them asked for seconds.

After dinner, Jonah went outside on the patio to call Marcus.

"Hello, Jonah. I didn't expect to hear from you so soon."

"I know where the Protector's Ring is hidden."

Marcus let out a startled breath. After a moment, he asked, "How do you know?"

"My mom and dad sent it to Aunt Imma. It's in her Halliwell Sphere sculpture. Right in the rec center." Jonah spoke in a rush. "We think Deyanira will try to take it on Thursday night."

Marcus muttered something under his breath. Jonah wondered if the Fallen Reaper would believe him.

He relaxed when Marcus said, "That explains things."

Jonah blinked. "What things?"

"Deyanira and her agents have become very active over the last few days. My people are spread far and wide. I see it was a diversion."

"What about the ring?"

"Have you seen it? This could have been a planted misdirection by your parents. They did a lot of that, which is why we have to follow all the leads."

"I'm sure. This has to be it." Jonah heard the desperation in his own voice. He never knew his parents had set up an entire plan to fool everyone else.

"Well, either way, you leave that to us."

"But we need to watch it, in case she tries to take it. We can let you know."

"Jonah…"

"I know, keep my head down."

"It's too dangerous for you and your cousins to get involved."

"We're already involved."

"Jonah, please. I'll send a couple of people down there."

"That's all?"

"If we pulled everyone back, that would alert Deyanira that we think you're right about the location. In that case, Mount Vernon would become a battle zone. It's delicate, but we need to keep a low profile ourselves until we can confirm the ring is there. Understand?"

Jonah tightened his grip the phone. He knew he was right, but he could also see Marcus's point. They didn't want Deyanira to bring all her people. The idea of facing her alone was bad enough.

"The rest of us will be there as soon as we can," Marcus added.

"Okay." Jonah let all the bitterness come out in his voice. They were the ones to discover its location, not Marcus and his people. He could feel it in his bones. This is where his parents hid the ring.

CHAPTER THIRTY-FOUR
SUMMER'S END

The Summer's End Festival hummed with the atmosphere of a county fair. Carnival vendors set up rides and games in and around the parking lot of the recreation center. Because the parking lots were taken, cars lined the streets for several blocks into the surrounding neighborhoods. The town provided a couple of school buses as shuttles to make rounds through the neighborhoods. The rides were free.

Jonah was amazed at the transformation as he walked the outside crowds, handing out flyers for the various clubs. Even with the constant activity, he began to feel a little lonely and scanned the throngs of people in a vain attempt to find Mike. Jonah suspected he still worried about the duel and wanted to hide that fact. But Jonah would welcome an argument with Mike over not hanging out at all.

Both Robert and Lynn worked inside the recreation center. Robert helped out with the teen art show while Lynn worked a booth featuring the center's youth programs. After an hour and a half of walking through the outside attractions and handing out brochures, Jonah had enough and headed for the main building.

A Native American magician roamed the festival attracting a crowd wherever she stopped. She wore a tunic of light brown material with the darker shapes of animals woven into the fabric. As Jonah drew close, he picked out the story the woman weaved around each trick she performed. It was about the fabled phoenix. The cadence of her voice rose to a climax just as she produced a fist-sized version of the mythical bird in mid-air.

Jonah and the crowd gasped, spellbound as the fiery bird flared and burned out. Enthusiastic applause erupted, drawing even more attention. But the magician simply bowed and nodded as she folded her arms. Soon the crowd began to move away, and the woman turned to catch Jonah's gaze. She bowed to him, her two long braids nearly touching the ground.

Caught off guard by the formal greeting, Jonah returned the gesture with an awkward bow of his own. He straightened, and that's when he noticed the symbol stitched into the left front of her tunic. It was three circles with wings stretched over the center one. Even though it was done in golden thread, it was just like the symbol branded into his godfather's long coat. This woman was part of the Alliance.

Jonah opened his mouth, but the woman turned and slipped through the crowd. He considered following her until he realized that wasn't necessary. She worked with Marcus, which meant she was here to keep a watch on the ring. That thought relaxed Jonah as he changed direction and headed toward the center.

Long banners were strung from the atrium ceiling and hung down between the art pieces. In the East wing, the game rooms were being used as booths for civic and county organizations, most focused on teen-related activities.

Lynn sat at a long fold-up table with two other girls. She wore a teen center shirt and had her own stack of brochures beside her.

As Jonah approached, the girl to Lynn's left smiled up at him. She had neat black curls and large loop earrings that matched her deep green shirt. "You want to join a club?"

"He's with the Practice Club already, Tamara."

Tamara looked between Jonah and Lynn and her eyes widened. "Is he your little brother?"

"He's my cousin."

Tamara pulled a rainbow-colored ribbon out of a small box and stood to pin it on Jonah's chest. "I'm with the Rainbow Coalition."

"What's this for?" Jonah tweaked the little ribbon.

"We promote tolerance and anti-bullying efforts. We have a chapter at the High School. We call ourselves Upstanders. You want to join? You're a freshman, right?"

Lynn laughed. "He's still in middle school."

That news seemed to animate Tamara even more. "Oh, well, middle school is the perfect place to teach tolerance." She leaned over the table. "You can start a chapter there."

Jonah shrugged and stuffed his hands in his pockets. Thankfully, a couple of older kids came over, and Tamara busied herself with them.

Lynn reached out and straightened Jonah's rainbow ribbon. "Have you heard back from Marcus or his people yet?"

"He sent someone, a magician. She's walking around outside." Jonah glanced around. He had hoped to see Kevin again, but so far, nothing.

Lynn looked impressed with the news. "Really? Did you talk to her?"

"No." Jonah frowned. "I was going to when she moved off like she didn't want to talk to me."

Lynn shook her head. "Well then, I say we go ahead with our plan."

Tamara finished with the other kids and glanced at Jonah again.

Jonah knew she wanted him involved in her group, but he wasn't ready for something like that. Besides, Mike would make a better Upstander, he thought. "I think I'll go see what Robert's doing."

He waved to Tamara and hurried toward the atrium. Jonah paused inside the open space and glanced up at Aunt Imma's sphere. He couldn't believe that the Protector's Ring floated above his head, in plain sight, and none of the people walking by had any clue about any of these things.

He shook his head and continued on into the West wing. The library's transformation surprised Jonah. The bookshelves remained in place, but all the chairs and study carols were stacked along the back wall. Movable partitions stood in the space now, and all of them were covered with hundreds of pieces of art and photos.

Robert stood among other kids, talking about his own pieces. As Jonah approached, he saw a big blue first place ribbon on a stark watercolor piece. Jonah lingered, impressed with how confident Robert sounded when dealing with art and computers.

Soon, the press of people entering this section became too much, so he waved goodbye to Robert and went back to the atrium. He received a warning buzz in his head just as he spotted Deyanira standing in the center of the atrium, gazing up at the Halliwell Sphere. Her bright red hair stood out in the sunlight and in stark contrast to her black pants and shirt.

Even though Jonah stopped, she must have sensed his presence because she turned to look directly at him. Would she try something around all these people, Jonah wondered? Deyanira's attention was drawn to the magician, who had just entered the atrium. Even Jonah could sense power in her.

Deyanira flicked her hand. At first, Jonah thought that had been a fluke until the cables holding two of the heavy banners snapped. As they began to fall, the magician raised her own hand and the banners stopped in mid-air. Jonah doubted that anyone milling around realized the woman had just saved them from getting hurt.

Using the diversion as cover, Deyanira stalked through the front doors. Jonah caught the magician's eyes and the woman gave him a slight shake of her head. He only took a second to decide to follow Deyanira anyway. He couldn't let the sorceress get away.

Jonah ran outside and caught a glimpse of her slipping through the crowd and hurried to catch up. She weaved toward the row of radio trucks along the edge of the carnival and dodged around the front of a radio station van. Her movement startled a heavyset employee sitting beside the vehicle.

"Hey! You can't jump the rope!" He struggled to his feet to follow.

The large speakers mounted on the truck sparked and popped. The van's music broadcast filled with electronic squealing, causing everyone nearby to cover their ears. Technicians rushed over to help, and Jonah slipped by them, unnoticed.

Deyanira headed toward the trees behind the center, and he followed. Just as she entered the cover of the trees, she waved her hand, creating a vortex. Instead of entering, she whirled to face him.

The move shocked Jonah and he skidded to a stop. "I know who you are."

"You've been talking to Marcus."

"I won't let you have the ring."

"You're so much like your father." She stepped toward Jonah, a curious look in her eyes. A second later, her demeanor changed. Moving faster than Jonah could imagine, her right hand blurred into motion as she cast a spell, right at him.

Pain from his Death Sense threatened to split his skull at the same time something slammed into Jonah from behind, taking him down. He expected the spell to fly past. Instead, it splashed against an invisible barrier right where his head would have been if he hadn't been tackled. The sudden lessening of his Death Sense buzz let Jonah know that Deyanira must have slipped through the vortex.

Someone hauled him to his feet and turned him around. Kevin stood there, looking serious. The Native American magician stood behind him, her hand still raised as if expecting Deyanira to reappear and attack again.

Jonah pointed at her, but whispered to Kevin, "Is… is she a Mage?"

Kevin nodded while giving him the once over. "That was stupid to chase Deyanira by yourself."

"She was getting away."

"So?" Kevin shrugged. "She didn't have the ring."

Jonah wanted to argue *so what* when something else occurred to him. "Why didn't she try to take it?"

"Deyanira couldn't," the Mage answered. She had a calm, serious voice. "I put a protective ward around your aunt's sculpture."

Jonah thought back to image of Deyanira staring at the sculpture. "Can she get through?"

"Not without a lot of power and alerting us." The woman crossed her arms, watching him.

For a moment, he thought she was angry with him for not offering to help back in the atrium and his ears reddened. "I'm sorry about the banners."

"You didn't break the cables and I was able to fix it without the mortals noticing anything."

Unable to decipher the woman's neutral expression, Jonah had no choice but to accept her words.

"Come on," Kevin said. He led the way back to the recreation center and inside, where they found Wick.

"Hey, Padawan."

Jonah hurried over to his friend. "Wick, she was here."

"Who?"

"Deyanira. I caught her looking at the sphere."

"Well, I doubt she could get it. There's a ward protecting the sculpture. I can sense it." Wick peeked over Jonah's shoulder, noticing the Mage for the first time. "You did it?" She nodded. "Whoa. Can we talk? Let's grab a table in the café."

Although the Summer's End had plenty of food vendors, the café tables were available to Festival goers if they needed to rest—or a table to sit at while they ate. Wick found a table close to the atrium and begin to ask the Mage all kinds of questions. The woman's cool expression softened into genuine interest as Wick talked.

After fifteen minutes, Jonah couldn't sit still anymore and hopped to his feet.

Kevin rose from his chair. "Where're you going?"

"I can't wait around."

"It won't do you any good getting all worked up." Kevin lowered his voice. "She's gone for now. The ring is safe."

Jonah flopped down in his chair and checked the time.

Kevin waved to get his attention. "This is Mage Trueblood, by the way."

The woman nodded to Jonah. "You shouldn't concern yourself. I'll check the ring on a regular basis."

"You're not gonna stay?"

"We have to report back to Marcus," Kevin answered.

"And I know my ward will alert me if Deyanira tries anything."

Wick patted Jonah on the shoulder. "Concentrate on the duel, Padawan."

Jonah tried, but that didn't help at all. In addition to worrying about Deyanira, his anxiety about the challenge also grew. After all that he'd been through, a duel with Brandon should be easy. Yet Jonah's stomach had developed a case of the butterflies by the time Robert and Lynn were ready to leave.

CHAPTER THIRTY-FIVE
THE DUEL

Jonah's butterflies turned into full-blown dismay when they arrived at the practice field. All of the club members turned out, along with extra kids Jonah didn't know. Lynn wore an *I told you* so expression on her face. Jonah tried to ignore her as he took out his practice blades and began warming up.

As duel time drew near, Lynn began muttering last-minute instructions to Jonah, which made him even more nervous. Wick came over and leaned close, speaking in a perfect Yoda voice. "Mind what you have learned. Save you it will."

"Wick!" Lynn punched him on the arm. "You're not helping!"

Jonah disagreed as he, Wick, and Robert all laughed. Lynn crossed her arms and muttered, "Geeks." Jonah didn't care. He needed to let off the tension.

Five minutes before six o'clock, Brandon, Drew, and Antwan arrived. Brandon had a large carry bag slung over his shoulder. He unzipped it, pulled out his own short blades, and strutted around, taking half-hearted swings and lunges.

Jonah fingered the edges of his practice blades as he watched. Brandon's blades looked sharp, whereas his tips and edges were blunt so as not to puncture clothes; however they could still deliver pain. Lynn had proven that more than once in practice.

At six, a hush fell over everyone. The sun hung low enough in the sky for the surrounding trees to cast shadows over the duel area. Jonah welcomed the shade. It would still be plenty hot during the challenge.

Alex broke away from the crowd and stepped into the center of the clearing. "If you're not here to see a practice duel, you're in the wrong place." He paused as a few kids laughed. "The duelers will use practice blades and the match will continue until someone submits." Alex glanced at Jonah and then Brandon. "Are you ready?"

Jonah moved immediately into the center of the clearing and stood in a ready stance. Brandon took his time entering. When he did, both boys bowed to Alex and then to each other. Despite the formal curtesy shown, Jonah's Death Sense buzzed at a continued low level.

His thoughts turned to Deyanira, and his anxiety about getting the ring increased. Maybe he could end this before it started.

"Brandon. You don't have to do this."

"Screw you, Jonah. You're not backing out."

"I just wanted to give you a chance to run home."

Brandon bared his teeth and nodded. Jonah returned the gesture. Both boys dropped into position. Brandon's blades were more or less in the correct positions as he bounced on his feet, ready to go. Jonah snorted; Lynn would crack his arms if she caught them like that.

Alex nodded to each boy, blew his whistle, and quickly moved back as they lunged.

Brandon pressed the attack, swinging his blades at Jonah's forearms and then his legs, forcing Jonah to defend himself repeatedly. He lost precious ground, but held the blades as Lynn had taught him, knocking each attack away. Brandon continued to concentrate on Jonah's legs. As soon as Jonah settled into the repetitive defensive moves, Brandon switched up. He whacked Jonah hard against the head with the butt of his blade. Jonah stumbled back, slightly dazed.

Brandon shot his friends a big smile. The crowd murmured because club members never openly gloated. Jonah prepared himself and waited as Brandon returned to the center.

At Alex's signal, they lunged. Brandon came on strong again, but Jonah stood his ground this time. When Brandon brought his blades around from either side, Jonah reared up and blocked each one. Then he reversed his own grip and struck out at Brandon, forcing the boy on the defensive. That's when Jonah noticed it: Brandon didn't bother to bring his blades back to protect his forearms. That gave him an idea.

When they lunged at each other for a third time, Jonah went in with both blades attacking Brandon's right side. As expected, Brandon moved to block that side, using both blades in a forward grip. In a flash, Jonah reversed the angle of his attack and struck Brandon's unprotected left side, scoring painful hits on the boy's left forearm. Brandon's face twisted into equal parts surprise and pain as he spun away from Jonah.

For a brief moment, Brandon left his back exposed, and Jonah considered taking advantage of it. The cheers of the practice club members registered and, remembering his training, Jonah dropped into the ready position. Brandon took his time coming back to the center. The smug look on his face was gone as he eyed Jonah.

Brandon pointed a blade at him and sneered. Without waiting for Alex's signal, he attacked. Jonah was ready, and he blocked Brandon even better than before. After a particularly messy flurry of thrusts that were easily countered, Jonah began to feel confident that he would win this duel. That proved to be a mistake, as he didn't account for Brandon's frustration. The boy's added height and longer arms allowed him to move in and elbow Jonah in the face.

Jonah heard, and felt, the sickening crunch a moment before pain exploded across his face. He fell hard to the ground, clutching his nose, blood running freely down his chin and onto his chest. He sucked in a startled, painful breath as the crowd roared its disapproval.

Robert and Wick's yells were the loudest among the shouts. When Brandon turned to face him, Jonah knew the boy was gonna ask him to yield. He struggled to his feet again, wiped his nose, and stared at the scarlet smear across the back of his hand.

The anger rose inside Jonah, but then his gaze fell on Lynn. Unlike the others, she remained quiet, her arms crossed, watching him. She hadn't run out to see if he was okay. This was his fight, and she couldn't help. No one could. He had to overcome Brandon's tactics on his own. Jonah sucked in a painful breath, causing his nose to throb.

Remembering her warning, he clamped down on the anger. As he dropped into his stance again, Jonah noticed something about Brandon, something he wouldn't have seen if he had allowed the anger to get the better of him.

Even though Brandon strutted back and forth, sneering at him, the boy breathed hard and took his time getting ready.

So Brandon cheats when he gets tired. It's time to change things up.

Jonah moved first, the tactic throwing Brandon off balance as he kept attacking the boy's arms and legs. He caught one of Brandon's blades and twisted it painfully from his grip. However, the move put Jonah too close. Brandon hit Jonah's arm with his own and then caught Jonah with an upward elbow in the stomach.

The force of it lifted Jonah off his feet and he toppled to the ground, clutching his stomach. The crowd booed and hissed. Fearful that Brandon would attack him while down, Jonah grabbed his blades and stumbled away from where he thought Brandon was. He didn't have to worry because Brandon stalked over to his bag, shaking his injured hand. Antwan grabbed Brandon's arm, and they argued. When Brandon yanked his arm free, he held a real sword.

An abrupt silence spread through the crowd.

Alex blew his whistle and hurried over to Brandon. "You can't use real weapons."

Many in the crowd voiced agreement. Jonah ignored the real sword in Brandon's hand and focused on Antwan. The boy didn't have his usual sneer on his face anymore. In fact, Antwan looked worried. His eyes met Jonah's for a moment. Then Antwan gave a slight shake of his head and pulled Drew back. Brandon didn't even notice the subtle distance his friends were putting around him.

Lynn called out from her spot beside Robert and Wick, "Practice weapons only, Brandon. You've cheated enough already."

Once again, more than one person offered agreement. Brandon ignored them all as he took a few practice swipes with the sword. Then he faced Lynn. "We didn't have that in writing. I won't cut him. I promise."

"No."

Lynn broke away from the crowd and marched over to stand beside Jonah. "Don't fall for it, Jonah." She tightened and loosened her fists.

Jonah knew his cousin wanted to teach Brandon a lesson. He touched her arm to get her attention. He sucked in a painful breath, his swollen nose making it harder to breathe. "It's cool, Lynn."

She opened her mouth to protest, and Jonah tapped his forehead. "I'd know if he really threatened me." Lynn realized what he meant, but she folded her arms and didn't move. "Let me use them." Jonah held out his hand. "I know you have the real blades. Please."

Lynn glanced at the blood covering the front of his shirt and the smear of red on his open palm. Then she raised her gaze to Brandon, huffed, and marched back to her bag. Jonah noticed that she activated the blades inside the bag just before taking them out.

She held out the blades, hilts first. "You better be right."

Alex saw her and stomped over. "Lynn, you can't be serious."

"It's up to Jonah."

"But…"

Lynn whirled on him, her braids whipping around with her. She grabbed Alex by the hand holding the whistle and pulled him off to stand among the crowd. Jonah noticed Mike Littleton watching him with wide eyes. In fact, everyone in the crowd now watched him.

He pushed that out of his mind as he tested the blades. They felt lighter than the practice ones. He tried a move he'd seen the older kids do and twirled the blades. They seemed to hum and move of their own accord as they stopped in position. He could feel the warm metal against his skin.

Brandon stood in the center of the clearing with the sword held loosely in his right hand. Jonah moved forward, watching Brandon's stance. He could tell when the boy would move. Again, he decided to change things. As soon as he saw Brandon's leg tense, Jonah began to circle. Brandon's face showed momentary surprise as he moved to keep Jonah away.

Jonah grinned, and Brandon attacked. Jonah's hands moved swiftly into place as he blocked Brandon's sword jabs. When Brandon brought the sword around in a low arc toward his right leg, Jonah reversed his blade to block it.

Letting go of his semi-controlled attacks, Brandon just came at him. Jonah blocked every swipe, thrust, and poke of the sword. He anticipated Brandon's moves, and that made the boy more frustrated.

When Brandon pulled back, then rushed forward with an overhead strike, Jonah brought his crossed blades up and blocked the blow. He twisted and forced Brandon's sword off and down to one side. Jonah followed up by flipping one of his blades around and banging Brandon hard on the forehead. The boy stumbled back and fell on his butt, his face twisted in fury.

The crowd cheered, but Jonah didn't smile or acknowledge them. He simply dropped into the ready stance. Brandon didn't bother to ready himself. He grabbed the sword and charged as soon as he got up, and Jonah easily parried a low swing at his legs. Reversing a blade, Jonah scored a solid hit to Brandon's upper arm and the other to the side of his head. Brandon screamed in rage, on the verge of tears, and charged again. Jonah moved to parry when Brandon suddenly reared back and tried to ram him with the sword.

Jonah knew what to do. As Brandon came forward, he caught the sword at waist height with both of his own blades. He immediately applied a little twist and his blades locked around the sword like a vise. With a twist of his upper body, Jonah snapped the weapon in two.

He reversed his twisting motion and landed the hilts of both blades on Brandon's forehead, watching in satisfaction as the boy fell to the ground. The broken sword flew out of his hand.

In one smooth motion, Jonah reversed his blades again, leaned over Brandon, and put the point of the right blade against his neck, just below the Adam's apple.

"Submit." When Brandon hesitated, Jonah applied a little pressure.

"Okay! I submit!"

Jonah stood and whirled the blades so fast, they appeared as a bright blur. When he stopped, the blades were in perfect position. He slipped both into his left hand. It was only then that he registered the crowd had erupted in applause and wild cheering. Robert, Lynn, and Wick broke away from the throng and rushed up to him. Lynn hugged him while Robert and Wick patted him on the back.

"How did you do that, Jonah?" Lynn sounded amazed. "I never taught you all those moves."

"I just knew when I held them," Jonah said in a low voice. He handed the blades to Lynn.

She gasped. "They're hot!"

Robert gave her a funny look. "He just used them. It has to be natural body heat." Lynn held the blade out and Robert touched it. He pulled his hand back. "Wow." They both looked at Jonah.

Wick reached out and touched the blades. "It's power."

Jonah heard someone yell his name. A split second later, Mike collided with him, giving Jonah a playful punch on the arm.

"That was so scary," he gushed. "But, oh my God, you were great!"

"Thanks," Jonah stammered. "I didn't think you would come to a duel."

"You stood up to Brandon." Mike gave an embarrassed smile. "I couldn't skip that."

Jonah's Death Sense gave a little twitch. He turned and saw Brandon glaring at him as Antwan helped him to his feet. Brandon shrugged off the help and yelled at Jonah, "Freak!"

Unlike all the other times, admirers surrounded Jonah now. That simple fact finally registered on Brandon. He looked nervously around at the crowd, then pushed past his friends toward his bike.

Lynn thumped Jonah on the shoulder. "He's just a bad loser. Don't worry about him."

Jonah wasn't worried about Brandon. He'd just beat him, and right now, he was on top of the world.

CHAPTER THIRTY-SIX
BUSTED

Jonah didn't like waiting, and it proved to be sheer torture, as expected. His nose had healed by the next morning, but it was still a bit swollen. He hid out in his room until Aunt Imma headed off to work, then dressed and hopped on his bike and rode to the center.

Vendors and county volunteers dismantled the booths and rides while center personnel cleaned up the surrounding area. Robert and Lynn were among the volunteers helping out. Jonah rode past the recreation center several times.

When Lynn caught him on his eighth trip around the parking lot, she recruited him, putting his nervous energy to better use. Every chance he got, Jonah would slip into the atrium to make sure his aunt's sculpture was still there. So far, he hadn't seen Mage Trueblood, but Deyanira never appeared again, either.

They came home that evening exhausted from the work and ate dinner in a hurry. Claiming they wanted to go to bed early, Jonah, Robert, and Lynn all went off to their rooms. Jonah was about to close his bedroom door when someone knocked.

Lynn poked her head in and whispered, "Black shorts, shirts, and sneakers. Got that covered?"

"Yeah."

"I suggest you get a few hours' sleep."

"Lynn? You think we should ask the Mage?"

Lynn stepped inside the room. "We thought about that, but do you know how to contact her or Kevin?"

"No. And if I call Marcus, he'll tell us to stay out of it."

"Then it's settled. Wick's sure he can take down the ward."

"I bet Deyanira can do the same thing."

"That's why we need to get there first. Are you having doubts? It was your idea."

"I know. I'm in." Jonah sat down on the edge of his bed. "If Trueblood is right, they'll come as soon as Wick tries anything. My godfather's gonna be pissed."

Lynn twisted a finger in one of her braids as she gazed out the window. "We'll deal with that when it happens. At least we'll know about the ring." She opened the door. "See you in a few."

As soon as Lynn closed the door, Jonah pulled a bag from underneath his bed, took out his clothes, and quickly changed. Then he lay down, never expecting to sleep, yet the next thing he knew, Lynn crouched over him in his darkened room.

"Wake up, sleepyhead."

Jonah sat up. "Sorry." He rubbed his eyes and touched his nose, noting that it felt normal after the short sleep. Kevin was right. Resting did help the healing process. Jonah wondered about the Fallen Reaper as he shuffled out of the room behind Lynn. He wished that Kevin was here with them. At least the young Fallen Reaper had been trained to fight. They didn't want to face Deyanira, just beat her to the ring. But things seldom worked out as planned.

Robert waited by the kitchen door with a black backpack on. Another sat on the floor.

Lynn slipped that one on, caught Jonah's curious expression, and said, "Robert has his computer gear and I have my blades and a few things we might need."

Jonah nodded and glanced at the time on the game console; twenty minutes 'til midnight. They grabbed their bikes out of the shed and met Wick at the end of the street.

Riding through the neighborhoods this late at night was a little surreal. The only sounds Jonah could hear were the hum of their tires against the street top. Without warning, a shiver went down his spine as he recalled the Grim Hound chasing him through these very streets. Jonah shook off the memory and concentrated on the ring.

Everyone seemed charged with nervousness. Or was it excitement, Jonah wondered. He found it interesting that they were able to take every hill without slowing down.

When they reached the center, Jonah paused by the bike rack.

"What are you doing?" Lynn called out as she rode by. "We can't park our bikes out front."

Robert stopped beside him. "We're gonna lock them up on the other side of the tennis courts. That way, a security patrol won't see them."

As Jonah followed his cousins around to the far side of the tennis court, he agreed that it made sense. They were furthest from the main building, and the bikes would be invisible in the shadows.

Once they were done with that, Lynn and Robert led the way to a gray side door. Wick kept an eye on the main road while Robert positioned himself.

Lynn took out a key. "You ready?"

Robert nodded.

Jonah felt the change in air pressure right before Kevin appeared. He held onto Trueblood's arm, giving her a ride.

Lynn paused with the key ready to unlock the door, her mouth hanging open. Robert and Wick looked just as stunned.

Kevin crossed his arms, ignoring the others while glaring at Jonah. "What are you doing?"

Jonah's moment of shock and then embarrassment over getting caught evaporated. "We're gonna prove the Protector's Ring is inside."

Trueblood stepped forward. "How were you planning to get around my ward?"

"I planned to short it out with my shield bracelets," Wick answered.

Trueblood whirled to him, her face showing surprise. "You have shield bracelets?"

"Yeah," Wick hunched his shoulders. "I made them." He held out his right arm toward Trueblood.

"That's impressive." The woman inspected the bracelet, running her fingers over the pieces of polished wood. She gazed into Wick's face. "Why aren't you in training to be a full Mage?"

Wick gaped at the woman until Lynn cleared her throat.

"I'm glad you're impressed." She motioned to the door. "Move out of the way, or you could just take the ward down for us."

"We have to know," Jonah added. He faced Kevin. "My parents died because of the ring."

Kevin didn't answer for a long moment. "Fine. I'll take you and Trueblood inside and--"

Everyone spoke at the same time. Lynn succeeded in voicing her concern the loudest. "You don't know the code and will set off the alarm."

"Tell us the code."

Lynn crossed her arms, refusing to give the information to Kevin. Robert and Wick stood with her. After a moment, Jonah joined them.

"We go inside, too," Lynn said. She made a point of holding up her watch. "Time's wasting. Deyanira could be here any minute."

Kevin exchanged a quick glance with Trueblood before stepping away from the door. Lynn unlocked it and opened it wide so Robert could duck inside. She held up her hand when Jonah started to follow.

"Robert has to turn off the alarm at the other end of the hall, and he only has thirty seconds to reach it."

The door opened a minute later and Robert stuck his head out. "All done."

Trueblood slipped inside the building first. Kevin motioned Jonah next, but he held back, staring at his cousins.

"How did you get the key and code?" Jonah asked Lynn.

"A while ago," Lynn whispered. "Wick swiped the director's keys." She held up the key so it reflected in the weak security light over the door. "We made a copy and use it sometimes when we have a tight deadline."

"And I pulled the code from the director's computer about a month ago." Robert gave him a smug grin. "She kept a whole list of codes on there."

Lynn crossed her arms. "Anything else you want to know, Jonah?"

"No, ma'am."

Lynn balled a fist and held it under Jonah's chin, causing Wick to laugh.

Robert gave his sister a mock bow. "After you, ma'am."

Kevin snorted. "You guys are such geeks."

Lynn gave him an appraising stare as she pushed Robert and Jonah ahead of her and into the darkened building.

CHAPTER THIRTY-SEVEN
HALLIWELL'S SPHERE

Jonah watched as Lynn and Wick positioned a fifteen-foot ladder under Aunt Imma's art piece. Robert stood off to the side, clutching his archive box in his hands. Trueblood stood in the entrance to the East wing. Kevin covered the West wing entrance, his Reaper blades activated.

Wick got everyone's attention by tapping on the ladder. "Who wants to go?"

Everyone turned to Jonah. He gulped and gripped the ladder while Lynn and Wick positioned themselves to either side to hold it in place.

When Jonah reached the top, he paused to stare at the sphere. Recessed lighting gave the atrium a soft nighttime illumination, and pale blue moonlight shone through the skylights. The angled display lights caused many of the rings to glitter. Even with that, Jonah knew it wasn't enough.

He glanced down at Lynn. "I'll need a light."

Lynn took a flashlight out of her backpack and tossed it up to him. Jonah flicked it on and tilted the light so just a little of it touched the rings. And then he heard a growl. Jonah froze in place and listened.

Robert noticed his hesitation first. "What's wrong, little cousin?"

Jonah peered into the darkened café below and the corridors leading off the atrium. He met Kevin's gaze. "Did you hear that?"

The Fallen Reaper nodded and started to prowl back and forth, his eyes darting everywhere. Robert clutched the archive box to his chest, staring around him. Lynn moved away from the ladder to stand at the entrance to the café.

Finally, she came back to the ladder and shook her head. "I don't hear anything."

Wick gulped. "I don't either, but it's the Witching Hour. Midnight."

"Wick. This is creepy enough." She glanced at Jonah. "Keep going."

Jonah moved the light back and forth over the rings. "It's gonna take forever."

"I have an idea." Wick glanced at Lynn before he continued. "Do you think you can sense the ring?" Everyone, including Jonah, stared at Wick. "Your father owned it for a time, right?"

"Sometimes," Trueblood said, "that creates a connection with an object. The young Mage has a point."

Lynn looked around the atrium again. "Well, do something. We're wasting time."

Jonah closed his eyes and thought about his dad wearing the ring. He pictured it clearly in his mind. And then he thought of all the power and good the ring represented.

Jonah held on to those images and concentrated. He sensed something, like a pulsing heartbeat.

Gasps came from below him. When Jonah opened his eyes, he understood why. A single ring, high on the opposite side of the sphere, glowed with a pulsing amber light.

"You did it!" Lynn thumped the ladder.

"Very cool." Wick smiled up Jonah, but he wasn't listening. The pulsing of the ring echoed his racing heartbeat. He deliberately calmed himself, and the ring's pulsing slowed to match.

"Jonah?" Lynn peered up at him. "Should we move the ladder?"

"Huh—oh. Yeah." Jonah climbed down.

"Maybe I should get it," Lynn offered after they repositioned the ladder. She placed a foot on the bottom step.

Wick stopped her. "I think Jonah should be the one to do it."

Jonah glanced up at the pulsing ring and thought Lynn might have a point. He would have to really stretch; the ring was near the top of the sphere.

I made the ring glow, not Lynn. The pulses matched my heartbeat. I should be the one to get it.

Wick gave him an encouraging tap on the shoulder, and Jonah climbed the ladder again.

Once he reached the top, he stretched out a hand. As his fingers brushed against the ring, it pulsed brighter. A surge of satisfaction shot through him. At long last, after the attempt on his life and the half-truths, he had found the Protector's Ring. Jonah stretched further.

As soon as he'd enclosed the ring in his fist, the atrium skylights exploded inward and two huge Grim Hounds crashed through. They barreled straight at Jonah from two directions, leaving him no time to move out of the way.

I need a shield.

The thought was instant, and the ring pulsed brighter as a sharp prickling sensation rolled up Jonah's arm and away from his body. A pale blue circle of distortion snapped into existence around him a split second before the Grim Hounds hit.

The barrier flared where the creatures struck it and deflected them in opposite directions. One smacked into the far wall and slid to the ground. The other tumbled into the hanging tennis racket sculpture, causing rackets to explode in all directions.

Jonah grabbed onto the sphere to keep from falling to the floor. His shoelace got tangled in the top step of the ladder, which yanked hard on his leg as it toppled sideways. Jonah's hands slipped along the sphere's metal rods for a few terrifying seconds. He managed to grab onto the ends where the rings were welded in place, groaning in pain as they cut into his palms. "Help!"

But no one could help him at the moment. Wick held his right arm up, and Lynn and Robert huddled beside him. Broken glass smashed against Wick's own activated shield, falling in a circle around them.

Kevin and Trueblood were busy because a vortex formed just inside the front doors. Four men in grey tunics and with glowing white eyes stormed out of the opening. Each carried a jet-black scythe. Kevin blurred into motion, snatched a side table, and hurled it across the atrium into the new arrivals. Trueblood began casting spells at the men. These actions served to hold the attackers away from Jonah and his cousins.

One of the Grim Hounds had rolled to its feet and ran toward the stairs, getting in position to jump on the sphere from the second floor landing. "Help!" Jonah shouted.

Robert grabbed the ladder and stood it under him. Wick took a fistful of glittery powder from a small brown sack and blew on it. A huge cloud of sparkly silvery dust blossomed into the air. The second Grim Hound, which had slammed into the far wall, ran straight through it.

The dust acted like metal drawn to a magnet as it attached itself to the hound's body. The creature stumbled and rolled around, knocking café tables and chairs in every direction. After a few frenzied moments, it gave up trying to dislodge the dust. Its claws slid on the smooth marble as it regained its feet and charged for the stairway.

By that time, Lynn stood in its path, her silver blades in hand. She whirled and struck the now-visible Grim Hound across its snout. It growled furiously, baring its doubled row of teeth as it scrambled backward.

Lynn tossed her braids over her shoulder. "Thanks, Wick, but I kind of wish I couldn't see it."

Wick didn't answer because he and Robert stared in shock at a real Grim Hound.

"Get down." Kevin's shout stirred the boys into action. The Fallen Reaper charged past them to take on more attackers, who came out of a new vortex near the West entrance.

Jonah lowered his weight onto the ladder and sucked in a breath as his injured hands gripped the top. He watched, amazed at Kevin's skills. But he only had a second to catch his breath before the first Grim Hound launched itself from the second floor landing.

Jonah gazed at it in morbid fascination as the creature sailed through the air, hit the sphere and scrambled for a hold. The impact snapped two of the holding cables, allowing the entire sphere to swing away.

Jonah sprang into motion and made it halfway down the ladder before the sphere swung back toward him. The Grim Hound slipped, its hindquarters smacking into the top of the ladder, sending it spinning in one direction and Jonah in the other. He landed on the polished marble floor and grunted as pain blossomed along his shoulder and arm.

Wick overcame his shock and ran to help. "Lucky you were halfway down."

"Yeah, just great."

A snapping sound came from above as the Grim Hound tried to claw its way around to the still-glowing ring.

Oh no! He had created a beacon for the creature to follow.

The mounting plates couldn't support the added weight and the remaining cables tore themselves from the ceiling. The entire sphere fell like a meteor and hit with a huge, ground-shaking bang.

Hundreds of pieces of sphere, rings, and metal rods flew everywhere. Several pieces of debris nicked Jonah's arms as he shielded his head from the worst of it. Silence rolled across the atrium, and only Kevin moved. He turned to kill the Grim Hound.

As he lunged for it, a bright sphere appeared in front of him. He impacted and bounced back, dazed. A tall man with dark curly hair, black tunic, and pants had stepped out of another vortex, his thin fingers raised like claws. "Don't touch Deyanira's pets." His mouth curved into a devilish grin. He waved his hands to cast another spell at Kevin. Trueblood dodged between them, deflecting the attack.

She stood straight, looking dignified and unruffled. "I'll deal with him." And she did, casting a series of spells at the sorcerer. His smile faded as he had to defend himself. They circled around each other, but Trueblood managed to maneuver the sorcerer into the West wing. Their continued fight shook the floors.

Jonah had never seen anything like it. Even the silvery-dust-covered Grim Hound paused in its attempts to reach the stairs. Kevin, though, was engaged again with another set of attackers who had followed the sorcerer through the vortex.

Robert made use of the general confusion to edge around the distracted silvery-dust-covered Grim Hound to crouch near a tangle of parts. He put something in the archive box, and the locks clicked shut.

The second Grim Hound turned at the sound and stepped toward Robert. Lynn jumped between them and nicked the Grim Hound across the jaw with a blade. The creature growled in pain as the cut sparked.

"Stay behind me, Robert."

The Grim Hound growled in frustration but didn't approach her. Jonah sensed and understood its basic desire. It needed that ring or Deyanira would punish it.

Robert took a step toward the stairs, drawing Lynn's attention. "Don't move!"

"We can't stay here all night, Lynn." Robert held up the box. "I want to put this in the safe. We drew protective sigils on it. The Grim Hound won't be able to touch it."

Lynn huffed. "Fine. You stay right behind me."

They edged toward the stairs together, with Lynn carefully keeping her body between the Grim Hound and Robert at all times, her blades ready. When they reached the foot of the stairs, Robert sprinted up them. The Grim Hound let out a fierce snarl and Lynn poked it on the nose, forcing it back.

Robert and Wick's planning impressed Jonah. It also helped that Lynn had real Reaper blades, which could hurt anything supernatural, including Grim Hounds. Something would have to give soon; Jonah could sense it. He opened his mouth to warn Lynn when the Grim Hound crouched and leapt.

It soared over Lynn's head and grabbed hold of the second floor railing, which sagged under the weight. Jonah prayed the creature might crash back down to the atrium. Instead, the Grim Hound managed to pull itself onto the landing. Lynn screamed in frustration as she ran up the stairs.

The Grim Hound wasted no time in smashing through the door to the attic and bounded in after Robert.

CHAPTER THIRTY-EIGHT
THROUGH THE VORTEX

Lynn reached the broken attic door and charged inside. Knowing he'd never get up the stairs in time, Jonah gripped Wick's shoulder and phased.

When they reappeared in the attic, Wick stumbled away, rubbing his arms. "Whoa! That's wicked, dude."

Jonah shook off the slight dizziness and scanned the attic. His jaw dropped. Lynn had the Grim Hound backed into the office section of the attic amidst destroyed computers and overturned desks.

Jonah couldn't understand her actions until he heard a moan. Looking up, he saw Robert holding onto a rafter over the club area. He still held the archive box, even though his arm dripped blood onto the ground. "Finish it, Lynn."

The sounds of heavy thumps drew closer. Jonah's Death Sense screamed just before the second Grim Hound bounded into view. It bulldozed Wick in the back and sent him flying into Lynn. Before Jonah could dodge to the side, the creature knocked him into the wall.

Jonah slid to the floor and watched in horror as the Grim Hound leapt up and swatted at Robert with a massive paw.

His cousin yelled, dropped from the rafter, and landed on the old sofa.

The archive box fell right in front of the Grim Hound and was scooped up in its powerful jaws. The silver Grim Hound leapt over Wick and Lynn and tried to help its mate tear the box apart. The creatures acted like real dogs fighting over a bone, but the archive box defied their efforts.

Robert moaned from the other side of the sofa. "Stop them. Get the box."

Lynn untangled herself from Wick and rose to her feet. The first Grim Hound, with the box in its jaws, turned and crashed through the attic window, ripping the blue curtain. The silver Grim Hound leapt out of the opening behind its mate.

Lynn ran to the window. "Dang it!"

Jonah stepped past a dazed Wick to look out the shattered window. "We have to go after them."

"Won't they phase?"

"They can't. They need a vortex, and Deyanira hasn't opened one yet." Jonah closed his eyes. "I can feel the ring." He ran for the staircase.

"Jonah, wait!" Lynn wrapped her arms around his shoulders just before he phased. A second later, they both reappeared beside their bikes. Lynn released him and stared at her arms. "That was freaky."

"You grabbed onto me," Jonah said, unlocking his bike. Lynn didn't hesitate to unlock her own and they set off after the Grim Hounds.

Speeding down the moonlit hillside on his bike seemed stupid and suicidal to Jonah, who couldn't see anything until he was on top of it. He sensed Lynn right behind him and knew she focused on the silver-dust-covered Grim Hound, which seemed to glow in the moonlight. He tried to weave faster through the trees and smacked his head against a low-hanging branch for his efforts.

The second Grim Hound had paused to bang the box against the trees in an attempt to get it open. That gave Jonah an idea. He concentrated on that Grim Hound, waiting for it to throw the box against the tree. When it did, he phased.

A moment later, he reappeared beside the Grim Hound and caught the box just as it bounced off the tree. The silver Grim Hound responded faster than he had expected. It raked a paw across his back, ripping his shirt and almost knocking him from the bike. Jonah screamed as he kept pedaling.

"Go, Jonah!" Lynn shouted from behind him. The Grim Hounds howled as if to answer her.

Seconds later, he burst into the creek-side clearing. Before he could adjust, his wheel hit one of the large rocks and sent him flying into the water. His bike tumbled across the creek and onto the opposite side. The archive box splashed into the water several feet away.

Jonah pushed himself toward the half-submerged box, but a huge, silver paw splashed down in the water right in front of him. Jonah stumbled back and fell on his butt.

The silver Grim Hound stepped toward him, ignoring the archive box. The red eyes glowed eerily bright in the dimness as it stalked closer. Jonah expected the creature to attack. When the Grim Hound hesitated, he waved to it.

"Hi, ugly."

The Grim Hound bared its double row of razor-sharp teeth. Jonah knew he should have been more frightened, but he wasn't. The creature appeared to recognize him, making Jonah wonder about the beast's intelligence.

"Sorry about the silver dust."

The Grim Hound cocked its head to the side like a real dog, as if watching something interesting. Or listening to something, Jonah thought. Was Deyanira communicating with it? She could do that. He'd seen that for himself in his strange dream-walk the first night here in Mount Vernon. Then Jonah sucked in a startled breath. *Could this be the same Grim Hound?*

He had thought Kevin decapitated that one. Or had the Fallen Reaper? As Jonah concentrated on the beast, he knew it wasn't the same one that had chased him from the Teen Center. This one felt different, familiar to him. It had to be the one from the dream-walk. Did riding along inside the hound's mind create a connection? Almost like the one with the ring?

The creature shook its head, let out a whine, and pawed at the ground. *It doesn't want to attack me.* Jonah suspected that Deyanira shouted her attack command into the creature's mind. As if confirming his thoughts, the Grim Hound focused on him, and Jonah inched backward. It crouched low, muscles tensed to spring, and Jonah's Death Sense spiked.

Lynn burst into the clearing, rolled off her bike, and came up slicing at the silver Grim Hound. The creature leapt aside, its huge paws dripping mud and water all over Jonah. Lynn positioned herself in front of him.

"Forget about me." Jonah smacked his hand down in the muddy water. "Get the box."

"Don't be crazy, Jonah." Lynn reached down and hauled him to his feet.

The first Grim Hound scooped up the box. Both creatures became rigid as statues, focusing on the same spot on the opposite side of the creek.

Jonah thought he could feel a change in the air. "Deyanira's opening a vortex."

A moment later, it blossomed into view, giving off its own shimmering, greenish light.

Lynn let out a frustrated scream. Her blades flashed as she rushed the Grim Hounds. The silver one leapt first through the vortex. The second, with the box in its jaws, turned to follow.

"No!" Jonah reached out for the ring with his mind. He could feel it, and he refused to let it go. The Second Grim Hound leapt for the vortex, then twisted around almost comically in midair. Its body disappeared in the vaporous opening of the vortex while its head stayed on this side. It tugged furiously at the box, trying to yank it through.

Jonah called on the ring. "You won't take it!" He could feel it pressing against the inside of the archive box, trying to come to him.

"Keep it there!" Lynn shouted to Jonah. She readied herself to strike the creature just as Jonah's Death Sense spiked.

"Lynn, look out!"

A ball of green supernatural fire spewed out of the vortex, singeing the Grim Hound. Lynn ducked as soon as Jonah warned her, but he hesitated and barely made it out of the way in time.

The fireball hit the stream, and a fog enveloped the clearing. Jonah lost sight of the Grim Hound, and his concentration faltered. He could feel it go as the Grim Hound took the ring through the vortex. "Dang it!"

The vortex snapped closed, plunging the area into moonlit dimness. Jonah slumped in muddy creek water. Lynn seemed to materialize out of the fog. Several braids were loose, giving her an impressive silhouette as she stood over him. Jonah glanced up at her. "I'm sorry I couldn't hold on longer."

"Don't apologize, Jonah. You were awesome. Sorry I took so long. I got tangled in vines."

Jonah lowered his head, feeling defeated. "Deyanira has the ring."

"That's not a problem."

"But we don't know where Deyanira is hiding."

"Yes we do. Robert searched the county records." At the mention of her brother, Lynn grew serious. "Let's head back."

As they turned, Jonah felt the change in the air that told of someone phasing. He tensed and Lynn drew her blades. Kevin stepped through the fading fog with Trueblood, Robert, and Wick trailing behind.

He searched the clearing before turning to Jonah. "What happened?"

"Deyanira opened a vortex and the Grim Hounds ran through."

Kevin nodded to Trueblood. "Can you detect it?"

The Mage, with one of her braids unraveling and hanging loose, stepped to the water's edge and raised a hand. "Yes, I can. She's opened so many that I can follow the magic back to the source."

Jonah was impressed with the quiet, powerful woman. As he caught Kevin's look, something occurred to him. "What took you so long?"

"We had to clean up and get out of the center. We couldn't leave injured mortals laying around."

"It's part of what we have to do," Trueblood explained, "to keep mortals oblivious to the supernatural world around them."

Robert, his arm bandaged with a torn piece of his shirt, stepped around Kevin.

Lynn gasped and rushed over to look over the bandage. "How is he, Wick?"

"He's okay. We turned on the alarm and then cleared out." Wick gave Trueblood an awed look. "She opened a vortex so Kevin could carry the… mortals through. It was wikid awesome." Jonah opened his mouth to ask a question, but

Wick beat him to the answer. "When someone sees that damage, they're going to wonder why the alarms didn't go off. We don't want any of the workers getting blamed for it not setting it."

Lynn finished checking Robert's arm. "Did you clean up everything?"

Robert surprised everyone when he answered, like he'd been turned on. "We wiped off the doors and security locks." Robert shook his head and continued in a numb voice, "The Summit is a total loss."

"It's time to get even, Robert," Lynn said. "Tell me you have Deyanira's location."

"Of course I do."

Lynn thumped Robert's backpack. "Do you have what you need?"

"I can deal with the door."

"And I can deal with the wards." Wick held up his arm to show more than one bracelet on it. He handed Lynn her backpack.

She slipped it on just as Kevin raised his hands.

"You guys aren't going anywhere."

Jonah had been expecting this from the moment Kevin and Trueblood showed up. "We have to go after the ring."

"Deyanira could have taken the ring to the Grim Reaper by now," Kevin countered.

"I don't think she'll go anywhere," Lynn cut in. "She has to make sure the ring is in the archive box."

Jonah's eyes widened. "She won't be able to open it." He glanced back at Robert, who smiled at him.

"Hey, I have good ideas sometimes."

Trueblood gave him a curious look. "You have a Seeker's box?"

Robert shrugged. "Jonah's parents gave it to me."

Jonah smiled at the Mage's astonished expression, but a problem presented itself. "Deyanira lives fifteen miles away. That's too far out for bikes."

"That won't be a problem." Kevin glanced at Trueblood. "Open a vortex."

"Are you sure? Maybe we should wait for the others."

"They're right. Deyanira won't take the box over, not until she's sure. This is the best chance."

"This is also dangerous, Kevin."

He shrugged. "I think Deyanira sent most of her people already. If not, well, I'll be with them. You bring Marcus when you can."

Jonah felt a wave of appreciation toward the older boy for standing with them. He was sure Marcus wouldn't agree if he were here. But at least now, they had a fighting chance to get the ring.

Trueblood raised her hand, her brow furrowed. Within seconds, a large bluish vortex opened. She raised an eyebrow to Kevin. "Be careful."

Kevin faced the group and activated his blades. They shone a pale blue in the vibrant light of the vortex. "I'll go first. Jonah, you come behind me. Wick and Robert come next. Lynn, you bring up the rear, blades ready."

Lynn slipped out her blades and activated them.

With a final glance at Trueblood, Kevin stepped into the vortex. Jonah's fear and excitement built to a crescendo as he moved forward. He didn't know what he'd face on the other end, but he felt ready with Kevin, his cousins, and Wick with him. Taking a deep breath, he stepped into the swirling mass of magical vapor and left the clearing behind.

CHAPTER THIRTY-NINE
STATUES, WARDS, AND STEEL

Going through a vortex was similar, yet different, to phasing. It was different because the trip took longer since you had to walk or run. However, the vapor was like a dense fog or mist touching every inch of your body, just like a phase.

Seconds after entering the vortex, Jonah exited onto a dirt road outside an old rusted gate directly in front of the house. Vapor from the vortex clung to him for a few moments, causing him to shiver.

Wick didn't seem bothered at all as he exited and leaned against the gate. "No lights on inside."

Lynn started through the gate, but Wick blocked her path. "Before we attempt the house, I have an idea." He turned to Jonah. "Can you still sense the ring?"

"I can't feel it."

"Maybe because it's in the box."

"More likely Deyanira has it in a warded location," Kevin concluded. He opened the gate. "Let's go."

The paint peeled off the walls of the deteriorated plantation house, exposing crumbling masonry underneath.

The shutters were rotten and hung at severe angles to most of the windows, which were all shattered.

But it wasn't the depressing appearance of the old house that made Jonah and the others edgy. Without warning, fear gripped Jonah's stomach. As they drew closer to the house, the fear became an intense urge to turn back.

"Do you feel that?" Wick's voice caused everyone to jump. He didn't seem to notice their reactions as he faced the eerie mansion. "Deyanira set up a deflection charm. It's designed to keep curious people away." Wick started to walk on, following Kevin but had to pause when he realized no one else followed. "Don't worry. It'll stop affecting us once we're inside."

Kevin snorted and continued toward the house, Wick right behind. Robert, Lynn, and Jonah traded dubious glances and kept going.

When they mounted the porch, Jonah followed Wick to one window while Lynn and Robert chose another. Each step was accompanied by a growing sense of dread. The urge to run away intensified. Wick scrambled through their window without any apparent problem, but Jonah required an act of pure will to place a leg through the opening. Voices kept shouting in his head that his parents were in trouble and would die. Above it all, he heard a cold, inhuman laugh. The fear morphed to dismay until a small voice spoke in his mind. *Don't be afraid.*

Halfway through the window, Jonah felt a jerk on his inside leg, as if someone had given him a yank. Suddenly, he was falling. As he made contact with something hard, the huge pressure lifted from his shoulders. He blinked and tried to focus as Wick helped him off the floor.

"See?" Wick patted him on the shoulder.

Jonah rubbed his sore arms and looked around. Kevin had a haunted expression and his shoulders shook as if he was in pain. When he saw Jonah watching, he stood tall and moved off, searching the room.

Lynn was across the room, gripping the window frame to keep from falling.

Robert held out a steadying hand to his sister. "Are you okay?"

"I'm fine. Just give me a minute." She wandered a short distance away.

Wick hurried over and tugged Robert in the opposite direction. Robert whirled on his friend. "First we find out about wards and now deflection charms?"

"I know, Bobby. Deyanira was a sorceress in her first life." Wick gave Jonah a troubled look. "We should be ready for more magic."

Robert threw his hands up as he looked around the decaying house. "Where to now?"

Lynn came up and leaned on her brother's shoulder. "Look for a door to the basement, genius. Right, Kevin?"

The Fallen Reaper motioned to a door down a narrow hallway. It showed signs of recent use. The dust on the floor in front of it had been swept away in a long curve. Several sets of footprints were visible, too.

Lynn eyed the door. "Do you sense anything, Wick?"

"No."

"What about you, Jonah?"

"I can't tell."

Kevin opened the door and grimaced when it creaked loudly in the silence. "Here goes." He took a breath and stepped into the darkened stairway.

Jonah felt like he was swallowed by the pitch darkness; the only sound was their footsteps. He thought they had descended three floors before they reached the bottom. Lynn entered a wide, torch-lit hallway with an arched ceiling and a broken stone floor. Jonah thought the dark recesses halfway down the hallway might be the entrances to side tunnels.

Lynn spoke from the back of the line. "Does any of this look familiar, Jonah?"

"No, it doesn't. There must be another stairway at the other end."

"Great," Kevin muttered. "Everybody stay alert." He started forward.

Jonah sensed the heightened tension around him, but nothing happened as they continued down the tunnel. Still, Jonah was certain that something was wrong, besides being in Deyanira's hidden tunnel.

Jonah tugged on Kevin's shirt as they reached the bottom of the next stairway. "This is the hallway I saw in the dream-walk."

Kevin nodded and looked over Jonah's head at Wick. "It's your turn to do your thing."

Wick raised his hand and took one step forward, and then another. After the third step, he paused. "Just as I thought. These wards are designed to stun, not kill."

Jonah inched his way forward until he stood beside Wick. "Can you get through them?"

Wick held out his wrist, showing Jonah the bracelets. "That's why I have these."

"But these wards are different from Trueblood's," Robert objected, directly behind Jonah.

"Calm yourself, Bobby. I'll be able to set them off."

Even Lynn tossed an unsure look over her shoulder before she went back to watching the stairway. "Isn't that dangerous?"

"There's only one way to find out."

Robert tried to step in front of his friend, but Wick pulled him away from the invisible ward.

"Whoa, dude. Don't get to close or you'll set it off. And you don't have a shield. I'll be all right." He looked at Jonah. "I think everyone should step back."

When Robert hesitated, Jonah tugged on his cousin's backpack to get him to move. Wick raised his hand to activate his shield. The telltale blue haze surrounded him, making the hairs on Jonah's arm rise. He shivered from anticipation or anxiety; he wasn't sure which.

When Wick stepped forward, a bolt of energy hit him. The air popped and sizzled. After a few more seconds, the fireworks abruptly died out. Wick lowered his arm and sniffed the air. "That one's down. I tripped it."

Jonah released a breath he hadn't realized he held. Wick's plan was like deliberately exploding mines to clear a path.

"Jonah, how many did you say there were?"

"Four."

Wick prepared himself and started the whole thing all over again. He set off two more wards in the same fashion as the first. Jonah noticed that each time, the boy's expression grew more concerned. Wick's arm begun to tremble, and the bracelet blackened and smoked.

Wick held up the bracelet afterward and inspected it. "It's about done. It may take one more."

He stepped forward and tripped the fourth ward. This time, his bracelet sparked and started to burn. Wick ripped it off and threw it to the ground before the ward completely dissipated. The remaining power zapped him, and he fell to his knees.

Robert didn't wait for the okay. He rushed forward and helped his buddy to his feet. Wick flashed him a lopsided grin. "I'm cool. Truth is, those bracelets lasted longer than I expected." He nodded toward the metal door. "Your turn, Bobby."

Wick reached out and Jonah's Death Sense spiked through his persistent headache. Before Jonah could open his mouth, Wick brushed his hand along the door. Jonah thought he saw a shocked expression on Wick's face a second before another ward went off with a loud bang.

Energy raced up and down Wick's arms and legs and even made his twists crackle with energy. He collapsed to the ground, shook violently for a few terrifying moments, and then didn't move.

Lynn and Robert screamed his name in unison and ran to his side. Lynn turned him over, pressed her ear against his chest, and let out a sigh of relief. "He's still breathing. Thank God."

Robert whirled on Jonah. "Why didn't you warn him?"

"I'm sorry, Robert."

Jonah looked at Lynn for help. She stepped forward, grabbed Robert's shoulder, and shook him. "Robert."

"What?" He rounded on his sister but Lynn didn't back off.

"Robert, you need to open the door. Wick told us the wards only stun. He'll be fine." Lynn leaned so close, their foreheads nearly touched. She looked directly into her twin brother's eyes. "I'll stay with him. You unlock the door. Okay?"

Robert nodded and stalked to the door without looking at Jonah.

"I'm sorry I couldn't warn him in time. My Death Sense is on overload."

Lynn pulled Jonah back and lowered her voice so Robert wouldn't hear. "He doesn't blame you." She glanced at her brother. "Is your Death Sense really that bad now?"

"I just have a huge buzz in my head and a blinding headache. I'm fighting to keep things straight."

"We better finish this and get out of here." Lynn knelt beside Wick.

Robert had his backpack off and his small laptop on the floor in front of him. He detached the door's colored keypad from the mounting and connected his computer to the exposed wires underneath.

"This may take a few minutes," Robert explained as he worked. "I have to find the combination while keeping the security system from issuing an alert." Robert typed on the small keyboard. Jonah peeked over his shoulder but couldn't understand the code that scrolled up the computer screen.

One of the lights on the dangling color keypad lit up.

"That's one. Five more lights to go." Robert glanced up at Jonah. "You didn't see the code in your dream?"

"The clerk moved too fast. I'm sorry."

"That's okay. I'll have this door opened in no time."

Jonah relaxed; his cousin didn't sound angry anymore. Talking about these things seemed to keep Robert from worrying about Wick.

Three more lights on the panel lit up. Robert frowned, speaking as he typed. "I'll have to stay here to keep the system from sounding the alarm."

Wick surprised everyone and mumbled something. Robert didn't miss a beat. "What did he say?"

Lynn lowered her ear to Wick's mouth which still moved. "It sounds like he's saying, 'Too late.'"

Robert glanced at her while his fingers flew over the laptop keys. "Oh, boy. I've heard him say that wards can be like security alarms. You set one off, and the person who made it gets a warning."

Lynn stood. "Then I should stay here, too. In case someone comes. Wick can't be moved until he's awake, anyway."

"But-" Jonah began but he stopped when the final two lights lit up. The lock mechanism in the door clicked and it swung open. Kevin pulled Jonah back and stood ready with his blades activated. Nothing happened. Clearly visible inside the chamber, Robert's archive box sat on the center pedestal, well lit and inviting.

"I don't like this," Kevin said. "It's a trap."

"At least Deyanira doesn't want to kill me." Jonah knew that wasn't totally true. Deyanira had commanded the silver Grim Hound to attack, he was sure of it. He kept that information to himself as he moved around Kevin to face the open metal door. As he did, they heard a distant growl from the direction of the stairs.

Lynn drew out her blades and positioned herself between the stairway and Wick. "You and Kevin should go, Jonah."

"No," Kevin said. "We should take care of whatever they send first, then we can check out the chamber."

Jonah agreed with Lynn. This was the reason they had come here, and he didn't want to stop now. The sudden spike of his Death Sense caused Jonah to wince. Before he could warn the others, a pair of hands gripped him from behind and yanked him into the chamber. The metal door slammed shut.

CHAPTER FORTY
THE PROTECTOR'S RING

Jonah experienced a moment of pure fear as he sprawled on the floor just inside the chamber. His reflexes were ready and waiting for the person to attack. Nothing happened. The room remained silent. He strained to see into the room's few shadows.

"Who's there?"

In answer, a shape moved, causing Jonah's heart to leap into his throat. The store clerk, or rather the Wraith, stepped into the light and gazed down on him. Dull thuds came from the metal door, breaking the eerie silence in the chamber.

Jonah expected that was Kevin and Lynn trying to get in. He bet that Robert wouldn't be able to override the lock this time. This had been a trap, set just for him. The most unnerving thing was the continued silence from the store clerk, as if he waited for something.

He's waiting for Deyanira, Jonah decided.

As the initial panic receded, he took the opportunity to scan the chamber. It appeared exactly as he remembered it from the dream-walk. The curved metal walls arched high overhead toward a much smaller circle at the apex. The stone portal Deyanira would use stood opposite the metal door.

Robert's archive box sat atop the stone pedestal in the center of the room. Spotlights high on the wall shone down on it. Crossing the chamber, Jonah reached out to touch it with his right hand. He sensed the ring inside and relaxed, running his fingers along the edges. As he did, a familiar rush of coldness reached him and Deyanira's stony voice floated through the chamber.

"Jonah Blackstone."

Deyanira stood in front of the portal, which showed a dark cavern on the other side. The former sorceress wore a red dress this time, her hair pulled so tightly back against her head that her square black glasses seemed to pop off her face.

She strode slowly toward the pedestal, watching Jonah intently. When she reached the pedestal, she, too, touched the archive box with a finger. Jonah pulled his hand away, fearing she would discover his connection to the ring.

Deyanira smiled and started to circle around the pedestal toward him. He moved away, maintaining their distance.

"You've caused a lot of trouble for one so young." Her voice was mild. "Why, you're just a little boy."

Jonah's tempered flared at her mocking tone. At the same time, he remembered Lynn's warning: Don't let her get to you.

"Hmmm. Someone has been learning self-control. Admirable." She made a full circle around the pedestal and stopped. "Tell me, Jonah Blackstone, why have you broken into my house and caused so much damage?"

"I want the ring."

Deyanira frowned for a second and narrowed her eyes. "I could have you and your cousins arrested for breaking and entering. You wantonly set off my security alarms and broke into a secured chamber. Isaiah Blackstone would have been shocked that his son turned out to be such a delinquent."

"You don't know anything about my dad." Jonah spoke before he could stop himself.

Deyanira laughed. "Child, I spent decades with your father. He became one of us, one of the KIN. I will admit that he proved very good at his job. All the mayhem, all the pitiful souls he reaped from worthless mortal bodies. It was glorious!"

"Shut up!" Deyanira's gloating made him sick. "Shut up!"

"Watch your tone with me, Jonah Blackstone." Deyanira's voice carried an icy tone. "I know things about your father that would give you nightmares."

Jonah shivered. *Nightmares? Could she know about his dream-walks?* That thought scared him, and he decided to do something: he darted forward and grabbed the box. He strained and pulled, but it wouldn't budge.

Deyanira laughed again. "The box can't be moved."

Jonah gave up and stared at the dangerous Reaper. "Why don't you just take it to your master?"

Deyanira's smile disappeared instantly. "Don't insult my intelligence! We both know the box can't be opened except by the person who locked it."

"You want to make sure the ring is inside."

"Of course. Open the box for me, Jonah Blackstone, and I'll let you and your cousins go. I have no interest in hurting you."

For a wild second, Jonah played with the idea that Deyanira would let them go, but he realized that would never happen. She belonged to the KIN and wasn't into doing kind things for mortals.

"Sorry I can't help you."

"You're going to force me to get nasty, I see." Jonah stared at her. "I know what you're thinking. I have other options besides hurting you, Jonah Blackstone."

He heard a sound behind him and turned around. His heart sank. The clerk led Lynn and Robert into the room. Behind him were two more goons in the grey robes with white skulls on the chests. Their green-edged, black scythes hung from clips on their sashes. Jonah understood now. They were Wraith possessed. Deyanira had been working with them all along, even when she attacked his parents.

One of the Wraiths carried Wick over his shoulder and dumped him onto the cot. Robert and Lynn were stopped a few feet away. Behind the goons came the two Grim Hounds from the rec center. Kevin shuffled along between the beasts, his hands in a pair of heavy cuffs. The silver Grim Hound continued to shake its head, trying to dislodge the glittering dust while the other nipped at Kevin.

Jonah's Death Sense spiked, and he thought his head would split open. He turned back to Deyanira as he tried to keep from vomiting. "I can't open it."

Deyanira held up a hand and let her index finger point at Lynn, then Robert, and back as if playing a game in her head. Finally, her finger stopped on Lynn.

"I'll ask you one last time, Jonah Blackstone. Open the box."

"He can't open the box!" Robert moved forward. The clerk grabbed his arm and jerked him back.

Deyanira shook her head. "Pity."

She flicked her hand in a quick, fluid motion and shot a bolt of supernatural lightning at Lynn. It hit her square in the chest. She let out a strangled huff as if punched and then began screaming in pain. Robert and Jonah screamed at the same time. The clerk held Robert tightly, and one of the goons grabbed Jonah when he moved to help. The man took his scythe and pressed it against Jonah's neck.

A tear rolled down Jonah's cheek as he was forced to watch Lynn convulse. The energy played up and down the length of her body. It took several horrible seconds for the effect to dissipate.

When it finally did, Lynn curled up in a ball and began to sob. Tears streaked Robert's face, and Jonah's breath came fast. He couldn't believe it.

Deyanira turned on him. "If you don't want your cousin to suffer more pain, then open the box."

"I–I can't open it."

She gave a dramatic sigh and shot Lynn with another lightning bolt. Her screams were even more anguished this time. Jonah couldn't do anything. The Wraith-possessed goon wisely pinned his arm behind his back and pressed the scythe into his neck, drawing blood.

When the second bolt faded, Lynn's screams abruptly died away. She didn't move.

Robert's voice was raw from shouting and crying. "Stop it! He's telling the truth. He can't open the box because it's mine!"

"Robert."

"No, Jonah! I can't let her hurt my sister anymore! First Wick and now Lynn." Robert spoke with so much pain that Jonah thought his own heart would burst.

Deyanira advanced on Robert, looking him up and down. "So." She let the word drag out. "The Seeker's box is yours? Where did you get it?"

"It doesn't matter. I'll open it. Just don't hurt my sister anymore. Please!"

Deyanira watched Robert for a moment until he pleaded with her again. She gestured to the clerk, who let Robert go. Jonah struggled in the Wraith's grip when his cousin hesitated, looking at his sister. Deyanira pointed sharply at the box.

"Open it."

Robert wiped the tears from his face and walked to the pedestal. He touched the lock mechanism, causing the locks to click and slide back into their recesses. Robert's hands shook as he activated the release on the lid and opened the box. Faint, pulsing amber light reflected off his skin.

He dropped his hands to his sides and looked around, but Deyanira's attention remained on the opened box. He took one step, and when no one stopped him, ran to Lynn's side and sat beside her. Placing Lynn's head in his lap, he began rocking back and forth, muttering to her.

Deyanira gazed into the opened archive box.

"The Protector's Ring. All this trouble over one ring." Despite her clear fascination, she didn't reach in and take the ring. Instead, she snapped at Jonah, "You. Come here and take the ring out of the box."

"Why don't you do it?"

Deyanira sneered and raised a hand toward Robert and Lynn.

"Wait! I'll do it." At a nod from Deyanira, the Goon lowered his scythe. Jonah yanked his arm free and walked over to the box.

Deyanira gave him plenty of room as he reached in and gripped the ring. It was warm to the touch and the pulsing was like an actual heartbeat. Jonah held the ring up. "It's beautiful."

"Here!" Deyanira held a small sack in her hands. "Put it in here, now!" She raised a hand toward Robert and Lynn to back up her command.

Jonah's rebellious side wanted to do something, but that would cause his cousins more pain. He reached out to drop the ring in the bag when he sensed the increase of pressure a second before he heard a familiar metallic swishing sound. Jonah thought someone had activated Lynn's blades until he heard Marcus's voice.

"I told you, Deyanira. You will never have the ring."

Jonah's heart leapt as he saw Marcus, Omar, Trueblood, and Emily standing around the edge of the chamber. He couldn't understand how they had managed to phase inside.

Wick hissed at Jonah to get his attention and pointed down at the symbol on the floor. He had rubbed out a small portion of it.

The Grim Hounds attacked. Emily blurred into motion and sliced one of the creature's head cleanly off. A spray of blood splattered the floor, but it and the creature soon dissolved into puddles of ecto goo. Emily turned and cut Kevin's cuffs with follow-up slices of her blades.

Trueblood had attacked the second Grim Hound with supernatural lightning. The creature was bathed in the glow of it, howling in pain. Kevin, with a pair of blades in hand, took down the second hound just as Emily had taken out the first.

Jonah ducked and rolled toward Lynn's backpack and drew out her blades. He whirled and managed to block first one swipe of a scythe, and then another. When the man prepared to strike a third time, Jonah dodge forward and stabbed him in the arm holding the weapon. The man screamed as he flailed backward, the scythe dropping to the floor. Marcus didn't miss a beat and sliced him across the back. Sparks flared out of the guy's mouth and eyes as the Wraith inside died.

Marcus whirled around to face the second goon, blocking swipes of his scythe. Marcus blurred into motion, cutting him across the chest with both blades and leaving a blood-stained X in the grey tunic. The goon's eyes flashed as one more Wraith was killed.

Meanwhile, Omar and Wick helped Robert and Lynn to the door. They had to duck aside when a third goon charged inside the chamber.

The man lunged straight at Jonah. The Wraith was so focused on the blade in Jonah's left hand, gripping it with both of his and trying to crush it, that he didn't give Jonah's free hand any mind. Jonah grabbed the man's head just as he had seen Deyanira do in the dream-vision.

He didn't know if he could suck out a human soul. He just hoped he could suck out a Wraith, hopefully before the man broke his wrist. He held on to the Wraith's head, digging his fingers into the skin, unsure of what to do next. Just as he feared he'd made a mistake, he sensed something, like a burning flame.

It was the person's soul, but the flame was wrapped in what looked like a spiky dark vine. *That's the Wraith!*

Jonah pushed against the angry spirit. The Wraith resisted and howled in response. Jonah's Reaper side swelled with authority and he shouted, "Out!"

The Wraith howled again, in obvious pain as it was sucked from the man's body. For a second, Jonah wondered if it was painful for a Wraith to be wrenched out of a mortal. He didn't care, but that thought stopped him from grabbing the Wraith as it broke free and soared up through the grate at the top of the chamber.

Jonah stared at his trembling hand. *I forced a Wraith out of a body.*

He only had seconds to exult in his accomplishment because the man's body sagged onto him. Jonah thought he would hit the ground under the added weight, but

Marcus grabbed the man's collar and lifted him away. He gave Jonah an intense stare before barking orders to the others. "Get these people out of here, now."

Emily grabbed hold of the man's body and phased. Trueblood already grasped the one Marcus had cut down, and she opened a vortex to drag the man from the chamber. Kevin and Robert held up Lynn, and all three phased a second later. Only Jonah, Wick, Omar, and the third unconscious goon remained behind.

"Move back." Marcus positioned himself between Deyanira and the others. Just like the dream, they readied themselves and blurred into motion. The fighting style alternated between blinding-fast movements and short pauses. Jonah thought that Marcus had to use an incredible amount of his stored energy to keep up with Deyanira.

Marcus's black long coat whipped around as he attacked with slashes and precise thrusts of the blades. For a moment, Deyanira fought defensively. Then she did what Jonah hoped she wouldn't do: she began to morph into her true form. She became at least a foot taller, more skeletal, and she wore the blood-red robe.

Wick sat up on the cot. "Whoa!"

Jonah would have thought fighting in a robe would hamper Deyanira. However, she seemed to get even stronger and faster. *Of course*, Jonah thought. The portal had been opened during the initial confusion. Deyanira was drawing power from her Master.

Jonah didn't know what he could do because Deyanira and Marcus continued to move with an odd fighting cadence. He thought about keeping the clerk at bay. Yet when he turned, he found the Wraith calmly watching the fight. His milky white eyes missed nothing.

Marcus made a desperate attempt to slash Deyanira and over reached. She delivered a devastating blow to his midsection. Jonah heard loud cracks, and Marcus fell to the ground. Blood seeped from the side of his mouth.

"Marcus!" Omar ran forward. Deyanira hit him with a blast of supernatural lightning, sending the man to his knees. Omar raised his head, pain etched in his face as he tried to crawl forward.

Deyanira stepped over Marcus and kicked his blades across the chamber. She planted her foot on Marcus's neck. "Stay where you are, Omar." She turned to Jonah. "Now, young Blackstone, bring me the ring or I'll snap this pathetic fool's neck!" She gave her foot a little twist. Marcus gagged and reached feebly for her foot.

The ring pulsed furiously in Jonah's pocket. He took it out but paused when he heard Wick whisper to him.

"Don't do it."

"Silence!" Deyanira glared at Wick, but he ignored her.

"She can't touch it, Jonah. She's a Reaper and afraid of it."

Deyanira roared in frustration.

Jonah feared she would snap Marcus's neck at any moment out of sheer rage. He couldn't stall any longer. He took a quick step toward Deyanira as she snapped her fingers. The clerk scurried over to pick up the discarded sack near the overturned pedestal and brought it to her.

Jonah held the ring up and Deyanira's eyes widened with triumph. "Put it in the sack, child."

Jonah's rebellious side won out, and he tightened his grip. The Protector's Ring was supposed to give the wearer power, and it had responded to him. Didn't that mean he was a Protector?

At that moment, Jonah made his decision. He didn't know if it would work, but he wanted to wipe that smirk off Deyanira's face. Too many people had died to keep the ring out of her hands. He wouldn't let her win.

Jonah held up the pulsing ring and slowly put it on the index finger of his right hand.

Time stopped.

CHAPTER FORTY-ONE
GRIM FINALE

Did time stop or did I speed up?

Jonah didn't know which as he looked around the chamber. Everyone appeared frozen in place. Omar wore a terrified expression as he watched Marcus suffer. Deyanira looked shocked. Marcus grimaced as she pressed her foot against his throat. Wick sported a suspended relieved expression as he watched Jonah put on the ring. The clerk's eyebrows were high on his forehead in amazement. Everyone was fixed in place and unmoving.

Then the familiar sensation rolled along Jonah's skin and Deyanira's chamber disappeared. In the next moment, he stood on a mountainside overlook. Across the valley, on another mountain, was an immense building. *Is this a dream-walk?* He jumped when his thought echoed across the valley as if spoken aloud.

Something appeared at the corner of the platform. Jonah whirled toward it, and his breath caught in his throat.

"Dad?"

His dad didn't respond. In fact, his dad's body was semi-transparent, and he wore the ring. Jonah looked down and saw the ring on his own finger. He took a step toward his dad, and the image wavered and disappeared, replaced by an old man in classic hiking clothing. He held the same ring in his hands as if holding a precious treasure. *Mr. Halliwell.*

Jonah recognized the reclusive artist from a picture Robert had found. Halliwell disappeared and another person appeared. In fact, a whole series of people came and went in faster and faster succession. Jonah understood they represented every person who had ever worn the ring. The parade of people finally ended with a tall, strong-looking man with rich, ebony skin who wore a royal blue, toga-like garment.

Unlike all the others, this man turned and mounted the platform. He raised an imposing arm and waved his hand in the air. *Behold.* His voice boomed across the hilltop, even though his mouth never moved.

A glowing symbol appeared, hovering about ten feet away.

Jonah stepped onto the platform and walked to the rail. His eyes widened as he took in the symbol. It was a bird of some kind, its long neck turned so that the beak faced backward. Deep down, he knew this symbol, something his mom or dad had shown him once. But he couldn't pull the fragment of memory into focus.

The man regarded Jonah. *Do you know the term* Sankofa?

Jonah sucked in a breath as that word ignited the memory. His parents had returned from one of their trips abroad. The symbol had been one of about fifty on a tablet from Ghana.

"Yeah. I've seen it before." He recalled his dad's rich voice explaining that the bird's beak was turned backward so it could see as well as get something from behind. "It means to learn from our past."

The man nodded, then pointed down into the valley. *Behold and learn.*

Jonah leaned over the railing, and his jaw dropped at what he saw far below. Instead of a true valley floor, he gazed upon an impossibly large crystal viewing surface divided into football-field-sized segments. Varying images of a magnificent city were displayed across many of them. The man's words seemed to form in Jonah's mind.

Sumer, the first civilization on the planet.

When it was destroyed, more images of other civilizations appeared. Again and again, the humans were destroyed until they were given powerful objects.

Watching the history lesson was like viewing bits of several shows at the same time. Jonah focused on an image of ring bearers, and the large screens obeyed. All switched to images of the people with rings. This allowed Jonah to catch the flow of the story. The humans with the powerful rings rallied mortals and restored the balance. Again, speaking directly into Jonah's mind, the voice floated to the surface.

Children of Light.

The images turned grim as the ring bearers were hunted down and killed. In the final images, the rings were gathered and hidden by the being who stood beside Jonah. The final image showed the same man with a powerful woman wearing a gleaming medallion and surrounded by four sons, all wearing rings.

Destiny.

The scenes changed again, this time to images of the Grim Reaper and another being in a grey robe standing on this very platform, looking out at the building across the valley. Jonah lifted his own gaze to the building. It was impossibly large, the upper portions hidden in the clouds. Understanding seeped into his mind. That was the Central Archives, storehouse of the recorded lives of all human beings who ever lived, and of all mortal knowledge.

Like a dam breaking, the entire history of the ring and its purpose rushed forward, downloading into Jonah's mind. Fearing he'd lose himself and his own memories, he staggered under the information assault. *Help,* his very soul pleaded. In answer, a part of him surged forward and lifted him away. As the tidal wave of knowledge flowed by, a cool remoteness descended over Jonah, allowing him to watch and learn without fear.

He relaxed into the cool yet strange power until the scenes changed again. A gasp escaped his lips and he leaned against the railing. He saw his mom and dad fighting their way through grey-robed attackers and into an amphitheater. As they reached the stage, a young guy wearing the Protector's Ring caused it to explode, killing all the attackers. Jonah's parents hid under his dad's long Reaper's coat, somehow protected from the blast.

Deyanira was there, and his dad refused to give her the ring. The next scene showed Marcus taking the oath of the Alliance Council and finally his mom and dad embracing while discussing hiding the ring. Jonah knew the rest of the story because he and his cousins found the ring.

Tears ran down his cheeks as he watched the super-sized image of his mom and dad together. And he understood their last message in the dream-walk. They did everything to protect him for as long as they could.

He soaked it up like a dry sponge and experienced a pang of regret as he sensed most of the specifics fading. But he would hold on to that last image of his parents for the rest of his life.

As the screens turned a pearlescent color, the being next to him answered the unspoken question. *You may not be able to access the information now. Yet someday, you will be able to recall it all.* He pointed to the ring on Jonah's finger.

Jonah held up his hand and asked, "Am I a Protector?"

No.

"Then what am I?"

You're something much more. That is the reason the ring has responded to you.

The man stood tall, his expression blank. He waited, still as a statue.

Jonah was at a loss until the ring pulsed. Untold numbers of voices began to echo through his mind, all making the same pledge in different languages, but Jonah understood them. *Forever standing in between, I maintain the balance. I am a Protector.*

The urge to repeat the pledge was strong, but Jonah reminded himself he wasn't a Protector. There was something else he needed to do. He gazed at the ring, sensing the increased pulse that didn't match his own heartbeat for once. It was if the ring anticipated something. *What?* He asked himself.

An image of what he did in the chamber came back to him. He'd been able to expel a Wraith from a mortal body. His Reaper side did that. *Of course!* The answer flooded into his mind. Covering the ring with his left hand, Jonah summoned his Reaper power. "Come out," he commanded. "I set you free."

When he spoke the last word, a pulse of energy shot out of the ring, up his arm, and over his entire body. The ring bucked, causing Jonah's arm to twitch. A ghostly shape detached itself from the ring and floated into the air.

Jonah's jaw dropped. It looked just like the quiet man standing beside him. The ghost swooped down and entered the man. He sucked in a startled breath and his skin seemed to glow with life as his chest heaved up and down.

It seemed like his body had been awakened from a long sleep. When he turned and leaned closer, the distant look was gone from his dark features, and Jonah sensed the first real emotion: sadness.

The man opened his mouth and spoke with a rich, deep voice. "You're so young to have this responsibility." He blinked. "I was older than you when I was chosen."

"Are you a Wraith?"

"No. I bound my spirit to that ring. For two thousand years, I waited for you to come. Now, I can move on and rest."

Jonah didn't understand. He pointed down at the display screens. "What about the last guy who wore the ring? He was a Protector. Why didn't he release you?"

"As you said, he was a protector, a mortal. They can't cross over to the Afterworld as you did. So I had to wait for you." The man patted his own chest. "I was never a Protector, either. My destiny was greater, to gather the rings and medallions in order to hide them from the darkness covering the world."

Jonah's eyes went out of focus as he recalled the Seer's words. "I'll change everything..."

"You'll restore the order."

"What are you?"

"I've had many names: The One, The Repairer of the Breech, and The Deliverer."

"And that's what I am?"

The man nodded. "If you believe in yourself."

That answer caused all kinds of questions to surface. But the image of his dead parents popped into his mind, overriding all the rest. "Were your parents... like mine?"

"My mother was a fallen one. My father was a mortal."

"Did they die?"

"Yes. It's a terrible burden, but it's your destiny." The man raised his strong chin to look off into the sky as it opened to shine a bright light on his body. He turned back to Jonah. "Remember that you're special, young Blackstone. This is just the beginning for you. Someday, you'll understand what you are and all that you can accomplish." The man rose into the air, his arms spreading wide, welcoming the light. He paused in mid-air, gazing at Jonah. "Listen to the ring. It will protect you and guide your actions."

With that, he soared off into the midst of the light. The opening, or whatever it was, snapped closed.

Jonah imagined he'd feel alone with the stranger gone, but power and confidence swelled inside, and he knew what to do. He held the ring close to his mouth and whispered, "Take me back."

Jonah phased back to the dark chamber. Everyone remained frozen in time, but Jonah knew that would change in a second. With the ring's encouragement humming in his mind, Jonah raised his hand, thought *Sakoto*, and a torrent of wind rushed through the opening in the ceiling. Jonah sent the blast of wind directly into Deyanira.

Everything snapped into motion as she tumbled across the chamber. She was quick to roll back to her feet. When she saw the Protector's Ring on his finger, she screamed. "You can't use the ring!"

Deyanira's blades were in her hand in a flash. Jonah merely thought, and two flaming blades appeared in his hands. He met Deyanira midway. As they fought and whirled, Jonah allowed the ring to guide his hands. Each time their blades connected, brilliant flashes of light erupted and the sounds shook the chamber.

Jonah matched Deyanira, blow for blow. She might have been fast, but she wasn't adaptable, and before long, he began to outmaneuver her.

Enough of this, he thought. He swept his blades up and out, slicing through Deyanira's. The move nearly took her hands with the weapons. Before she could recover, Jonah used another blast of wind to pin her against the wall. Deyanira's scream of frustration was cut short as a petrified look transformed her face.

The Grim Reaper, taller and more massive than Deyanira, stood on the other side of the portal. His crimson robe writhed and moved like a living thing. Coldness, hatred, and anger emanated directly from him.

Deyanira crawled to the portal opening.

"He shouldn't have been able to use the ring. He's not a Protector."

The Grim Reaper ignored her, raised a skeletal red hand, and pointed at Jonah. When he spoke, his gravelly voice grated on Jonah's nerves. "Give me the ring and I'll let you live."

Jonah's eyes were drawn to the Grim Guards standing behind their Master. Each wore what Jonah hoped was a bone-white skeleton mask clearly visible underneath their hoods. They held large black scythes in their hands. Fear bit down on Jonah, and doubt nibbled at his mind.

The Grim Reaper's voice sliced through the air. "Yes. Yes. This is too much for you. You're just a boy. Take off the ring."

Jonah's rebellious circuits fired, and the fear receded a bit. Hackett's comments about the Grim Reaper bubbled to the surface. The Scythes were just symbols of fear. And the Grim Reaper fed off fear and misery.

Jonah grunted as the mental assault intensified, forcing him to his knees. He raised the ring close to his mouth with a trembling hand. "Help me. Please."

An energizing warmth sprang up around him. The horrible headache and pressure subsided. He could think clearly as confidence surged back into his body. Standing, he positioned himself to protect his friends.

The Grim Reaper raised his hands and held them still. A huge red ball of supernatural fire appeared and shot at Jonah.

A sudden rage took hold of Jonah's body as he deflected the fireball up and into the chamber. It exploded against the upper portion, dislodging a piece of metal and warping the others. Jonah ignored that as rage built inside him. He'd only seen red fireballs once: the day his parents died. He knew, at that moment, that the Grim Reaper had personally killed his mom and dad.

Jonah screamed, conjured his own green fireballs, and sent them through the portal. The Grim Reaper deflected them back through and into the chamber.

Omar pushed Wick out of the way of one of the fireballs. "Jonah!"

Jonah spared a glance around the chamber and realized he had been tricked into destroying it himself.

The Grim Reaper chuckled, and a shiver went down Jonah's spine when he spoke. "Embrace Death, young Blackstone, as your father did. Who knows, maybe you'll be reunited with your parents when you die."

Jonah grew even angrier. He didn't care if he brought down the chamber; he would make the Grim Reaper pay.

Marcus's weak voice penetrated Jonah's fog of rage. "Resist him, Jonah. He can use anger as well as fear and doubt." Marcus coughed. "Remember your father…"

Jonah gasped. If Marcus was right, why didn't the ring block the Grim Reaper's mental attack? The answer rang out in Jonah's mind like a bell on a clear day. He had allowed the anger to goad him. He had opened the door.

But how could he overcome the anger that still burned inside of him? His mind latched onto memories of his parents' bravery. Pride in their ability to face their enemies surged through him, displacing the anger. Once again, the pressure ebbed and Jonah could think clearly.

He shouted at the Grim Reaper, "My dad resisted you!"

The Grim Reaper roared in response and shot balls of red-tinged, sizzling lightning through the portal.

Jonah was prepared. Instead of deflecting the balls of lightning, he created a powerful shield directly in front of the portal. That surprised the Grim Reaper and forced him to dodge his own attack as it rebounded.

Jonah took advantage of the distraction to pour a burst of fire through the portal. The Grim Reaper staggered backward under the assault, totally enraged.

In a moment of clarity, Jonah understood that the Grim Reaper reminded him of Brandon, only a hundred times worse. He also pushed people's buttons and fed off the anger and misery he caused.

As the Grim Reaper retaliated with another fireball, Jonah reached out and shouted in a voice deeper than his own and much more like his dad's voice, "*Sakoto!*"

The fireball stopped in midair. Jonah started to weave his hands in a circular motion above his head, and the fireball went into a graceful spinning orbit around the interior of the chamber.

Wick stared at it. "Unbelievable. You've got to teach me that trick." He and the clerk huddled to avoid the intense heat of the fireball.

Once again, the Grim Reaper fired. Jonah increased the speed of his hand movements, and the second fireball joined the first as they coalesced into one ball. It streaked around the chamber in a perfect, tight circle like an angry red comet.

Jonah added his own power to it. He let his anger, frustration, and hatred bleed out. He didn't stop until he had drained himself of the hurtful emotions. By then, the fireball was twice its original size.

As it completed the last circuit around the chamber and neared the portal, Jonah prepared himself. "You may have killed my parents, but you won't kill me or my friends."

At precisely the right moment, he released the fireball and scored a perfect three-pointer through the open portal. The fireball exploded like a bomb on the other side.

Jonah watched in satisfaction as red-robed beings and Grim Guards dove for cover and the structure on the other side shook and began to fall apart. A thick smoke rose up, obscuring his view.

Somehow, through all the noise, he heard Marcus's voice again. "Jonah, shut the portal. This is too dangerous, even with the ring on."

Marcus coughed up more blood. Omar cradled Marcus's head gently in his lap and spoke softly to him.

Jonah wondered how to close a portal, and the answer came to him. He raised his hands, and after a second, he could feel the power around the opening. He imagined himself gripping the edges of it and brought his hands together. The portal resisted as the Grim Reaper fought to keep it open.

"Jonah!" Omar warned.

"I'm trying, Omar."

The Grim Reaper rose to his feet and raised a hand. Supernatural electricity crackled as he conjured a ball of lightning. Jonah concentrated with all his might and, just before the Grim Reaper attacked, slapped his hands together. The portal closed.

Jonah staggered a bit as the oppressive coldness and evil vanished. He took deep breaths and glanced around just as the chamber begin to collapse on their heads.

CHAPTER FORTY-TWO
HEALING POWER

"We have to get out of here." Wick pointed at the opening. "The door is toast."

Jonah saw the scorched and melted door and wondered if he had deflected a fireball right into it. More and more pieces of the chamber began to fall, and the entire thing began to vibrate.

"We need a shield, Wick."

"I don't have another bracelet. Besides, you made a shield at the rec center."

Jonah knew that, and he was sure he could do one now. However, he was very aware of the silent store clerk watching everything he did. He wanted to confront the Wraith within, before it could get away. He doubted that, even with the ring, he could do both.

"You can do it without one."

Wick shook his head. "I'm not powerful enough."

Jonah grabbed Wick's wrist. The boy gave him a funny look.

"Huh, Jonah?"

"Shut up."

Jonah concentrated, causing the ring to flare in response. Energy flowed from the ring, through Jonah, and into Wick, who let out a startled gasp.

"Dude!" Wick closed his eyes and a moment later, the blue distortion of a shield snapped into place around them. Debris began to bounce off it. Wick opened his eyes, amazed. "I'm not even straining! This is too cool."

Jonah turned and faced the clerk, who huddled against the wall, watching him. As soon as Jonah took a step toward him, the clerk fell onto his knees.

"Please, don't hurt me. That evil spirit left my body."

Jonah gave him a slow smile as he lightly tapped his temple. "I know you're still in there."

The man's shaking stopped, and he stood tall and straight. His eyes changed from their natural green color to milky white. Despite being in the body of a clerk, the dignity of the ancient Egyptian warrior came through. The Wraith raised his hand to stop Jonah and spoke in a deeper voice. "You've beaten the Grim Reaper with the power of the Protector's Ring. My king will want to know what happened here today."

"Is that why you helped me escape from Deyanira?"

The Wraith inclined his head. "Yes. Your actions change everything."

Jonah paused in mid-step, bathed in the sudden memory of the Seer he'd sat beside on the bus. She had prophesied he would change everything. "I spoke to a woman. A Seer. Is she one of you?"

The Wraith shook his head. "The woman is a priestess, one who can summon our Seers, allowing them to communicate through her."

"She said the same thing you did, about me changing things."

"The prophecy." The Wraith smiled. "Wraiths possess far more knowledge than mortals."

Jonah had opened his mouth to ask about the prophecy when a huge piece of the upper chamber broke free and slammed into the shield. Wick's arm bent in response to the force of the blow. Jonah stepped toward the Wraith again, and the man gave him a genuine salute.

"We will meet again, Jonah Blackstone." With that, the clerk fell to the ground and the Wraith exited his body.

Wick let out a snort. "Wow. He literally gave up the ghost."

The Wraith didn't fly away or disappear. Instead, the ghostly warrior hovered inside the shield. Jonah understood and turned to his friend. "Wick, it can't get out. You'll have to lower the shield."

Wick nodded, and his brow drew together as he concentrated. A second later, the blue, hazy distortion of the shield winked out of sight. The Wraith saluted Jonah, then flew up and out of the enlarged hole in the ceiling. When pieces of the chamber thudded to the ground near his feet, Jonah whirled to find Wick had moved.

He knelt beside the overturned pedestal. Jonah hadn't noticed until he saw it from this angle that the top was made of a clear crystal. Inside was a pulsing dome, undamaged by the fighting. The setup reminded Jonah of a computer desk he'd seen once, the kind with sunken monitors, leaving the entire desk's surface free for work.

Jonah's attention was snapped back to reality as Wick stood, holding Robert's archive box under one arm. He hurried back and activated his shield just as a large warped section of the upper wall crashed down.

He noticed Jonah's exasperated frown and shook the box. "You heard Deyanira: it's a real Seeker's box. Even she couldn't open it. That means it'll come in handy later."

"Whatever," Jonah said and turned to Marcus and Omar. His irritation dissolved, replaced by fear.

Omar stared up at him, perhaps sensing his unspoken thought. "He's still alive, Jonah. We should go now." His African accent was strained with worry. "You have to phase us."

"But I never phased this many people."

"You have the power of a Protector. Remember everything Marcus taught you and you'll be able to do it."

Jonah closed his eyes and thought about the clearing on the plantation grounds. The ring pulsed brighter. Jonah sensed when Omar stood and lifted Marcus. He kept his eyes closed. "Don't worry about touching me. I can get us all out."

His could do this. His Reaper side could touch their souls, which burned bright like stars. He raised his hands. Energy flowed from the ring, through him, and connected with every soul under the shield.

Jonah willed himself to phase. Cool predawn air touched Jonah's skin a moment later. He lowered his arms and opened his eyes. He knew without looking that everyone had made it out with him.

A low rumbling vibrated the ground. Someone yelled, and everyone watched as the earth buckled and collapsed in an expanding fissure that headed straight for the plantation house. The decayed Antebellum columns wobbled and fell into the fissure, along with half the house. A thick layer of dust rolled over the clearing, causing everyone to cough. As the dust began to settle, the sun broke over the horizon. The first morning rays allowed Jonah to see the devastation.

The house looked like someone had cut it in half and scooped it away, leaving the insides exposed. The sound of loose earth tumbling into the fissure punctuated the otherwise quiet morning.

Emily let out a startled gasp and pointed at Omar, who lowered a bruised and battered Marcus to the soft ground.

The Fallen Reaper's hand moved, beckoning Jonah to his side.

Omar knelt over Marcus, gripping his hand. "Don't try to talk."

Marcus shook his head, in a movement that was little more than a jerk. He reached out his free hand, and Jonah didn't hesitate to take it. "Well done, Jonah." Marcus paused to take a painful breath. "You saved us all."

He tried to say more, but it turned into coughs. His head drooped and his eyes closed. Omar touched his head to Marcus's, and his shoulders shook with quiet sobs.

Marcus's patterns, visible through the ripped and blooded-shirt, turned a lighter shade of red. They were nearly gone, and Jonah thought it strange that Marcus would become fully human again at his death.

Without warning, something deep inside Jonah roared out in anger at the very notion. He had lost his parents to the Grim Reaper. And now the man who had pledged to protect him and train him would die because of the same being. The anger over the unfairness of it all boiled up inside Jonah and a single word tore its way out of his mouth.

"No!"

Jonah's shout shook the ground, causing everyone in the clearing to jump and stumble about. He pressed his palms flat against his godfather's chest.

Omar looked on, dazed. "Jonah. It's too late."

"I can save him!"

The ring started to pulse brighter and brighter. Jonah closed his eyes, willing it to draw in more power. He would save Marcus. He would not lose another person. The ring pulsed so bright, no one could even look at it. When Jonah could no longer hold the energy, he let go. Power flowed out of him and into his godfather.

Marcus's body jerked and his back arched. Omar stared in open shock as the cuts and bruises began to heal. Jonah could feel the broken bones knitting together beneath his hands. After what seemed like an eternity, the patterns began to return. First, they grew deep red, then brown, and finally black. Once they had fully returned, to Jonah's amazement, they began to glow with light.

Jonah pushed the last bit of power into Marcus and let go. Marcus sucked in a deep breath and his eyes snapped open. He took several more breaths before he was able to sit up. His hands fumbled around, slipping off his long coat and then ripping the mangled shirt off. He stared down at his glowing patterns.

"Marcus!" Omar's deep voice boomed across the clearing in relief. The two men embraced, rocking each other back and forth for several minutes.

"Whoa!" Wick's jaw dropped.

Robert sounded just as shocked as his friend. "You mean they're together?"

Jonah had begun to smile when the world tipped sideways and an intense rush of dizziness hit him. He swayed and pitched forward. The ground, rushing toward his face, stopped less than an inch from his nose.

Kevin spoke softly, in his ear. "I got you." He pulled Jonah back to his feet and wrapped a protective arm around him.

Jonah tried to pull the ring off his finger but missed; his right hand trembled too much. Kevin gripped the hand and held it steady until Jonah could slip it off.

Relieved at having the ring off, Jonah shook his head to clear it, which only made him dizzier.

"Take it easy, Jonah." Kevin held up a butterscotch candy. Jonah smiled up at him as he took it.

Omar and Marcus were on their feet now. Marcus moved his arms around, testing them out. He ran his hands along his healed ribs and only stopped when he realized everyone watched him with awed expressions.

Omar motioned to Jonah. When he tried to move, Kevin refused to let go.

"I'm alright."

Kevin slowly released his hold and Jonah walked, a little unsteadily, up to Omar.

The big African pulled Jonah into a bear hug and lifted him off the ground.

"Thank you, Jonah. I owe you so much." Omar set Jonah down and added, "I just hope you'll forgive me someday for what I've done."

"What did you do?"

He tapped Jonah on the forehead in response before turning back to Marcus, who was still checking over his mended body.

When Marcus finished, he nodded to Emily. "You, Kevin, and Trueblood, take care of Deyanira's people. Omar, you go with them."

"I'm staying with you, Marcus." Omar crossed his arms.

Marcus gripped the man's muscled forearm and smiled. "I'll be fine. I have to get the kids home."

Omar let out a deep laugh that seemed to relax everyone.

Kevin turned and raised a closed fist to Jonah. "See you later, little man." He helped Emily march two of the groggy people out of the clearing.

Omar lingered, pointing at Marcus, who stood bare-chested. "At least put on your long coat. You look like a walking neon sign." Omar smiled and hurried to follow Kevin and Emily.

Through it all, Jonah remained in a kind of daze. He appreciated Kevin saying goodbye to him, but frankly, Omar's apology still rolled around in his mind. Had Omar really suppressed one of his memories? Jonah didn't know how to respond at the moment, and he didn't get a chance to consider it because Lynn called to him.

"Jonah, please tell me you kicked in Deyanira's teeth."

"Yeah." Jonah gave her a smile.

Lynn nodded as the energy seemed to flood out of her, and she settled against her brother.

Robert frowned. "We need to get her home."

Marcus buttoned up the long coat, the glow from his Fallen Reaper patterns unable to seep through the dark fabric. After that he motioned to Trueblood, who had stayed behind.

The Mage opened a vortex and everyone piled through without being told. Jonah wasn't surprised to find the vortex opened into his relatives' backyard, near the shed. Robert had already helped his sister into the house by the time Jonah arrived. Wick had followed.

However, Jonah stopped at the kitchen door to watch the vortex snap closed. That's when he noticed that his godfather had paused to stand in a ray of morning sunlight that peeked its way between the houses.

Marcus tilted his chin up toward the rising sun, his eyes closed. "Thank you, Jonah."

"You're welcome." He glanced inside the house. "I need to get inside before my aunt or uncle…" When he turned back, Marcus was gone.

Jonah stumbled out of his bedroom late in the afternoon. Robert and Wick were already up and playing video games. They glanced at him and nodded without stopping play. Jonah went into the kitchen to get a bowl of cereal and noticed the blinking message light on the phone.

"Anyone checked the messages?"

"We figured they were all from Mom calling to tell us about the rec center." Robert looked a little uneasy. "Lynn called her."

"And?"

"Mom asked if we knew anything about it. Lynn convinced her we didn't, but Mom's not stupid. We asked about the sphere, then, two days later, someone destroys it. She'll keep an eye on us from now on."

Jonah didn't argue as he sat down on the sofa with his bowl of cereal and watched Robert and Wick battle each other on the screen. It took him a minute before he noticed Lynn's opened bedroom door. He tapped Robert's shoulder.

"Where's Lynn?"

"She went for a walk."

"I thought she should get some more rest." Wick blasted one of Robert's men and snorted. "She told me what I could do with my suggestion."

Jonah laughed and, of course, Lynn walked through the kitchen door at that moment.

"What's so funny, geek boy?"

"Uh, nothing." Jonah slipped into the kitchen to rinse out his breakfast bowl while Lynn took his seat on the sofa.

Jonah thought his cousin looked tired, and he couldn't stop the wave of guilt that threatened to overwhelm him. He also wanted to apologize. When Lynn saw the look on his face, she gave him a slight shake of her head.

After a few minutes of watching her brother and Wick play their video game, Lynn sat forward. "You two are pathetic."

Robert held the controller out to his sister. "Can you do better?"

"Easily. Let's do teams. Jonah's with me."

"Deal."

CHAPTER FORTY-THREE
BULLY TAMED

Jonah, his cousins, and Wick spent the weekend cleaning debris out of the Summit clubhouse. Even Robert, with all his computer skills, couldn't salvage the equipment. The center's director promised to consider buying new computers once she had the insurance estimates.

By Monday, most of the heavy lifting was done. The remaining furniture was pushed to the center of the clubhouse so the walls could be repainted. After that, there was nothing left to do except clear out.

Robert and Lynn decided to head over to Wick's house while Jonah stayed at the center. He couldn't believe the damage to the atrium. A large section of the marble floor had been removed to make way for replacement tiles. The overhead skylights were covered in heavy plastic. The center of the atrium was roped off and had an extendable construction crane parked there.

Jonah edged around the obstructions and walked into the café.

"Jonah, over here!"

Mike sat at a blue-topped table. As soon as Jonah took a seat, he started in. "What happened?"

"Huh?"

"Don't play dumb with me." Mike lowered his voice. "I know you have something to do with that mess in atrium."

"Can't I get a soda first?" Mike crossed his arms and waited. When Jonah returned, he told Mike everything that had happened.

Mike leaned across the table and punched Jonah in the shoulder.

"Ow!" Jonah said, shooting Mike a scandalous look as he rubbed his shoulder. "What's up with you?"

"Why didn't you tell me any of this earlier?"

Jonah blinked at him. "Everything happened so fast. Besides, you didn't want to go with us, did you?"

"Maybe." Mike slumped in his chair, crossing his arms. "I guess not. I don't want to see the Grim Reaper or anything like that."

"So what's the problem?"

"I wish I could have helped you, Jonah. The discussions with your cousins and Wick sound so interesting."

Jonah stared at his friend and thought he understood. Mike was smart and knew a lot about everyone else. Aside from his broken friendship with Drew, Mike didn't seem to have that many friends of his own. In fact, Mike reminded Jonah of himself.

"I'm sorry. I'll tell you more the next time."

Mike's eyes grew wide. "Do you think there will be a next time?"

"Yeah, I do." Jonah nodded. "Deyanira and the Grim Reaper are still out there. You heard your uncle. There are thirty-five rings, not just one." Jonah glanced around the café, having a hard time believing that just a couple days ago, they had fought Grim Hounds in here.

"I think this is just the start." He gave Mike a smirk. "You sure you want to be my friend?"

Mike blew out an exasperated breath. "Are you kidding? I never had this much fun."

When school started on Wednesday, Jonah wondered if his cousins would use that as an excuse to put the destroyed clubhouse out of their minds. Robert and Lynn would continue to collect stories, but the blog was on hold for the week.

As for the police, they concluded their investigation into the bizarre break-in at the recreation center and labeled it an act of random vandalism. So far, they hadn't been able to explain how the vandals managed to get through the skylights without any gear. The only evidence found were strange gouges on the roof's surface.

The police detective in charge never questioned Aunt Imma. Jonah thought that very fortunate because his aunt took her Christian faith very seriously, and she would have felt honor-bound to mention her conversations with the kids. Just for good measure, Robert managed to hack into the county computer system and release a virus into the donation database. They'd have to work out a way to get the hard copies.

The center requested Aunt Imma and the other artists resubmit pieces for the atrium. Aunt Imma announced she would go with her original idea and use kayaks.

Marcus, Emily, and Kevin remained silent. Jonah didn't expect his godfather to call. He imagined Marcus off somewhere with Omar, enjoying his power boost. Even though Kevin had helped in their rescue, Jonah still felt the warm glow from his promise, deep inside. Did that mean that Kevin would return? Jonah hoped so because he wanted to see the young Fallen Reaper again.

Jonah entered the attic clubhouse after school on Thursday and grimaced. A painter's cloth covered the old sofa, conference table, and rusted filing cabinet. The center had chosen to repaint the attic walls a light grey. They also replaced the busted attic window and frame.

Jonah's footsteps echoed off the dark wood floors and exposed rafters as he crossed to the new window. The painters had left it open to air out the paint fumes. Jonah enjoyed the fresh breeze as he looked out onto the ravine below him. This was all his fault. He had brought this danger and destruction into his cousins' lives.

A sudden change in air pressure surprised Jonah as much as the voice behind him. "A penny for your thoughts."

Marcus stood near the top of the attic stairs. Instead of wearing his trademark black long coat or even a suit, he wore a long-sleeved black shirt and tan pants. He looked rested, Jonah thought.

"Where have you been?"

Marcus spread his long arms, revealing a black onyx and ivory bracelet around his right wrist. He also held a small gift bag in his left hand.

"I've been using the power you gave me. I feel like my old self." Marcus smiled as he lowered his arms. "Actually, Omar made us take a mini-vacation." He strode over to Jonah. "You look worried."

"I'm just thinking how all of this is my fault. Lynn and Robert don't even come in here anymore."

"Don't blame yourself, Jonah. In fact, I'm the one who should apologize to you."

"Why?"

"I never told you the whole truth about the ring. I thought if I could find it, I could use it--"

"You wanted to use the ring to give yourself power without the binding spell. I know. I understand."

"I appreciate you understanding." Marcus looked out the window. "But the ring would not have worked. In fact, I don't think the ring has worked for anyone in a while, not even your father."

"It worked for me."

"You're half-human, so the ring responded to your human side. That's incredible, when you consider it."

"I don't feel incredible. I almost got us buried alive."

Marcus turned Jonah so he could look him in the eyes. "You faced the Grim Reaper, Jonah, and prevented him from winning. Because of you, the Protector's Ring remains here in the mortal world, where it belongs. You've no idea how much can be changed. Don't ever underestimate what you've accomplished."

Once again, Jonah was reminded of the Seer's prediction that he would change things. He gazed out the window until Marcus cleared his throat and handed him the gift bag. As soon as Jonah took it, Marcus held a hand over the top to keep him from looking inside. "We recovered a fireproof safe from your old home."

Jonah's eyes widened. "Really? What did you find?"

"We found copies of legal documents, and this."

Jonah tried to peek around Marcus's hand. "What's in the bag?"

"I hope you'll forgive me, Jonah. I kept this from you because I thought it might be too much for you. After seeing all the things you've faced, I realize that you're far stronger than I would have imagined."

Marcus removed his hand and Jonah peeked inside. A jeweler's box sat at the bottom.

"It's from your parents, Jonah," Marcus whispered,

Jonah's stomach clinched. "My parents sent this? But…"

Marcus leaned down to peer into his eyes again. "It's the birthday present they meant to give you."

Jonah couldn't speak and his hands shook as he reached in the bag and lifted out the box. Inside was a gold-and-silver compass. It appeared ordinary except for a strange dial around the face.

It's beautiful, Jonah thought as he removed the compass from the box. A folded piece of paper slipped free. Marcus caught the paper before it hit the ground and handed it to Jonah.

When he opened the note, he couldn't believe his eyes. It was a riddle in his father's handwriting. Both his parents had signed *Happy Birthday* at the bottom.

Jonah's eyes blurred, and he hastily wiped them with the back of his hand. "Thank you." When Marcus didn't respond, Jonah looked up and saw an awed expression on his godfather's face. "You know what it does?"

"Yes."

"Can you tell me?"

"You should discover that for yourself, Jonah." Marcus took his eyes off the compass. "I'm sorry I held on to it. Omar was livid with me when he found out. He said it was yours, and I was wrong to keep it from you. I hope you'll accept my apology."

As Jonah turned the compass over in his hands, he realized he wasn't angry with Marcus. "I accept it."

Marcus let out a breath and looked at his watch again, but he didn't seem ready to leave.

Jonah decided to take advantage of that. "Can I ask you a personal question?"

Marcus cocked an eyebrow and nodded.

Jonah hesitated a moment, then asked, "Why did you become a human if you miss your power so much?"

Marcus abruptly turned to look out the window again. "Your father asked piercing questions like that."

Jonah nodded and waited.

"I was convinced of the error of our ways. After that, I felt compelled to change, even though I didn't like the idea of becoming mortal again." Marcus stared down at his hands, his brow furrowed. "Sometimes, Jonah, you'll find that staying where you are is impossible and you have to move, even if you don't like the options available to you. Most people require a lifetime to learn that. I suspect the things you've been through have already taught you that lesson."

Jonah considered that. He'd lost everything he knew and been sent here to Georgia. He had never wanted to come here, but now that he was, he wouldn't give up his relationship with his cousins or his new friend for anything.

"I've gotten used to it." He leaned against the window. "I feel like this is home now."

"You see? You've learned a lesson that even I haven't." Marcus crossed over to the old sofa and sat down on the cloth-covered arm. This allowed the Fallen Reaper's eyes to be level with Jonah's. Marcus gave him the Reaper stare, but only for a brief moment before he lowered his gaze.

"Jonah, do you remember the day you left for Georgia? You asked why Omar and I didn't take you in. I wasn't totally honest with you." Marcus laughed softly. "I seem to do that often." A worried expression returned to his face. "Your parents asked me to be executor of their estate instead of your aunt and uncle because they knew I would become like a surrogate father to you."

"I don't understand."

"Think about it, Jonah. You are half-Reaper. When you needed phasing lessons, you called me. When you experienced the dream-walks and needed help with

Deyanira, you called me. There's going to be more and more things in which your mortal relatives can't help you. Each time, you'll turn to me. Your parents knew this."

"Are you saying you don't want to help me?"

"Of course I want to help you. I'm attempting to explain my thoughts on the night I realized your parents would…" Marcus paused. "When I realized they would die and leave me to watch over you. They were my best friends, and I lost them. My promise to your father required me to do something I never anticipated doing: help raise a teenager."

Marcus allowed Jonah to absorb everything he said before going on. "Jonah, you're going to elevate the whole angst-ridden teenager thing to a new level. You're not just a teenage boy; you're also a teenage Reaper. As your mortal side grows and develops, your Reaper side will also grow and develop. If anyone needs a father to guide him through the coming changes, it's you. And who will you call on in the future?"

"I'll call you."

"Yes, you will, and I'll always help you. I do that because it's the right thing to do and because I admire you. Never doubt that."

"I won't." Jonah held the compass up to the window, watching the light reflect off its surface as he thought about everything Marcus said. "Hey, if you're going to teach me a lot of things, will you teach me to drive?"

"No." Marcus sounded so serious about it that Jonah actually laughed. Marcus cocked an eyebrow at him, and that made it even funnier.

"You have a cool car."

"My car will continue to be cool and stay in one piece because I will not have an underaged driver behind the wheel. That is one thing your relatives can teach you."

Jonah cocked his head to the side. "Maybe I'll ask Omar."

"You will not ask Omar, and that reminds me. These little conversations are just between you and I. Attorney-client privilege. You understand that?"

Jonah nodded and couldn't hide the smile that tweaked the corners of his mouth. He could already detect the differences in Marcus's voice. One day, he just might persuade his godfather to let him drive his car.

Someone cleared their throat. Marcus and Jonah looked up to see a delivery driver at the top of the stairs, holding an electronic notepad.

Marcus stood and brushed a bit of lint off his pants. "Finally." He waved the man forward and signed the pad. The deliveryman looked around the attic.

"Where should I put the boxes?"

"I'd say over there, on the other side of the stairs."

Jonah watched as the delivery guy and a helper carried several large boxes into the attic. When they left, he hurried over to look at the labels.

"What are these?" For a wild moment, he thought Marcus had found a hidden stash of books that belonged to his parents.

"I felt responsible for what happened to the Summit, so I asked the company to purchase new computers and work desks for you."

"Wow! Thank you."

"You're welcome." Marcus clapped his hands together. "Well, my work is done here. Tell your cousins I said hello."

"Wait. Where are you going?"

"I have to get back to Washington."

Jonah hurried to his book bag and pulled out a small used jewelry box. "Take this. It's the ring."

Marcus stared at the box. "Are you sure?"

Jonah nodded. "I'm not a Protector. Find the real ones and give it to them. I'm sure the company can keep it safe."

"We can certainly do that." Marcus took the box from Jonah and turned it over in his hands. "There's a legend that says any one of the rings can be used to find the others."

"That's great. Use it to find the others."

Marcus subjected Jonah to a long stare—but Jonah realized it wasn't a Reaper stare this time. It was all human, and unless Jonah was wrong, Marcus looked impressed.

"You are a special young man, Jonah."

"Maybe." Jonah lowered his head and stuffed his hands in his pockets. Marcus laughed and patted him on the shoulder.

"Take care, Jonah, and enjoy the school year."

With that, Marcus waved and vanished.

Jonah made it to the end of his first week at Eddie Middle School before he came across his least favorite classmates: Brandon, Antwan, and Drew.

Brandon spoke loudly as he approached Jonah and Mike in the hallway. "Hey, freaks."

Jonah stood his ground, more than ready to face Brandon and his buddies. The boys seemed insignificant compared to raging Grim Hounds, a mad sorceress, and the Grim Reaper. However, Jonah didn't need to deal with Brandon alone.

Mike stood tall next to him, along with their practice club friends Rodney, Lorraine, and Anthony. Rodney had made the football team and had a couple of his football buddies with him. In short order, Brandon, Antwan, and Drew were surrounded.

Brandon looked wildly around, realizing his mistake. Antwan and Drew took a step back, leaving space around their friend. A month ago, Jonah would have liked to kick Brandon's butt; however, he didn't feel the need to do that anymore. Jonah didn't have any buttons for Brandon to push. Yet, he did want something from the would-be bully.

Jonah smiled. "My name isn't freak or DC. My name is Jonah."

Although Brandon looked as though he had swallowed something sour, he nodded and said, "Jonah," in a very low voice. As soon as the word passed his lips, he whirled on the spot and pushed his way through the crowd. A few students gave Brandon grief as he passed out of sight. Drew and Antwan slouched after their friend.

"That was brilliant, Jonah." Mike punched him on the arm. "Can I call you DC?"

Jonah laughed. Having the other kids standing with him was something he'd never imagined could happen. In that moment, he understood exactly what his mom had meant. The connections he made in life are the really important things. Jonah wasn't a loner anymore. Despite being a half-Reaper, he had made friends in Mount Vernon, Georgia.

John Darr is a native of the state of Georgia. As a graduate of Columbus State University with a B.A. in Communications, and with work on his M.F.A. degree at Howard University in Washington, D.C., John has over twenty years of experience as a writer, screenwriter, independent filmmaker, and educational television producer. He loves long walks in picturesque locales, playing tennis, and helping others realize their creative dreams. John currently resides in Arlington, VA. Visit him online at www.johndarrbooks.com.